BONE
CRIER'S
DAWN

BONE CRIER'S DAWN

KATHRYN PURDIE

 KATHERINE TEGEN BOOKS

An Imprint of HarperCollins *Publishers*

Katherine Tegen Books is an imprint of HarperCollins Publishers.

ISBN 978-0-06-279880-0 (trade bdg.)
ISBN 978-0-06-308046-1 (special edition)
ISBN 978-0-06-308680-7 (special edition)

Typography by Joel Tippie
21 22 23 24 25   PC/LSCC   10 9 8 7 6 5 4 3 2 1

First Edition

To my mother, Elizabeth,
for pure faith in me from the beginning

1
Sabine

"WATCH OUT, SABINE!" JULES'S LOW and scratchy voice calls from a mineshaft above. I barely have time to move aside before she drops into the tunnel. A rush of air hits Bastien's candle, and the flame sputters out. We're thrown into absolute darkness.

"*Merde*," Bastien curses.

"Relax," Jules says. "Marcel always has a tinderbox in his pack."

"And another candle," Marcel adds.

"Excellent," Jules replies. "The thunderstorm is loud enough now. It's time to blow that wall."

We're in the mines beneath the catacombs close to Beau Palais, the castle where Prince Casimir lives, where he's holding Ailesse captive. Not for much longer. My heart beats faster.

Today, we rescue my sister.

A few seconds later, flint and steel strike together. The soft glow meets a candlewick and snaps into a brighter flame.

Bastien and I elbow forward for the candle. The alliance I've made with the boy who loves Ailesse—who she somehow loves in return—is tenuous at best. Just because he and his friends are helping me free her from her abductor doesn't mean I've forgiven them for also holding her captive.

"I'll do this myself," Marcel says.

"Wait!" Jules's eyes widen at her younger brother.

It's too late. He lowers the candle to the powder.

Whoosh.

Fire streaks an angry line toward the cask.

Jules yanks Marcel to his feet. Bastien spins and runs the other way. I shove him faster. Ailesse would never forgive me if he died.

We race until the dense atmosphere eats up all light and sound behind us. My nerves sting, waiting for the explosion. Did the fire burn out before it reached the cask? I glance over my shoulder.

BOOM.

A massive burst of flames zips toward us and throws me backward. I hit Bastien. We crash onto the ground. A second later, Marcel and Jules topple onto us. Chalky smoke and debris flash by. Sharp rubble scrapes against my sleeves. The chaos finally settles into fat flakes of twirling ash.

No one moves for a long moment. We lie in a tangle of legs, arms, and heads. Finally Marcel slides off our piled bodies, and his floppy hair bounces. "I may have misjudged the impact of the blast."

Jules groans. "I'm going to murder you." She rolls off and shakes dust and ash from her golden braid. "You better hope that sounded like thunder, or any moment now all the soldiers in Beau Palais are going to flood this tunnel."

We've been waiting for the perfect storm to mask the noise of the explosion, and as poor luck would have it, it fell on the same day as the new moon. Ferrying night. If this rescue attempt fails, I'll have to lead my *famille* on the land bridge myself and ferry the souls of the departed—the sacred duty of each Leurress, given to us by the gods of the afterlife, who we descend from. But I can't lead my *famille*. Ailesse is the only person alive who knows the song on the bone flute that opens the Gates to the Beyond. She was meant to be *matrone*, not me.

I scoot off of Bastien and offer a hand to help him up. He hesitates, then exhales and takes it. Despite our bickering, I want his assistance. We'll find Ailesse faster if we work together.

We stand side by side and stare into the hazy gray light shining in from the blasted hole. I inhale a deep breath. After fifteen long days, we finally have access to Beau Palais.

"Everyone ready?" Bastien cautiously rubs his back where my mother stabbed him. The wound is still healing. Only in the last week has he been able to walk without grimacing.

Jules nods and adjusts her cloak. I tighten my fists. Marcel settles into a comfortable position. He's going to serve as watch. If the tunnel is compromised, he'll light a small explosive filled with sulfur and pepper seeds. The stench will warn us not to come back this way. Meanwhile, Jules is going to guard our point of entry into the castle above.

Bastien waves Jules and me forward. The three of us advance to the end of the tunnel. I reach the wall first and climb the rubble. Through the blasted four-foot hole, I stare inside a dry castle well lined with river rock. Its construction isn't yet complete. King Durand, Casimir's father, commissioned it to replace a more vulnerable well outside the castle keep.

While Bastien and Jules have been spying in Dovré and gleaning these facts about Beau Palais, I've been forced to spend most of my time at Château Creux with my *famille*.

The Leurress are shaken by the news of Odiva's death. All I told them is our *matrone* died ferrying alongside Ailesse on an ancient bridge in an underground cavern. If they knew Odiva ran through the Gates of the Underworld to join her true love—my father, a man who wasn't her sanctioned *amouré*—it might spark anarchy. Once Ailesse comes back and rightfully replaces me as *matrone*, I'll let her decide what to reveal about our mother, and I'll retreat to the comfort of her shadow.

I leap to the opposite side of the well, grab an iron rung, and climb a ladder built for the well diggers. They're not at the castle today. No one labors during La Liaison except entertainers and those preparing food for the three-day festival.

We'd hoped to sneak in through the main entrance, but King Durand isn't holding a public celebration. According to rumor, he's too ill. But he was ill before Ailesse was taken captive, and the castle gates have only been locked since Prince Casimir brought her here.

Jules leaps onto the ladder after me. I envy the leather leggings she's wearing. My shoes keep tangling on the hem of my simple blue dress.

Bastien follows last, and the three of us rise sixty feet to the top of the well. It's covered by an iron grate, which scrapes loudly as we slide it off. A clap of thunder muffles the sound. For now, the rainfall doesn't reach us. We're in the tight quarters of the castle well tower.

I creep to the tower door and peek through a small window at the top. I can't see much of the castle courtyard beyond the pelting rain—even with my far-reaching vision, thanks to the power from my nighthawk grace bone—but I make out the blue-and-gold-striped awnings that line the perimeter. They provide shelter for a few servants who scurry across the wet cobblestones to reach the other side. One awning caps an arched passageway that leads inside the castle—the entrance we'll use.

Bastien removes his dusty cloak and tosses it over to Jules. Beneath it, he's dressed in the simple garb of a castle dungeons soldier. I also throw off my cloak and tuck a few stray black curls into my servant's cap. I slip my grace bone necklace beneath the neckline of the uniform dress Bastien stole for me and hide my bone knife in the sheath under my apron.

Bastien turns to Jules. "See you soon."

She sits on the rim of the well, still a little breathless from climbing. "Promise to keep your head, all right? If you can't pull this off today, don't be reckless. We'll figure out something else. We still have ten and a half months before—"

"This will work." He flexes his jaw muscle. "Come on, Sabine."

He slips out the door before Jules can say anything else.

I'm quick to follow. I don't wish to discuss the soul-bond between Ailesse and Casimir, either—the bond Bastien thought he shared with her until I discovered the truth. Now Ailesse has to kill Casimir within a year from the time the gods sealed their lives together, or she'll die with him. I'll make sure it happens before we leave the castle today. I'll hand her the bone knife and persuade her to save herself.

Bastien and I head through the rain for the arched passageway. We've committed to memory the map of Beau Palais he pieced together after conversing with a retired castle servant. "After three cups of tavern ale, the man was an open book," Bastien told me.

We shake off the rain once we're inside the castle. We're standing in a stone foyer that intercepts a long corridor running left and right. Straight ahead is the great hall. Servants mill about, setting gold plates and goblets on a few gathered tables. Garlands of vibrant late-summer flowers twirl around towering columns that support a vaulted ceiling. Blue banners embroidered with the gold sun symbol of Dovré—an homage to the sun god, Belin—hang alongside green banners with the tree symbol of the earth goddess, Gaëlle. I'm told La Liaison is held to invoke their joint blessing on the upcoming harvest.

Bastien and I share a quick glance and nod before we part ways. He heads left, and I head right. His direction leads toward the dungeons entrance, and mine accesses the staircase to the third level. Ailesse could also be locked in one of the royal apartments up there.

I've only taken a few steps when a handsome boy with strawberry hair walks around a column in the great hall, fifteen feet away. My body goes rigid, my blood cold—then scorching hot.

Prince Casimir.

He's wearing a burgundy doublet over a loose linen shirt and fitted breeches. A simple crown made from a thin band of gold wraps across the middle of his forehead.

He hasn't laid eyes on me yet, but I still can't force myself to move. Images from the last full moon crash through my brain: Casimir taking Ailesse's grace bones, carrying her away in his arms; Ailesse struggling against him while her injured leg dripped blood; me seeing them from a distance as I fought his soldiers; Bastien, also helpless, lying on the bridge and bleeding out from his stab wound.

"Can you add more wildflowers?" Casimir asks a female servant while surveying the garland draped around the column. "Ailesse is fond of them."

"Of course, Your Highness."

"I want everything perfect for when she meets my father tonight."

My mind snags on his words. *Flowers for Ailesse? A meeting with the king?* I glance at Bastien. He's taken cover behind a potted tree at the corner of the great hall and an adjoining corridor. From his deeply furrowed brow, he's just as confused as I am. How can Ailesse attend a dinner with Casimir's father? Isn't she locked away?

"I understand, Your Highness." The servant bows, and Casimir starts to turn in my direction. I jerk around, shuffle to the nearest table, and fuss with a place setting. I itch to hold the bone knife. If I could stab him right now, I would. But that would kill Ailesse. Their lives are woven together. She must be the one to wield the ritual blade and kill her *amouré*.

The prince's footsteps slowly clip toward me. My pulse pounds faster. I lower my head and pray to the goddess of the Night Heavens. *Elara, don't let him recognize me.*

"Pardon me, but are you new here?"

I stiffen, keeping my back to him. "Yes," I squeak.

"What is your name?"

I could run. With my nighthawk speed, I could make it to the third level before Casimir had a chance to catch me. If only I knew which room Ailesse was in. By the time I find her, he'll have the whole castle on alert. "Ginette," I murmur, feigning to be shy.

"Ginette, I am your prince and future king." Casimir's voice is warm and carries the charm that made me lightheaded when we first met. I had performed a proxy ritual to summon and kill Ailesse's *amouré*, expecting Bastien to come, but Casimir came instead, and for several wonderful and terrible moments, I thought he was my *amouré*, not hers. "You need not be afraid of me," he says. "In this castle, I treat my servants with regard."

A scoff rips out of my throat. "And how do you treat your prisoners?" My subterfuge is pointless. Whether I run or confront him now, he's going to discover me. "You can't win Ailesse with flowers and gold and false honor. She will always see you as her abductor."

My jackal hearing catches his soft intake of breath. "Sabine?" he asks.

I lift my chin and turn to face him. Casimir gazes back at me with widened stone-blue eyes. I fight to keep the heat in my blazing stare. His restrained demeanor carries wisdom, depth, and strength. It makes it hard to remember he's the same person who felt entitled to steal my sister away.

"Where are you keeping Ailesse?" I demand. I pull out my hidden necklace and let my grace bones dangle, exposed, over the bodice of my dress. The three bones hang side by side—a fire salamander skull; a crescent-moon pendant, carved from the femur of a rare golden jackal; and the leg and claw of a nighthawk.

Two guards at the edge of the room take a step forward, but Casimir holds up a hand to stall them. He may not understand what I am—what Ailesse is—but he knows my bones hold power.

"Ailesse isn't my prisoner. I invited her to stay with me, and she agreed."

Lies. Ailesse would never consent to that. "Then tell her I'd like to pay a visit."

"You know I can't do that." His tone exudes a maddening level of calm. "You tried to kill me, Sabine. You are not welcome in this castle."

The golden jackal in me snaps. I whip out the bone knife beneath my apron. Casimir quickly draws a jeweled dagger. Our blades meet each other's throats at the same time. His dagger's sharp edge presses against the tendon of my neck.

"What would Ailesse think of you if you killed her sister?"

"No less than she'd think of you if you . . ."

An animalistic screech rings in my ears and drowns out the rest of his words. A small reflection appears in his pupils. A bird with a white heart-shaped face.

Somehow, as I'm staring at Casimir, the bird grows larger. I gasp. This is a vision. It has to be. I'm seeing the silver owl—the goddess Elara's bird. She hasn't appeared to me in her physical or transparent form since the night Casimir abducted Ailesse. Visions like this are unheard-of among the Leurress, but the silver owl has shown me two before, and both visions were in connection to saving my sister.

The owl grows to full size and hovers in front of Casimir with her wings unfurled. He can't see her; he's looking right through her at me. It's like she's protecting him.

I don't understand. The silver owl once wanted Casimir dead. She led me to kill the golden jackal, carve a flute from its bone, and use it to lure the prince during my proxy rite of passage. I could have killed him then without dooming Ailesse to die in return. The ritual would have protected her.

The owl beats her wings once, and my surroundings change. I feel the castle floor beneath me, but I see the cliffs overlooking the Nivous Sea above. It's the night of the last new moon. Ailesse is playing the siren song on the bone flute, trying to open the Gates of the Beyond.

She keeps playing. The harrowing melody floats to my ears and burns through my mind. I've remembered snatches of it before, but not every measure. Now all the notes pulse vividly inside me and plant deep roots. I doubt I'll ever forget them.

What's happening? I came here to rescue Ailesse, not see a memory, not learn a song. I came here to help her kill Casimir. Why isn't the silver owl helping me?

She beats her wings again. Now Ailesse is in the underground cavern on the fragile soul bridge. She moves toward the Gates of the Underworld with headstrong determination. I hear myself shouting for her to stay back, but she won't listen.

I blink and see Casimir again through the body of the owl. My bone knife shakes at his neck. Maybe the owl isn't protecting him from me. Maybe she's protecting *Ailesse* from me.

I could threaten Casimir, fight off his soldiers, find Ailesse, free her . . . but what if my sister shouldn't lead the ferrying tonight? She barely resisted stepping through the Gates of the Underworld last time. The only thing that distracted her was Odiva stabbing Bastien.

Perhaps . . . perhaps my sister is safer in Beau Palais. For now.

My eyes blur with infuriating tears. Casimir's brows hitch together. He doesn't know what to make of my reaction. For the longest time, all I've been trying to do is save Ailesse. Why am I prevented at every turn?

I pull the bone knife away. The silver owl disappears. I curse the goddess's messenger, but I've learned to trust her. She warned me about Odiva before I knew my mother's crimes. She led me to Casimir, who helped me finally find Ailesse. She'll help again when the time is right, when Ailesse's freedom won't lead to her death. She knows more than I do.

Casimir's dagger holds steady at my neck. He opens his mouth like he wants to say something, but his expression is torn between anger and pity. I harden my glare on him, even while my tears fall. I still hate him. My actions don't change that.

One of his soldiers clears his throat. "Shall we take her to the dungeons, Your Highness?"

The tip of Casimir's blade slides to lift my chin as he deliberates. He swallows. "Yes."

The soldiers advance. Casimir lowers his dagger down my neck. He's going to cut the leather cord of my necklace. With nighthawk speed and jackal strength, I grab his wrist and slam the hilt of my knife into his upper arm. His dagger tumbles from his grip. Before it clatters to the stones, I drive my knee into his gut. He buckles forward. I shove him to the ground and jab my elbow in his back. I pluck up his fallen dagger. The first soldier swings low for me. I jump over his blade and spring off Casimir's body. I bolt away before the second soldier can attack.

Casimir shouts my name. He's back on his feet and chasing after me. His soldiers follow. I run toward the long corridor, past Bastien's hiding place.

He shoots me a livid glance. "What the hell are you doing?" he hisses.

"Leaving. Tell Ailesse I know the siren song. I can open the Gates."

I spin around and fling the jeweled dagger at Casimir, but purposely throw off my aim. It sails above his head and clangs against a stone column. While Casimir is distracted, I toss the bone knife into a potted tree opposite Bastien's. "Tell Ailesse to finish him," I say. His eyes narrow on the barely exposed hilt of the knife. He'll have to come back for it later. He gives me a determined nod before he slinks away in another direction.

I run past the arched passageway that leads to the courtyard. I can't leave the castle through the dry well. I'd endanger Jules and Marcel and expose Bastien's safe exit.

Casimir shouts for more soldiers. Boots pound closer down an adjacent stairwell and branching corridor.

A large man emerges and grabs for me. I narrowly dodge him and keep sprinting. I focus on a stained-glass window thirty yards ahead. The late afternoon sunlight beats in through the colored panes and lights up a majestic image of Belin, the sun god, riding his white stallion through the sky.

I cast off my servant's cap and apron and pick up speed. I yank loose the ties at my shoulders that hold up my hemp-spun over-dress. It falls away from the chemise I wear beneath, and I kick it aside. I can't have it dragging me down.

"Stop!" Casimir calls after me.

The stained-glass window is five yards away. I grit my teeth and leap off the ground. My nighthawk grace heightens the jump. I cast up my arms to protect my face.

My body hits the glass. The window shatters in a rainbow of shards.

Sixty feet below me, the Mirvois River rushes by.

I tumble toward the whitecap currents.

2
Ailesse

LIGHTNING FLASHES THROUGH THE MULLIONED windows as I race down the corridor. Or *attempt* to race. My trailing gown isn't helping. Neither is my crutch. But I set my jaw and hobble as quickly as possible.

The ornate door is only fifteen feet away now. I ignore the pain in my shattered knee and keep moving. I'm not supposed to bear weight on my leg for another month. When that day comes, I will burn this wretched crutch. Being held captive in the catacombs was nothing compared to being a prisoner in my own body.

I pass another window on the third level of the castle. A bolt of lightning streaks like a jagged finger and illuminates an ancient bridge just beyond the city wall. *Castelpont.* I halt. I haven't seen the bridge since the night of my rite of passage. The night I first met Bastien.

Tu ne me manques pas. Je ne te manque pas. You're not missing from me. I'm not missing from you.

The phrase he taught me has been my mantra since I've come to Beau Palais. Soon I'll be with Bastien. I won't need Old Gallish words to hold his memory or help me visualize his sea-blue eyes and dark tousled hair. He's alive. He has to be.

I press forward for the door. My knee jostles from each painful limp with my crutch, but I finally set my hand on the lever. I'm about to turn it when a shout echoes throughout the castle.

I freeze. Strain to hear what's happening. I can't make out the words above the thunder. I try to brush off my worry. The affairs in this place are none of my concern. I open the door, shuffle inside, and shut myself in the room.

I'm standing in a private library near King Durand's chambers. I've never been here before, but I've been making subtle inquiries among the servants. I haven't been idle while waiting for my knee to heal. I've gleaned the basic layout of the castle, including this room, which is only used by the king and Prince Casimir. Apparently a larger library exists on the second level.

Aside from an arched window letting in the gloomy light from the storm, each of the four walls is lined floor to ceiling with shelves. They're mostly filled with books, but a few treasures rest among them: a marble bust of King Durand, a framed map of South Galle, a collection of exotic feathers, a gold vase, jeweled goblets, a few bottles of wine, and a small chest. . . . My gaze lingers on the chest—a perfect hiding place for my grace bones. Once I have them back, I'm leaving this castle.

My heart thrums faster. I abandon my crutch—my armpit aches from it—and I brace myself against a large lacquered table. I hop alongside it toward the shelf with the chest on the far wall. I've already searched every corner and crevice of my own room—Casimir's room—and the room he's been sleeping in since he brought me to Beau Palais. This private library seems the next logical place where he would have hidden my grace bones. According to the servants, he comes here often.

I reach the shelf and pull down the small chest. Its lid is carved with a beautiful tree nested inside the circle of a great sun. Symbols of Gaëlle, the earth goddess, and Belin, the sun god. Beau Palais overflows with them, while Tyrus's golden jackal and Elara's sickle moon are glaringly absent.

I sit on the edge of the table to take the pressure off my leg. My hands shake as I struggle to pry open the stiff latch. *Please, Elara, let my bones be in here.* I can almost feel their coolness resting above my chest, where they belong: a pendant carved from the sternum of an alpine ibex, the wing bone of a peregrine falcon, and the tooth of a tiger shark.

None of them can heal me, like Sabine's fire salamander skull can, but they'll make me stronger, faster, more agile. I'll need every advantage in order to make it to the land bridge tonight. I'm the *matrone* of my *famille* now. I'm the only one who knows the song to open the Gates to the Beyond. No one will be able to ferry the souls of the dead without me.

I finally pop the latch. At the same moment, the door to the library swings open. I startle, and the chest topples out of my grasp. Its contents spill across the table.

My shoulders slump. My grace bones are not among them.

"What are you doing in here?" Casimir says, aghast.

I look up, and my heart pounds, my primal reaction whenever I see my handsome *amouré*, but this time the reason isn't because of my innate attraction to him. Something's wrong. He's panting, and a bead of sweat rolls down his temple. He holds his dagger at the ready. My lips part. "I was only . . ."

He barges into the room, checks behind the door, and glances under the table.

I frown. "What's going on?"

"Have you seen anyone else?" he demands.

"Who would I—?"

He's about to answer when three guards burst into the room, swords drawn. Once they see me, they freeze and throw Casimir confused glances. He composes himself and shakes his head. "Not in here. Search the royal apartments, starting with Ailesse's room. Bring me word once you find out those places are safe."

"Safe from who?" I ask.

His eyes lower to his dagger, and his thumb idly rubs the blade. He waits for the guards to leave before he answers. "There's a . . . a growing band of dissenters in Dovré. People who blame my father for the recent plague. Some of them snuck into the castle."

I know about the dissenters. The servants say they're angry because the gates of Beau Palais have been closed for over two weeks and they aren't able to petition King Durand about their troubles. "Why do they blame your father?"

"Kings are always to blame when anything terrible occurs in the land. That is the burden of being monarch. If the gods really did anoint someone to rule, that person should hold enough sway with them to prevent mass tragedy from happening. If it does, that king or queen must have fallen out of divine favor. They're no longer fit to rule . . . or so say the people of other kingdoms who have succeeded in overthrowing their monarchs. North Galle has practically made a sport of it."

Something is off about Casimir. He's speaking faster than usual, and with a forced nonchalance that's unlike him, even though these dissenters sound like a serious concern.

He sheathes his dagger. "It's nothing for you to worry about. I have the situation well in hand." He offers me a small but reassuring smile and passes me my crutch. I take it without letting our fingers brush.

I don't blame the prince for bringing me here fifteen days ago. He thought Sabine was a threat—she threatened to kill *him*, after all. Besides, I agreed to stay here of my own volition. But he's lying about my grace bones. He said he lost them on the journey to Beau Palais, a direct deception. He won't meet my gaze whenever I mention them.

"I wish you would allow yourself to rest more and give that leg a proper chance to heal," he says. "If you wanted another book from the library, all you had to do was ask."

"I'm sick of being in my room."

"I know." He sets his hand on mine, and I stiffen. I won't let his warmth stir my blood. I don't care if he is my *amouré*, perfectly designed for me, and I for him.

"I'm trying my best to please you, Ailesse," he says. "You'll see more of the castle tonight, I promise." The dimple in his right cheek deepens with his grin, and I curse Tyrus and Elara for how charming it makes him. "It's the first feast of La Liaison. Even as we speak, servants are decorating the great hall and . . ." His eyes lower to the toppled chest and its spilled contents: a string of pearls, a folded letter, a lock of strawberry hair tied with a lavender ribbon, and a miniature painting of a woman bearing a striking resemblance to the prince.

Casimir's brows tug together. "What were you doing with my mother's things?"

Heat scalds my cheeks. "I—I was bored and . . ." I shake my head. "I'm sorry, I didn't know what would be in there." Queen Éliane died during the great plague when Casimir was a young boy. He was her only child, and King Durand's as well, as he never remarried.

Casimir grows quiet and slowly returns the items to the chest. I pick up the string of pearls to help. "I can do it," he says, and reaches for them. But then he hesitates to take the jewels. His fingers hover over mine. He finally exhales and closes my hand over the pearls. "You should wear them tonight." His stone-blue eyes lift to take in my face.

"No, I can't," I blurt. I feel like a thief for even touching them. "They're too precious."

"I'm not say I'm giving them to you. I'm just letting you borrow them." He cracks a grin. "Maybe I'm not as generous as you think."

I burst into laughter. I can't help it. I've been a coiled ball of tension for days, and I didn't think Cas had a sense of humor buried beneath his deeply earnest nature.

He chuckles along with me, shyly rubbing the back of his neck. "Do you know this is the first time I've heard you laugh? It sounds . . ." He searches for the right word. "Healthy."

"Healthy?" I snort. "Are you saying I come off sickly when I'm moody?"

"It's difficult to say. You're always moody."

"Oh really?" I catch his dimple flashing again.

"But laughing suits you. You should allow yourself to indulge in it much more often."

"Hmph." I lift my chin and toss my hair over my shoulder. "Well, you should know I *do* laugh often." Sabine can give me one wry look, and I double over in a fit of giggles. "You just don't know me well enough yet."

"Fair point." His eyes take on a mischievous gleam. "I'm working on that."

I sober as his gaze warms, and I fight to tame the heat fluttering in my belly. The pearls weigh heavier in my hand. "What do you like about me?" I ask, speaking before thinking again. I squirm, feeling foolish, but still wanting to know the answer. Casimir had no choice but to be drawn to me after I played the siren song during my rite of passage, but the luring spell would have faded quickly, its effects gone after that night.

His brows lift, and he chuckles again, though more nervous. "Forgive me, you've caught me off guard. The reason is . . ." He scratches his arm. "Well, it isn't the easiest thing to put into words."

Lightning flickers outside and swiftly brings me to my senses. "Never mind." I slide off the table and lean against my crutch. I don't have time to solve the mystery that is my *amouré*. I need to leave the castle before nightfall. "I'm going to return to my room now," I announce. After Casimir sees me settled there, I'll make one last attempt to find my grace bones and flee this place.

"Ailesse, wait." He shifts to block me. "You are so . . . so captivating," he haltingly begins.

I roll my eyes. "You don't have to—"

"When I first saw you, I felt as if I'd known you all my life."

"You saw me from afar."

"But the song you played—your talent on the flute astounded me."

"Of course it did." I try pushing past him. These are all remembrances of the luring spell.

"You're fiercer than any girl I've ever met," he continues.

I pause. "Sabine was the one who held you at knifepoint."

At the mention of her name, his nostrils flare, and I understand why. She brought him to the cavern bridge and told me to finish my rite of passage. Casimir couldn't have known what that term meant, except that Sabine wanted me to kill him. "Your sister didn't fight your mother on a narrow bridge with no weapons like you did," he counters.

"She would have." Sabine was changed that night, no longer

the girl with only a salamander skull and deep reservations about the need for blood sacrifice. She had three grace bones and a new-found fire in her eyes. She was ready to do anything to protect me.

Casimir exhales. "Why are we talking about Sabine?"

"I don't know." Exasperated, I manage to elbow past him.

He catches my arm briefly, and I turn around. The strand of pearls swings, dangling from my fist. I've unthinkingly kept hold of them. "You remind me of my mother," he says.

I stare at him, unsure how to respond.

He swallows and repeats softly, "You remind me of my mother."

A sharp pang strikes deep inside my chest. He could have said, *You remind me of your mother.* The words were so close.

He bites his lip. "Is that strange to confess?"

I slowly shake my head, though I wouldn't know. Growing up, no one in my *famille* ever said I was like my mother, no matter how hard I trained or tried to prove myself. *You're better than the* matrone, *at least in the ways that really matter,* Sabine once said, trying to comfort me. All it inspired me to do was hunt harder for a more powerful grace bone.

"If her hair had been darker, it would be like yours, thick and a little wild." Casimir gazes at a wavy auburn lock spilled in front of my shoulder. "But your similarities go beyond resemblance. You're *alive* like she was. Radiant. She would walk into a room, and people would flock to be near her. They laughed when she laughed. They danced all night if she did."

I'm lost for a moment, thrown off by the differences between his mother and mine. Odiva also wielded a lure over people, but it stemmed more from intimidation than charm. "She must have been remarkable."

His mouth curves. "She was."

I lower my eyes. Casimir witnessed *my* mother's true nature at the cavern bridge. I picture her stabbing Bastien again and wince. "You can't compare me to her, Casimir. I've been sullen since the first day you brought me here." *I've been heartsick.*

"Anyone would be after what you've endured. That doesn't diminish your light."

Again, I'm rendered speechless. Does he mean light or Light? He can't mean Light. Only the Leurress know about the energy from the goddess Elara's Night Heavens. All mortals carry its life-force, but the Leurress need to replenish it just as they must nourish their bodies with food and water.

"I'm leaving now," I say. Casimir doesn't know what I am or what I need to survive. "I need to rest before tonight, Cas."

He smiles. "You finally called me Cas."

I curse myself. "It just slipped out."

"I'm glad. You know I prefer it."

My heartbeat quickens in the way I hate, the way that reinforces why the gods knew what they were doing when they chose the prince for me.

I hobble closer on my crutch and place the pearls in his hand. A look of hurt crosses his face. I don't care. I won't allow myself to feel guilt over a boy who is hiding my grace bones. "I'm not like your mother. I can't be." I'm meant to be a Ferrier of the dead, the *matrone* of my *famille*. . . .

I'm meant to kill you, Cas, just like my mother tried to kill Bastien.

I turn away and move toward the open door. But I can't leave yet. One of the soldiers has returned and is standing on the threshold.

"Your Highness." The stout man bows to Casimir. "Mademoiselle Ailesse may safely return to her chambers now. We have found no sign of more intruders."

"Thank you." Cas's voice rings dully, without its usual warmth and vibrancy. "Tell the castle guard they may return to their posts."

As the man leaves, I pivot to Cas, unable to help meeting his eyes once more. They've lost their luster, though not their kindness. Why can't he be more villainous? It would help me make sense of his reasons for deceiving me. He'd be that much easier to hate. *Or kill.* "I'll see you at the feast tonight," I tell him, compelled by some inexplicable need to cheer him up.

His expression brightens by a slight measure, a tiny lift of his brows and subtle softening of his lips. "The servants will bring you a dress for the occasion," he says. "I hope it doesn't cause any offense. I had it newly commissioned, so it never belonged to anyone else." He glances at the string of pearls in his hand and returns them to the chest. He closes the lid gently. "What I'm trying to say is that the dress doesn't come with any expectations."

He can't really mean that, even if he wants to. Where there's affection, there's always expectation.

"If that's the case, then I'll be honored to wear it," I reply, careful to tread the fine line of being considerate but not giving him false hope at the same time. I'm protecting *my* heart, as well, keeping it safe for Bastien.

My words spark a true smile from Cas, and I quickly glance away before I can dwell on his dimples. I rush out of the room on my crutch.

It's only a dress, Ailesse. No false hope given. No expectations.

3

Bastien

I CAN'T STOP STARING AT one of the maids in the great hall. It's her hair. Red. Nowhere near Ailesse's perfect shade of auburn, but it's long and waving like hers. Plus, every now and then when she stands in dim places, where the light of the massive chandelier can't reach her so well, her hair seems a bit darker. Like right now. If I squint hard enough, she looks just like—

"Everyone stop what you're doing!"

I suck in a sharp breath. A man marches right past my hiding spot. I slink backward from the edge of the tapestry into the space between the fabric and the wall. If the man hadn't been carrying a crate that blocked his face, he would have seen my head poking out.

I press my back against the cool stones. Flex my clenched hands. I've been stuck here for too long, waiting for the right moment to sneak over to the potted tree where Sabine hid the bone knife. But the great hall is crowded with servants preparing for the first feast of La Liaison.

"We have an emergency!" the man declares. *Thunk.* He slams the crate down on a table. "Take a look for yourselves. Tallow candles, not beeswax." He pauses, probably waiting for gasps to reflect his panic. None come. "Apparently the candlemaker never received our order, and all the other shops in Dovré are closed for the holiday." Another pause. His toe taps the floor. "Well, are we to allow smoking candles to stink up the first occasion His Royal Majesty has attended in weeks—as well as insult the prince's special guest?"

Special guest? I hold back a scoff. Is that what Casimir calls his favorite prisoner? I picture Ailesse seated beside him tonight, a chain binding her ankle to her chair, then another image flashes to mind: Ailesse in the catacombs, her hands and ankles bound in the rope I tied her up with. My gut twists. Yes, I also abducted her, but I thought she was a heartless murderer then. I never pretended to be saving her, like the prince did.

"The answer is no," the man—probably the high steward—continues. "So here's how we'll salvage this travesty. Each of you will scour the castle for any beeswax candles in sconces, lanterns, and any taper holders. Take them even if they've been lit already. We'll use the tallest ones for the head table and make do with the rest." He claps his hands twice. "Be off, then! Make haste!"

Feet patter. The murmurs of the twelve or so gathered servants fade as they scatter in different directions. The determined clip of the steward's footsteps follows last.

Now's my chance.

I sneak out from behind the tapestry, make sure the room is empty, and dart for the potted tree on the other side of the great hall. Thankfully no soldiers are in sight. Casimir has his guards searching the castle in case Sabine didn't come alone.

Sabine. My teeth grind together. Did she really need to leave so suddenly? She had the skill to fight off the prince and his men. She could have kept them distracted while I freed Ailesse. Now I have to do it on my own—after Ailesse kills Casimir.

I grab the bone knife from the potted tree and whirl in the opposite direction. I head for the corridor that leads to the staircase on the third level. Sabine was supposed to check the royal apartments up there while I searched the dungeons. But after overhearing what Casimir said—that he wanted more wildflowers for Ailesse tonight—I'm guessing he's made her a more comfortable prison in one of Beau Palais's finer rooms. Doesn't mean he's considerate, just manipulative.

Up ahead, the staircase comes into view, a hulking mass of limestone with marble posts and ironwork rails. A forest-green velvet runner lines the steps. Probably cost more than the food it'd take to feed every street kid in Dovré for a solid month.

I jog up the stairs two at time. My stab wound throbs, but I don't slow down. I can't have much time before the soldiers and servants return and—

A servant boy with a stubborn cowlick comes around the corner of the next flight above. Looks to be three or so years younger than me, maybe fourteen or fifteen. He hops onto the landing, five beeswax candles in his hands. His eyes are lowered as he idly hums.

I freeze eight steps below. I'm holding the bone knife in plain sight. My arm tenses to hide it. Too late. His eyes lift. They're a ruddy brown color, one shade darker than Ailesse's burnt umber. I see her in everyone. But her face would never pale at the sight of an armed stranger. It would harden. She'd take a defensive stance and prepare to fight.

"I'm not going to hurt you," I say. "Just promise not to—"

"Help!" he cries at the top of his lungs.

"—shout." My shoulders fall.

Raised voices and trampling boots echo from above and from the corridor below.

Merde.

I spring up the stairs toward the boy. He pelts me with two candles.

"Ouch!" The third candle bounces off my forehead. "Stop that!" I whack the fourth one away before it stabs me in the eye. I climb the last three steps and try to grab him. He beats my hand back with his last candle. I yank it out of his grip and toss it over the banister.

"Help!" he shouts again.

"Quiet now." I pin him against the corner wall and raise the bone knife to his throat. "I told you I wouldn't hurt you." But I *will* have to take him hostage. Just for a little while. It's my only leverage.

He shakes violently. He's thin and frail looking. He wouldn't know how to fight me with his fists if he tried.

The soldiers' boots pound louder. They're calling to warn Prince Casimir. The servant boy whimpers. His nose starts running. *Please*, he mouths. The tendons of his neck tighten as he cringes away from my blade.

I flush with hot sweat. Adjust the hilt of the knife. My grip is clammy. I can't do this again—take another person captive to get what I want.

I lower the knife. Trip a step backward. Nod once. "Go." My voice is thick and rough. How will I free Ailesse now?

The boy tears away and rushes past me down the stairs. Two soldiers race up them, dodging him to get to me. Another three men storm down from the flight above.

"Arrest the thief!"

I glance up. From the third level of the castle, Prince Casimir leans over the railing. The lines of his shoulders are broad and hard.

I whip out my second knife. Consider my odds of escaping. Not good, especially with my injured back. Here goes nothing.

I quickly sheathe the bone knife and hold the second knife between my teeth. Just as the first soldier below reaches to grab me, I swing over the banister and hang on to the railing from the other side. The toes of my boots balance on the barely protruding edges of the steps. I pick my way down, hurrying as fast as I can.

The soldiers have already wheeled around for me.

Once I'm eight feet from the ground, I jump. My stab wound spasms when I land. I pull the knife from my mouth and force myself to keep moving.

I bolt down the corridor, back in the direction of the great hall. The foyer across from it leads to the courtyard and the castle well.

I'm sorry, Ailesse. My chest gives a sharp pang. *I'll come back for you, I promise.*

Here's hoping next time her best friend doesn't ditch me and leap through a stained-glass window.

Sabine better have survived that fall. I saw how far the drop was to the river. After Casimir and his guards left, I snuck to the edge of the shattered window and took a good look below for myself.

The soldiers close in from behind. I run faster, passing the first column of the great hall. It's wrapped in garlands with the wild-flowers Casimir requested for Ailesse.

His words to Sabine ring through my head. *Ailesse isn't my pris-oner. I invited her to stay with me, and she agreed.* I scoff and swallow a bitter taste in my mouth. What a smooth liar South Galle is going to have for a king.

I run past the second column. A large soldier jumps out from behind it and rams into me. I crash backward onto the floor. My hand slams the stones. The knife falls from my grip and skids several feet away.

I fight to breathe. My back is on fire. The soldiers from the corridor are almost upon me. The one who knocked me over stalks closer.

Looks like I'm not escaping.

I kick my heel into the shin of the nearest guard. Crawl back to the second column. Pull the bone knife from my sheath. Another soldier grabs my left arm. At the same time, I slip the bone knife under the garland at the base of the column. I won't let them take it. Ailesse needs it to kill Casimir. She needs it to keep living.

A third soldier yanks me up by my collar. His thick fist flies at my face.

Pain bursts through my skull.

Everything goes black.

4
Ailesse

"IT'S A SHAME ABOUT YOUR crutch," my maid says, passing
it to me as she helps me stand. She positions me in front of the
mirror that hangs from my bedroom wall. "Otherwise you would
be able to dance tonight."

I squint at my reflection. A pool of still water would serve better
than this sheet of polished silver, but I faintly make out hints of my
maid's careful work: white powder to conceal my scattered freckles,
something called rouge she lightly dusted across my cheeks, and a
waxy lip balm that smells like wine and looks the shade of wild ber-
ries. She failed at plucking my eyebrows thin. After she yanked out
the first hair, my reflexes took hold of me. I grabbed her tweezers
and hurled them outside my window into the pouring rain.

I bend closer to the mirror. I'm not fond of how pale my skin looks or the darkened color of my lips—they remind me too much of my mother's stark beauty—but I do like the way my maid has styled my hair. The top half is woven into a bun with ribbons that match my moss-green dress, and the bottom half falls into long spirals she formed around heated tongs. Sabine's hair is this curly by nature.

Sabine . . .

A stitch of pain lodges between my ribs. I have to find a way to leave the feast early tonight. Sabine and my *famille* must be frantic about how to ferry without me.

"I wouldn't want to dance, anyway," I reply to my maid, and turn my back to the mirror. Dancing means death—rites of passages and blood sacrifice on secluded bridges under a full moon . . .

. . . though dancing also means Bastien's hands on my waist and hips, my fingers tracing the planes of his face, and the softness of his mouth. I won't diminish that memory by dancing with another boy, even if he is my *amouré.*

My maid clucks her tongue. "You're a peculiar girl, mademoiselle."

I shrug. "So I've been told."

Three knocks sound on my bedroom door. My maid startles. "It must be the prince!" She fusses with my brocade-and-velvet dress one last time. It clings off the edges of my shoulders, just like my rite of passage dress did. Perhaps Cas commissioned it to resemble that one on purpose. He saw me from a distance at Castelpont the night I lured him with the bone flute . . . the night I thought I had lured Bastien.

Satisfied, my maid crosses to the door and opens it a few inches. "Your Highness." She dips into a low curtsy. "Mademoiselle Ailesse is ready to accompany you to the feast."

The door opens wider, revealing Casimir. I grit my teeth and stand taller. *Stop racing,* I command my heart. Curse the gods for choosing such a handsome *amouré* for me.

Cas is wearing a wine-red doublet that perfectly complements the green shade of my dress, and his strawberry hair is slicked back and held in place by a thin gold crown. His eyes rivet to mine, then slowly travel over my dress, face, and hair. He drifts forward, his movements tentative, like he's walking on a bridge that might collapse at any moment. When he reaches me, he takes my hand and kisses it. Heat surges into my cheeks. My maid could have saved herself the trouble of applying any rouge.

"You're a vision," Cas says, breathless.

My toes curl in my fine slippers. There goes my heart again. "Are you hungry?" I ask, and his brow furrows. "For the feast, I mean." Better to get this party over with so I can get back to the hunt for my grace bones.

"Yes, of course." He cracks a smile. "Ravenous, in fact. Shall we?" He extends his arm. I don't know how to take it without abandoning my crutch. Besides, I don't want *him* being my crutch tonight. I stubbornly hobble past him.

We make our way out the door, down the corridor on the third level, and finally to the head of the staircase that winds down to the main floor. The rain patters on the mullioned windows as I stare at the flights of velvet-lined steps below. They seem to go on for miles. Curse my broken leg.

Cas tilts his head at me. "Would you permit me to carry you?"

My eyes fly wide. "Absolutely not."

"You should save your strength for the feast."

"How much energy does sitting and dining require?"

"I wouldn't want you to be exhausted when you meet my father."

"I'm *fine*." I plant my crutch on the first step and hop down. "I'm more than capable of—" I pitch forward. *Merde.* My crutch is pinning the skirt of my dress.

Just when I'm sure I'll tumble and break another limb, Cas swoops me into the cradle hold of his arms. My breath catches as I stare into his eyes. I'm still in shock from nearly falling.

"Careful." He chuckles. "These stairs are notorious for twisting ankles." He summons a servant to take my crutch and begins carrying me down the flights himself.

My body is stiff, my jaw clenched. I can't stop thinking about my carved crescent-moon pendant. I wouldn't have been so clumsy with my ibex grace bone strung around my neck. I'd have been agile, perfectly balanced, even elegant.

I *will* find where Cas has hidden my grace bones. Perhaps they're in the great hall, at the very center of the feast. They could even be tucked under the throne—somewhere Cas would never think I'd dare to search.

"I've already told my father so much about you," he says. "I would have introduced you to him by now, but he can't bear the indignity of being bedridden when you two become acquainted. Thank the gods he's feeling better today."

My ears are only half open. I'm too distracted by the thumping of his heart against my shoulder. Perhaps the real reason I haven't left this castle is because, deep inside me, I know what I must do. Kill Casimir. Stop that very heart from beating.

"Did you know my mother's favorite holiday was La Liaison?" Cas says as he steadily carries me down the stairs.

Maybe I wouldn't need a ritual knife. Any blade might do. He's wearing a jeweled dagger on his belt. How difficult would it be to swipe it off him and complete the ritual?

"Tonight will be a small gathering, I'm afraid, but when my mother was alive, she would open the castle to anyone who wished to attend the first feast. She'd offer them sweet breads and sugared almonds."

His words linger in my ears for a moment. I picture Queen Éliane alive again, her beautiful stone-blue eyes, so like her son's, widening in horror as his life bleeds out of him. I picture Casimir's father, King Durand, learning of his son's death. Would his heart fail at the news? Would I just as well have killed him, too?

"The dancing lasted all night, until morning. My father would always reserve the first and last dance with my mother. The great hall would hush as everyone watched them."

What if I can't kill Casimir? I promised myself I'd spare his life when I first agreed to stay here. If I don't, I'll be betraying Bastien. It would be just like I'd killed his father.

"I was supposed to be in bed by then, but I'd sneak out of my room and hide under a banquet table." Cas laughs. "I'd stuff myself with glazed tarts and spy on all the party guests. I'd smile, watching my mother smile. She was never happier than on the night of the first feast."

We're on the last flight of stairs. My body has softened in his arms. I'm listening to every word he says now, enchanted by the story he tells of a loving family living in peace together. It's easy to see Sabine in that setting, but not Odiva, maybe not even me. Perhaps I'm more similar to my proud mother than my tender sister.

Cas slows his descent on the last few steps. "I wish you had been able to take part in the celebrations the way they were back then. What I've prepared tonight seems vastly inadequate by comparison."

"I'm sure it will be lovely." The words are out of my mouth before I think better of them. It's all the encouragement he needs, and his right dimple appears. My heart flutters.

"My father will be there . . . and you will be, too. That's all that really matters."

Strains of cheerful music drift down the main corridor from the great hall. My head turns toward the sound. I briefly set aside thoughts of my grace bones and deadly soul-bond. "Has the dancing begun?" I ask, curious to watch the guests. I only ever learned the *danse de l'amant*. What are other dances like?

"Yes, I'm afraid so." Cas reaches the bottom of the stairs. "So has the celebration. Forgive me, but it was my intention to escort you in late. I've always found the beginning of the feast rather dull, and I didn't want to bore you. Now all the heralding of the guests will have taken place, and the king should have received the homage of each noble. We won't have to idle away any time before you're able to converse with my father."

He carefully lowers me to my feet. The servant he summoned is waiting for us and passes me my crutch. I reluctantly take it. I balance my weight on my good leg and stare down the long corridor, fidgeting.

"What is it?" Cas asks.

I turn and study him. He isn't winded from lifting me down the flights of stairs. If anything, he looks rejuvenated. His cheeks have a healthy glow, and his posture is strong and stable. I bite my lip. "You could carry me again," I say quietly. "I wouldn't mind this time. But only until we reach the great hall."

His brows rise ever so slightly, and his mouth curves into a gentle smile. He steps closer and places his hand against the small of my back. My skin heats at his touch, and I release a tremulous exhale.

"I regret that I'll be unable to ask you for the first and last dance tonight," he says, giving a nod at my crutch. "Perhaps this can be our dance instead."

Before I can answer, he sweeps me into his arms again. I let my crutch fall to the care of the servant. "And what is my part?" I ask with a teasing grin, hoping to establish a lighter mood between us. Cas keeps glancing at my lips like he has a mind to kiss me, but I won't let him. I'm only consenting to this dance because it can't really be considered dancing. "Doesn't a dance require two partners?"

"I suppose." He carries me down the main corridor.

"Well, my arms are free." I smirk. "Should I wave them in the air, like this?" I sway them back and forth to the music.

He chuckles. "Yes, perfect."

"What else should I do?"

Both of his dimples flash this time. "You must clap your hands so my feet stay on rhythm."

"Very well. Try to stay on *this* rhythm."

I clap erratically, speeding up, slowing down, whatever I can do to make the beat more difficult. He grins and does his best to follow. He races and pauses and skips and hops. I can't stop laughing as I jostle in his arms. The poor servant with my crutch trails behind us, struggling to stay in step.

We keep "dancing" down the corridor until Cas runs out of breath. He laughs, almost wheezing, until he stops twenty feet away from the first garland-draped column of the great hall. The glow of bright candles shines from within.

"We better compose ourselves," I whisper, giggling. I motion for the servant to bring me my crutch. When he does, I thank him and he excuses himself promptly. "I think I'm his favorite person," I say to Cas. He smiles, but doesn't laugh. He doesn't put me down, either. His eyes lower to my lips again. His head bends closer.

My pulse quickens. My nerves spring to life. For the briefest moment, I want to truly understand why the gods chose him for me. I want to feel it in his kiss. But suddenly I'm in another place—a tunnel, not a corridor. I'm in the arms of another boy, one with sea-blue eyes and dark tousled hair . . . a boy who opened his heart to me when he had every right to hate me. *You never needed to play a song for me, Ailesse.*

I turn my head before Cas's mouth touches mine. His breath heats my cheek as he exhales softly and pulls away. "I'm sorry," I say, sensing his disappointment. "You're gentle and you're kind, but—"

40

A man steps into the corridor from the great hall. It's Briand, one of Cas's young captains. I recognize him from the cavern bridge a month ago. Cas takes one look at his troubled face and hurriedly sets me down. I lean on my crutch.

"Have more intruders infiltrated the castle?" Cas walks forward to speak with Briand privately, but every word bounces back to me in the resonant corridor.

Briand shakes his head. "It isn't that, Your Highness. As your friend, I only wanted to prepare you before you joined the feast."

"Prepare me for what?"

Briand sighs and combs his fingers through his short-cropped hair. "Your father . . . he isn't here. He wasn't able to attend after all."

"Did he take a turn for the worse?" Cas's body tenses.

"Not exactly. I spoke with his manservant. Apparently your father wasn't even able to stand upright after bathing and getting dressed tonight. His physician insisted he continue to rest for a few more days."

Cas falls silent for a long moment. "I see." His head drops, and the sight of his wilted shoulders makes my chest ache. More than anything, he wanted to please his father tonight. I understand that kind of yearning. I always wanted to please my mother, and I almost always failed. But Cas's disappointment must be so much harder. Until now, he believed his father was recovering.

"But you have my word there are no more intruders," Briand says, in a weak attempt to comfort his friend. "No other accomplice was here but the thief."

My heart beats out of cadence. "Thief?" I hobble closer on

my crutch. "What thief?"

Cas stiffens. He won't turn around to look at me. Briand shoots him a nervous glance and carefully replies, "No one that should trouble you. We've taken care of him."

"What thief?" I glare at Briand when Cas still won't give me an answer.

The captain swallows and looks to his prince for permission. Cas blows out a heavy breath and nods. "Bastien Colbert," Briand replies. "But you are safe, mademoiselle." His next words almost drive me to my knees. "The thief will hang. His Highness locked him in the dungeons."

5
Sabine

My knees tremble as I guide the thirty-three Ferriers of my *famille* from our home at Château Creux to the cliffs above the arm-shaped inlet in the Nivous Sea. Everyone except for the five novices too young to ferry and the six aged Leurress too old to battle the dead are here with me . . . here to witness if I succeed or fail.

The ferrying dress I changed into is dripping wet from the storm, and my arms throb from my grueling swim through the river below Beau Palais. The closer I lead the Ferriers to the land bridge, the more my doubts prey on my mind. Can I really open the Gates?

I quietly hum the melody the silver owl imprinted on my mind.

"Hush, Sabine," Roxane whispers behind me. "That song must only be heard coming from the bone flute."

My cheeks flush, and I nod. The Leurress are forbidden to sing any ritual songs; Odiva taught us that our voices would defile the sacred music. But I have a tendency to hum or sing when I'm nervous.

Once we reach the cliffs, we take the secret passage between two boulders to the carved limestone stairs that descend to a cave off the shore. We walk from the cave out onto the rain-drenched sand of the beach.

My pulse beats faster. It's midnight. It has to be. The tide is at its lowest, and the rocks of the land bridge have emerged from the water. They form a forty-foot pathway that runs half the length of the inlet. It's already time to ferry.

I let the Leurress pass me and take their places at even intervals on the land bridge. The skirts of their white ceremonial dresses flap about in the lashing rain, but each woman stands strong with her staff ready. They look to me to join them. I'm still on the beach, my feet sinking in the wet sand.

"Come on, Sabine." Isla shivers, her ginger hair plastered to her face. She's taken position at the foot of the bridge for no other reason than to goad me, I'm sure. She's the youngest Ferrier, aside from me—if I even count as a Ferrier. I may have three grace bones, but I never had a rite of passage.

The Leurress spent the earlier part of the evening debating whether I should be allowed here. A small majority finally won because I have the only bone flute still in existence—and now

I know the ferrying siren song. I had to prove it by awkwardly humming each nuanced phrase. Roxane didn't chide me for defiling the music then. She deemed it necessary, and the other elders followed her lead.

"What are you waiting for?" Isla asks.

I look to the high cliffs jutting up from the shore. Ailesse isn't anywhere. Which means Bastien wasn't able to free her on his own.

I should be relieved—the silver owl warned me what might happen if my sister ferried tonight—but my stomach won't stop roiling. Ailesse would have thrived on this opportunity to lead the ferrying, while all I want to do is bury myself in the sand.

Pull yourself together, Sabine. Do this for your sister.

I tighten my grip on my quarterstaff, turn back to face the inlet, and take my first tentative step onto the land bridge.

Isla arches a brow as I walk past her and move toward Maurille, the next Ferrier in line. The middle-aged Leurress places her bronze hand on my arm and squeezes. I muster a smile in return. She's one of the few who have supported me from the beginning.

I slip by her on the twelve-foot-wide rocky path and approach two of the elders, Roxane and Milicent. They step back to give me space to cross a more narrow section of the bridge. A generous action, though diminished by their wary expressions. They were ready to follow any order from Odiva, but not from a sixteen-year-old girl—a girl who isn't even the *matrone's* blooded heir. To them, I'm just the girl Odiva named as heir when Ailesse went missing. I've kept the truth a secret; otherwise, I'd have to explain that

Odiva was my mother, as well as Ailesse's, and that she had conceived me with a man who wasn't even her own *amouré*. My *famille* doesn't need one more reason to disregard me.

I continue advancing toward the end of the bridge. The rain pelts my face as I walk by the remaining Ferriers: Isabeau, Vivienne, Alainne, Giselle, Chantae, Élodie, Jacqueline, Maïa, Rosalinde, Daphné, Fleur, Valerine, Adélaide, Orianne, Rochelle, Séraphine, Alette, Jessamyn, Nadine, Damiana, Joselle, Clémence, Laurinne, Cecille, Désirée, Zoelie, Bernadette, Dolssa, and Pernelle.

All of them are older than me, more experienced, more committed—I never even wanted to be a Ferrier. My foot slips on the wet rocks, despite the agility from my salamander grace. I steady myself and take the last step to claim my position at the end of the bridge—the *matrone*'s position. I release a trembling breath and unwrap the bone flute from a piece of lambswool.

Pernelle, closest to me on the land bridge, comes to my side. She smoothes the dripping honey-blond hair off her face and holds a woolen blanket over my head. That way my notes won't burble in the rain. I bring the flute to my mouth, squeeze my eyes shut, and try to concentrate.

"Relax, Sabine," Pernelle says. At thirty-nine, she's the youngest of the elders, and the only one who supports me. "This isn't the first time the Leurress have ferried in a storm. I'll stay beside you. For now, focus on playing the siren song."

A lump forms in my throat—from guilt, not gratitude. Pernelle trusts me, but I've told so many lies, even though I had good intentions. I haven't wanted to make things worse for my *famille*.

They're still mourning Odiva, and they don't trust that I can lead them. They don't know Ailesse is in Beau Palais and soul-bound to the prince of South Galle. Or that Odiva sacrificed thousands of souls to Tyrus—the Unchained dead who deserved Paradise but who my mother ferried to the Underworld instead. They don't even know I slaughtered the golden jackal we were all desperately searching for last month. I told them the flute I'm holding is Odiva's, and that she found and killed the jackal, then carved this flute from its bone before she died, when in reality I was the one who did those things.

Ailesse will take my place soon. She'll make everything right again.

But what if I can never bring her back? How will I tell my *famille* the truth?

For now, focus on playing the siren song. I inwardly repeat what Pernelle just told me. I breathe in and out and start to play.

The melody of the siren song pierces the roar of the rainfall. Each achingly beautiful note beckons and urges and instills desire. If more people besides the dead had ears to hear it, all might come and glimpse the dark wonder of the Beyond.

The music sails high in its last measure, then dips low for a final reverberating note. I pull the flute away from my mouth and wrap it back in the lambswool. I *think* I played it right.

"Well done." Pernelle lowers her makeshift canopy. She points to the end of the land bridge, eight feet away, where the rocks drop away into the water. There, a low wave begins to froth and gurgle.

My heart drums. I hurriedly stuff the bone flute into the sodden pocket of my dress. I've never seen the Gate of water before. I've only seen its strange counterpart, the Gate of dust, at the end of the soul bridge in the underground cavern. Each of those Gates, here and there, leads to the same place: Tyrus's Underworld.

The wave ripples higher without spilling over onto the land bridge. It keeps rising until it's thirteen feet tall and hangs from the air like a billowing veil. The water continues rushing upward, but it never crests, and its midnight-blue color darkens to a sheer silky black.

The purest siren song begins to play, not from my bone flute, but from both realms of the Beyond. It's so captivating I'm almost breathless. Layered over the deep melody from the Underworld comes a soaring descant from Paradise.

I glance to Elara's Gate, which has just risen as well. It stands a few feet to the right, where it also adjoins the bridge. The Gate is barely visible, only a shimmer of silver, like a fogged-up window embedded in the slanting rainfall. It looks just as it did at the other soul bridge, except the spiral staircase beyond it, leading to Paradise, doesn't disappear against a cavern ceiling; it extends all the way into the sky, past the storm clouds pulsing with lightning.

A slow exhale purges out of me. My mouth curves upward. I've done what my mother couldn't do last time she was here: I've opened the Gates. My siren song was accepted. Which means it's also unlocked all the other ferrying Gates in the world. Now the Leurress, near and far, can perform our sacred work.

For the first time in my life, I feel a flicker of pride at being born a Leurress.

A shriek echoes off the cliffs surrounding the inlet. The warmth inside me vanishes. The dead are coming.

I turn and hold my quarterstaff ready and ground myself on the bridge. My role is critical tonight. Beyond opening the Gates, I'm required to deliver each soul through one of them. The final act of ferrying is the *matrone's* duty—my duty.

Nearby, Pernelle also takes a defensive position. The other Ferriers along the land bridge do the same, every woman wielding a staff of her own. Swords and daggers would be pointless. We can fight the rebellious dead, but a soul can't be killed; it can only be ferried.

The cliffs start to light up with flares of *chazoure*. Without my nighthawk vision, I wouldn't be able to see the glowing color of the souls. The other Ferriers also have sight to perceive it from their unique grace bones. Their heads turn and bodies shift, watching the souls scale down the cliffs and pour out from the cave off the shore.

The first soul to reach the bridge is Chained, marked by the gods for his unforgivable sins. He's a giant of a man—at least two feet taller than me. And he's fast. He bolts down the bridge and dodges most of the Ferriers' staff swings and blows. The hits he takes don't faze him. He keeps barreling forward, his *chazoure* eyes clapped on mine. He's after me because I played the flute. The Chained man, like all souls, can't resist being summoned here, but he's still desperate to avoid an eternity in the Underworld.

Elara, help me. I'm not ready.

Pernelle twirls her staff to span the twelve-foot width of the bridge. She's trying to stall him and buy me time, but I'm only backtracking.

Tyrus's siren song thrums against the vertebrae of my spine.

I glance behind me and gasp. I'm only inches from the Gate of water. I stumble forward to distance myself. The Chained giant shoves past Pernelle and lunges for me.

"Feint, roll, and jab!" she shouts.

I immediately fall into the counterattack pattern drilled into me as a novice. The movement works. I trick the Chained man long enough to somersault in front of him, then I swing around and slam the end of my staff into his back.

His tangible body lurches forward, but then he digs in his feet. He growls and spins to face me—fast. He grabs my staff before I can strike again. His gaze drops to my grace bone necklace. His eyes flash wide. I'm not sure what's overcome him, but I yank my staff away and ram it into his chest. He tumbles backward through the silken black water of the Gate.

I catch my breath. Nod my thanks to Pernelle. She nods back and runs down the bridge to help Dolssa wrangle a fitful child— Unchained, but still terrified of the afterlife. The other Ferriers are also busy encouraging, cajoling, and battling other souls. I wait at the end of the bridge for them to prod someone toward the Gates, keeping my defenses raised against the lure of the Underworld.

It's powerful, but ultimately resistible—at least for me. Ailesse's struggle was undeniable, but she was always the thrill seeker between us, driven by her passion more than reason.

"*Sabine.*"

I frown. Where is the woman calling my name? She's barely loud enough to be heard above the rolling tide and falling rain.

"*Sabine.*"

Her rich voice ripples like music.

"*Sabine, turn around. I am here.*"

My insides thread together. It can't be . . .

I turn. Look. Stare past the black veil of the Underworld. I feel blood trickle from my face. My mother . . . she's standing just beyond the Gate of water.

Odiva is still serenely—severely—beautiful. Palest white skin, a sheet of raven hair, lips red as blood. She wears her majestic grace bones, just as she did in life. Her three-tier necklace holds the claws and claw-shaped bone pendant of an albino bear, along with the tooth band of a whiptail stingray. The feather epaulettes on her shoulders rustle against the talons of an eagle owl. One of the talons, like the bear-claw pendant, is also carved from bone. Most intimidating of all, the vertebrae of an asp viper and the skull of a giant noctule bat form her *matrone's* crown.

But my mother can't be . . . she can't be alive.

"You're dead."

My hoarse voice is only a scratch of sound, but my mother must hear me, because she replies, "Do I glow with *chazoure?*"

I shake my head. My thundering heart echoes the sky above. "But how are you—?"

"Where is your sister, Sabine?"

I blink. "She's . . . she's . . ."

The Unchained child stumbles into me, sobbing. She's even smaller than Felise or Lisette, the youngest of our *famille*. I numbly take her hand and escort her to Elara's Gate. My mother's black eyes follow the child. After I ferry her, I drift back to Tyrus's Gate, unbidden. I feel strangely disconnected to my mind and body. None of what's happening can be real, yet it must be real. I'd never willingly imagine this.

"I am trapped here, Sabine." Odiva places her hand against the Gate of water. "I need my firstborn daughter to set me free. Where is she?"

"Ailesse isn't . . ." I press my lips together. I shouldn't be talking to my mother. I take a backward step and glance around for Pernelle. She'll tell me what to do. But the youngest of the elders is grappling with two Chained. None of the other Ferriers notice me, either. They're busy with oncoming souls.

"Why isn't Ailesse ferrying as *matrone* tonight?" Odiva surveys my position at the end of the land bridge. Tyrus's siren song swells behind her, and its dark beauty loosens my tongue.

"Her *amouré* is the prince of South Galle. His father, the king, is dying, so . . . so Ailesse will be soon be queen." I'll let my mother believe that if it protects my sister, though I refuse to let Casimir win his way with her. "She prefers a gold crown over being *matrone*," I can't help adding to provoke Odiva, though I'm sure it isn't true. Ailesse prepared all her life to lead our *famille*.

Odiva tilts her head with an elegance uniquely her own. "And what of that crown when Ailesse must kill her *amouré*?"

I lift a shoulder, feigning more boldness than I have. "She'll still be queen."

Her lip curls. "Bring her to me, Sabine. All she needs to do is touch my hand, and then Tyrus will release me."

I can't believe her arrogance. "Why would I help you? Why

would I want you back, after what you've done?"

"What a *god* asked me to do, you mean."

I scoff.

"I am not evil, child. Do you see me wrapped in chains?"

"Only the dead wear chains."

Odiva doesn't acknowledge my remark. She touches the necklace she wears, but not the one with her grace bones. My father, whoever he was, gave it to her—a crow skull with a ruby caught in its open beak. "Your father desires to meet you, Sabine. If Ailesse releases me, I can bring him back, too."

"No." My voice cuts sharper than my bone knife, and my legs start shaking. I finally understand what my mother wants. Her pact with Tyrus is incomplete. The god still requires my sister to be sacrificed before he'll release my Chained father from the Underworld. "I don't wish to meet him. And Ailesse will *never* come here. I'll make sure of it."

Her onyx eyes bore into me. "Will you? Beware the grace you bear, daughter. Tyrus's golden jackal is cunning. He will prey upon your weaknesses."

My stomach gives a hard twist. Tyrus must have told her I have the golden jackal's grace bone. When she was alive, I had claimed my pendant was carved from a black wolf. "The jackal makes me strong."

Odiva's hand reaches toward me, her palm pressed again to the veil of water between us. "I want to help you, Sabine. I have learned many things in this realm. We can share your grace together."

"That's impossible."

"Not for me. Not anymore. I can teach you how to reach your potential with the jackal. Without my guidance, its power will consume you."

I swallow. Could a grace really be that dangerous?

Tyrus's siren song grows louder, faster.

Growls of the Chained close in behind me. I need to ferry them, but I can't look away from my mother's penetrating eyes. "Come to me, daughter," she says. Her raven hair swirls. Her midnight-blue dress sways about her ankles. "All you have to do is touch my hand."

"Sabine, what are you doing?" Pernelle shouts. "Ferry them!"

I gasp. My hand is just an inch from the veil. I don't even remember lifting a finger. I jerk backward and spin around. I can't see Pernelle. Two Chained are in my face. One swipes for me. The other reaches for my neck. He startles when he sees my necklace.

I dodge them both and rush the opposite way down the land bridge.

"Sabine, come back!" Pernelle cries.

I can't. She'll have to ferry the souls through the Gates for me. I have to get away from my mother.

The other Ferriers don't see me until I race past them. I dart around their swinging staffs and the *chazoure* souls they battle. "Stop, Sabine!" Maurille calls near the foot of the bridge. "The Gates will close!"

I keep running. She's not making sense. The Gates stay open as long as there are souls left to ferry.

I pass Isla last. She tries to grab me, but she can't reach me with the Chained woman between us. "You're the *matrone!*" she says as I leap off the rocks toward the shore. "You have to stay on the—"

My feet hit the sand.

"—bridge!"

The Gate of water crests into a high wave and crashes onto the far end of the bridge. It doesn't rise again. The silvery shimmer leading to Elara's realm also vanishes.

Everyone on the land bridge—Ferriers and souls—comes to an abrupt halt.

The souls gape at the place where the Gates no longer stand. Cries of confusion ring out. They build into riotous roars.

The souls flee the bridge. Dive into the water. Run onto the shore. Climb the hidden stairs. Scale the limestone cliffs. The Ferriers and I try to stop them, herd them. But we can't contain the chaos.

No, no, no. What happened last ferrying night can't be happening again.

The dead are loose, the Chained and Unchained. They're heading toward Dovré, toward the biggest population in South Galle.

But this time it's directly because of me.

6

Bastien

I curse Casimir for the hundredth time as I kick aside the straw in my dungeon cell and tap the paving stones with my boot. Another prisoner could have hidden something thin and sharp in here. I need it. The soldiers confiscated my lock picks after they knocked me out. I woke up with a splitting headache and an even deeper grudge against the prince.

Bastard. He threw me in this reeking cell himself. I have a foggy memory of the gloating look on his face when the barred door clanged shut. "Thief," he called me, like that one word summed me up. I used to take pride in that title. I've been a wanted criminal in Dovré for years, but I've never been caught until today.

A thick-necked dungeons guard walks by and catches me

prodding at the stones. "What do you think you're doing?" He crosses his arms.

I cross mine. "Dancing. Can't help myself." I tip my chin at the ceiling. "I blame the party music." It has to be well after midnight, and from the faint sounds drifting down here, the first feast of La Liaison is still in full swing. "I'm surprised you're not doing a little jig yourself."

The guard scowls. "Careful, boy. We kill the smart-mouthed even faster down here."

I hold my grin steady until he stalks away. As soon as he's out of sight, I exhale and drag my hands through my hair. I have to get out of here. Free Ailesse while I'm at it.

Thunder rumbles outside. I step up on a stone bench at the back of my cell to reach a small grate at the end of a chute in the ceiling. It let in a little daylight before sunset—not that there was much light to be had. This storm won't quit.

I wrestle with the grate to pry it free. Maybe I can use it as a weapon. It won't budge. I ignore the wrenching pain from my stab wound and keep yanking. *Come on.*

"Bastien?"

My muscles go stiff. That voice. *Ailesse.* I hold my breath and turn around. She stands five feet past the bars of my cell. Her auburn hair glows red under the torchlight. Her creamy skin gleams soft and radiant—almost too perfect. I miss her freckles and the natural flush of pink on the tip of her nose. She's all dusted in powder. It doesn't matter. She's still more beautiful than I remember. A green dress hangs off her bare shoulders, and a gold-and-emerald belt droops low from the slender curve of her waist.

Her umber eyes fill with tears. "You're alive," she chokes out. "How are you even . . . ?" She swallows. "My mother stabbed you."

"I'm fine." I can barely speak. *She's really here.* "Doing much better now."

She looks me over to be sure, then her eyes harden, her jaw stiffens. "You shouldn't have come."

"Ailesse . . ." The tension freezing me in place releases. I'm suddenly desperate to hold her. I jump off the bench and rush to the bars. She moves slower, staggering. Her nostrils flare. She's angry. I don't blame her. All I've done is complicate everything.

As she limps closer, her loose sleeve slips back. A crutch rests beneath her left arm. I stretch out my hand to help her. She's still beyond reach, just like she was on the soul bridge when she crushed her leg. I was bleeding out and close to dying. I couldn't stop Casimir from taking her away.

She hobbles another step, and our fingers touch. Then they're grasping, pulling. She's flush to the bars now. There's just enough space for our mouths to come together. She lets the crutch fall. Her hands grab at my sleeves. Her fingernails dig into my arms. I hold her face. I brush away the wetness on her cheek. I don't stop kissing her. *Damn these bars.* She's not close enough.

"How did you get down here?" I find ways to speak around her mouth on mine, pulling back just enough to form a few words at a time. "You have to be careful. That guard . . . he'll return any moment."

"He's preoccupied." She kisses me harder. "There's another entrance to the dungeons. I saw Sophie sneak in to meet him."

"Who's Sophie?"

"Servant girl."

I try to muster a reply, but can't. Ailesse smells amazing. Fresh earth and wildflowers and dizzying *life*. My hands tangle through her hair. I can't get enough of her. We slide down the bars until we're kneeling. She finds a position more comfortable for her broken leg. Some buried part of my brain tells me we should stop, escape first, wait until later to get lost in each other like this.

Later is hard for me to think through now that I'm finally holding her.

"Ailesse . . ." I murmur.

"Mmm?" Her hands crawl under my shirt, and I shiver.

"Do you have anything . . . sharp?"

"Sharp?" Her laugh is breathy and warm.

"And thin . . ." I run my fingers across the smooth skin of her shoulders. "So I can . . . pick . . . the lock."

She pulls back and blinks. "Oh . . . um, I think so." Her lips are puffy and red, and her face is flushed. She paws through her mussed hair, searching. "I can't believe you got caught."

"I'm not exactly in top form right now."

Ailesse releases a tight exhale. "You really shouldn't have come here. You could have been killed."

"Tell me you would have stayed behind if our situations were reversed." Her guilty silence says everything. "That's what I thought."

She glares at me, pressing her lips together against a grin. She plucks a decorative comb from her hair. "Can you pry off one of the teeth?" She passes it to me.

I apply some pressure, and the comb starts to bend. "I doubt the teeth are long enough. Gold is too pliable, anyway. It usually jams up a lock. Do you have any hairpins?" She shakes her head. I examine her dress. "Any whalebones sewn into the seams of that bodice?"

She wrinkles her nose. "Women wear whalebones in their clothes?"

I chuckle. "I can't believe that shocks you, of all people."

She smiles, but then the corners of her mouth fall. She rubs her neck. "I don't have *any* bones right now."

"Casimir took them?" I scoff. "Doesn't surprise me." Another reason to hate the prince. I turn the hair comb over in my hands. "What's he doing giving you gold?"

Ailesse shrugs and lowers her eyes. "He's offered me far more than that."

My stomach twists. "The offer can't be so sweet when you have no freedom . . . can it?"

"Casimir gives me freedom. That's not why I decline."

"What do you mean, he gives you freedom?" A low roll of thunder echoes through the dungeons corridor. "The prince abducted you."

"No, Bastien. I chose to stay here from the beginning."

"You call that a choice? You had a broken leg and no grace bones."

"I still could have left if I wanted."

I don't believe her. "Why can't you just admit the prince gets whatever he wants—*whoever* he wants?" My voice rises. "He thinks he's entitled to it."

"Shh, the guard will hear us."

"Then let him."

She sighs. "You don't understand the situation."

"Why don't you enlighten me?"

"Casimir is a good person. When he brought me here, he asked me to give him a chance."

"A chance at what? Winning your heart?" I can't believe what I'm hearing. "Is that what this is?" I wave my hand at the dress she's wearing. It must have cost a fortune. She's practically being groomed as a queen. "You giving him a chance?"

"Maybe not in the way he meant, but yes. He's my *amouré* and—"

"So have feelings for him now?"

Her eyes narrow. "I was thinking of *you* when I made my choice not to kill Casimir."

My mouth goes slack. I can't even speak for a moment. "You . . . *what?*"

"What if I had killed you when we first met at Castelpont? What if your *father* had been given a chance and hadn't been killed so rashly?"

A vivid image of him being stabbed by a Bone Crier grips my mind. "Don't compare Casimir to my father." My jaw muscle tenses. "That isn't fair."

"I'm trying to make you understand." Now her voice grows louder. "Your father deserved to live. So does Casimir. That's why I can't kill him."

"But you'll die with him."

"I'll find a way to break the soul-bond, the same way you and I—"

"We were dreaming, Ailesse. We were *deluded*." What's the matter with her? She knows this. She already lived through it once. Why can't I make *her* understand? "There's no way to break the soul-bond."

Her lips purse stubbornly. "You can't be sure of that."

"Ailesse, please . . ." I reach past the bars and hold her arms with shaking hands. "Don't argue with me about this. I can't—" My voice cracks. I'm suddenly a child again, holding my father's dead body. "I can't lose you, too."

Her eyes shine, and the anger fades from them. She slips closer to me. "You won't, Bastien." She strokes the side of my face. "We'll figure this out, I promise. We have time. I planned to leave here after my leg healed." She lifts a shoulder. "I was actually going to leave tonight—it's ferrying night."

My stomach sinks. "But then I came."

Her mouth flickers into a small smile. "But then you came. And I couldn't leave knowing you were locked up down here."

My head droops forward against the bars. *Merde*, I've made a mess of things.

She combs her fingers through the back of my hair. "I snuck away from the feast as soon as I could. I told Casimir I didn't feel well."

I look up. "You left a dinner with the prince and the king that easily?"

"King Durand couldn't come after all. He was too ill. And Casimir drank his disappointment away with several glasses of wine. It wasn't so hard to excuse myself."

I exhale heavily. "Sabine is going to be sick when she finds out I'm the reason you stayed here tonight."

Her eyes widen. "You've been talking to Sabine?"

"She was here today. Planned this whole break-in with Jules, Marcel, and me."

Ailesse gasps. "Well, is she all right? What happened?" She grips my hand. "Bastien, tell me everything."

I sum up the last two weeks in as few words as possible, including today's adventure with the black powder. "Hopefully Jules and Marcel abandoned the castle well," I say. "The soldiers will be searching for the way we broke in."

When I explain what happened with Sabine—her run-in with Casimir and how she bolted from the castle with no explanation, Ailesse crinkles her brow. "Maybe you didn't hear everything they said."

"Maybe," I admit.

"Sabine had to have a strong reason to leave so suddenly like that."

I rub my jaw. "She *did* ask me to tell you something."

"What?" Ailesse leans forward.

"Apparently Sabine knows the siren song to open the Gates."

She draws her head back. "What? How?"

"She didn't say. She was too busy staging the most dramatic exit possible."

Ailesse grows quiet as she thinks over everything. She seems . . . upset. Understandable, given how overprotective she is of her sister.

"Sabine will be fine," I reassure her, kissing her palm. "She has a working bone flute. It's how she lured Casimir when she brought him to the cavern bridge—some kind of proxy ritual, she said. So you don't have to worry about the ferrying tonight. She'll lead it just like she's been leading your *famille* all this time you've been away."

Ailesse's eyebrows shoot upward. "She's been leading the *famille*? As *matrone*?"

I don't understand why she's so worked up. "Just until you come back."

Her shoulders sag.

I brush the back of her hand with my thumb. "What's wrong?"

"Nothing, it's just . . . my *famille* wouldn't let Sabine take charge like that unless my mother had already declared her as her heir. She must have done that when I was with you." Ailesse forces a grin, but the look in her eyes is hollow. "It was all part of my mother's plan to sacrifice me to Tyrus."

Odiva had made a deal with the god of the Underworld two years ago: her firstborn daughter's life in exchange for the man she loved. Not her *amouré*, but Sabine's father. The pact was supposed to resurrect him, but it didn't because Odiva didn't keep her end of the bargain. She never killed Ailesse. She sacrificed herself instead.

"But you're still alive—you're still her heir," I say, trying to comfort her.

"I know," she murmurs, but her eyes stay empty.

Footsteps echo from the dungeons' corridor. The guard is returning. Ailesse startles and grabs her crutch. I reach through the bars and help her to her feet. "I'll come back soon—later tonight," she rasps. "I'll bring a proper lockpick."

She starts to turn, but I tug her back and kiss her mouth. She pulls away quickly, shrinking into herself. She shakes her head apologetically. "I—I have to leave."

"Wait." I try to pin what I've done to offend her. There's a new rift between us that wasn't there a moment ago. "Sabine brought a bone knife." I hurriedly explain where I hid it. "Please, just think about what I said. You may not get another chance to be near Casimir after we leave Beau Palais." *I wish I could kill the bastard for her.*

She hobbles backward on her crutch. "Bastien, I . . ."

"Please, Ailesse."

She presses her lips together and glances toward the sound of the approaching guard. She finally nods, pivots on her crutch, and rushes into the shadows past the torchlight.

I blow out a shaky breath. What I've asked her to do is a betrayal to my father's memory, but I'm still desperate for her to do it and kill Casimir to save herself.

7
Ailesse

THE HILT OF THE BONE knife digs into my spine. I slipped it under the laces of my dress after I snuck it out of the flower garland, the hiding spot at the entrance of the great hall Bastien told me about. I managed to retrieve it without having to return to the celebration and without anyone seeing me. Now my long hair conceals the blade, but my heart still beats a frantic rhythm.

Calm down, Ailesse. Just because you took the knife doesn't mean you're really going to kill Cas.

But you should, another voice speaks to me. It has Bastien's lower register, though when it echoes again, it sounds like Sabine. My closest friends care about me—of course they want me to live—but they don't know Cas. It's easier to say someone should die when they're a stranger.

I hobble down the corridor as quickly as possible. The occasional guards on the third level of Beau Palais don't trouble me. Neither do the servants who are still awake. They bow and curtsy like I'm a princess. They don't know who I really am. They don't realize that when I wear a crown it will be made of bones.

I'll be the one to lead my *famille* on the next ferrying night, even though my mother named Sabine as her heir. I'm supposed to be *matrone*. Sabine knows that in her heart. My *famille* does, too. They'll find me worthy and restore me to my rightful position . . . won't they?

My stomach clenches. I curl into myself for a moment, the way I did with Bastien in the dungeons. I don't know what's the matter with me except I suddenly miss my *famille* more than ever. That divide feels like a physical tear through my body. I've been gone too long. After I free Bastien, I need to return home.

I stare down the long corridor. My room is still several doors away. I curse my shattered knee and slow pace and missing grace bones. My peregrine falcon could be giving me speed right now, my tiger shark strength and endurance, my alpine ibex agility and balance on this crutch. I exhale, trying not to think of what I don't have. Instead, I make a mental inventory of the items in my room. Is there anything Bastien could use for a lockpick?

I take another step just as a faint sound reverberates though the castle. A woman's laughter. It's wild with abandon, but eerie in a way that raises the hair on my arms. I glance behind me and see no one. This stretch of the corridor is empty.

". . . wish you could have met her."

Cas? I look in the other direction. *His* voice I recognize. It comes from within the nearest room, beyond a tall and ornate door that has been left wide open. King Durand's chambers. I have to pass them to get to my room.

I cautiously press forward, trying my best to be quiet. If Cas finds me, I'll have to explain why I lied about having to leave the feast early.

"Don't worry," he says. "I know you need to save your strength. We'll find another way for you to meet Ailesse."

As I pass the door, I can't help peering inside. Cas is seated on a chair beside the king's four-poster bed. Its velvet drapes are drawn closed except for one open panel, through which Cas leans forward, elbows on his knees, and holds his father's extended hand. I find myself lingering. This is the first time I've ever seen King Durand.

He might have been handsome once—his face has a fine bone structure—but his skin is a sickly grayish color, even under the candlelight. And he's so thin he looks almost skeletal. His light green eyes are his best feature. Perhaps that's because of the loving gaze he gives his son. He opens his mouth to speak but then starts coughing. Cas quickly presses a cup of water to his lips. It dribbles down his chin as he struggles to drink.

I glance away. Cas wouldn't want me to see his father like this. I start to creep past the doorway, hoping he won't see my shadow, but I don't make it to the other side. The eerie laughter returns. It cackles in my ears and tears right past me, entering the room. But I don't see the woman anywhere.

Cas turns. His brows pull tight. "Ailesse, what are you—?" He jerks sideways as the bodiless laughter rushes by him. "What was that?"

Icy dread hits my veins. I finally understand. "No, this can't be happening. Not again."

"What can't be happening?"

I sweep my hair aside, yank the bone knife from the laces of my dress, and charge into the room, using my crutch to propel me. "Protect your father, Cas!"

He stands and whips out his jeweled dagger. His eyes rove over the tapestries and shadowy corners of the room. "Who's in here? I can't see her."

"She's a Chained." *She has to be.* Which means Sabine couldn't open the Gates to the Beyond tonight. The unferried souls are loose again. My *famille* needs me after all.

"Chained?" Cas repeats.

"Some people call them ghosts."

His eyes widen. "Pardon?"

"Ghosts," I repeat. He knows nothing about the dead. He'll have to learn quickly. I rush around the bed so the king is guarded from both sides. "But she's a bad one." I'd be able to see her *chazoure* color if I had my peregrine falcon vision—or feel her location if I had my tiger shark sixth sense. "Don't let her reach the king. He's already weak."

The window flashes with a bright pulse of lightning. Deafening thunder immediately follows. I can't hear anything else for a moment.

"—off him, you fiend!" Cas rages.

I throw aside the velvet drapes. King Durand is sitting upright, but suspended at an odd angle. The Chained woman is lifting him.

He weakly bats at his invisible attacker, his eyes round with terror. Cas blindly slashes his dagger, but his blade doesn't hit anything. He doesn't dare aim closer to his father.

I flip my bone knife and hold it by the blade. "Cas, move!" He swiftly angles away. I throw the knife. It stops in midair, an inch above the king's face. The woman's terrible shriek rings out.

The king drops onto his pillow. The hovering knife yanks back and falls. At the foot of the bed, the velvet drapes billow apart. The Chained woman has burst through them.

Everything goes quiet except the rain pelting the window glass. I strain to hear where the woman went. Cas's face is in utter shock. He's never witnessed an attack from the dead. Sabine brought him to the cavern bridge after I'd finished ferrying souls. "How is it that a ghost can be stabbed?" he whispers. He's standing just as still as I am, his dagger at the ready.

"The Chained are tangible." I lean on the mattress with my good knee. I pluck up my bone knife. "All souls are."

Cas nods, though his brow stays furrowed. "And these Chained don't bleed?"

"Or die."

He swallows. "Marvelous."

King Durand starts coughing again. Cas quickly props him up with another pillow.

An awful thought seizes me. "When did your father first become ill?"

"About a month ago."

"When other people in Dovré also became sick?" The second plague, some call it. They know nothing about the Chained, who are invisible to them. They don't realize that the reason so many people in the city are still weak and suffering is because the Chained stole Light from them last time the dead were loose and unferried. And stolen Light can't be replenished.

"Yes." Cas studies my face in the candlelight. "Why?"

The drapes at the foot of the bed gust apart. I swipe out with my knife, but I'm not fast enough. I'm kicked in the ribs and hurled back several feet.

"Ailesse!" Cas shouts as I topple over. My crutch flies out of my grip. My bone knife spins across the floor.

The Chained woman laughs. Cas leaps toward the sound, but he grabs on to nothing. Another peal of laughter rings from the other side of him.

I gasp for air. I don't have any breath to warn him.

He turns and stabs with his dagger, but then his hand stills. She's caught his wrist.

"Foolish prince," the woman purrs. "You'll be just like your father, won't you, comfortable here in your castle and blind to everyone else who suffers?"

She's one of the dissenters, I realize. She blames the monarchy for the recent plague.

Cas glares at the spot where her face should be. "Does my

father look comfortable to you?"

His dagger hand twists roughly, forcing him to drop the blade. The moment it's out of his hand, he's thrown backward. He slams into a stone wall, and his head whips back, cracking against it, too.

Panic overwhelms me. If Cas dies, I die. I drag myself toward my bone knife. I don't have time to grab my crutch, and no help is coming. The castle soldiers won't be able to hear our struggle above the howling thunder.

The mattress caves. The Chained woman is on the bed. "The gods are punishing you for cursing the land," she tells the king. Durand's head lifts off his pillow, pulled up by her again. He moans, eyes wild. "I'm going to help them."

"Let him go!" My knife is five feet out of my reach now. I scramble faster. "Cas, help!"

The prince struggles to stand, dazed from hitting his head.

"Your father has already lost too much Light," I say. The king must have been attacked before, when the Chained were loose in Dovré. "She'll kill him! She'll kill his soul!"

Cas's face turns ashen. "Is that possible?"

"Yes!"

He blanches even paler and fumbles for his dagger. I finally reach my bone knife. I grab it and pull myself up on my good leg. I take aim and throw the blade. It flies near the king's head again, but this time it sinks into the bedpost just beyond him. I've missed the Chained.

King Durand's eyes roll back until they're nothing but white. His chest heaves like he's being sucked dry. Horror floods me. I desperately hop toward the bed. "Hurry, Cas! It's happening!"

He charges forward. I've never seen him so ferocious. He leaps onto the mattress and throws a vicious punch. I hear it connect with the Chained, and the king droops to the bed. Cas immediately grapples for the woman. He stabs her over and over. My stomach turns, even though she's invisible and won't bleed. Cas keeps stabbing, but he can't fend her off forever.

I glance at the window. It's just like the one in my room, with glass panes that are fitted into shutters. "Cas, bring her over here!" I hop toward the window, ignoring my throbbing knee. "It's the only way to get rid of her." *At least for now.*

He drags her off the bed, continuing to stab while she shrieks. Scratches appear on his face as she claws at him.

I reach the window, fling back the latch, throw open the shutters. The curtains lash wildly in the wind. Rain beats into the room. Cas yanks the invisible woman closer. "Won't she just fly back in here?"

"Souls don't fly."

"Naturally," he mutters.

I reach to help wrestle her over when Cas's boot slips on the wet floor. He quickly regains his footing, but his dagger is knocked from his grip. "Ailesse, she . . ." He stiffens and starts to choke and gag.

Then his eyes roll white.

No! I grab at the air. My hands latch onto the Chained woman's shoulders. I shove and punch, but she doesn't budge. I curse Cas. "Why did you hide my grace bones? I need them!"

His mouth twitches, but he can't speak. I yank the woman toward the window ledge. She drags Cas with her. My back hits the sill. The three of us struggle while the rain pummels us. I'm about to strangle the Chained when I start to choke. I don't understand. The woman doesn't have me by the neck. The suffocating sensation spreads throughout my body. I buckle to the floor.

My heartbeat thrashes in my ears. I'm losing Light, like Cas. Somehow, the Chained is stealing mine, too. I writhe, desperate to make it stop. My fingers nudge against wet metal. Cas's dagger.

I grasp the hilt. Summon my last reserves of energy. Aim for what I hope is the woman's calf. I swing up on my good knee and stab with all my graceless strength. The blade strikes true. The Chained screams and releases Cas. He catches himself on the windowsill. We suck in a ragged breath simultaneously. "Now, Cas!" I cry.

He shoves the space where the Chained woman should be. At the same time, I grab her invisible legs and sweep them off the ground. Together, we hurl her out the window.

Her unearthly shrieks rage out, then fade as she falls three stories to the ground. The storm muffles the sound of her crash.

Cas releases a huge exhale. He slides down to the floor beside me. We sit with our backs against the wall, panting side by side, completely soaked from the rain.

"What . . . just happened?" he asks.

"I think we lost some of our . . ." I swallow. "Our souls."

"We?"

My teeth chatter. "You're my *amouré*." I know he heard that word at the cavern soul bridge, but I never explained what it means. "We're linked by a soul-bond. What happens to you also happens to me." I'll leave it at that. I can barely comprehend the revelation myself. I had no idea I could lose my soul if he did.

Cas nods slowly, his gaze losing focus as he struggles to accept this reality along with every other strange truth he's learned tonight. "Are we going to be all right?" he asks. Rain drips from his thin circlet crown. "Our souls, I mean."

I think back on what happened to Jules. She wasn't just attacked like us. A Chained soul actually possessed her for a few hours. "We should have only lost a small portion of Light," I reply. "We were lucky."

He looks to his father's bed and springs to his feet. "I should check on him." He hurriedly brings me my crutch, then goes to tend to the king.

I stand and close the window in case the Chained woman decides to scale the castle walls. I'm fastening the latch when I hear a broken sob. I turn around.

Cas is quietly weeping. His hand is on the side of his father's brow. King Durand's eyes are closed. I hobble nearer, but once I see the king's face, I stop. He's utterly changed—not only lifeless, but terribly hollow, although his features look the same. There's nothing inside him now . . . somehow, that's apparent. His soul isn't dormant in his body, awaiting the call of the next ferrying night. His soul is gone forever.

"Oh, Cas." My throat tightens. What's just happened is horrific, almost beyond comprehension. Souls are sacred, meant for eternal life. I can't imagine losing a loved one like this. I walk around the bed on my crutch and place my trembling hand on his shoulder. "I'm so sorry."

He hangs his head. He looks smaller somehow, like an abandoned child. "I've lost all my family now."

A male servant with graying hair appears at the open doorway. He holds a tray with several tinctures and herb potions. His eyes grow large as he looks at the king, and he sets down his tray on a table, bowing deeply. "My sincerest condolences, Your Royal Majesty."

Cas lifts his head. "What did you say?"

"My sincerest—"

"No, what did you call me?"

I realize what Cas is stuck on, what he's struggling to accept. The servant didn't address him as Your Highness, the honorific of a prince.

"Your Royal Majesty," the servant repeats, and prostrates himself even lower. "Long live King Casimir."

8
Sabine

RAIN LASHES INTO THE OPEN cavern under the ruins of Château Creux. I stand with three of the elder Leurress at the edge of
the space we call the courtyard. Here, the rainfall can't pelt us.
"I'm sorry," I say for what must be the hundredth time. "I was never
taught that the *matrone* needed to remain on the soul bridge."

"You weren't taught many things." Nadine sighs, refastening
the eel skull comb in her hair. Her chestnut locks are still dripping.
We've returned home to warn our *famille*, while the rest of the Ferriers are still out in the storm, trying to herd what souls they can.
"Ailesse was raised to be Odiva's heir, not you."

Her tone isn't scornful, but it still stings. "I'm very well aware of
that." I bite my trembling lip. Hunting, fighting—every skill prized

by the Leurress—came more naturally to Ailesse. "I didn't ask to be *matrone*."

"Of course you didn't." Pernelle touches my arm.

Chantae rubs her ebony brow, impatient. "What happened tonight, Sabine? I saw you fight when the Chained were loose last time. You were far more adept."

I shake my head and squirm backward, my chest squeezing in a vise. I can't even draw strength from my jackal pendant to help me push past my anxiety. I don't know how to explain that my mother is alive, even though I saw her in the Underworld. Then I'll have to explain why she's there to begin with—how she'd had a lover besides her *amouré* and a second child with him. Me. It's enough to spark anarchy. I can't handle a rebellion right now.

Pernelle reaches for me. "Where are you going?"

I keep backtracking. I can't breathe. I don't know how to do everything at once—rule my *famille*, ferry the dead, free Ailesse, deal with my mother, stop the Chained.

Nadine frowns. "We haven't even made a solid plan."

"We need to prepare a place to hold the Chained," Dolssa adds. "You haven't even awakened the *famille* yet, Sabine. You need to speak with them."

"I know, but . . ." Black spots flash in my vision. I brace my hand against the cavern wall. "I just need a moment to . . ." I hasten toward the tunnel leading outside. "I'll be right back."

I bolt through the tide-carved tunnels. The echoing of the waves crashes against my ears, louder with my jackal hearing. I can't stop picturing Odiva behind the rushing veil of water, the noctule bat skull on her bone crown staring down at me. How will I be able to ferry again with my mother's black eyes looking over my shoulder?

I reach an upper level where the cave tunnels meet the ancient castle's corridors. Engraved crests of Château Creux keep catching my eye. They're repeated in the archways and along the walls, the crow and rose symbol of the monarchy that once ruled South Galle. The images nudge me like a warning, but I'm too overwhelmed to make sense of them. I hurry toward the collapsed archway my *famille* uses as an entrance, then up the crumbling stone staircase. My feet sink into the wet grass outside.

I bend over, lean my hands on my knees, and try to force my lungs to open up. The rain drizzles onto my hair and face and drips off the end of my nose. *Calm down, Sabine. Just breathe.* This day won't end. It's all been too much.

"Sabine?"

My head jerks up at Jules's low and gritty voice. Fifteen yards away, she rises from behind the ruins of the castle's garden wall. Her hood is drawn up against the rainfall, but my nighthawk vision catches her shoulders' shiver. I rush over and pull her back toward the castle, under the shelter of an overhanging battlement.

"What are you doing here?" I hiss. "If my *famille* sees you . . ." I don't want to imagine their anger. No outsiders are supposed to know where we live. The people of Dovré have always stayed away. They believe these castle ruins are cursed, haunted by the former king of South Galle. Casimir's father didn't always rule this country.

"What am I doing here?" Jules places a hand on her hip. "You abandoned me and Marcel."

I briefly shut my eyes. Did I do *anything* right today? "I'm sorry. I wasn't able to rescue Ailesse and . . . well, it was ferrying night. I had to . . ." I trail off, distracted by the sickly pallor of Jules's skin. "You really shouldn't be here, you know—or outside at all." Bastien told me how she had already lost a great deal of Light. "Ferrying was a disaster. Chained souls are loose again and—"

"Bastien was arrested."

My eyes widen. "What?"

Jules casts off her hood, glaring at me. "You weren't there to help him. I overheard the soldiers. They said you ran off to save yourself."

"That's not what . . ." I rub my brow as guilt overwhelms me. "I thought he was safe when I left."

"Well, he's in the dungeons now, thanks to you. And the law isn't lenient toward thieves." Her hard expression cracks, and her chin starts to quiver. "They could execute him if we don't act quickly."

I wince. I can't let Bastien die. I owe it to Ailesse. "Was our route through the castle well discovered?"

She nods. "Marcel and I barely escaped with our lives."

"Then how else can we infiltrate Beau Palais?" Our plot via the well route took us a fortnight to prepare.

She draws a long breath, like she's been rehearsing her answer. "I think I know a way. The first night that Bastien, Marcel, and I took Ailesse to the catacombs—"

"You mean when you abducted her?"

"Yes, yes." Jules waves a dismissing hand. "Odiva made an attempt to set her free—a diversion meant to give Ailesse the opportunity to break away. It almost worked." She quickly explains how a colony of giant bats raided their catacombs chamber.

I think back to that night. "Odiva was chanting, praying to Tyrus," I murmur. When the elder Leurress were out searching for Ailesse, Odiva stayed behind in Château Creux. "I saw her cut her finger on the teeth of her noctule bat skull. Her blood must have been part of the ritual." Of course it was. As her daughter, Ailesse shared her blood. The ritual magic sent the bats to the place she was being held.

"Excellent," Jules says. "Then you already know how to do it."

"Maybe." It might be similar to the proxy ritual I had performed. "But we shouldn't resort to a blood ritual with Tyrus unless we're desperate."

"Didn't you hear me a moment ago? Thieves hang. We're desperate, Sabine."

My mouth runs dry, and I force a swallow. "Well, I don't think a flock of nighthawks or a herd of salamanders is going to be quite as threatening as giant noctule bats."

"What about golden jackals?" Jules asks.

"They're not native to South Galle." The one I killed was extremely rare. Who knows how the gods had brought it here? "Leurress rituals are powerful, but they can't create new life."

"I figured." She tilts her head. "So the animal should be common to these parts if we want a whole nest of them to attack the castle?"

I frown, wary of the eager gleam in her hazel eyes. "I already have three grace bones, Jules. I can't—"

"Odiva had *five*."

"I'm not *matrone*. Not really. Ailesse will be back soon and—"

"You're *matrone* in the meantime. So claim another bone." She shrugs. "You can toss it out once Ailesse wears the crown. You'll bring her home even sooner once the snakes create a diversion."

"Snakes?" My stomach twists.

She leans closer. "Don't you see? Ailesse and Bastien will understand it's Bone Crier magic. They'll seize the opportunity and find a way to spring free during the madness."

A harsh laugh escapes me. "Unless they're poisoned by venom."

"We don't have to worry about that. I'll show you." Jules rushes back toward the garden wall. From behind it, she lifts a sack of rough-spun cloth that's knotted at the top. *Oh no . . .*

She hurries back, her wide grin revealing the small gap between her front teeth. She's already panting from such a short run. She's so much weaker than the girl I fought under the bridge during Ailesse's attempted rite of passage. She'll never recover from the Light she lost. None of the people in Dovré who were attacked will.

I grimace at the wriggling sack. "What have you caught in there?"

"A Gallish whip snake." She flings her golden braid behind her shoulder. "They aren't poisonous, but Marcel says they're often mistaken for venomous meadow vipers. Their scale markings are similar, and they flatten their heads in a triangular shape to look like a viper when they're threatened."

I knead my temples. I feel a headache coming on. "I don't know, Jules." The elders are expecting me back inside. Though maybe if I return with another grace bone, they might believe I'm trying harder to become a good *matrone*. "I want to free Bastien . . . but what if Ailesse is safer in Beau Palais?" I picture my mother's cunning face again. Her words ring to mind: *All she needs to do is touch my hand, and then Tyrus will release me.*

"Safer?" Jules scoffs. "You said the Chained are loose now. Ailesse was a beacon to them last time."

"That's because she played the siren song to open the Gates." I did the same tonight, but I seemed to repel the Chained instead of luring them. Once they saw my necklace, they startled.

"It's still dangerous," Jules insists. "We need to take cover underground again. When Bastien and Ailesse return—"

"Ailesse can't return!" I snap. "My mother is alive, Jules!"

Her brow wrinkles. "You told me she ran through the Gate and—"

"I saw her through the Gate tonight. She said she's alive, and I believe her." I blow out a long breath. My problems are far from solved, but it feels good to finally have that off my chest. "Odiva is trapped for now, but she wants Ailesse to set her free."

Jules takes a moment to absorb this. "Well, don't you think you should warn Ailesse?"

I drag a hand over my face. "I don't know." I had my own warning today. I thought the silver owl was protecting my sister from the lure of the Underworld, but maybe the owl knew my mother would be at the Gate tonight, waiting for Ailesse to come.

Jules nibbles on her lip, glancing in the direction of Dovré. If the high towers of Château Creux were still standing, we would be able to see the ramparts of Beau Palais from on top of them. "Look," she says, "I'm not sure what to say about your mother and Ailesse, but Bastien is my best friend. You left him stranded today, and now you need to do something to make it right." She holds the sack out to me. The cloth writhes from the whip snake inside. "So do something, Sabine. Make it right."

I sigh. I need to make a thousand things right. Maybe I should start with this. I steady myself and take the sack.

"Good," Jules says. "Now hurry."

I murmur a quick goodbye, then rush back inside Château Creux and climb one of the small still existing towers that leads to my mother's old chambers. She had a collection of ritual blades— bone weapons she used to sacrifice animals for their graces. I grab the bone sickle that killed her asp viper.

I unknot the sack and drop it on the ground. I hold the sickle high, ready to strike. The old Sabine would be sick to her stomach, but instead my belly growls. If I'm disgusted, it's with myself. I hate the craving for flesh the jackal grace has given me. And the graces I'll obtain from the snake will probably only make that craving worse. I shudder. What other "gifts" will I receive tonight? My mother had the graces of a snake—an asp viper. How did they change her?

The snake peeks out of the sack. Its pupils are round, but its head is flattened and triangular. It's feeling threatened. Of course it is.

Don't think, Sabine. Rely on the jackal grace and do what you have to do.

My bloodlust heightens. I swing my blade. *Thwack.* The snake's head rolls away.

I don't look. My mouth is already watering. I slit the snake's belly, peel back its skin and flesh, and expose the edge of one of its vertebrae. I cut my palm with the bone sickle, then press the vertebrae against my blood. The snake's graces rush into me with a wave of prickling heat. I don't pause to analyze them. I want this over with.

I squeeze my fist. Drip my blood onto the stone floor. Spread my arms with my hands cupped downward to the Underworld. I chant a prayer similar to my proxy ritual. "Hear my voice, Tyrus, my soul's siren song. Find my sister through the blood we share. Summon other creatures like this one. Send them to attack the castle where my sister resides."

There. It's done.

I quickly wrap my hand in a cloth and grab another one to mop up the mess on the floor. As I pick up the snake's head, I gasp. Even lifeless, it's still triangular. And its pupils are no longer round from the dimness of the sack; they're slitted like all other venomous breeds.

This isn't a Gallish whip snake. It's a deadly meadow viper.

Marcel may have explained the difference to Jules, but I doubt he went hunting with her. She caught the wrong snake.

I stare at my spilled blood on the floor, horror coiling inside me. I can't reverse what I've done. Bone-and-blood rituals are binding.

I've just sent a nest of vipers to attack Beau Palais.

9

Bastien

I PACE ALONGSIDE THE BARS of my cell, my eye on the shadows past the torchlight on the other side. Dawn is a little over an hour away. Ailesse still hasn't returned. Now would be the perfect time for her to sneak down here. The feast is over—at least the music has stopped—and my guard is sleeping. His snores rattle down the corridor in the quiet between thunderclaps.

Come on, Ailesse.

Even on her crutch, even with all the flights of stairs, she should have been back by now. I flip her gold hair comb over and over in my hand. What if Prince Casimir found out she came to see me? If he didn't lock her up before, would he lock her up now?

I drag my hands through my hair. I've got to find a way to get out of here on my own. Free her, too. Break us both out of this damn castle. But how? I pace my cell two more times, and then it comes to me.

I lean against the iron bars. "Hello there! Guard!" When I don't hear a response, I whistle, loud and shrill.

"Oy!" The guard's voice is gruff and throaty from sleep. "None of that, unless you want a beating, boy." An idle threat, because he doesn't come. He starts snoring again.

"I'm bored senseless!" I shout. "Come and keep me company. We can talk about your girl, Sophie." I chuckle. "Does your captain know what you two are doing down here?"

A pause. Then tramping boots. The guard's panicked face appears. "Who told you about—?" His jaw muscle tightens. "I don't know any Sophie."

"You talk in your sleep, friend." I wink.

In three quick strides, he's at the bars. His meaty hand reaches past them and grabs for my throat. I jump back and grin. "Relax, I won't snitch. Especially if you're willing to make a trade. I found myself a little treasure buried in the straw." I flash the hair comb at him. "This is real gold. Emeralds, too. It's worth enough francs to unlock this cell door, don't you think?"

The guard looks at it, and his fingers twitch. "You think you can bribe me?" He huffs. "The captain will have my head if I set you free."

"So we make it look like I got the best of you." I shrug. "I blacken your eye and leave your key dangling in the lock. You have a cozy nap in the straw, and when the captain makes his rounds, he'll find you a little worse for the wear, but also the picture of innocence."

The guard grumbles. "Give me the comb first, and I'll think about . . ." His eyes pop wide. A look of terror comes over him. He gapes at the ceiling behind me. I twist around just as a snake drops through the chute grate. It rapidly slithers off the stone bench and under the straw on the floor.

I shuffle backward. That was a damn meadow viper. "Unlock the door," I tell the guard, but he stands frozen. "Hurry, or the deal's off!"

He fumbles for the key ring at his belt. Something streaks over the toe of his boot. He curses and kicks like a madman.

I glance behind me. The straw in my cell has gone still. I have no idea where the snake's hiding now. "You got a viper problem down here?"

The guard shakes his head. "Never seen so much as a garden snake."

Down the corridor, the shadowy floor starts to writhe like it's made of black water. *Don't react, Bastien.* I don't want to spook the guard and have him run off on me. "The gold comb for your keys," I demand, keeping my face straight as one of the vipers starts to coil up right behind him. One bite isn't fatal. "Now. We make the trade at the same time."

The guard nods and shifts closer. Sweat beads on his forehead. He lifts the keys. I hold up the comb. "Ready?" I ask. "One, two, th—"

The coiled viper strikes. Sinks its fangs into the guard's leg. He cries out. Slams into the bars. Drops the keys. I don't grab them; I whip the guard's sword from its sheath. The viper in my cell hisses. I spin around and slash. My blade severs the snake just as it springs from the straw.

The guard howls and falls down. Another viper has bitten him. *Merde.* More slither toward him—toward me. "Get up!" I shout. I slice my sword past the bars. Another snake shrinks back. I struggle to pull up the guard. He's dead weight and moaning, but I finally get him up on his feet. Two more vipers lunge. I cut the first with my blade. The second darts into my cell. Wonderful.

I bear up the guard and keep an eye on my cell. I carefully slip my boot between the bars, trying to reach the keys. A snake lashes at the guard from his other side. Latches onto his left hand. He buckles. I can't hold him up. He thuds to the floor, bitten three times now. My chest falls. Nothing can remedy that much venom.

The viper in my cell coils. Bares its fangs. I strike before it does, but it gets away, streaking aside like lightning. Another snake drops from the chute grate. Two more slither past the bars. *Merde, merde, merde.*

My sword flies in all directions. The snakes hiss. Open their jaws wide. Snap at me. I keep thrashing, fighting. I know what this is now—Bone Crier magic. I've been attacked this way before. I toss another glance at the corridor. Where is Ailesse? We have to leave here together.

I decapitate two vipers and hurry to the bars. Snakes swarm the guard's lifeless body. I swallow a rush of bile and focus on his fallen keys. I bat away another three snakes and hook the key ring on the tip of my sword. I kick off a snake circling my ankle and race to the cell door.

The ring holds six keys. The first two don't fit. I'm fumbling with the third key when a viper drops from above. *Merde.* It was coiled around the bars. Before I can jerk away, its fangs puncture my wrist. Blinding pain rips into me. I shout and drop the keys.

"Bastien!"

Ailesse.

Black dots scatter across my vision. Past them, I see her. Her auburn hair is wet. Her dress is soaked and ripped in a few places. She's holding her bone knife. It's bloody. Casimir's blood? "Sh-shouldn't have come down here." I speak past gritted teeth. "Too dangerous."

She spares a glance at the dead guard, and her creamy skin pales.

"G-go," I croak. I can barely talk, barely move. The pain won't let up. She needs to save herself. But she doesn't leave. She rushes to my cell, moving fast on her crutch. Maybe it's a trick of my muddled brain, but the snakes seem to part around her. Then I remember—the noctule bats never attacked her in the catacombs, just me, Jules, and Marcel.

Ailesse snatches up the keys and quickly tries them in the lock. A viper lunges for my leg. She beats it away with her crutch and turns back to the keys, hands shaking. "Why would Sabine send meadow vipers if she knew you were here, too? I thought you were friends."

More like allies, I think past my throbbing pain. "Sabine . . . sent them?"

Ailesse finds the right key. The lock tumblers clang. She yanks the door open and shoves the bone knife into my grip. She grabs my sword and hacks at a snake lashing toward my ankle. "Hurry, Bastien. Concentrate on walking. I'll keep the vipers away."

I stumble out of my cell and down the dungeons' corridor. She hobbles around me, swinging and stabbing. "It has to be Sabine," she finally answers my question. "No other Leurress has meadow viper graces, and she's *matrone*—at least for now." A dark expression crosses her face. "And as *matrone*, Sabine could obtain more grace bones. Besides, I've only seen my mother practice this kind of magic. Maybe you have to be *matrone* to access it."

The dungeons' stairs come into view. Ailesse heads for them. I clench my jaw and follow close behind her. She clears a path with her sword like she's scything wheat. Once we reach the first step, we instinctively link arms. She bears me up to keep moving, and I balance her on her crutch. I kick away the snakes that slither from the upper level. Ailesse stabs two others.

We reach a cracked door at the top of the flight. I shoulder it open. We're in a narrow hallway. Vipers dangle from the sconces and zigzag along the floor. Ailesse wards away the nearest snakes. We rush forward, trailed by sharp hisses.

"I should warn you," she says between gasps of air. "Sabine didn't open the Gates to the Beyond."

A viper strikes for my leg. I slash its body with the bone knife. "How do you know?"

"A Chained woman"—Ailesse severs the head off a snake— "attacked the king tonight." Her eyes grow pained. "He's dead, Bastien."

Coldness grips my feverish body. We hurry into an adjoining hallway and enter the long corridor that runs the length of the castle. I struggle to absorb the implications of what she's just said. If one Chained is loose, many more will be. And if King Durand is dead . . . "The prince is still alive, isn't he?"

Ailesse glances away. "As far as I know."

Merde. Then Casimir is the king of South Galle now. Which means he's more powerful, more important . . . maybe even more desirable to Ailesse. She'll have an even harder time killing him. My stomach knots. "You have to hide underground again." I can't think about their soul-bond right now. I have a more pressing worry. "The Chained will find you like they did before and—"

"I didn't play the siren song this time." She grimaces, hobbling slower on her crutch. Her knee must be killing her. "I'm no more endangered than anyone else is."

At least there's that. She should still get out of here. She swipes away another charging viper, and I link arms with her again to support her leg. My wrist throbs harder, but I square my jaw against the pain. She holds her sword pointed forward, ready to defend me, but the snakes slither out of my path now, as well as hers. As long as we're physically connected, I'm safe from them.

Exhausted, I lean against her. Some of the tightness in my muscles eases as I feel the steadying warmth from her body. "Head for the new castle well," she says. "The soldiers would have abandoned it because of the vipers."

I press forward down the corridor. It's mostly empty of people, except for a couple of slumped figures that look horribly like the dead dungeons guard. I swallow. It's hard to imagine that Sabine was willing to accept these casualties when she sent the snakes. Hopefully most of the people in the castle are hiding in closets or wherever else they can protect themselves.

We finally reach the great hall. What's left of the feast is now ridden with vipers. They writhe over tables and around goblets, their forked tongues jutting past their sharp fangs. When morning comes, these monsters will be gone. Dawn is what broke the spell when Odiva sent the bats into the catacombs. I glance past the windows at the brightening storm clouds. I'm betting the sun will rise in the next half hour.

Ailesse and I move through the foyer leading to the courtyard. The rainfall lets up to a steady drizzle. Vipers slither on the stones and around the puddles that haven't drained. I kick a couple of snakes out of my path, ones that are too slow to dart out of the way. We reach the door to the well tower. I fling it open and stagger inside.

Dizziness racks my head. I'm panting, and the stab wound on my back throbs worse than my snakebite. But I can't stop now. I have to get Ailesse down the well. Snakes are wriggling out of it, working their way up the ladder. She still needs my help, and I need her protection.

"I have an idea," she says. "Pass me the bone knife." When I do, she drops her sword and crutch and nicks her palm with the knife. On purpose. She smears some of her blood onto my forehead.

I wince. "What are you doing?"

"Trying to trick the snakes. All Leurress rituals involve blood and bone. Sabine shares my blood. I think that's what drew the snakes to Beau Palais. So it makes sense that my blood is what's protecting me—and hopefully you, too, now." She dabs more blood onto my neck. "Let's see if I'm right."

We carefully pull away from each other. She steadies herself against a wall, and I quickly grab the fallen sword and spin around to attack. No vipers strike. The ones at my feet scatter when I take a step. Even the snake that drops from the rafters swings away from me. I exhale and hand Ailesse her crutch. "You're brilliant." I kiss her cheek.

Her smile is fleeting. She grabs a torch from a sconce. Soldiers must have left it burning. "Dawn will be here soon," she says, and passes me the torch. "You better leave while you still have the chance."

I stiffen. "You mean *we* better leave."

She shrinks back a little, like she did in the dungeons. She won't meet my gaze.

"Ailesse, look at me." I wait several moments until, at last, she lifts her beautiful eyes. They're golden in the torchlight, fierce and unshakable. "You need to come with me," I say. "You don't owe the prince anything."

"He just lost his father."

"He's been preparing for that. Everyone knew the king wasn't long for this world."

"There are still the vipers to think about. If Casimir dies, I die and—"

"If he's survived the night so far, he's going to make it till

94

morning. You said it yourself—dawn is almost here."

She releases a slow exhale. "I've lost Light, Bastien."

My gut folds on itself. "What?"

"The Chained woman, she attacked Casimir, too. She drew out some of his Light, and when that happened, it drained out of me as well."

I can't breathe for a moment. The thought of Ailesse losing her soul is too terrible. "A-are you all right?" Everyone needs Light, but it's even more critical for the Leurress. If they can't take it in regularly from Elara's moon- and starlight, they starve and weaken. And no one gets back Light that's been stolen by a Chained. "How much did you lose?"

"Not much. I'll be fine." She sets her jaw. "But don't you see? I have to stay here until I can find my grace bones. Then on the next ferrying night, I can force the Chained to move on." She draws herself up taller. "I'll fix everything once my *famille* takes me back as *matrone*."

I stare at her, my pulse crashing fast. Ailesse was torn from me at the soul bridge, and I've clawed my way back to her. "So you just want me to leave you here with all the Chained loose and your soul draining of Light whenever Casimir's does?"

She narrows her gaze at my sharp tone. "Fighting the Chained is what I've trained to do all my life."

My eyes sting. I'm furious with her. I'm more furious with myself for not being her *amouré*, even though that's irrational and impossible and solves nothing. I hate that she has to endanger herself to guard another boy's life and soul—especially when he's the one hiding her grace bones. "How can I—?" My voice breaks. I suck in a deep breath. "How can I let you go?"

"By *trusting* me." She sounds as exasperated as I do.

"Ailesse, please . . ." She flinches when I reach for her, and takes a small step backward. I feel that new rift widening between us, and I don't understand what put it there.

"You know how I feel about you, Bastien. No matter what happens, that's never going to change."

"No matter what happens?" A terrible ache builds inside me. "What do you mean?"

She shakes her head like she needs to explain something, but she doesn't even know what it is. Then suddenly whatever's restraining her snaps. She rushes forward and slides her arms around my torso. She embraces me fiercely, arms trembling. I can't even hold her back with the torch and the sword in my hands. I still feel her slipping away. It's too easy to picture her wearing a crown and seated on a throne beside Casimir. She was born to be a queen.

Is that what her gods have plotted all along—for her to rule the Leurress *and* South Galle? Then I curse her gods. Ailesse isn't their pawn, but they're still blocking her at every turn, forcing her to move in the direction they want. They won't let her choose her own life.

But what if she *could* choose? What if no one else's life was on the line?

Would she still choose me?

She inhales, long and deep, and unfolds her arms from around me. "Go, Bastien." She brushes her mouth against mine, then hardens her face like a shield. My chest weighs unbearably heavy. What if I never see her again?

It takes all my strength to step away from her. I slide my sword under my belt, climb into the well, and step down the first three rungs of the ladder. I pause. Force myself not to look at her. It will make this goodbye feel more permanent. "When you decide to leave here—"

"I *will* leave."

"—you can find me with Jules and Marcel at Birdine's apartment." I explain where to find it above Le Coeur Percé, in the brothel district. The tavern's name means The Pierced Heart. Damn ironic.

I step down another rung, and my willpower crumbles. I look at her. Her eyes are wet. Her auburn hair is thick and wild in the humidity. Snakes writhe around her feet, but they don't dare come too close, like her beauty is untouchable. "I love you, Ailesse."

She releases a tight breath. "I love you, too, Bastien."

My throat aches. "Goodbye."

I descend into the well.

10
Ailesse

EXHAUSTED AND HEARTSORE, I FINALLY reach the third level of Beau Palais and hobble into King Durand's chambers. But Casimir isn't here. I sigh. I don't have the energy to go searching for him. *He has to be alive*, I tell myself, *or else I wouldn't be*. Besides, morning has broken. The vipers are slithering away, fleeing as quickly as they came, and beams of golden sunlight scatter the storm clouds past the windows. It should feel like hope, but it doesn't.

I collapse into a chair beside the king's four-poster bed. His body is no longer here. The servants have already taken him away. I pray his soul finds peace, but then my stomach wrenches. He has no soul.

I lean forward on the mattress and press the heels of my palms to my watering eyes. I may have saved Cas from the Chained woman and Bastien from the snakes, but the king still died . . . and likely several more people in the castle. None of this would have happened if I hadn't stayed here as long as I have, if I'd been the one leading my *famille*. And yet I continue to stay. I have to.

Again, that awful feeling of being torn in half seizes me. Maybe it's even my soul ripping apart. Sabine would be able to tell me what's wrong. She'd say something wise, and then make me laugh. That's the healing I need.

Ailesse . . . Ailesse . . .

Mother?

Her silky voice calls to me, but it's muffled like she's under-water. Have I fallen asleep? I can't see her, so I move toward the sound. Everything around me is catacombs black, without even moonlight or starlight, until Odiva's starkly beautiful face appears. She's wearing all five of her striking grace bones, and her sapphire-blue dress undulates and ripples like the ends of her raven hair. "Ailesse, my firstborn child," she says, "my fierce and faithful daughter."

I'm weightless, though I try to ground myself. I *have* to be sleeping. This is a dream. My mother never smiled with such affection. She never gave her praise so easily, not to me.

She reaches out her hand. I reach back, even though I shouldn't. How is it possible I still want her love?

Our fingers almost touch when a bird screeches and flies between us. The silver owl. She beats her wings once, and my mother fades. In her place, an unfamiliar crown appears, made of onyx-carved feathers and glimmering rubies. Beau Palais rises behind it, and the crown's feathers and rubies multiply, staining the castle's limestone walls black and red.

"Ailesse . . . Ailesse . . ." It isn't my mother's voice anymore. "Ailesse . . ."

Someone nudges my shoulder. I startle and open my eyes. Casimir's worried face bends over me. I push back from the king's bed. Light-headedness grips me. "Are you all right?" I ask.

"Am *I* all right?" He laughs, miserable and exasperated. "What were you thinking, running off like that?"

"I'm . . . sorry." I'm still reeling from my dream and wondering what it means. It takes me a moment to notice his slightly bloodshot eyes and weary posture. Just a few hours ago, he lost his father in this very room, and then the castle fell under attack. More people died. I can't fathom what he must be feeling right now.

I'm about to ask how many casualties there were when he says, "Tonight you called me your *amouré*."

My stomach tenses. I can't meet his eyes, so I stare down at my hands.

I feel him studying me. "I'm tired of you pretending you're a normal girl. I'm more tired of trying so desperately hard to believe it. Nothing about you is ordinary, Ailesse. I've known that from the moment I saw you again on that cavern bridge. You and your mother and sister . . . you all had power I didn't understand."

When I remain silent, he continues, "You spoke of Chained souls and Light that could be forever stolen." His voice catches, and he's unable to talk for a moment. I glance up and find him gazing at the sunken spot in the bed where his father died. "What does it all mean?" His eyes cut back to me. "Who—*what*—are you?"

Part of me wants to tell him. Would the truth be consoling? But I can't. Casimir is king now. What would he do with his power if he knew I'm one of forty-six women and girls with dangerous bone magic, a *famille* that lives within the borders of his kingdom? Would he really trust me, a Leurress born and raised to ferry the dead, a girl who must earn that right by sacrificing her *amouré*— him? He doesn't even trust me with my grace bones. "I'm a friend," I say. "I hope I proved that last night."

He contemplates me, softly gnawing on the edge of his lower lip. "Yes, you did. And I think it's time I also proved I'm your friend." He fidgets with his jeweled ring. "That is, if you can forgive me first."

"Forgive you for what?"

"Deceiving you." He inhales a steadying breath and crosses the room to a mahogany wardrobe. He opens some kind of trick drawer and retrieves a small bundle from within. I stifle a gasp when I realize what it is—a leather coin pouch hanging from a necklace cord. "I never lost your grace bones," he confesses, walking back to me.

My heart thunders. I jerk to my feet. My bandaged knee pangs, but I don't care. I grab the pouch with fumbling fingers and loop the cord over my head. My graces rush into me, a thrilling burst of sensation. I close my eyes and try to soak them all in.

"What do you feel?" Cas asks tentatively.

His nearness buzzes along my spine and awakens my tiger shark sixth sense. I'm falcon buoyant and ibex balanced and shark invigorated. I'm as I should be, at one with three powerful and incredible animals. "Whole," I finally answer, and breathe in deeply. Everything is going to be all right now. I'll be able to protect Cas until the next ferrying night, then I can leave here and be with Sabine and my *famille* and . . .

My blood runs cold. "Cas," I hiss, clutching his arm. "Move behind me. Now."

He doesn't. He draws his dagger and spins around to face the room, ready for any danger. But he doesn't have my peregrine falcon vision. He can't see the flare of *chazoure* five feet in front of him—the soul of a balding man with a gaunt face and crooked back. The man's expression is solemn, but also severe. I expect to find chains wrapped around him, but none are.

"Why are you here?" I demand.

He tilts his head at me, as if he's surprised I can see him. "Rumor reaches the dead fast," he rasps, his voice reedy. "King Durand has finally met his death, so I've come to take a hard look at his son. See if he's up for the job."

Cas shifts on his feet, startled at the bodiless voice. "Of course I am. I—"

"Don't speak to him," I whisper, and grab my crutch. Chained or Unchained, I have a bad feeling about the man. He was probably one of the dissenters in Dovré when he was alive. "His Royal Majesty needs time alone to pray for divine guidance," I tell him, remembering what Cas said yesterday: the dissenters believe the recent plague was a sign of the gods' displeasure with King Durand. I don't want them thinking Casimir is also out of favor. "Please respect his privacy."

Cas and I cautiously advance into the corridor. The gaunt-faced man's eyes trail our movement. With any luck, he won't follow us. Once he's out of sight, I release a pent-up breath.

"Was that another Chained?" Cas whispers.

I don't answer. My mouth goes suddenly dry. Down the corridor, two more souls drift toward us. Four more come from behind. Some wear rich robes. Others are in simple clothing. Heavy *chazoure* chains hang from three of them. My heart pounds. How many of the dead have been gathering in this castle before I had eyes to see them?

"Stay right beside me," I tell Cas under my breath. I head left, toward the two oncoming souls. One of them is Chained, but that's better than our odds the other way. I don't look directly at them, praying they'll let us pass without incident.

The Unchained, a young woman, turns her head at Cas and sneers. "He doesn't deserve to be so handsome."

Cas jerks around. "Did you hear that?"

The Chained man curls his lip. "Handsome is worth little if the gods spit upon your bloodline."

"They should curse him like they cursed his father." The young woman's *chazoure* eyes glitter coldly. "I would have lived to care for my child if the Trencavel dynasty hadn't brought about the plague."

More dissenters, I realize, deceased ones finally able to infiltrate Beau Palais and challenge the monarchy.

Cas's nostrils flare. "My father was a devout man. He provoked nothing."

"Oh yes? And what about his son?" The Chained man steps into Cas's path. Cas stumbles into him. "I could have a taste of what the gods really think of you, leech a little of that proud soul and find out."

"Stay back!" I prod the Chained away with the end of my crutch.

He chuckles. "So, the pretty girl can see us. Where is she hiding her bones, I wonder?" He eyes the pouch around my neck and tries to snatch it. I dodge him and grab Cas's arm. The four other souls are crowding in. We hurry farther down the corridor. The souls keep right behind us. Now the gaunt-faced man from the king's chambers has joined them.

Cas and I reach a place where a varnished railing overlooks a velvet-draped sitting room below. My nerves jump. At least seven more souls are wandering about down there. They can't all be dissenters. Two are dressed like servants and silently follow living servants who have cautiously returned to their duties. But the other five catch sight of Cas and make their way toward the staircase leading to this floor.

"There are too many," I gasp. Why did I ever think I could protect him *here*? I had no idea the dissenter movement was gaining such momentum in Dovré. If this many have already died, weakened from losing Light, there must be several times more still living. "We have to leave."

"Leave?" He frowns.

"I can't keep you safe here."

"But I'm king."

"Exactly!" I swipe my crutch at a Chained lady who comes close to him. "And the dissenters don't want any Trencavels on the throne. They'll try to kill you, and I can't kill them. They're already dead."

I tug his arm to keep him moving, but he resists. "No, Ailesse. The castle has just been attacked, and it's already under threat again. I can't begin my reign by running away."

His bravado is infuriating. "It would only be until the next ferrying night." Just two weeks away, if I dare to use the fragile cavern bridge again.

"I have no idea what that means."

The gaunt-faced man leers nearer. "You think a fine weapon engraved with Belin's sun will prove your worthiness, boy?" He strokes a symbol on Cas's jeweled dagger. "You can't just look the part. You have to be truly anointed by the gods."

I shove him back. "Come with me," I plead with Cas. "Trust me." I'll take him underground—hide him, like I hid with Bastien.

"Trust you? You won't even explain what you are."

The other souls press closer, mocking him. They smell his hair, touch his rich clothes, whisper like a swarm of chittering insects. My sixth sense crawls with them. Cas struggles to hold still, keeping his eyes fast on me. Perspiration flashes across my skin. I have to tell him. "I'm a Bone Crier."

"That tells me nothing."

The four Chained circle him like tiger sharks. Adrenaline pounds through my veins. I reach up my sleeve and draw my bone knife. We don't have any more time to argue. My *amouré* is more stubborn than I am.

With falcon speed, I swing the knife and set its sharp edge against Cas's neck. "I'm the girl who's supposed to kill you." My voice lashes like a whip. "And if you don't come with me now, I swear to you I will."

11
Sabine

I NERVOUSLY SING A GALLISH folk song as I stare at Beau Palais from Castelpont. Or is it Castelpont? The riverbed beneath this bridge should be dry—it has been so for over a decade—but now it flows with sparkling water. Meadow vipers slither through its currents like eels. More bask on the bridge's stones, which are beginning to warm in the morning sunlight.

I don't understand. The break of dawn should have made the snakes scatter. I glance at the road that leads around the bend to the city gates. Where are Ailesse and Bastien? They should have escaped by now. They were supposed to come meet me here.

Someone laughs at me. I lean over the parapet and see my reflection in the water. *You never told them to meet you here, my* mirrored self tells me. *You're dreaming, Sabine.* There's a ring of gold around my brown irises that doesn't belong there, and a row of knifelike teeth that slide down over my lower lip. Maybe I *am* dreaming. Graces can't cause physical changes like this. *It's best you sleep right now, anyway. You should hide from the deaths you caused last night.*

I push back from the parapet. Bile rises in my throat. "I didn't mean to kill anyone."

"I believe you."

I startle. The voice that answers me now is silky, and more slippery than the vipers hissing at my feet. "Mother?" I say, though I can't see her anywhere.

"I am waiting to bring you comfort. Come to me, my gentle child."

At her words, a golden jackal pounces onto the west end of the bridge. He yips at me, but then a rasp-screech comes from the east end, where the silver owl flies in and lands on a post. Both animals beckon, but it's the jackal I follow. He belongs to Tyrus, and my mother dwells in the god's dark kingdom. I have to tell her to leave me alone.

Don't go, Sabine, and she won't trouble you.

I'm speaking to myself again. But I don't trust myself.

I bound away with the jackal. No matter how fast he runs, I keep pace with him. His speed is my speed. His endurance my endurance.

He brings me to the hollow with the stream where I buried him. My mother stands above his unmarked grave. Her raven hair and sapphire blue dress float and sway like they did when she stood behind the Gate of water.

The jackal comes to sit beside her. She sinks her pale fingers into his golden hair. "My poor daughter," Odiva says to me. "I warned you the jackal would play upon your weaknesses."

I bristle. "Was it weak to send an army of meadow vipers into Beau Palais?"

"Is rashness strength?" Her bloodred lip curls in the semblance of a smile. "You meant to send a nest of Gallish whip snakes. A Leurress should know better."

"At least I have another formidable grace now."

"Which was not wise to claim when you had not yet mastered your third grace." Her fingernails drip blood as she scratches the golden jackal deeper.

"I am *matrone* now. I'll decide what measures need to be taken for the good of the *famille*."

Odiva sighs and kneels on the grave mound. Her raven hair ripples and fans around her shoulders. "If only you and Ailesse could feel the strength of your mother's love . . ." She starts to dig a hole, scooping up the earth with her hand. ". . . you might understand that I desire the very best for you."

"Love," I scoff. "You don't know its meaning."

Three more scoops of earth. Somehow the hole is already a foot deep. "You sound like Ailesse." Her voice is light, but her black eyes are cold. "She chided me for the same, even after I spared her life countless times."

"She would have chided you worse if she knew all your

betrayals." My sister felt enough heartbreak when she found out Odiva had bargained with Tyrus to resurrect my father. The pact came at the expense of Ailesse's life. I didn't know how to tell her that our mother had also sacrificed thousands of souls meant for Paradise. A futile attempt to appease the god. I stand taller. "I came here to tell you to leave us alone."

The hole is four feet deep now, though Odiva has barely lifted a finger. "But I am the only person who can help you. Let me, gentle Sabine. The jackal is too great a burden to shoulder on your own."

"You don't want to share my grace; you want to steal it. And you don't want to help Ailesse; you want to trade her life for my father's."

Five feet deep. "It is the jackal that spurs these doubts. Beware his cunning. He will bury you, daughter."

It's then I realize the golden jackal has gone missing from my mother's side. The sound of flapping wings catches my attention. Just past the stream in the hollow, the silver owl hovers, trying to fly toward me, but she's caught midair against an invisible force.

Six feet deep. "Come and see his carcass," Odiva says.

I don't want to, yet my feet slip forward through the grass and overturned earth. I lean over the hole my mother has dug in mere moments. It's not only deep, but also long. It exposes the length of the jackal's body. Only it isn't the jackal.

It's me.

I'm in my white ferrying dress, but it's ripped with bloody claw marks. My olive skin has turned the color of brackish water, and my black curls are choked with dirt. Worms crawl out of my nose and mouth. Worst of all, my eyes are open and coated in a film of grisly white. I stumble backward, my hand pressed to my stomach. I'm going to be sick.

"Do you see now?" My mother rises to her feet. Her dress floats around her ankles. "This is the fate I wish to prevent. All you need to do is bring Ailesse to me on the next ferrying night. It can be done on the full moon. You can open the Gates on the cavern bridge."

"Why do you need her so you can help *me* with my jackal graces?"

"Is your sister not at the very heart of your weakness?" The silver owl screeches, but my mother doesn't regard her. "Think of all the terrible things you have done in the name of saving her." My mother tilts her head. "Perhaps you and I have more in common than you are willing to believe, Sabine."

"No." I step back.

"All Ailesse must do is touch my hand to set me free." She comes closer. I shrink away. The silver owl screeches relentlessly. "Then I can help you bear the jackal grace. I can save *you*."

She reaches to stroke my face. "Get back." I recoil. "I don't need saving. I can bear this grace on my own."

I whirl around and sprint into the forest. My mother doesn't chase after me. I glance over my shoulder and catch a flicker of her victorious smile. My jaw locks. She's been toying with me, showing me gruesome things that aren't real, spinning lies so I'll sacrifice my own sister. She must be mad.

The silver owl swoops in front of me, finally free. She rasps in my ear, and I bat her away. I don't need her telling me what to do, too. I race faster, past a copse of trees, then down a gulch, through another stream, and up a hill. I'm hunting, I realize. I need a fifth grace bone, something to give me power against the jackal's influence. The meadow viper only agrees with him, and the nighthawk and salamander are too timid.

I'm in the forest now. The spruce-and-pine canopy is so thick it crowds out the sun. A flare of light dashes by on my left. It's too warm to be *chazoure*. It must be my new heat vision. Meadow vipers use it for hunting. The light I just saw was an animal.

I veer for it and pick up pace with nighthawk speed. A spear with a ritual bone tip appears in my hand. Have I been holding it all this time?

You're dreaming, Sabine, I remind myself. That knowledge unleashes an inner savageness. If I'm dreaming, I'm allowed to be vicious and raging.

I scream a guttural cry. Release my fury at my mother. Yell at the elders of my *famille* who don't believe in me, at the silver owl who never explains enough, at the Chained who can't be killed. I shout at Jules for losing so much Light, at Bastien for getting arrested, at Ailesse for breaking her leg and being better than me at everything. My throat burns from cursing Casimir. If he were my *amouré*, I would have killed him already.

I keep chasing the glowing heat of the animal. Whatever it is, it's large and fast. I smell its heady musk, its robust dominance. I want it all for my own.

I shut out the voice at the back of my mind that pleads, *Be cautious, Sabine. Be patient. You told yourself you'd select an animal more wisely.*

I can't. I need more graces *now*. I shake from the irresistible urge to make this kill. Whether the reason is the jackal's bloodlust or my own desperation for more power against him, I can't tell.

The animal leaps over a deep crag in the earth. I leap, too. It darts back and forth, zigzagging around trees and blazing a fiery path for me. I follow until the forest abruptly thins into a clearing and the animal bounds into the wild grass. Its ruddy hide glistens in the sunlight. I finally have space. I take aim. Hurl my spear with graced strength.

The animal crashes to the ground. I bare my teeth and bolt after it. I scarcely see what it is, only that it's still breathing. I yank out my spear and stab again. Terrorized eyes blink back at me. I scream. Cry. Keep stabbing. *Die, you beast.*

Tears flood my vision. I hate myself for the thrill of adrenaline in my veins, for the failure I am at leading my *famille*, for killing each and every creature that has given me their graces: my bone knife through the spine of the fire salamander, my arrow through the chest of the nighthawk, Ailesse's bone knife through the heart of the golden jackal, Odiva's sickle to decapitate the meadow viper, and now this spear—is it also my mother's?—through the side of the red deer.

I see him for what he is now. A stag. Majestic, with sixteen tines on his antlers, surely the king of this forest. And now he's dead, nearly gutted from my attack. *Do not weep, Sabine.* I am not my mother's gentle child or Ailesse's fragile sister. I'm more than second born, second best. I'm *matrone*. And I deserve to be.

I cut my palm, scarred four times now from claiming my other graces. I press the red deer's antler to my blood. A swell of new graces, bold and proud, course into me . . . and they're what break me.

A low keening rises from my chest, and I fall to my knees. I've stolen a life, a powerful and noble one. I've sacrificed, just like my mother sacrificed thousands of souls.

I look down at myself. I'm barefoot and still wearing the ferrying dress I fell asleep in at Château Creux. It's streaked and splattered with the stag's blood.

But you're only dreaming, Sabine. You're only dreaming.

I open my eyes—no, they were already open—and everything is just as it was. I'm kneeling beside a slaughtered deer, and my dress bears the guilty crimson stains.

I swallow a sick burning in my throat. Perhaps I *was* dreaming when I spoke to my mother. But now I am very much awake. And I've made my fifth kill.

For better or worse, I've claimed my five grace bones.

12
Bastien

I RUB MY ACHING BACK and duck into a narrow alleyway. My stab wound is on fire, my lungs burn for air, and I'm dizzy from my viper bite. *Merde,* I miss the old me. I've trained most of my life to fight powerful Bone Criers. Now I can barely outrun two run-of-the-mill soldiers.

"He went into that alley!" one of them shouts.

I groan. I have to get them off my tail. They were near the castle well, patrolling the mines. I only scraped past them when I jumped down a shaft. I didn't expect them to follow me all this way, but they're more dogged than a horde of Chained.

I jump onto a barrel and climb three tiers of washing lines. I cut each down with my sword as I clamber higher. Wet clothes and ropes flop down on the soldiers. They bat them away and curse me.

I swing inside an open window, nod at an old woman kneading dough, and race through her apartment. A rickety staircase in the hallway catches my eye. I race up it two steps at a time, practically wheezing. The soldiers yell from below. They're already in the building.

I kick open the door at the top of the flight. I'm on the roof. The crumbling spires of Chapelle du Pauvre are in sight, less than a quarter mile away. I bolt for the church ruins. I have no time to wheel back for Birdine's apartment. The soldiers have chased me in the opposite direction of the brothel district. I'm in another poor district now, this one on the west side of Dovré.

The soldiers emerge on the roof. I race faster and gauge the distance to the next rooftop. I'll never make the jump. I scan around for a plank of wood or length of rope or—a flagpole. I shove my sword into my belt, veer for the flagpole, and yank it out of its stand. I don't bother tearing away the tattered sun flag of Dovré; I run to the edge of the roof, ready to catapult. On second thought, I'd rather live.

I lay the pole down like a bridge between the rooftops. I hang from the pole and haul myself across, hand over hand. It takes more strength than I bargained for. My arms throb. My grip shakes. The pole rolls left and right. *Come on, Bastien.*

The guards' boots pound nearer. I'm almost to the neighboring rooftop. The pole jostles. They've grabbed the other end. I quickly swing for the roof and let go of the pole. They kick it into the alley.

My body slams against the edge of the building. I grab the lip of the roof. Clamber onto it, panting.

The soldiers shout curses at me. I drag myself up and flourish a bow. "It's been a real pleasure, boys. Better luck next time."

As soon as I turn away, my grin vanishes. I prod my back and grimace. My wound is wet, and my fingers come away with blood. *Merde.*

I keep heading for the disused church. The rooftops leading to it are spaced closer than the last two, thank the gods. I need somewhere to rest.

Once I slip inside the chapel, I make my way to the alcove behind the altar. The frayed rug is buckled, but the hatch door beneath it is still hidden. I smother a prickle of unease, throw back the rug, and go down through the hatch.

In the cellar, I light a candle—I can't find the lantern I usually stash down here—and take the door that leads to the catacombs and my secret hideout.

The bone-lined corridors soon open up to an old limestone quarry. After my father died, this place was my home for two years. Once I met Jules and Marcel, I rarely came back, and when I did, I came alone. Everything that once belonged to my father, I brought here with me. Everything I could salvage, anyway. City officials auctioned off the few valuables he owned to pay his debts. No money was left over to bury him, so his body was tossed into an unmarked mass grave. I can't bear to think of him there, so I think of him here.

I lower myself down the scaffolding ladder at the edge of the forty-foot pit. When my father couldn't afford to pay for any lime-stone to sculpt, this was where he came to quarry his own blocks. I'd often tag along and keep him company. He'd tell me stories of Old Galle between the strikes of his chisel and hammer. I thought the tales were myth. Maybe my father did, too, or he might have never told me about Bone Criers. He didn't know the half of it. Neither did I, even after all my studying with Jules and Marcel. Nothing could have prepared me for Ailesse.

My chest suddenly pulls tight, and I struggle to breathe. *Ailesse* . . . I rest my forehead against one of the rungs of the ladder. When I close my eyes, I see her beautiful face again. I feel the last kiss she gave me in the well tower. I can't believe she stayed. I can't believe I really left her behind. I'll still do whatever it takes to protect her. That hasn't changed. I'll help her survive her soul-bond. I'll gently persuade her to accept that Casimir has to die.

I square my jaw and move down the scaffolding ladder again until I reach an eight-by-ten-foot quarry room, open to the pit on one side. I freeze. The missing lantern is lit and resting in the middle of the floor. It barely casts enough light to fill the space. A split second later, I see who's lying at the base of the far wall, beneath the relief my father carved of Château Creux. A boy. No, not a boy. A damn king.

I yank my sword from my belt and charge into the room. Any warmth I felt a moment ago is gone. Acid burns through my veins. "What the hell are you doing here?"

Casimir jerks into a sitting position—a feat, seeing he's tied up from shoulders to ankles with strong rope. His stony eyes narrow. "You escaped."

"Of course I . . ." *Wait a minute. If he's here, then—*

I spin around and call into the pit. "Ailesse!" My pulse races. I can't see far enough. The light of my candle only shines a few feet into the darkness. "Are you down there?" She's the only other person who knows about this place.

"She's gone." Casimir sighs wearily. "She's out searching for you."

I frown at him. "Why didn't she bring you with her?" I told her where to meet me if she left Beau Palais—at Birdine's apartment.

He winces as he shifts to get comfortable. "Apparently I'm safer underground."

I study him, trying to solve the puzzle. If Ailesse refused to leave the castle with me, what changed her mind? "Were you attacked by a Chained again?"

His brows jut up. "You know about the Chained?"

"Fought them myself."

"But how did you know I was attacked?"

I don't answer him, and I don't need to. The moment he figures it out is clear by his slow exhale and the downward tilt of his mouth.

"Ailesse was the one who helped you escape."

I smirk. "Pretty impressive considering she was on a crutch the whole time. What's harder to string together is how she got *you* out of the castle." I tip my chin at his ropes. "From the looks of things, you didn't come willingly."

"Yes, well, I'm certain her grace bones provided her the advantage," he grumbles.

"So you gave them back?" I snort. "She really has you wrapped around her finger, doesn't she?"

Casimir's grin is tight and thin-lipped. "I'm not the only one who has taken extreme measures for her."

A muscle tics in my jaw. "Don't pretend you and I have anything in common, Your Highness." I sheathe my sword and stride across the room to the right wall, toward the ledge with my father's figurines. I set my candle beside my dolphin statue, a gift he carved just for me. I make sure it hasn't been disturbed. All my nerves are wound up. I can't believe Casimir is here, of all places. He mutters something as I dig through a crate, searching for a drink. "What was that?" I turn and glare at him.

"It's *Your Majesty* now," he murmurs, no pride in his voice. "My father is dead, murdered by those merciless Chained."

My stomach twists. I bite the inside of my cheek, struggling to hold on to my hatred. It's hard when I know the pain behind his bitter and broken expression. I've lived with it for eight years.

I shove my hands in my pockets. Shift from foot to foot. "My, um . . . my father was murdered, too."

Casimir's brows slowly pull together. He says nothing for a long moment, just stares back at me with slightly widened eyes. I try to look away, but I can't. It's like the moment I found Jules and Marcel after what felt like being forever on my own. They understood me. Their father had been stolen from them, too.

Casimir finally raises his voice, but it's quiet and solemn when he asks, "By another Chained?"

I shake my head and sit down five feet away, my back to the corner wall. "Bone Crier."

He swallows, nodding heavily.

We fall quiet again. The dense air of the underground quarry thickens the silence until he says, "You could let me go."

I chuckle. "Says the person who had me arrested."

"All your charges would be dropped, of course."

"Ailesse brought you here for a reason. I have to respect that."

"She plans to keep me sequestered here until the full moon."

"Makes sense if the Chained are on your tail."

"I'll miss my father's burial."

My gut twists. "That can't be helped."

Casimir's composure cracks. "I'm the blasted king!" he shouts. "I *have* to go home! I haven't even had my coronation yet. *Someone* must rule this country. We're being ravaged by the dead, border wars are on the rise, and North Galle is a constant threat—not to mention a growing population of dissenters who are all too anxious to see me usurped. If my enemies discover my throne is empty, they will seize the opportunity and strike hard."

"Not my problem."

He stares at me in disbelief. "That's right. I'm sure a thief like you has never had to think beyond taking care of yourself."

I scowl at him. What does *he* know about living off the streets? "Save your arguments for Ailesse. I'm not going against her in this."

"Ailesse is a Bone Crier, Bastien."

"What of it?"

He looks at the ceiling and shakes his head slowly. "I think she means to kill me."

A twinge of sympathy pricks me, again not so easy to brush away. I know his fear. I've felt it myself. But I desperately need Ailesse to live. And for that, Casimir has to die. I can't give him any false hope otherwise. He understands me now. He would know I was lying. "I think she has to."

13
Ailesse

RELIEF SWEEPS THROUGH ME AT the sight of a painted sign swinging from an iron bracket. It depicts a dagger plunging straight through a heart. Le Coeur Percé. I've finally found it.

I shield my eyes from the noonday sunlight and survey the tavern and its second story. The building is patched together from odd chunks of limestone, mortar, and wooden beams, but its ruggedness is balanced by the beauty of creeping honeysuckle and cornflower-blue shutters. Which of those windows looks into Birdine's apartment? Is Bastien inside? I need to explain where I had to take Cas. He won't like it.

I hobble to the door and linger for a moment on my crutch. Am I supposed to knock or just walk in without invitation? Growing up, I never learned the etiquette of people outside my *famille*. I nibble on my lip and decide to knock.

Just before my knuckles rap on the door, an elderly man with a knitted cap opens it wide and walks past me, giving me a second glance with raised brows. I've been getting similar reactions from other people in the city. Maybe it's my dress. I tug at the off-the-shoulder sleeves of my velvet-and-brocade gown. Perhaps it's too fashionable for everyday wear. At any rate, no one else in the brothel district is clothed like this.

The elderly man has left the door open, so I tentatively crutch-limp inside. Dust motes glitter about me from the sunlight, but when I shut the door, the charm I found outside vanishes. My tiger shark vision swiftly adjusts to the dim interior. I'm surrounded by oak, stone, and iron—aged not in the hauntingly beautiful way of Château Creux, but by soot and grime.

Ten or so tables are scattered about beneath hulking iron chandeliers, and a bearded man in a filthy apron stands behind a counter propped up by large barrels. Bottles of brackish-looking liquid and small casks line the shelves at his back. "What is Madame Collette up to now?" His Gallish accent is harsh, nothing like Cas's or even Bastien's.

I blink. "P-pardon?"

He snorts and dries a pewter mug. "Dressing up her girls like princesses, now, is she?"

"I'm not sure I—"

"Go back to La Chaste Dame." He slams his mug on the counter. "I don't need you stealing my paying customers."

My mouth hangs open. I understand his meaning now. I passed La Chaste Dame on the way here. It's a brothel house, and not a very reputable one, judging by the bawdy remarks I overheard from those loitering nearby.

Low chuckles echo in the tavern. I glance around at the few people I felt with my sixth sense the moment I walked in: two men, one woman, and—my muscles tense—two *chazoure* souls. At least they don't wear chains.

"I don't work for Madame Collette." I limp toward a staircase past the counter. "I came to see . . ."

Someone gasps from above. I look up past the railing of the upper story and find Jules staring down at me. Or at least a version of Jules. She's notably thinner and has dark shadows beneath her hazel eyes. "Aileen," she addresses me with a scowl. "I told you never to come here."

Aileen? I stare stupidly at her until she gives me a subtle but pointed look. "Oh, I'm . . . sorry."

"Don't be sorry. Be gone." She marches down the stairs.

"You know this girl?" the bearded man asks her.

"She's my cousin, but we're forbidden to speak. Bad blood between our fathers." Jules takes me by the arm—her grip is weaker than it used to be—and ushers me toward the front door. "Stay out of this district, or you'll start a street war," she says, loud enough for everyone to hear.

"All right" is my best response. I need a good lesson in subterfuge.

She follows me outside and kicks the door shut behind us.

"Hurry," she hisses, and pulls me into a tight alley on the side of the tavern. "The prince's soldiers will be looking for you. We need to be covert." She sighs, glancing over me. "You should have worn a hooded cloak." She rushes deeper through the alley and waves a hand for me to follow.

I hobble after her. "I didn't have time to change clothes."

"It's not just your dress, Ailesse."

My hand drifts to my hair, wild and tangled from my fight with the vipers and the Chained. "I'll bathe before I go out again."

She groans. "You're insufferable, do you know that? You could be wearing rags and dripping mud, and you'd still turn heads in Dovré."

I'm not sure whether to say "Thank you" or "I'm sorry," so I say nothing.

Once we round the back of the tavern, she points to a warped wooden door. "Go through this entrance. On your left, you'll see a ladder. Take it to the loft, then come back down to the second story. Birdine's room is in the northeast corner. I'll meet you there." She hurries back the way she came.

I hastily follow her instructions, despite the awkwardness of my crutch. It isn't too long before I find Birdine's door and turn the latch. Jules is already inside and waiting. She tugs me into the room and locks the door behind me.

I turn and look at the simple but pretty room, decorated with yellow curtains and a vase of cheery golden coneflowers—clearly Birdine's additions, though she isn't here, either. The only other person in the room is Marcel. He's sprawled out on a bed by the window and snoozing with an open book in his lap. "Where's Bastien?" I ask.

"I was just about to ask you the same." Jules crosses her arms.

"But he told me to meet him here."

"Didn't he escape?" she demands. "I thought the whip snakes Sabine sent would have—"

"Whip snakes? They were meadow vipers."

"No, they only *looked* like meadow vipers."

"People died, Jules," I say emphatically. "They were vipers."

She blanches. "I didn't mean to . . . That—that was a mistake." She rubs her brow and paces away from me. "Bastien, did he—?"

"He was only bitten once. I helped him escape."

"Then why isn't he with you?"

"I . . . I had to take care of some things before I left Beau Palais."

"Things?" Jules frowns. "What things?"

Marcel sits up, his floppy hair bedraggled. "Ailesse?" He smiles crookedly. "You made it. You're welcome for the whip snakes." He chuckles and winks a droopy eye. "That was my idea."

A miserable laugh escapes Jules. I'll let her explain what he missed later. "We have to find Bastien," I say, praying for my knee to stop throbbing. I can't rest just yet. "He must be in danger."

Jules tenses. "Was he followed?"

"Not that I'm aware of, but—"

"You don't think that the Chained . . . ?" Her eyes widen.

A sick wash of anxiety chases through my stomach. I can't bear to imagine Bastien losing Light or, worse, his soul. "How did you know they're loose again? Were you attacked?"

"No, Sabine told me."

Sabine? I keep forgetting my sister has been in contact with my former abductors. My two separate worlds won't stop colliding. "Where is she?"

"With your *famille*," Jules says. "She has her hands full with the Chained, too."

Heat scalds my cheeks. I still can't believe Sabine is *matrone* when I should be. "Yes, of course." I turn away and walk purposefully to an open chest. I dig through a pile of clothes and blankets, my jaw clenched. "Do you have a spare cloak?"

"Take mine." Marcel shifts off the bed and grabs it for me.

Jules fetches her own cloak. "Stay here until Birdine gets home," she tells her brother. "And pack up. It's time for us to move underground."

Good plan. I give it my full focus and banish any more thoughts of returning home and reclaiming my birthright. At least for now. I need to deal with the problem of my captive *amouré* first. "We should all stick together in Bastien's hideout." Jules can't afford to lose any more Light.

"Which hideout?" She tucks her golden braid into her hood and grabs a water flask, slinging its rope over her shoulder.

"The one off the catacombs and quarry beneath Chapelle du Pauvre."

Jules exchanges a puzzled glance with Marcel. "I don't know what you're talking about."

I forgot Bastien kept it a secret from them. "It's where he hid me when the Chained were loose last time . . . as a last resort, of course. It's a special place for him."

She scoffs. "Bastien has a special place we don't know about?"

Marcel scratches his jaw. "It's possible. It wouldn't be the only church in Dovré that led to the catacombs. It must have made a good hiding spot."

"It still does." I fidget with the strings of his cloak around my shoulders. "Casimir is there now. He, um . . . might be tied up."

Jules gapes at me. Marcel bursts into laughter. "You abducted the prince?"

"The king, actually."

Jules shakes her head, and a slow grin forms on her mouth. "*Merde*, Ailesse."

"The Chained were after him and . . ." I cross my arms defensively. "It's for his own good." *And mine.*

She blows out a long breath, trying to process what I've done. "Well, I suppose it serves him right."

Does it? I don't know. But I'm not overly concerned with Cas at the moment, not when Bastien is missing and Sabine is trying to manage a near-impossible situation without me. "Ready?"

Jules nods and turns to her brother. "As soon as Birdine is back, hurry to Chapelle du Pauvre. I don't want you out in the open much longer. If you hear a Chained, don't fight. Run."

I quickly tell him how to find Bastien's quarry room.

"You mean I can bring Birdie with me?" Marcel asks Jules, like he didn't hear anything else we said.

She rolls her eyes. "I guess. I don't trust that girl to keep her mouth shut otherwise." She tosses me a hard look. "You know you've committed treason, right?"

I lift my chin. "It was that or let the king die."

She huffs.

Marcel opens the door for us. His lazy grin doesn't falter, despite our talk of crimes punishable by death. I squeeze his arm as I hobble by. "It's good to see you again."

"You too, Ailesse," he says warmly.

As Jules follows me out, Marcel nudges her with his elbow. "Are you going to tell her?"

I glance between them. "Tell me what?"

She bites her lower lip. "Sabine wasn't sure you should know just yet."

My pulse jumps. All my earlier frustrations with my sister vanish. "Did something happen to her? Is she all right?"

"Sabine is fine, but when she was ferrying—"

"She *didn't* ferry. The Chained wouldn't be loose otherwise."

"Well, she must have at least opened the Gates for a bit, because she saw your mother."

I rear back slightly. "What?"

Jules draws a steeling breath that rattles in her chest. "Odiva is alive, Ailesse. Trapped. And she wants *you* to set her free."

14
Sabine

Is your sister not at *the very heart of your weakness?* The words my mother spoke in my dream call back to me as I keep watch on Château Creux. I'm hidden where the plateau meets the forest, a distance where none of my *famille* should be able to sense me with their graces. I haven't returned home since I walked in my sleep last night. I'm still wearing my bloodstained ferrying dress.

I glance at the path that leads to Dovré. The late afternoon breeze kicks up the scent of lavender from the fields and salty brine from the Nivous Sea, but nothing human, certainly nothing like Ailesse's earthen and unique wildflower smell. *Where is she?*

Earlier, I ventured near Beau Palais, hoping to catch some rumor that might help me learn if she escaped last night, but the castle is even more closed off now. They wouldn't even open the gates for regular couriers. I later checked Birdine's apartment to see if Jules or Marcel had any news, but everyone's personal belongings were gone. I have no idea where they've all run off to.

A cloud passes over the sun. My meadow viper's heat vision flickers and catches the glow of nearby life. Again, nothing human, only a fox with a hare in his mouth. Sharp pangs of worry twist through my stomach. What if Ailesse didn't escape with Bastien? Did I kill them both with the vipers I set on Beau Palais?

Ailesse is blood of my blood, bones of my bones. There is magic between a mother and daughter that even the gods cannot explain. Again, my mother's voice comes to mind, and this time I'm desperate to believe she's right. Can that same magic extend to sisters? Ailesse can't be dead. I would feel it. She's alive, just like she was when my mother declared her dead before.

I look back to Château Creux and shake out my hands. My *famille* needs a *matrone*. Ailesse would want me to lead if she couldn't.

I whisper a prayer to Elara and cross the plateau to Château Creux. I draw on the majesty and boldness of the red stag—or is it the jackal that helps me carry myself like a queen? *I'm not just any sixteen-year-old girl*, I remind myself. *I'm Odiva's daughter by all rights, too.*

I walk down the crumbling stone staircase and enter the ancient castle, passing the engraved crow-and-rose crest, the symbol of the dynasty that ruled South Galle before its last monarch, King Godart, died and Château Creux fell into ruin.

I descend to the lower levels and weave through the tunnels. By the time I set foot inside the open cavern courtyard, most of the Leurress have already gathered there. Perhaps they sensed me coming, because this feels like an intervention. All the elders who are present—Nadine, Pernelle, Chantae, Roxane, and Damiana—stand where Odiva used to preside, at very center of the limestone ground, above the carved face of Tyrus's golden jackal—my jackal—nested in the curve of Elara's sickle moon. The rest of the Leurress are assembled against the curving edges of the courtyard, giving those with more authority a wide berth.

My *famille* turns the moment I enter. Maurille gasps. Isla's eyes narrow, and Pernelle's grow round. Little Felise and Lisette startle and hide behind Hyacinthe's skirt. I'm a terrible sight in my blood-streaked dress, but I hold my head high.

I've fashioned my red stag's antlers into a crown worthy of the *matrone* I need to be. Roxane, one of the strongest elders, also wears a stag wreath, but its antlers only have eight tines. Mine have sixteen. I used Odiva's ritual spear to saw them off today, and then wrapped a ring of twigs around them so they jut up like fangs. My meadow viper vertebrae and nighthawk leg and claw are woven among them at the base of the crown, and I've threaded the waxed cording from my old grace bone necklace around two of the antler tines so my fire salamander skull and golden jackal pendant hang down across my forehead.

With Odiva's ritual spear in my grip, I walk to the center of the courtyard to take my place, but the only elders who step aside are Pernelle and Damiana. Roxane stands where I should stand, and she draws herself taller. We're like two stags facing off in battle for the rights to the harem.

"Your timing is impeccable, Sabine." She arches an ash-brown brow. "Those of us who are not out contending with the dead *you* failed to ferry have gathered to discuss your premature role as our *matrone*."

My jaw muscle flinches. "Odiva named me as her heir. You all bore witness."

"We do not dispute that," Nadine replies. "But surely Odiva expected to live many more years."

"You are so young, Sabine," Chantae adds. "What happened at the land bridge is proof you're not prepared to fulfill your duties."

Heat flushes my face. "You would have run away, too, if you had seen—" I exhale and clamp my mouth shut.

"There's a reason the rest of us had to sacrifice our *amourés* before we were allowed to ferry," Isla says.

"Stay out of this." I glare at her. "You're not an elder." Isla is barely twenty years old, the youngest of the Ferriers.

Roxane holds up a hand. "Isla may have spoken out of turn, but she isn't wrong. It was a mistake to let you lead the ferrying so soon." Isla smirks once Roxane looks away.

"I have five grace bones now, and each death cost me. I am committed. I don't need to sacrifice an *amouré*."

"Oh, but we all do," Chantae says. "That pain is necessary, and we bear it together. It strengthens our sisterhood."

"It proves our loyalty to the gods," Nadine adds.

"And it gives us power against temptation." Roxane glides a step nearer to me. "If you had cultivated that resistance, you wouldn't have fled the land bridge."

"That's not why . . ." I struggle to breathe. No one's giving me a chance to speak. They've already made up their minds. "Now isn't the time to discuss my rite of passage. We need to focus on how to manage the loose Chained. Luckily, we've dealt with this situation before, so we know how to—"

"We have declared you unfit to rule, Sabine," Roxane cuts me off.

My legs turn to water. "What?"

"Don't take it personally," Chantae says. "None of us could have ruled at your age."

But Ailesse could. That's what everyone's thinking, but not saying.

"We've decided to appoint a regent in your stead," Nadine tells me.

"Regent?" I frown. "No, that's not— We've never had a regent before."

"We've chosen Roxane." Chantae clasps her hands together. "She will rule until you're sufficiently prepared. Perhaps in ten years—"

"Ten years?" My voice pitches higher. "No, no, no. You can't take away my power." *Ailesse's power.* If the elders do, it will be much more difficult for her to wrest it back again. She'll never forgive me. "You don't have the right."

"We believe we do," Roxane says.

"Well, you're wrong!" I look from her to the others—to everyone in my *famille*. Why aren't they listening to me? I'm supposed to be graced with indisputable abilities of a leader. I've killed a stag with sixteen antler tines. I'll never be clean of his blood. "If Ailesse were here—"

"She isn't here," Roxane snaps, losing patience. "She's missing, probably dead."

"Thank the gods," Isla says under her breath. My graced ears catch it, and I whirl on her, tightening my grip on my spear.

"What did you say?"

She lifts her chin. "You heard me." She flips her ginger hair over her shoulder. "Who am I to argue with Tyrus and Elara? If they can choose our *amourés*, they can certainly choose who should rule us. Apparently Ailesse wasn't cut out for the job."

I lunge for her, teeth bared, spear raised.

"Sabine, no!" Pernelle cries.

Isla yelps, unprepared for how viper-fast I strike. She barely dodges my attack.

"Just as I thought." I spin back for her. "You're all words and no muscle. I can solve that." I grab hold of her chin and yank her forward. "We'll be grateful when you've lost your tongue."

"Let her go, Sabine!" Roxane commands, but she doesn't have authority over me.

I set my spear tip at the corner of Isla's mouth. I'm not going to hurt her, just teach her a lesson. "I'll tell you who the gods find pathetic," I snarl. "Someone who can't let go of her jealousy, even though she believes her rival is dead."

Tears spring to Isla's eyes, but her glare is vicious. "I'm not the one who skulked in the shadows, thinking I could never measure up to Ailesse."

My blood catches fire. The elders shout at me, but my pulse thrashes in my ears and drowns out the sound. My spear tip trembles against Isla's lip. One little yank, and I could tear a gash through her cheek. An image from my dream flashes to mind. My reflection in the water below Castelpont. Me with jackal teeth and yellow eyes.

I jerk back from Isla and swing my spear away.

Someone shrieks. It's Hyacinthe, the oldest Leurress. Her eyes fill with horror. She clutches the side of her throat. Blood seeps through her fingers. I gasp and drop the spear. I've cut her by accident. "Hyacinthe!" I trip forward.

She collapses to her knees. Pernelle rushes to her side and applies pressure to her neck. The other elders swarm to assist her. Little Felise and Lisette start crying.

"I didn't mean to—" I can't breathe. "Will she be all right?"

Pernelle, who has always been supportive, turns fearful eyes on me. "You should go, Sabine."

"But I—"

"Just go!"

I turn on my heel and run out of the courtyard. I rush through the tunnels, the crumbling corridors, the stairwells. Pernelle probably meant for me to go to my room, but I race outside instead. I can't remain here. I'm too dangerous. They'll take away my grace bones—the punishment when one Leurress attacks another in the *famille*.

I was a fool to think the red stag could keep my golden jackal grace in check.

What if I gave it up?

No, I can't. The dead are afraid of it. I need it to help me rein them in.

The jackal is too great a burden to shoulder on your own.

I cry out, raging against the words my mother spoke in my dream. She wants me to hand over Ailesse before she'll help me. I refuse to.

I run faster until I can no longer see Château Creux or sense all the panic within its walls. "She'll live, she'll live," I chant, willing Hyacinthe to stop bleeding.

Ailesse will return soon. That's what I want, isn't it? She'll fix this. She'll fix everything. Until then, I'll fight what Chained I can. I'll draw them out from Dovré.

I wipe the tears from my eyes and grit my teeth.

I *will* conquer myself. I *will* master this grace.

15
Ailesse

"Watch your feet on the scaffolding right here," I tell Jules. "The wood has rotted." She dodges the weak spot, and we continue to descend the side of the quarry pit beneath Chapelle du Pauvre.

The day is almost over. We searched all afternoon throughout Dovré for Bastien and found no sign of him. My stomach is in knots.

"We're almost there." I hop down to the second-to-last scaffolding platform on my good leg. I'll give Cas some food and water; then I need to continue my search. Maybe I can persuade Jules to stay here and guard him. She needs to rest. The neckline of her shirt is drenched in sweat.

"Do you need me to hold the candle?" I ask. The one we found in the cellar keeps dripping hot wax on her fingers. There was no spare lantern.

"I'm fine," she grumbles on a thin breath. "You're worse than Bastien with all your coddling."

I bite my tongue. Showing strength under duress is admirable, but Jules's strength is feeble at best. *Admitting you need help isn't weakness*, Sabine often told me.

Sabine. The knots in my stomach cinch tighter. Did she really see our mother past the Gates of the Underworld? Maybe that's the real reason I've lost my appetite. The person I thought was my mother will be dead forever. She never existed. My true mother is a stranger, a betrayer, a murderer. What would she do if she broke free of the Underworld? A flush of cold dread races up my spine.

"Here we are," I say, and step off the scaffolding. The small quarry room is already lit with the lantern I left for Cas. He's bound up where I left him, although a second candle glows from the ledge with Bastien's father's figurines. My heart gives a hard pound.

"Bastien?" I rush over to where he's lying asleep in a corner of the room. I set aside my crutch and crouch beside him. Thank the gods he's safe.

His eyes slowly bat open, and his mouth curves. "Hey, beautiful." Warmth flutters through my chest. "You came back." His voice is a little spell-drawn from sleep. Then he blinks, and his eyes grow large. "You . . . you really came back."

"Of course I did." I grin. "I sort of had to." I steal a glance at

Cas, who's glowering at both of us. The warmth inside me vanishes. What a tangle I've gotten myself into.

Bastien sits up and winces, reaching for his back. I gasp when I look at the dark red spot on his shirt. "Did your wound reopen?" I touch the stained fabric. It isn't wet. "Do you need to be stitched up again?"

"Nah. Bleeding's stopped. More stitches will just cause infection."

I bite my lip and nod. "How long have you been here?" I curse myself for not checking this place sooner. I could have left to find Sabine already.

He scratches his head. "You'd have to ask His Royal Specialness over there. I'm not sure how long I've been out."

Jules saunters into the room. "His Royal Specialness doesn't look too eager to speak at the moment." Her smirk is half sardonic, half amazed as she gawks at Cas, whose brows are lowered in a highly unamused line. "May the gods save the king," she adds, dipping into an awkward curtsy. "Or if they won't, I guess we will."

Cas blows a strawberry curl out of his eye. "You can start by untying me, unless you also want to be charged for treason."

Jules shoots me a sharp glance. "I told you this was treason."

"No one's untying him." My tone is adamant.

"Ailesse, the abductor." She nods approvingly. "I like this look on you."

Bastien chuckles, sliding closer beside me. I tense with the sudden urge to scoot away. I'm not sure why. For hours, I've longed to see him. Now I know he's safe, all I want to do is run home. Which is not so easy now that I've taken the king captive.

"I'm serious," I reply. "Cas isn't safe in Beau Palais—or anywhere else aboveground. Don't let him persuade you otherwise. The dissenters in Dovré would be happy to see him dead. Some of *them* are dead and far too dangerous. This is for his own good."

"Is it?" Cas narrows his eyes. "Or is it for *your* good, Ailesse?"

"Hey, now, take it easy," Bastien says. "Ailesse has a right to protect her own life, too. And her soul, for that matter." He slips his arm around my waist, and I squirm on instinct, unable to hide my reaction this time. He immediately lets go, his ears tinged red.

What's the matter with me? Ever since I learned my mother had named Sabine as heir, my head has been muddled. Anything that pulls focus from my *famille* overwhelms me, even Bastien.

"And what of the souls of *my* people?" Cas demands. "Are you really intent on hiding me here while they remain defenseless against an army of the dead?"

I meet his gaze squarely. "I haven't forgotten about your people. My people have been protecting everyone in South Galle since long before your family took the throne. I'm certain they're doing everything in their power right now to rein in the dead and—"

Bastien stiffens. "Jules, don't touch—!" He lets out a tense breath. "Just put that down. Please."

She returns the dolphin sculpture to the ledge and holds up her hands. "Good to see you, too. I'm alive and well, thanks for asking."

Bastien sags back against the wall, careful with his wound. "Sorry, I'm not used to this much company down here."

"I can see that." She prods a mug filled with wilted wildflowers and eyes all the unlit candles in the room. "Looks like it was cozy enough for two, though."

He groans. "I brought Ailesse here as a last resort, all right? Besides, this was my home before I ever even met you."

"So." She crosses her arms. "Explain why you made Marcel and me sleep in reeking alleys in this very district when you had a better place nearby."

He opens and closes his mouth. "I was . . . This is . . ."

"It's a sacred place for him." I touch his leg defensively, then catch myself and pull away. "Can't you see his father's things are everywhere?"

Jules glares at me. "He has lungs and a voice, you know. He can speak for himself."

"How would Bone Criers protect people?" Cas asks, still stuck on that fact and ignoring the rest of our conversation.

I sigh and turn to Bastien. "I'm sorry I brought him here. It was the closest place I knew of."

"It's fine." He musters a kind smile, even though I keep jilting him. "I'm just glad you're here and safe."

That's part of my problem, I realize. I don't want to be anywhere that feels like another prison. I don't want to be shut away from Elara's Light or tied to an *amouré* or even obliged to anyone. Suddenly it's all too suffocating. I never asked for these complications that keep dragging me away from my birthright.

Jules scoffs at Bastien. "Unbelievable."

He rolls his eyes and waves her over to him. "Come and sit

down, all right? We're all tired. Let's save the arguing for—"

"Protecting is the opposite of killing," Cas says, belligerently pressing his point. "You said you were the girl who was supposed to kill me, Ailesse."

I sigh, massaging my temples. "He doesn't really know what Bone Criers are," I murmur to Bastien. "Apparently not everyone was told this story by their fathers."

"What story?" Cas asks.

"Folktales," Bastien replies. "Women in white on bridges who kill men they lure after sharing a dance."

Cas is quiet for a moment. "You meant to kill me, Ailesse?"

"Oh yes," Jules chimes in. "A great honor for you, too. And don't worry, you would have thanked her for it one day in Paradise."

I cringe. Did I really once believe that justified the blood ritual?

"But why?" Cas's brow furrows. "None of this makes sense."

"He doesn't know about Ferriers, either?" Bastien asks me.

I shake my head, and Jules laughs. "I think I *will* sit down." She plants herself in the middle of the room and tucks her knees to her chest. "This is getting good."

I take a deep breath and start at the beginning—with Tyrus and Elara, a new groom and bride separated at the dawn of time by the mortal world that formed between them.

I explain about Belin and Gaëlle, who caused that to happen and divided the two kingdoms of the dead. Then a Leurress was born, the first and only child of Tyrus and Elara. She was charged with bridging the gap between the mortal world and her parents' realms and bringing them the souls of the departed . . . and so was every Leurress daughter in her line forevermore.

But in order to bear daughters, they needed fathers, so the gods gave them *amourés*. The Leurress couldn't lose themselves to love, however—they had a divine mandate, after all—so the gods asked them to sacrifice their *amourés* within one year from the time they were soul-bound, and in reward Tyrus and Elara would grant them the right and the strength to ferry their dead. If the Leurress failed, the soul-bond would become a curse. Their *amourés* would die at the year's end, and the Leurress would die with them.

"But if you had killed me that night," Cas says, "I could have never fathered your child."

My cheeks set on fire. "That was never going to happen."

"Damn straight," Bastien grumbles.

"Some of the Leurress choose to become Ferriers without first becoming mothers," I add. "That was my plan."

"But you're next in line to be *matrone*," Jules replies, and my chest tightens. I should be *matrone*, anyway. My mother had no right to replace me with Sabine. She knew I was alive. "Don't queens need heirs as much as kings?" she asks.

"No one's making heirs," Bastien says.

"I was going to name an heir instead." I fidget. "It seemed kinder than . . . well, I didn't wish to become involved on such a level with my *amouré* before I had to . . ." I release an exasperated breath. "Intimacy before blood sacrifice is just cruel." My ears burn, but my anger blazes hotter. "It isn't fair, what the gods demand. I deserve a better life." I swallow and look at Bastien and

Jules, adding softly, "Your fathers did, too."

Jules brows wrench together, and she blinks back moisture from her eyes. Bastien's gaze drifts to the ledge with his dolphin statue. His jaw muscle flexes. "Then let's stop this—all of it. Let's find a way to end blood sacrifice."

"How?" I ask. "I can't just decide to stop it. You know what will happen if I don't kill Cas."

"Isn't there a way to break the soul-bond?" Cas shifts uncomfortably.

"Just thinking about that makes my head ache," Jules moans. "You haven't met my brother yet, Your Majesty, but believe me when I tell you he's something of a prodigy, and if he can't figure out how to break the soul-bond, I'll be bowled over if anyone else can."

"Maybe the problem isn't the answer; it's the question," Bastien says.

"How do you mean?" I frown.

He leans closer. "All this time we've been asking ourselves how to break the soul-bond, when maybe we should've been asking how to break the system that requires blood sacrifice in the first place."

I'm still not following. "The world needs Ferriers, Bastien. What's happening right now in Dovré is proof of that."

"I'm not saying we get rid of Ferriers. I'm saying we get rid of *all* soul-bonds that end in blood. Not just for you, but for everyone, forever. That way no one's father, no one's king"—he nods in Cas's direction—"would have to die the way mine did. That peace would be worlds better than revenge."

"What you're inferring means waging war on the gods." Cas's voice drops to a grave whisper. "Is that wise? Is it even possible?"

"It isn't war," Bastien says. "It's—"

"—outmaneuvering them." Jules catches on.

"Like a bargain?" I think of my mother's pact with Tyrus. "Bargains with deities come at a high price." *I was to be that price.*

"Not exactly." He drags a thumb across the stubble on his jaw. "Look, I'm not sure what the solution is, but we're on the right track. I can feel it. And with Marcel's help, we'll find the answer soon enough. Meanwhile, we keep the king here and . . ."

His voice becomes distorted and tinny. The air shimmers in front of him, rippling like a silver mirage. I've seen this before, back in our old catacombs chamber when I first glimpsed—

The silver owl.

As soon as I think of her, she appears in a radiant wash of Light with her wings unfurled. She beats them once, and I'm sucked inside a vision. It's so rapid-fire I can scarcely comprehend the images flashing by. . . .

Sabine. Castelpont. A bounding wildcat—no, a jackal. Sabine's arrow in the jackal's heart. A new grace bone. A pendant carved like a crescent moon. Sabine wearing it as she breaks through a stained-glass window.

Then a storm in the sea. The land bridge. Ferriers and chazoure flares of oncoming souls. My mother's black eyes. The Gate of water holding her back. Her hand reaching for Sabine. Sabine fleeing the bridge. Another flash of the pendant.

Sabine in Château Creux now, a crown of antlers on her head. Her face ferocious, but scared. A swinging spear in her hand. A great commotion in the courtyard. Shock on her face. Tears as she races outside, sobbing.

The silver owl rasp-screeches. I'm thrown out of the vision, and her wings close. The silver Light vanishes. The owl's gone. I'm shaking, gasping for breath. Cas and Jules and Bastien all stare at me.

Bastien's hand is on my back. "Ailesse, what—?"

I jerk away and grab my crutch. "It's Sabine," I stammer. "I—I saw her."

Jules's brow wrinkles. "How did you . . . ?"

I can't explain or stay here a moment longer. My sister needs me. I need her.

I race out of the room, quick with my falcon grace, even on one leg.

"Ailesse, wait!" Bastien says.

I don't. I spring up the scaffolding, ibex agile and tiger shark strong.

I'm coming, Sabine.

16

Bastien

"Ailesse!" I call. I can't believe how fast she's able to move, in spite of her broken leg. With her graced strength and ability to jump, her crutch has become a more of a vaulting pole. I chase her through the alleys of Dovré, but she stays out of reach. She springs off barrels and crates, and bounds for the west wall of the city.

"Can we talk about this?" I have no idea what set her off so suddenly, except it's something to do with Sabine. Honestly, I have no idea what's setting her off about a lot of things. Including me.

She leaps up a steep and narrow stone staircase that runs along the side of a building. "Go back, Bastien." She pivots at the sheer edge of a step, incredibly agile and balanced. She looks down at me. "Stay in hiding. If the royal guard finds you—"

"They'll be searching for you, too." I rub my throbbing stab wound. "Please, just tell me what's going on. Is Sabine—?"

"She's not meant to be *matrone*." Ailesse rushes up the stairs again, three steps at a time. She hisses as her long dress snags beneath her crutch. "Sabine never prepared herself like I did."

"She's with your *famille*. They can protect each other at Château Creux." I race up the stairs. "That's over seven miles away. We shouldn't travel that far with the Chained on the loose."

"I'm doing this alone, Bastien. I can fight the Chained." She hurries across a rooftop and leaps the six-foot gap to the next building. She grunts as she lands. "Go back. Please."

Before I can say anything else, she bolts across the next rooftop. Its far edge is thirteen feet from the city wall. "Ailesse, stop! That's too far!" Graces or not, she's only got one good leg.

Her jaw is set. She doesn't hesitate. She hurtles forward. Her crutch propels her faster and faster. I jump the gap between the first set of roofs. She's too far away. I'll never reach her in time. If she falls, she'll fall thirty feet. "Ailesse!"

She lifts her dress to her knees. Pushes off the roof's edge with her strong leg. Catapults toward the wall. Her cry of exertion echoes back to me. I keep running. Desperate adrenaline pounds through my veins. *Please, please, please.*

Her right foot catches the wall, but she doesn't have enough traction. She can't hold her landing. She drops her crutch. Scrambles to grab the wall with her hands. Her long sleeves are in the way. She tumbles over the wall on the side of the forest.

"Ailesse!" I grind to a stop. She doesn't call back. *Merde, merde,*

merde. I wheel around and race back for the other rooftop. I run down the stairs and sprint for the west wall on ground level. There's a weak spot a quarter mile away. I've used it to make quick exits after thieving.

I find the place, make sure no one's watching, and slip behind the honeysuckle vines. I shove out a few loose bricks from the wall that need repair. I make a hole big enough for myself and squirm through it. "Ailesse!" I shout. I rush back to the place where she fell.

She isn't there, but a tall and thorny patch of underbrush is smashed in on one side. I find her tracks—the marks from her crutch aren't subtle—and follow them. For the first half mile, they point a steady course toward the coast and Château Creux . . . but then they veer off and zigzag in strange directions. What is she doing?

I pick up speed and finally see her from a distance. She's standing on a forest bridge. She leans on her crutch and looks down at the river. I know this place. It's one of the bridges I scouted during my search for a Bone Crier.

I creep closer, not wanting to spook her. I don't have the energy to keep up all this chasing. When I'm near enough, I notice that her dress—the same brocade-and-velvet dress she's been wearing since the feast for La Liaison—is shredded and torn from her fall in the thorn patch. Her face is scratched, too. She continues to stare at something—not the river, I realize, but a bird on the far bank.

"It's the silver owl, Bastien," she murmurs. I freeze, startled she knows I'm here. Of course she does. I forgot about her tiger shark's sixth sense. "Do you think she wants me to kill her?" She adjusts her grip on the bone knife in her hand. "Maybe that's why she sent me the vision. A *matrone* needs five grace bones."

She had a vision? I didn't know a Leurress could have those—or anyone, really. "You recognize this owl?" I set foot on the bridge and carefully walk closer. Its wood is rickety and old and creaks beneath my feet. "Has she sent you other visions?"

Ailesse nods without looking away from the bird, whose angled eyes stare back at us. Her feathers shine amber in the sunset. I've never seen an owl so close to water. They're usually in trees or roosting in barns. "The silver owl showed me Sabine once before." Ailesse wrinkles her brow. "Maybe I shouldn't kill her. Maybe she's watching over us."

I sidestep a broken plank. "What did she show you in your vision today?"

"I saw that Sabine is unstable. She killed a golden jackal and claimed its graces."

"Unstable? She told me the jackal makes her strong."

Ailesse darts a puzzled glance at me. "You know about the jackal?"

I nod. "It's her third grace bone."

She frowns and turns back to the owl. "That must be how she made a new flute—with another bone from the jackal." Ailesse bites her lip. "But now Sabine has *more* grace bones. In the vision, she wore a crown of stag antlers, and she must have meadow viper graces, too. She couldn't have set snakes on Beau Palais without sacrificing one first."

I finally reach her. I've never seen her eyes in the sunlight before. Her umber irises glow like liquid fire. She's close enough to touch, to hold close against me. I'm afraid if I do, she'll jerk away like she did in my quarry room. What happened to the girl who said just a month ago, *I can't imagine anyone else for me but you?*

"If Sabine has five grace bones, doesn't that mean she's officially the *matrone* now?"

Ailesse flinches. "I'm supposed to be *matrone*."

"But you told me the gods only give graces to those who make honorable kills." I keep my voice gentle, trying to be sensitive. She looks ready to gut me on the spot. "Maybe that means they've already accepted Sabine as the next ruler of your *famille*."

Her cheeks flush dark. "You believe she's more capable than me?"

"That's not what I said."

"She never even wanted to be a Ferrier."

"People change their minds. What if you did?"

She balks at me. "I would never . . . How can even you say that? This is who I *am*, Bastien—it's who I was always meant to be."

I nod slowly. "And why did *you* want to become a Ferrier?"

Her eyes are large and disbelieving. "I just told you."

I hold up my hands. "Just hear me out. Your mother held a strong sway over you, right? Sabine said you were always trying to impress her—even outdo her."

"Of course I was. I'm her heir."

"But you're not the only heir. Not anymore."

Her jaw clenches. "Why are you arguing with me? I thought you supported me."

"I do, Ailesse." I sigh. It doesn't seem like she feels that support anymore, no matter how much I try to show her. "I'm just asking . . . what do *you* want? You could be the *matrone*—hell, maybe the gods will let you have five grace bones, too. Or you could be the next queen of blasted South Galle." I swallow a bitter taste in my mouth. "But all that was chosen for you. The gods are shifting you around like a pawn on their chessboard. What if *you* choose the next move, not them?"

Her lips press together in a slight grimace. She glances at the silver owl again. The bird cocks her head. "I don't have that luxury. Sabine needs me. All my *famille* does. Why would the owl show me that vision if they didn't?"

Ever so gently, I take her by the shoulders. Her brows twitch, but she doesn't pull away. "Think about when that happened, right after we were talking about finding a way to end blood sacrifice. Your power, it comes from the gods, right? The owl could have showed you that vision to trick you. The gods don't want us rocking their boat. They want you back home, doing things like they've always been done—more death, more sacrifice."

"But the silver owl wouldn't trick me. She's appeared to me before when I needed strength. I think . . . I think Elara sent her. The goddess never tempted me on the soul bridge; it was Tyrus who wanted me to come through his Gate, and now my . . . my . . ." Ailesse's voice catches. She buries her head in her hands.

"What is it?" I draw her close.

"Don't." She shrinks back like I've burned her.

I exhale tightly and run my fingers through my hair. I have no idea how to act around her anymore.

"I'm sorry, I . . ." Her eyes fill with pain, like she's hurting more than she's hurting me. "Right now I just need you to listen, all right?"

I shove my hands in my pockets. "All right."

"Sabine talked to Jules." A tremor runs through her shoulders. "My mother . . . she's alive. She's trapped in the Underworld, and she wants me to break her free."

My mouth drops open. I can't breathe for a moment. My lungs are blocks of ice. I stare at Ailesse, but I'm not really here anymore. I'm at the cavern bridge again, lying in my own blood with my father's knife in my back. "Y-you can't—"

"Of course I wouldn't." She slips an inch closer. "But don't you see? I can't take the silver owl's warning lightly. What if Sabine is the one who's in danger? I don't think Elara is our enemy. My mother is our enemy—and through her, Tyrus. He's the one we have to stop."

I scrub my hand over my face and look across the river at the silver owl. My father taught me to believe in the four gods of Galle, at least in an easy and distant kind of way, but I never imagined how powerful and dangerous they really were—or that the true target of my revenge would be the god of the Underworld, not a Bone Crier.

I take a steeling breath. "So let's say you're right, and it was Elara who sent you these visions." I try to piece everything together. "What has she been trying to accomplish? Maybe she wants to show you Sabine is capable *because* of her five grace bones. She could be saying you're fine to focus on what you've already set out to do: protect Casimir—and yourself—until after the next ferrying night. Meanwhile, we work to break the chains Tyrus has you and your *famille* all wrapped up in."

"We're not Chained."

"He makes you slaughter your *amourés*, or he kills you otherwise. I think it's safe to say your lot in life is just as heavy."

Ailesse's gaze drifts to the silver owl. Her knife hand is trembling. "I don't think that's why Elara sent me the vision," she says, going back to my question. "I think she really does want me to kill the owl for her graces. That way I'll have abilities linked to a god, just like Sabine."

"Why would you need them?"

"I've told you why." She turns to me, exasperated. "I'm the one who should be *matrone*." Tears rim her eyes. "Who am I, if I'm not?"

The owl spreads her wings and pushes off into the air.

Ailesse gasps and yanks her knife up to throw it. The owl zooms northward.

"No, wait!" she cries. She steps back to take aim.

A section of the rotted wood breaks away.

"Ailesse!" I can't catch her in time.

She plummets through the bridge.

I hear her crash into the river. "Ailesse!" I shout again. I hurry to the edge of the hole. My heart pounds. *She'll be fine*, I tell myself. *She has the grace of a tiger shark.*

Her head emerges. She coughs and struggles to tread water. *Merde*, it's the dress Casimir gave her. It's pulling her down.

I throw off my boots and shirt and dive in after her. A shock of cold hits me. I surface and shake the wet hair from my eyes. Ailesse is seven feet away and fighting with graced strength to swim to the bank. The nearest side is a twenty-yard distance.

In three strokes, I'm right beside her. I wrap my arm beneath hers and kick hard. She's kicking, too, but with only one leg, and it's tangled in her skirt. Both our heads drag beneath the surface. We work together and push up again. "Your dress is too heavy," I sputter. "We need to unlace it."

"I can make it." She clenches her jaw. "I'm strong enough."

She could, I realize. She'd find a way to do it on her own. "I know you're strong enough." My teeth chatter. "But is it really worth the struggle?"

Her brows hitch inward. She blinks water from her lashes and fights to stay afloat. Her crutch bobs away toward the bank. She finally nods and swallows. "I'll take it off."

I reach around her to help with the laces. She pushes away. "I've got it, Bastien."

She tears off her long sleeves. Rips apart the seams along her torso. The top of her dress falls away over a strapless bodice. She spins the skirt of her dress so the laces are in front. She yanks them loose. The skirt slides off her chemise and sinks into the river.

She paddles against the current. Fastens her gaze below, searching. Her expression is hard. "I dropped the bone knife."

I kick to pull my mouth above the surface. "Ailesse. Please, don't."

Her nostrils flare. She slowly lifts her eyes to mine.

"Let it go. The knife, being *matrone* . . . let it all go."

Her soaked hair clings to her shoulders and fans wide in the water. *"No."*

She dives below the surface, right into the path of a swift current. *Merde.*

I dive right after her without thinking. The current is too strong. It hurtles me deeper downriver. I kick and struggle. It's no use. I can't pull free. My chest burns. Head throbs. I desperately need to breathe. If this is how I die, I'll be furious. I'll fight any Ferrier who dares to drag me to the Beyond.

An arm wraps around my chest. I'm jerked from the current. The last of my air leaves my lungs in a flash of bubbles. I'm hauled upward. Blackness crowds my vision. I'm on the verge of passing out.

My head breaks the surface. I suck in a ragged breath. Cough up the water I just inhaled. Dimly, I realize Ailesse has saved me. It's her body I feel behind mine.

She swims me to the bank, where her crutch is floating. I regain my strength by the time we reach a patch of reeds. I clutch a fistful to anchor myself and turn to Ailesse, panting. Her eyes are wide with worry. Her bone knife is between her teeth. She pulls it away and kicks close, pressing herself flush to my bare chest. One of her hands slips behind my head. Her eyes drop to my lips. She kisses me hard, her mouth wet from the river. Her fingers claw into my hair. Her good leg wraps around my waist.

My pulse races. Heat blazes deep inside me. Even then, I'm so shocked it takes me a moment to bring my stunned arms around her. Just as I do, she pushes away and drops her head. Her breaths come in quick gasps. I'm completely thrown off and have no idea what I've done wrong.

Her eyes are red when she finally meets my gaze again. "You're right, Bastien," she says. "I do need to choose the next move in my life, not anyone else." She exhales slowly and swallows hard. "And I think you and I should be nothing more than friends."

17
Sabine

I'VE BECOME A HISSED RUMOR among the soldiers who patrol Dovré's city wall. *L'esprit en blanc*, they call me. The spirit in white. Twelve days have passed since I left Château Creux, and the soldiers have learned to fear me, not fight me. I dodge their arrows with ease. I even caught one by the shaft as it shot at me. Last night, when I circled the city from the surrounding forest, one man saw my face and whispered to his captain, calling me by a new name. *Gardienne d'âmes*. Keeper of souls.

They think I'm trapping the ghosts here, that I've been sent by the gods to punish the people with a second plague. Some, like King Durand, have already died. South Galle is cursed, they say, and many blame the Trencavel dynasty. One thing is true, though: it's my fault the Chained are still here.

Thunder crackles, and a flare of *chazoure* crests the wall. A Chained peeks down and crawls over the wall like a spider. I steady my feet on the wet forest mulch and hold my staff ready. It isn't my usual staff, carved with woodland animals, sea creatures, and phases of the moon. I fled Château Creux too quickly to grab that. This is a simple staff I fashioned from a sturdy branch. Just as effective.

The Chained—a man, sinewy and tall—bounds for me through the slanting sheets of rain. I always draw a soul out if I linger near the city long enough. The siren song hasn't lost all its power, and I was the one who last played it.

The Chained jumps past the tree line and snarls at me. Lightning flashes behind him. "You squandered your chance to send me to Hell, Bone Crier. Stop trying."

I brush my dripping curls off my brow and lift my chin. The man sucks in a startled breath. His *chazoure* eyes clap on the crescent-moon pendant dangling from my antler crown. I'm not sure whether the Chained knows the pendant was carved from the bone of a golden jackal, but he senses the threat of Tyrus through me. I will bring him eternal suffering for the wicked life he led.

He turns and dashes back for the city. I chase after him, my feet splashing through puddles and mud. He climbs up the wall, but I leap like the red stag and knock him down with my staff. "I haven't squandered my chance," I sneer. The golden jackal in me wishes I could make him bleed, but I fight the bloodlust. "I'll call you again with my song, and you will meet your master."

The Chained shudders and tries to bolt. I jump over him, night-hawk high, and block his path. He races around me, but I shove him back. I prod him deeper into the forest, working fast despite the mud and downpour, and guide him toward his temporary prison. The busier I keep myself, the more my mind stays quiet. But as the days have crept closer to the full moon, it's becoming harder to shut out the images and voices inside me. . . .

Hyacinthe's bleeding neck. Pernelle's accusing eyes. Roxane's words. *We have declared you unfit to rule our* famille, *Sabine*. Then Ailesse, as she was in my vision, obstinately walking toward the Gates of the Underworld. My mother cautioning me about the jackal, *Beware his cunning. He will bury you, daughter*. Last of all, me—dead—in the jackal's grave. Me, with his yellow eyes and knifelike teeth.

I cry out with frustration and battle the Chained toward the trap I've made—a deep hole in the ground, cloaked by a covering of woven sticks and brambles. *What's the matter with me?* I thought I'd been doing better lately.

Will I ever master this grace?

The man lands a punch in my stomach. I stumble and gasp for breath. "Back the way you came, monster," I growl, and quickly prod him toward the trap again.

"Monster?" He winces as my staff thuds his chest. "You're the worst of us. You have Hell written all over you."

His jab strikes hard. I shouldn't emanate the Underworld. The Leurress are destined to dwell in Paradise. We're supposed to be filled with the greatest portions of Elara's Light.

Don't listen to him, Sabine. My staff whirls and lashes across his arm. He backtracks, and I keep striking, kicking, desperately trying to rein in my mind. *Be rational. Challenge your doubts.* It's not too late to regain my *famille's* trust. Hyacinthe survived. I caught word of it myself. I snuck back the day after I hurt her and spied on Château Creux. I stayed until I was reassured that the eldest Leurress was recovering well.

I've also spied on people in Dovré. I learned Bastien escaped Beau Palais the night I sent the meadow vipers, and a beautiful girl dressed like a princess was seen wandering the city the next day. Which means Ailesse is also free, although I don't know where she's gone. Birdine's apartment has been empty for days, and Ailesse hasn't returned to Château Creux.

I'm frantic to find her. The moon is full tonight. At midnight, ferrying will be possible again. But I'm scared to attempt it without warning her. It would be just like Ailesse to show up out of nowhere and interfere. I can't let that happen. Not when Odiva wants to trick my sister into setting her free.

The man and I reach my trap. Moans and shrieks rage from within. So far, I've caught sixteen Chained here, but last time I checked, only eleven remained. The mystery isn't unprecedented. My *famille* also had trouble keeping the dead trapped when they were loose before. The only way to be truly rid of them is to ferry them.

I quickly roll away the heavy stones that secure the bramble covering of my trap, all the while using my staff to keep the Chained man corralled nearby.

I remove the last stone, kick off the covering, and swing my staff to knock the Chained man inside. But just as I do, my foot slips on the muddy ground. I crash to my knees and lose hold of my weapon.

The man jerks it away, scrambles around me, and slams it into my back. I grunt and fall forward on my hands. My fingertips land an inch away from the open hole. I glimpse the thrashing souls within—ten now. Their *chazoure* eyes are wild. They claw at the earthen walls, desperately trying to escape.

I hurriedly scoot back. Push up to my feet. Whirl around to fight the man.

He's too close. No time to dodge him. He's going to ram me into the pit.

I dig in my feet. Reach to grab the staff's other end. Pray I have the strength to shove him off course.

He's thrown sideways ten feet. I gasp, watching him tumble across the wet grass. I never even touched him.

Dazed, I look in the other direction. Then freeze. My heart leaps in my throat. "Ailesse."

She's using a crutch but also racing for the Chained man. She plucks up the staff he dropped, yanks him to his feet, and roughly prods him toward the pit. Once he's at its edge, she shoves him hard. He cries out, arms flailing, and plunges into my trap.

I rush to replace the bramble covering and anchoring stones. Ailesse quickly helps, rolling two rocks back into place while I roll the other two. We finish at the same time. Look up at each other. My eyes grow hot. I can't believe she's really with me. I burst into tears.

Her hand flies to her chest. "Oh, Sabine."

The rain softens to a drizzle as we rise and stumble toward one another. We fall on each other's shoulders, weeping. I clutch her tightly and cry harder, hiccupping when I breathe. She snorts, laughing at me through her sobs. I smack her arm, and she smacks me back. The next thing I know, we're both giggling and sobbing, and it's the most ridiculous and perfect moment . . . and oh, how I've missed my best friend.

She finally pulls back and wipes her nose on her sleeve. "Where in the world have you been?" She shakes me by the shoulders. "I've been looking everywhere for days."

"What do you mean? You're the one who's gone missing. Why haven't you returned home?" I've snuck back to check for her.

"I could ask you the same thing. Our whole *famille* has been searching for you."

"Wait, you've been with the *famille*?"

"Not exactly. I *did* return home . . . almost. I came upon Felise and Lisette just outside Château Creux. They didn't sense me, of course. But I overheard them speaking."

I picture the younger girls, who have yet to obtain graces. "And?"

Beneath the folds of her loosely tied cloak, Ailesse fidgets with the laces of her burgundy bodice. It isn't Leurress-made. Neither is her creamy blouse or simple blue skirt. It's strange to see how well suited they all are to her. She tilts her head. "Did you really hurt Hyacinthe?" she asks gently. "Is that why you ran away?"

Heat rushes to my cheeks. "That was an accident."

"Of course it was." Her gaze flickers to my golden jackal

pendant. "Why don't you go back, then? You know the elders would never banish you."

That's only because they never banish anyone. They wouldn't want to risk exposing our secret way of life. But they could still punish me, take away my grace bones for a season. I can't be stripped of my power when the Chained are loose. "I'm just working to prove myself first."

"Why?" She shifts on her crutch. The movement is awkward, missing her usual agile elegance. "So they'll let you lead the ferrying again?" Her pensive eyes flash to my antler crown this time.

"Well, yes." I bite down on my lip. "You have to understand, I wasn't sure if you'd ever return home . . . no matter how much I desperately wanted you to."

"I was only waiting to find you first, but I *will* be coming home." She sets her jaw. Being held captive twice did little to tame her stubborn streak. "We should return home together," she amends, giving me another hug. The muscles in her arm are so tense they quiver. Or maybe I'm the one shaking. Am I ready to face my *famille* or give up my claim as *matrone*? Roxane can't rule as regent forever.

"I'd like that," I say.

Ailesse draws back, and although her smile wavers, it reminds me that my sister is the same person who prepared my salamander skull after I made my first kill and couldn't stop crying, and who offered me the killing blow to slaughter her tiger shark so I could be the one to claim its graces, even though I declined. No one has ever loved me as much as she has. No one ever will.

"But our mother *did* name you her heir." She swallows tightly. "So you will have to decide what that means for you and me."

My chest constricts. She's asking if I'll give her back her birthright or keep it for myself. She would actually let me have it if that's what I really wanted. Even if it would break her.

I don't know what to say—I'm too scared to examine what I want that closely—so I squeeze her hand and ask, "Will you walk with me? There's a stream nearby, and I'm thirsty . . . despite the rain."

She studies my face and nods, slowly linking arms with me. We leave the howling souls in my trap behind, as well as the question of who should be *matrone*. The fact that I didn't answer is answer enough for the time being.

We try to talk of light things, but there are none, so we talk of hard things in a lighter way . . . around little smiles, gentle footsteps, and the small hobbles of her crutch. I explain about the mix-up with the snakes, and she tells me how she still managed to help Bastien escape Beau Palais.

"You didn't leave with him?" I ask. "Then how are you here?"

"Well, for one thing, I was never locked in a cell. And I stayed to protect Cas from the Chained." I note how she calls Casimir by his nickname. "There are dissenters among them, and Cas and I found out the hard way that when he has Light stolen from him, I do, too. Before you say anything, don't worry. I'm fine. We just lost a smidge. But I couldn't take any more chances, so I had to abduct him from Beau Palais. Thankfully he gave me my grace bones back first."

I stop walking, dizzy from trying to absorb everything she's just thrown at me: *amourés* losing Light simultaneously, dead dissenters after the new king, and Ailesse actually abducting him. "So then Casimir didn't leave Beau Palais on a mission to find a remedy for the sick people in Dovré?" I ask, then feel compelled to add, "He's been writing letters to his councillors—I intercepted one from a courier. At least I thought the letters came from Casimir."

"Oh, they did." Ailesse smirks. "With a little urging on my part, anyway. It was my idea to paint him in a good light. Hopefully it improves his reputation among the people. Blaming the Trencavels for the so-called plague is absurd."

We start walking again. "And what about the public coronation he's promised as soon as he returns home?" I ask, remembering another line from the letter.

She shrugs lightly. "Well, I'm not going to hold him captive forever."

For the people's sake, I hope not. Beau Palais has been draped in gold and green bunting for several days, awaiting Casimir's return. Meanwhile, only a few sun-symbol flags and banners decorate the thoroughfares of Dovré. Those that do are tattered from the wind and rain. The people are losing faith that anything—or anyone—will be able to help them.

I'll help them. Tonight.

"No wonder I haven't been able to find you," I say. "You've been keeping watch on the king."

"I haven't had to do it on my own. Don't forget, I've been searching for you, too." She nudges me. "And since when did you become so difficult to track, anyway?"

"It must be my golden jackal graces." I wave a dismissing hand, though I stand a little taller. "No one in our *famille* was able to capture the jackal. I only did because the silver owl forced him right into my path."

The corners of Ailesse's mouth tug into a frown. She glances at my crescent pendant again.

We reach the stream. She sets down her crutch and kneels, not too ginger with her broken leg. It must be healing well. We cup our hands in the trickling water. I swallow extra handfuls, drumming up the courage to say what she must hear: "Odiva is alive in the Underworld."

"We have to ferry tonight," she blurts at the same time.

I blink. "Yes, I was planning on it."

"I know about Odiva." She speaks over me. "Jules told me what you told her. Wait, how were you planning to ferry?"

I shake my head. "You've seen Jules?"

"She and Marcel are helping me with Cas. Birdine, too. Do you know Birdine? We're keeping Cas in a hideout Bastien has below an old church. So Bastien's helping, too." Ailesse scratches her arm when she says his name, her cheeks flushed. "How were you planning to ferry?" she presses me. "Not on your own?"

I squirm. "I'm not sure what other choice I have. The cavern bridge is too fragile. It can't support all the Ferriers." I still haven't told the *famille* about the second soul bridge, the only place we can ferry on the full moon, unlike the land bridge, which can only be used on the new moon. I can't risk endangering anyone else but myself.

Ailesse crosses her arms. "Well, I'm going to help, of course.

We'll help each other. That's why I've been trying so hard to find you, so we can ferry together."

"No, you can't." I sigh. "That's why I've been trying to find *you*. Our mother wants you to free her and—"

"Jules told me about that, too."

"Let me finish." I twist my hands in my lap. "Odiva says all you have to do is touch her hand, but I'm worried it will be more than that. What if she's trying to sacrifice you to Tyrus again? She could still be striving to fulfill her pact to release my father from the Underworld."

"Even if that was her plan, that doesn't mean I shouldn't ferry again," Ailesse counters. "I'll be careful."

"Like you were last time on the cavern bridge?" I lift a brow. "You would have run through Tyrus's Gate if Odiva hadn't stabbed Bastien."

She flinches. "You don't know I wouldn't have stopped on my own."

"I saw you, Ailesse. Tyrus's siren song brought out all your weaknesses. And Odiva can be just as manipulative."

"Well, I've learned from my mistakes," she says defensively. "I won't repeat them. It's *you* I'm worried about tonight."

"Me?" I shrink back.

"You weren't able to finish ferrying on the new moon. The Chained are loose because of it."

"That's only because I saw Odiva in the Underworld. I was startled, unprepared for—"

"You'll face more startling challenges while ferrying."

"Yes, but I have five grace bones now."

"And how much have they helped you withstand your golden jackal grace?" She throws a pointed look at my crescent pendant. "That's what's bringing out all *your* weaknesses, Sabine. That power is tied to Tyrus. You always had the strongest Light, but I think the jackal is suppressing it."

I stand abruptly. "You don't know what you're talking about. You haven't even seen me since last month."

"I *have* seen you." She rises without her crutch and balances on her good leg. "The silver owl showed me how you've been suffering. I saw how you killed the jackal and claimed his graces, and how you've been unstable ever since—jumping through stained-glass windows, fleeing the land bridge, hurting Hyacinthe, running away from home."

My eyes sting. I turn my back to her.

"I'm sure the jackal gives you great power," she says, her voice a little softer now. "But is it worth the cost? Will it help you or endanger you when you try to ferry again?"

I look down at my hands, the dirt beneath my fingernails, the ragged skirt of my ferrying dress . . . I've been wearing it for over two weeks now. I must look wild and ferocious. No wonder Ailesse doubts me.

She limps closer and wraps her arms around me from behind. "Oh, Sabine, I don't wish to argue. Forgive me. You and I are going to be fine tonight, just as long as we're together. Surely that's all the silver owl wanted to tell me—that we should be ferrying side by side."

My shoulders relax, and I set my hand on her arm. She's right. We do need each other. Together we'll be safe. I take a deep breath. "When you see Odiva tonight, don't let her rattle you. Remember who you are."

"I'm my mother's firstborn daughter," she murmurs. "How will that help me?"

"You're more than just her daughter—or even the *matrone* one day, if that's what you really want. Odiva didn't make you. She may have given birth to you and influenced some of the choices you made, but she didn't compel you to be anyone other than yourself. Your soul is too bold to be shaped by someone else. You're your own person, Ailesse. *You* made you."

She falls quiet for a moment, her cheek pressed against the back of my shoulder. "Have I ever told you're the sweetest, wisest person I've ever known?"

"Don't forget 'kindest' and 'most loving.'"

"You also smell of mildew and deer droppings. No wonder I couldn't track you."

I whirl around and slug her arm, laughing.

"Ouch!" She bursts into giggles. "Careful, you're stronger than you realize."

"Oh, I know my strength." I lunge for her. She squeals, hopping backward to pick up her crutch. She fends me off with it.

We circle each other, laughing harder. The sky thunders, and the clouds unleash heavy rain. I pick up clods of muddy dirt and throw them at her. She dodges the first one, but the second one splatters her squarely in the chest. She wheezes with laughter. "All right, you win! Have mercy on . . ." Her eyes widen. Face blanches. She staggers, leaning heavily on her crutch.

My smile wilts. "Ailesse? What's wrong?"

She shakes her head, her brow furrowed. "I think it's my Light. This is how I felt when . . ." She stiffens. "Cas. He's under attack again. Sabine, I have to go."

My stomach tenses. "But how will you reach him in time?"

"I don't know. I have to try."

I hurry to her side. "I'll come with you." I don't care about the king, only that Ailesse is in danger because of their soul-bond.

"You can't. We don't have much time before midnight. You should return to Château Creux. We need more Ferriers. There must be a few you trust. They don't have to stand on the bridge with us; they can help from the ledge in the cavern."

"But—"

"I'll be fine." She swipes dripping hair off her face and sets her jaw in that obstinate way of hers. "We can't lose this chance to ferry, and we shouldn't thwart the opportunity by trying to do it on our own. It's too dangerous."

I hesitate. "Are you sure you'll be all right?"

"Yes." She waves me away. "And I'll have four friends ready to help me once I reach Cas. They can't see the dead, though. They need me." She sets off at a quick pace toward Dovré, using her crutch only lightly. "Go, Sabine," she calls over her shoulder. "I'll meet you at the cavern bridge."

I fight off a rush of uneasiness and race back to my trap, praying I've made the right decision to let Ailesse and me separate. The souls of the dead shriek from the pit. I roll each stone off the bramble covering so it's unanchored again.

I grab my fallen staff and hurry away from the pit toward Château Creux. The Chained will find a way to free themselves from my trap. Mad desperation will drive them to it after they hear the ferrying song.

I race faster and steel my nerves for what's ahead—returning home and, much more worrying, having to face my mother again. But I will, without shrinking. I'll have Ailesse by my side. The dead *will* be ferried to the Beyond. My sister and I will see it done.

The plague on Dovré ends tonight.

18
Ailesse

I RACE INSIDE CHAPELLE DU Pauvre, my cloak dripping with rain. I throw back my hood and rush down the hatch behind the altar, through the cellar after lighting a lantern, then the catacombs tunnels and down the scaffolding on the side of the quarry pit. My knee throbs—I'm barely using my crutch—but I can't pause to rest.

"Cas?" I call, clumsily slipping down the ladder despite my ibex grace. My muscles tremble, leeched of strength. I'm too drained of Light. "Bastien?" My heart pounds faster. What if I'm too late?

I don't know if they can hear me. I can't hear them or any sounds of struggle. That isn't comforting. The quarry is too closed off to echo sound. My friends could be battling three Chained down here, and I wouldn't hear any commotion until I was within several feet of them.

I jump off the ladder when I'm five rungs away from Bastien's room. I burst inside, my bone knife drawn.

"Ailesse!" Marcel jumps in front of me, and I startle. His eyes are as wide as saucers. "I'm so glad you're back. We need your help!"

I shove past him and scan the room. Bastien and Birdine aren't here. Only Marcel, Jules, and Cas. I whirl around and look behind me. I don't understand. I don't see any streaks of *chazoure*. "Where are they?"

"Who?" Jules crosses her arms. She stands by the open end of the room, near the drop-off into the quarry.

"The dead."

"The dead are coming?" Cas scrambles to his feet. I don't know how he thinks he'll defend himself. He's no longer tied up in excessive rope, but his wrists are bound together, and his ankle is attached to a ball and chain. Bastien and Marcel thieved it from a city prison a few days ago.

"Can't you tell when they're stealing your Light?" I limp back to the scaffolding and shine my lantern into the quarry. How are the dead hiding from me? "You need to pay closer attention. Some Chained are subtle. They might not attack you outright. They could sit silently by and drain your energy away."

Jules coughs into her fist. "None of the Chained are in here, Ailesse. I, for one, would know if I lost any more Light by force."

I stare at the sickly shade of her skin and how her once

tight-fitting clothes now look baggy. Her condition is worsening. "But . . . Marcel just said he needed my help."

"Yes!" He lumbers back to me. "You're our resident Bone Crier—er, Leurress—and so your opinion holds the most weight. I want to know what you think of my new theory."

I hear him only vaguely. I'm still struggling to slow down my racing heartbeat. "Where's Bastien?" I turn back to Jules, unable to shake the feeling that someone I care about is in danger.

"He's on a supply run." She coughs again, and it rattles deeper in her chest. "Should be back by now, but knowing him, he's probably stealing you another pretty outfit."

I ignore the jab and set down my lantern, limping toward Cas. Even though Bastien and I are just friends now, Jules hasn't given up the habit of goading me about his small kindnesses, like the clothes he brought me after I abandoned my La Liaison dress in the river.

"Have you ever considered that Tyrus's magic involves more than bones?" Marcel trails behind me. "What if it's tied to the elements, too?"

"Just a moment," I say. "Are you sure you're well?" I ask Cas. "I felt a sudden loss of Light, and it's still fading within me. Don't you feel it, too? I was sure the Chained had found you."

His brows hitch inward at the tender concern in my voice. A slipup. I've tried my best not to give him or Bastien any hope that I can return their affections right now.

"I *do* feel much weaker tonight," he confesses. "I feared you were the one who had been attacked."

"Isn't it obvious what's wrong with him?" Jules paces along the edge of the room. "He's desperate for Light, the same way you were when we abducted you into the catacombs."

"She could be onto something." Marcel absently shuffles behind me, waiting to share his theory. "Tonight is a full moon. Maybe Cas senses that on an innermost level, and it's made his need all the more insatiable."

"But he isn't a Leurress." I frown. "He shouldn't need sustenance from Light like I do."

"Maybe he does." Jules lifts a shoulder. "It's probably just another part of the soul-bond you share. Next thing you know, his hair will darken to auburn, and your voice will drop an octave. He'll take up ferrying the dead, and we'll start having to call you Your Majesty."

"Hilarious."

She smirks.

"I do think going outside would help," Cas says, "even if it's only for an hour." He licks his lips and shifts a step closer. "Could we try it?"

"You know we can't." I sigh. I know how it feels to be starved of Light. "It's too dangerous with all the dissenters. If the dead among them find you or discover where you've been hiding . . ." I shake my head. "I'm sorry, Cas."

His expression falls. He slumps back against the wall.

I try to nudge away my guilt. After Sabine and I ferry, I'll let him return home.

"I have to go." I brush some of the wetness from my cloak before it gets drenched all over again. "I'll see you tomorrow." I turn to leave, but Jules has already thrown on her own cloak, and she's holding the lantern I set down a moment ago. I freeze. "What are you doing?"

"Going to look for Bastien," she replies, as if the answer is obvious. "Three of us don't need to guard the king."

"But *I* have to leave." Midnight is a little over an hour away, and it will take almost all that time to travel to the cavern bridge. "I finally found Sabine tonight, and we—" I stop short. I can't tell Jules we're going to ferry. She'll tell Bastien, and he'll be furious.

The cavern bridge is one crack away from completely crumbling, he said three days ago, when I brought up reconsidering it. *Promise me you won't risk ferrying there.* The plan, as far as he knows, is to wait to ferry at the land bridge.

No promises were made; I evaded answering him directly. Bastien doesn't understand what it's like to carry the responsibility of protecting the living from the dead. How can I wait another fourteen days to ferry on the new moon?

Jules loses patience and steps onto the scaffolding platform. She climbs the first two rungs of the ladder. Her legs already tremble from weakness.

"Wait," I say. "You're not strong enough to—"

She casts me a murderous glare. "You don't know me, Ailesse. I'm always strong enough—in all ways. Maybe you can toss aside your feelings for Bastien, but that will never be me. I'm going to find out where he is and make sure he's safe."

I stand stunned, even after she's gone, and keep my back to

Marcel and Cas. I never tossed aside my feelings for Bastien. Is that what they all think? Is that what *he* thinks?

Marcel's footsteps approach lackadaisically. He taps me on the shoulder. "So, back to my theory on the elements," he says, oblivious to his bad timing. "Tyrus's Gate can be made of water, wind, and earth, right? At least wind and particles of earth held the Gate of dust together last month. And Elara's Gate is made of some kind of spirit, being transparent and all. But guess which of the five elements is missing from the Gates?" Before I have a chance to respond, he answers, "Fire," and grins smugly. "So what do you think? Could we use it against him?"

"Um . . ." I try to compose myself. "I don't see how." *What would we do, shoot flaming arrows into the Underworld while I make my list of demands?* "But it's an interesting idea." It's more progress than the rest of us have made toward outmaneuvering Tyrus, anyway. "You should explore it more."

"Thanks, Ailesse," he says brightly. "That's exactly what I was thinking. I have a book about the elements in one of our other hideouts. I'll see if I can find it. Bye for now." He ambles past me and grabs one of the lanterns.

"Wait, you can't leave, too. Who will guard Cas?"

"Birdine's here." He flings an easy grin. "She's taking a bath below." I fight an eye roll at her excessive habit of bathing in a pool of groundwater off one of the quarry tunnels. "I'm sure she'll be up soon."

I sigh roughly as he climbs the scaffolding ladder. My friends and I have a rule—my rule—that we never leave Cas alone.

I rethink how long it will take me to travel to the cavern bridge. I suppose I can spare a quarter hour to wait for Birdine and still make it there by midnight.

"You shouldn't let her upset you," Cas says.

"Birdine?"

"No, Jules." He settles down on a straw mattress and props one knee to his chest. "She strikes me as the type that can't stop picking at an old wound. It can make a person believe healing isn't within their own power."

It's such a wise thing to say—such a Sabine thing to say—that I catch myself staring at him. I smile softly. "You remind me of my sister."

His gentle expression fades. "Your sister tried to kill me."

"No, she wanted *me* to kill you."

"But you have no desire to; that's the difference. You're invested in finding a way to break our soul-bond."

"Please don't misjudge Sabine." I limp closer. "She was only trying to protect me. She respects life more than any Leurress."

Cas scoffs.

"This isn't the only time she's been tested. Did you know her mother died two years ago?"

"You said the woman on the cavern bridge was your mother— and hers."

"That's true." I sit on the floor in front of him. I haven't taken a long look at him in days. He's grown some stubble along his jaw, and it's redder than the lighter shade of his strawberry hair. It makes him look older, more kingly . . . more handsome. "But

Sabine was raised to believe another woman was her mother. And when that woman was killed ferrying, she was devastated. I needed a second grace bone, and she needed solace, so I took her on a great trip to the north to hunt an alpine ibex."

Cas idly tugs on the chain around his ankle. "And did it help her?"

"No." I laugh and pull my crutch into my lap. "She missed being home. I'm the one who craves adventure. Sabine likes steadiness and security, but that doesn't make her weak. She's also fiercely loyal to what she believes in, though careful about what she trusts. She's always questioned the cost of being a Leurress, the sacrifices necessary. . . ."

"Yet she's willing to sacrifice for you."

I pick at a splinter of wood. "I'm what Sabine believed in most. She had a harder time believing in herself, which is . . ." I struggle for the right word. "Astonishing."

He lifts a brow like he doesn't believe me.

"All the Leurress are filled with extra measures of Light, because we descend from Elara," I explain. "But Sabine always carried it stronger than the rest of us, whether she realized it or not. She has an inner strength I could never surpass. She climbed icy mountains with me, even through sleet and frigid air. She slept beside me in snow caves. She only cried when she thought I was sleeping, and even then, it was only for missing the woman who raised her."

We're quiet for a moment, and then Cas whispers, "I do understand that kind of grief. It can haunt you for a lifetime."

I search the heavy expression on his face. "Is it strange that I *want* to understand how that feels? I wish I'd been loved so deeply by my mother that the loss of her hurt me. That would be better than my resentment over not knowing how to mourn her."

I can almost hear her voice now. *I am not lost, Ailesse. You know where you can find me.*

"It's not strange at all," Cas says. "To be loved is the purest of all human desires. Anyone who says different is deceiving themselves."

I stiffen, realizing how close he's shifted toward me. Our knees are almost touching. I release a trembling breath. It's not so hard to recognize why the gods chose him for me. Cas is a calming influence, a steadying anchor, like Sabine. He could keep me grounded in the afterlife.

"I *do* know what it is to be loved," I reply with an edge in my voice. Sabine loves me. She would do anything for me. Bastien loves me, too, and his love is like a pair of open wings. It reveals the world, rather than planting my feet in one place. The trouble is, I'm supposed to be grounded; I'm supposed to be my mother's heir. If Sabine really does love me, she won't take that away.

I also love you, daughter. If I could return to you, I would rename you as my heir.

My blood runs cold at the sound of my mother's voice again, much more vivid this time. I glance around me, though her words didn't radiate from anywhere except my head.

"When I brought you to Beau Palais," Cas says, "you promised to give me a chance."

I struggle to focus on what he's saying and rein in my wild

imagination. My mother can't speak to me. She's trapped in the Underworld. "I *am* giving you that chance—the chance to live."

"What if I want more? I've offered you everything, Ailesse. Even now—even after you've imprisoned me—I would give myself to you. I would have you for my queen."

My stomach flutters before it tenses into knots. "Please don't say that. I can't be your queen. You're smitten with the promise of me, but I'm not your mother. I'm not even like the song you heard on the bridge. All of that is an illusion."

His jaw muscle tightens, and he shakes his head, staring down at his bound wrists.

"Please try to understand. I have nothing against you. I believe you have every quality that will make you a great king. I would fight to protect you even if we weren't soul-bound."

I pull myself up to stand with my crutch, anxious to be finished with this conversation. Cas will be fine. Birdine will come up any minute now. I need to hurry to the cavern bridge. "I'll return you to Beau Palais soon, I promise, and when I do, you'll be safe. The dead will be ferried, and the Chained won't plague your people anymore."

"What if all your struggle is in vain?" He rises, challenging me with his somber eyes. "What if the soul-bond can never be broken, and you and I are tied together throughout the eternities?"

"It *will* be broken."

I know how to break it, Ailesse.

My pulse jumps. "Impossible."

"Pardon?" Cas frowns.

I rapidly glance around the room again, searching for the silver owl or a shimmering tint to my vision or anything to explain why I'm hearing my mother's voice when I'm wide awake and not dreaming.

I love you, daughter. I do not want you to suffer any longer.

I won't listen to this. "Love isn't love if you never show it." My voice is quiet but scathing as I repeat the words I told her on the cavern bridge.

Cas blinks twice. "I—I *have* been trying to show you. I even offered you my mother's pearls."

Does he think love can be bought?

You did, Mother. I speak inwardly this time. *At the cost of my life.*

But I never paid that price, did I? I leapt through the Gates of the Underworld to spare you, child.

No, you abandoned me to be with the man you loved.

Oh, Ailesse. It wasn't abandonment. You, above anyone else, should understand the power of loving someone more than your amouré. *Is that not why you chose to stay here with Bastien rather than returning to our* famille *after you left Beau Palais?*

"If I have less than a year left to live"—Cas's bound hands slide around one of mine—"I wish to face it bravely. I'll quash the dissenters' rebellion and rule my country with honor, not by hiding. Most of all, I want to spend that time with you," he whispers, his breath warm on my face.

I barely comprehend what he's saying. My heart stampedes in my chest. My mother is wrong. I haven't returned home yet because I needed to find Sabine first and bring her back with me.

Bastien had nothing to do with it. I broke off our relationship because I was thinking of the needs of the *famille* first.

That must be comforting to believe.

My hands clench.

Cas's lips feather across mine. All my nerves stand at attention. *No, I don't want this.*

You no longer know what you want, daughter. But I understand what you need. I can help you.

She can't tell me what I want or need. What if I *do* want Cas? What if I do want to be grounded?

When I don't respond, he starts to pull away. I quickly grab his arms and lean into him, kissing him with conviction.

A rush of blackness consumes me. The candles in the room flicker like warning flags at the edges of my sight. I close my eyes and open them again, but I can't chase away the glittering darkness all around me. It's like the dust of Tyrus's Gate at the cavern bridge, except this time I'm in his storm, not safely outside it.

My mother appears. She glides on steady feet through the whirling wind. Her raven hair whips madly around her face, but her black eyes stay fast upon me. "Listen to me, Ailesse. We do not have much time."

"No." I step backward, but she catches my forearm. It's the strangest sensation, feeling her nails on my skin while Cas's mouth moves against mine. I kiss him harder, hoping to moor myself in the quarry room and tear away from this vision.

"I have learned many secrets of the Underworld," my mother continues. "I am penitent, and it is my earnest desire to make amends with you."

I can't speak or the kiss will break. If it does, I might be swept away into Tyrus's realm. Is that even possible?

"What I said is true." My mother's voice is so soothing and affectionate, it's almost a croon. She's never spoken like this to me before. "I *do* know how to break the soul-bond, and once that happens, you will be free to understand your heart and what it desires. That is what you wish for, is it not, daughter?"

The darkness scatters for just a moment, and I can picture it, a life of my own making: I'm wearing a crown of new grace bones and leading my *famille* onto the land bridge. I stand at its end by the great Gates of the Beyond. But then the image shifts, and now I'm doing more: I'm sailing away on a ship, exploring lands beyond Galle, scaling great mountains, swimming in clear water, seeing all the majestic beauty of the world.

"You will not find the answer in a book." My mother tilts her head, and the mirage ripples away. "You will die poring over those words while your Light fades and your one year with your *amouré* comes to an end. The secret to breaking the soul-bond lies with me, and me alone. But I must first be set free so I may show you how."

All my muscles grow taut. My mind strains. I cast up all my resistance, but her proposal sinks inside me and plants roots. What if there is no other way? What if she could teach me not only how to break the soul-bond, but also *all* forms of blood sacrifice? That's what my friends and I have been working toward, isn't it?

"Come to me tonight, Ailesse." My mother stretches forth her hand. Her eyes hold the challenge that's sparked the flame in me all my life, her great dare to be as brave, bold, and indomitable as she is. "I had the tenacity to enter the Underworld, but all you have to do is touch my hand. Then I will be with you again."

Is she belittling me? I was ready and willing to cross into the Underworld, but I showed even greater strength by resisting Tyrus's siren song.

"Come and join your sister. If she ferries without you, she will receive all the glory for saving South Galle. The *famille* will wish her to remain *matrone*."

No. My veins flare with adrenaline.

The blackness scatters again, and this time I see Sabine. She's standing under the battlements of Château Creux, just past the heavy rainfall. Pernelle, Maurille, and Chantae are with her. She's holding a bone flute and speaking rapidly. I can't hear what she's saying, but her brows are lifted like she's trying to persuade them. Maybe they won't be persuaded.

"If she told them you were alive and would be joining them soon, she might prevail upon them more easily."

What? Why wouldn't she tell them I was alive?

"You heard your sister today. She never wanted you to follow her to the cavern bridge. She does not trust you, just like she does not trust me. Perhaps she hopes you will not come."

Sabine's hand cuts through the air, like she's making a final statement. She marches off into the rain. Pernelle sighs, takes up her staff, and hurries to join her. Maurille and Chantae do the same.

Three Ferriers? That's all Sabine could gather? It isn't enough. I had my mother to help me on the cavern bridge, and she was worth at least six Ferriers.

"With you and me, they will stand a fair chance," Odiva says. "You are my true daughter when it comes to skill and talent."

Sabine and the others head eastward, away from Château Creux.

"You will lose her, Ailesse, if you do not allow me to help both of you."

I can't breathe. The darkness is more suffocating than drowning in my brocade dress.

"And if Sabine dies now," Odiva continues, "Tyrus will surely wrap her in chains."

"No!" The vision breaks. I jerk away from Cas at the same time. His lips are flushed from kissing me. I cover my own lips and breathe heavily. *This was a mistake. I shouldn't have—* "No, Cas . . ."

His brow wrinkles. "It's all right." He reaches for me, but I hobble backward on my crutch.

"It *isn't* all right. I will never care for you the way you want me to." I refuse to let the soul-bond dictate my life. "Love is a choice. It isn't written in the stars." I grab a new lantern and rush to the scaffolding ladder.

"Where are you going?" He rises, but he can't move far with the ball and chain around his ankle.

To break the bond, to claim my life back. "To help my sister."

Don't try to stop me, Sabine. I'm doing this for both of us.

I quickly climb the scaffolding. I have to set my mother free.

19

Bastien

I SLIP INSIDE CHAPELLE DU Pauvre and pull my hand out from within my cloak. I check on a small bouquet of wildflowers I've been protecting from the rain, rare yellow poppies I found growing under a giant pine. Will Ailesse like them?

I prod one of the flowers that hasn't opened yet. Maybe I shouldn't give them to her. What if she thinks I'm pressuring her to get back together? Despite what she said, after she kissed me in the river, she's been warmer toward me lately. It's given me hope that maybe we *can* be more than friends again. Or am I wrong? Is she too good a dream for someone like me?

I swallow hard and tuck the poppies back inside my cloak. I'm going to give her the damn flowers.

I adjust the pack of supplies on my shoulder and make my way through the church and the tunnels below the quarry. The wound on my back only twinges a little now, almost healed. That's something to be thankful for.

Once I'm halfway down the scaffolding and within hearing distance of my room, I call out Jules's name. I've brought her some soft cheese, not the usual hardened stuff that keeps for days down here. Hopefully she'll eat it. She's lost her appetite for almost everything.

She doesn't answer, so I call for Marcel, then Ailesse. "Birdine?" I say as a last resort, my gut prickling. Where is everyone? I hop down another rung and lower my head to peek inside the quarry room. It's empty. Except for Cas. He's tucked against the back wall and crouched on his mattress. But not in a casual way. His rolled-back sleeves reveal tensed forearms. And his legs are bent, ready to spring.

I frown. "What's going on?"

He doesn't say a word. My fingers flex near the hilt of my father's knife. I've started carrying it again, an itch I can finally scratch again. Revenge is near. My friends *will* find a way to outsmart Tyrus and put a stop to blood sacrifice. No more fathers are going to die. We just need to find the right bargaining chip. Then we can cut a deal with the god of the Underworld.

I take a cautious step into the room. A sliver of metal glints at Cas's feet. A hairpin? The shackle around his ankle is open by a gap, and the shelf with my figurines is missing the sun god.

Merde.

Cas leaps at me. I yank out my knife. He swings the small statue with his tied-up hands. I duck and roll, then launch up again. I nick his arm with my blade. I can't stab him. His life is tied to—

"Ailesse." I jump back when he strikes again. "Where is she?"

His brow twitches. "Does it matter?"

"Course it matters."

He hurls the figurine. I sidestep it, but it glances off my shoulder and shatters against the wall. My blood catches on fire. "My father carved that!"

Cas grabs another statue—the earth goddess, Gaëlle.

"Put that down, or I swear I'll—"

"You'll what?" He juts up his chin. "You're in no position to threaten me. You love Ailesse too much." He practically spits the words.

Something's set him off. "What did you do to her?" My voice shudders with deadly rage.

"What did *I* do?" He laughs scornfully. "I never asked to be her *amouré*. She's brought me nothing but misery."

I don't understand. He's never this spiteful toward her. "*Where* is she?" I take another step. He raises the goddess statue, a warning.

"Maybe it's Jules you should be worried about."

My chest squeezes. Jules is like family. "Did you hurt her?"

He balks at me. "I'm not the villain here. She went looking for *you*."

Merde, Jules. "And Marcel and Birdine?"

"Out for books and down for a bath, as usual."

I stalk closer. "Why won't you tell me about Ailesse?"

His eyes narrow. He adjusts his grip on the statue. "Let me pass, Bastien. I won't stay here another fortnight. Dovré is under threat. My people will lose faith without a king on the throne."

My pulse races. Ailesse is alive. She has to be, or Cas wouldn't even be breathing. I'm not going to waste my own breath arguing with him. He knows why he's our prisoner—and why he needs to stay here until the dead can be ferried again.

He's three feet away now. I hold up my knife. "A man can still live without a hand, an arm, a leg," I say.

A bead of sweat drips down his forehead. Sabine told me Cas trained in the art of warfare; he was dressed in a captain's uniform when they first met. But he's no danger to me, especially not with his hands tied.

I turn my blade so its sharp edge catches the lantern light. "*What . . . did . . . you . . . do . . . to . . . her?*"

He doesn't answer. He swings the statue at my arm, but I knock it away. It hits the stone floor. The goddess's head snaps off. I slash out with my knife. Cas kicks me back before I can cut him again. "I kissed her, Bastien," he spits out bitterly. "And I can assure you she wanted to be kissed back . . . at least at first."

My heart gives a hard pound. The poppies fall out from beneath my cloak, a pile of bent stems and crushed yellow petals. Then all I see is red. "At least at first?" I repeat. *What the hell did he do?* An animalistic growl rises from my throat. I ram my shoulder into his chest. He grabs my dolphin statue. My nerves sting. *Not that one.*

I shove him against the wall. He strikes my side with the statue.

I grunt and rear back. *Bastard.* I reach for the dolphin in his grip. Cas knees me in the gut and spins me around. Now I'm the one against the wall. He hits my wrist with the statue. The back of my hand slams against the limestone. Once, twice, three times. My knife fumbles out of my fist. Cas drops the dolphin. Its tail cracks.

I'll kill him.

He snatches up my knife and jumps away. He rapidly saws though his ropes. I lunge at him again. His hands are free now. He nicks my upper arm like I nicked his. I hiss and grab my wound.

"Let me leave." He backtracks to the ladder. "I have no wish to hurt you, Bastien."

Like hell he doesn't. I charge at him. The blade in his hand comes arcing down for me. I grab his wrist to stop it. We wrestle for control. "That knife you're holding belonged to my father," I say past gritted teeth. "Drop it."

Cas's brows spasm, but he doesn't let go. I drive him back against the scaffolding post. One of his feet slips off the sheer edge of the floor. He grabs a rung of the ladder. I finally wrench the blade away, but he hits my arm at the same time. The knife flings into the dark depths of the quarry.

I stop breathing. *That didn't just happen.* Blood rushes to my head. My vision blackens at the edges. My father is dying all over again, and I'll never be able to give him peace.

Another spike of rage rips through me. I swing my fist at Cas, and my knuckles clip his jaw. His head jerks to the side. He pushes past the pain and fumbles to climb the ladder. I grab him by the back of his shirt and yank him down to the scaffolding platform.

He punches me hard in the temple. White stars pop around me. I fall back on the platform, wincing. Cas pants. "You're overreacting, Bastien. Would you like to know how much Ailesse took pleasure in that kiss?"

"Go to hell." I spit at him.

He gives a humorless laugh and wipes his bloodied lip with his thumb. "She enjoyed it so much that she ran away."

I freeze. "What?"

He nods, jaw locked. "She said she would never care for me like I wanted. She said love isn't written in the stars."

I wait for relief to come, but can't find it. "I don't understand. Why would she run?"

He shrugs. "Some far-fetched excuse—a sudden need to help her sister."

My mind races. "Tonight's the full moon." I picture the fissured bridge and hear Ailesse's shriek when her knee shattered. "They wouldn't dare."

"Dare to what?"

I shove past Cas, grab a lantern from the room, and rush back to the ladder. "They're going to ferry the dead, you fool."

After a startled pause, he clambers after me. "On the cavern bridge?"

"Same one you saw."

"But it will break."

Now he's catching on. "How long ago did she leave?"

"A quarter of an hour, perhaps. You arrived shortly after she left."

"Then I can still stop her." Ferrying doesn't happen until midnight. If I hurry, I can make it to the cavern by then—as long as the Chained don't get in my way. Damn, I wish I still had my knife.

I climb one rung of the ladder, then pause, take a deep breath, and look at Cas. "Sorry I jumped to the wrong conclusions about you." I still can't stomach the thought of him and Ailesse kissing, but at least he didn't force anything on her. I shouldn't have attacked him.

He nods, lowering his eyes a moment before meeting my gaze again squarely. "Sorry about your statues and your father's knife."

My jaw stiffens, but what's done is done. "You coming, then?" I don't have time to argue with him about staying back. Truth is, between Ailesse and Sabine, I might need his help.

He answers by following me up the scaffolding and through the tunnels of the mines and catacombs. We reach the cellar, climb the ladder into the chapel, and rush toward the tall doors that open to the street. I pull up the hood of my cloak. The storm is still raging outside. "We'll have to be quick," I say. "Stick to the shadows of buildings and alleys whenever you can. And be quiet. The dead are cunning."

He gives a tight-lipped nod.

I bolt outside and launch westward, but Cas races away to the east—toward Beau Palais. *Merde.* I wheel after him, then force myself to stop. He's chosen his throne. Fine. I choose Ailesse.

I turn west again and break into a run. *Don't die,* I silently command Cas. Ailesse would want me to stay with him and keep him safe. But I can't. It's not just the fragile bridge that has my adrenaline pounding. It's Odiva, who wants to be freed. It's the power of the song Ailesse heard in the Underworld. Between her mother and that music, she's headed straight for a deathtrap.

The dead shriek and howl above the rainfall.

I clench my jaw and race faster into the shadows. I imagine I have Ailesse's falcon speed and her ibex agility on the wet cobblestones.

I *will* make it to her before midnight.

I'll save her from herself.

20
Sabine

I WALK FORWARD TO THE meadow in the forest west of Dovré until I find the circle of stones, nearly hidden by the wild grass. Moon phases are engraved on them. Within the ring, I point out the long gash in the earth to the three Ferriers who have come with me.

Pernelle steps toward the edge, watching her footing in the pelting rain. The full moon is hidden behind the storm clouds, but Pernelle's fox vertebra pendant gives her excellent vision in the dark, and her sea hawk wing bone also helps her see well at a distance. She should be able to focus on what I do—the soul bridge, over a hundred feet below.

She shakes her head. "How did our *famille* never know about this place?"

"We must have, once." I nudge a broken plank of wood with my staff. Bastien told me he blasted apart the cavern's patched-up ceiling here. At one time, the soul bridge must have been naturally open to the Night Heavens, but someone—probably our Leurress ancestors—hid it from sight, perhaps when the people of Galle began using the quarries and caves below Dovré as catacombs for their innumerable dead.

Maurille touches my shoulder, and I meet her deep brown eyes. They're full of a mother's concern, because that's who she has tried to be to me since Ciana died. The two of them were best friends. I wish Ciana had been my real mother. "Are you sure you're ready this time?" she asks me.

A tremor runs through my hands, but I shake it off. The weight of my antler crown is nothing next to the press of the golden jackal pendant on my brow. *The burden is a privilege,* I tell myself. And I will tell my true mother the same. I don't need her help bearing these graces.

"Yes." I contrive a reassuring smile.

I start humming to calm my nerves, and advance to the hatch that leads to the underground stone staircase, another relic of our people. It's made of limestone bricks that zigzag downward through a hollowed-out passageway.

I lift the hatch door and take the lead, my heart pounding. A flood of memories rushes back. Cas walking these same stairs with me, my skin flushed to be so near him. Then holding him at knifepoint and asking Ailesse to kill her true *amouré.* Watching my mother stab Bastien, seeing Ailesse almost die when part of the bridge broke away. Finally, losing my mother when she ran through the Gates of the Underworld, and losing Ailesse when Cas stole her from me, a terrible blow after how long I'd fought to save her.

My sister still needs saving. She's still locked in a soul-bond and in danger from our mother. But maybe she won't come here. Maybe Bastien was able to persuade her to stay away.

The stairs end. I stop humming, realizing I've slipped into the melody of the sacred siren song. Roxane chastised me for doing so last ferrying night. I'm not supposed to hum or sing it, only play it on the bone flute.

The three Ferriers and I walk out a tunnel to a ledge that's a few feet wide and extends halfway around the perimeter of the thirty-yard pit. The natural stone bridge crossing that gaping hole leads from our ledge to a dead end on the other side, where there is no ledge, just a massive curving wall of limestone. It stretches up a hundred feet, where it meets the open gash in the ceiling above.

I study the strength of the Night Heavens pouring in, along with the torrential rain. Elara's Light is heady enough, but we could still use more illumination—especially considering that Chantae doesn't have keen vision in the dark like me, Pernelle, and Maurille. "Light the torches," I tell her, since she's carrying our only lantern. I point out all the sconces on the back wall of our ledge.

Soon warm light fills the space and flickers over the long cracks and weak spots of the bridge. It's five feet wide and five feet thick. Below that bar of limestone is only air. The pit must be unfathomably deep. With a shiver, I remember when part of the bridge broke away. I never heard the large chunk hit the bottom.

I pull the bone flute from my dress pocket. My hands are clammy. Chantae murmurs a prayer and strokes her boar jawbone choker. She advances past me to take her place on the bridge. "No." I catch her arm and look at the others. "You three need to stay back on the ledge."

Chantae lifts her chin, her bronze skin shimmering in the torchlight. "We're accustomed to ferrying on wet rock, Sabine."

"I know, but this bridge is fragile. The souls will only add more weight. It's better if you guard the foot of the bridge instead. Try sending me only one soul at a time."

Chantae exchanges a tense glance with Pernelle. Out of all the elders, they're the two I trust most, but I'm still far from earning *their* trust. "We shouldn't be attempting this without more Ferriers," Chantae says. "Roxane would never have—"

"Roxane isn't *matrone*," I snap, then flex my hands to control my temper. It still flares easily from my golden jackal grace. "Our duty is to protect the living from the dead. We have to take this chance."

Chantae sighs. "Very well."

I steady my legs and take my first tentative steps onto the soul bridge. The rain beats down on my head, and I twist the bone flute in my hands. Should I wait another moment in case Ailesse comes? What if she *can't* come? What if she wasn't able to fight off the Chained attacking Cas, and they both died? My stomach clenches. I should never have let her go back for him on her own.

"It's midnight, Sabine." Pernelle looks up through the gash. I'm not sure how she can judge that without seeing the lodestar past the storm clouds, but I believe her.

I can't wait for Ailesse. *She's safe,* I tell myself, *and safer away from here.* I would feel if something terrible had happened to my sister.

In the middle of the bridge, I raise the bone flute to my mouth.

I play the siren song flawlessly, though I feel none of its beauty. I'm guarding all my emotions against what's to come. Tyrus's siren song. My mother watching me through his Gate.

The moment it ends, a blast of onyx dust shoots up from the pit. My dress and hair whip in the strange wind that gathers the dust together like unseen hands. It forms into an arched doorway of glittering black at the dead end of the soul bridge. For a moment, I can't breathe. I'm shaking, expecting to see my mother's midnight-blue dress, her bone crown, her chalk-white skin through that dusty veil. But so far nothing but the dark of Tyrus's realm stares back at me.

I glance at the three Ferriers on the ledge. Their eyes are round with awe and fear, but they stand tall, their staffs ready. Soon enough, the dead will be upon us.

I advance to the end of the bridge, my pulse beating in double time as the dueling siren songs rise above the rainfall, Tyrus's brooding melody and Elara's hopeful descant.

Stay focused, Sabine. Think of Paradise, not the Underworld.

My gaze travels right, and I catch a glimmer of the goddess's near-invisible Gate and silvery spiral staircase.

When I reach the end of the bridge, I turn around to face the foot of it. The dead will pour in through the tunnel we came through. But when the first flare of *chazoure* appears, it shines down a shaft beside the tunnel opening. I'd forgotten about that entrance; it's how Jules and Marcel arrived when they came for Bastien.

The soul drops through the shaft and advances toward the bridge. A teenage boy with shaggy hair and wide-set eyes. Unchained. Maurille steps out of his way with an encouraging smile. He looks to me, and I nod with a smile of my own, though I tap my toe. I risked ferrying tonight to rid South Galle of the Chained, not the Unchained, although I expected them, too.

When the boy is halfway across the bridge, my keen ears pick up a *swish, scritch* from above. I look up, but Maurille yells, "Behind you!"

I whirl around. Several yards above the Gate of dust, a flash of *chazoure* streaks down the cavern wall with unnerving speed. A man with a prominent square jaw and spindly fingers. Chained.

I backtrack to make space to fight him, but when he pushes off the wall, he jumps past me, leaping overhead with impossible strength. He's stolen Light. Great quantities of it.

He lands on the bridge right next to the boy and grabs him hostage by his *chazoure* collar. "Let me into Paradise," the Chained demands, glaring at me while the boy thrashes to free himself.

"It's too late for redemption." I stride toward him. "Tyrus has already claimed you."

The Chained's eyes flicker to my golden jackal pendant, and

his *chazoure* color pales a shade. He cries out in rage and throws the Unchained boy off the bridge. I gasp as he plummets into the darkness with a shuddering scream. What will become of him? I look to Maurille, but she shakes her head, horrified. She doesn't know either.

My shock passes. My fury ignites. I spring for the Chained. He races toward the ledge, but each step comes slower than the last. He can't resist the lure of the soul bridge.

I catch up to him and kick him hard in the back. His stomach slaps the wet limestone. I flip him over so I can see his rain-splashed face. "You will be punished for that," I say. The Underworld holds many places for sinners. A scalding river of blood that boils off flesh. The scorching Perpetual Sands, where murderers eternally thirst. I step on the man's neck and dig my heel into his windpipe. "The worst sinners burn forever in the Furnace of Justice. That will be your fate. Tyrus will wear your ashes."

"Sabine." Pernelle's voice sounds distant and tinny, despite my jackal hearing. I glance up at her. She looks sickened. "Just ferry him. It does not fall upon you to place judgment."

I blink twice and swallow hard. The Chained man beneath my heel writhes, his *chazoure* eyes rolling back in his head. Lack of breath can't kill him, but Pernelle is right. I shouldn't be torturing him like this.

My cheeks burn. I quickly release his throat and drag him up to his feet. He fights me as I haul him toward Tyrus's Gate, but I manage to keep him in tow, using the breadth of my red stag and golden jackal strength. It's the jackal grace that's the problem. It flows through me unbridled and exacerbates my worst tendencies. I didn't know I had it in me to be so cruel. But perhaps a *matrone* needs to be this formidable.

The Gate of dust billows as we come near, as if it's conscious of our presence. I try not to think of it and quickly hurl the Chained man through. When I do, I glimpse black eyes and a flash of bone white from the other side. My ribs constrict against my lungs.

"You came, daughter." Odiva elegantly sidesteps the Chained man and draws flush to the Gate. Her raven hair floats about her in an eerie underwater way. "You are ready to let me help you."

"I didn't come here for you." I force myself to breathe. "You sacrificed innocent souls to Tyrus. I'll never release you from your fate." I turn my back to her and put ten feet between us.

The other Ferriers don't notice their former *matrone*. They're busy with four new souls. Chantae shoves a Chained woman onto the bridge while holding another—her twin—back. As I run toward the first sister, aware of how she resists me, a fissure cracks wider on the bridge. I dart away from it and use my staff to prod the woman forward. Another Chained attacks Chantae, and the second twin gets past her. She bounds onto the bridge, and the fissure snakes longer by three feet.

"Go back!" I shout at her. "The bridge is too weak."

"Let me be with my sister," she pleads, though she doesn't have chains.

I fumble, wrestling with the first twin. "You would go to the Underworld with her?"

She nods. *Chazoure* tears spill from her eyes.

"You see, Sabine." My mother's whisper is spun of spider silk. It sticks to my ears and draws my unwilling gaze to her. "What I did was not so terrible. Not all of the innocent wish to be rewarded by Elara. They would rather be with their loved ones. And each of us loves at least one of the damned."

My heart drums with greater warning. I can't listen to her. She wants to distract me.

The bridge groans as another Chained soul bolts onto it. I throw the Ferriers a desperate look. "Hold them back! There are too many."

"We're trying!" Maurille's staff whirls left and right. She's herding three more souls while Pernelle and Chantae grapple with four each. "You have to be faster."

"I could help you." Odiva's voice spins a tighter web. "Let me do my part, daughter."

My muscles lock in resistance. With seven quick strikes of my staff, I bring the Chained twin back to Tyrus's Gate. I plunge the end of my staff into her stomach, and she's cast into the Underworld. This time my mother doesn't step aside. She catches the soul's arm and effortlessly flings her into the depths behind her.

"Lucille!" Her Unchained sister races forward through the rainfall.

"Let her come, if she is so insistent," Odiva says.

I take a defensive stance. The remaining Chained soul on the bridge is also running toward me, but his eyes are fixed on Elara's Gate, where he doesn't belong.

"Sabine, watch out from above," Maurille cries. I trust her

dolphin echolocation and swing up my staff. It thuds against flesh. Another Chained falls onto the bridge. *Crack.*

I kick him away, then jab back the Chained bolting for Paradise. I throw both souls into the Underworld. The Unchained twin leaps through after them while I'm preoccupied. *No!* I instinctively reach for the black dust. My mother reaches back for me.

"Sabine, I'm here!"

My breath catches. *Ailesse.*

I turn around. She's on the ledge. She throws off her wet cloak and squirms past the busy Ferriers. She springs across the bridge on her crutch. The limestone fissures slightly, but holds. Worry, determination, and ferocity dance over my sister's face. Most of all, I see her deep love for me. It's shining in her umber eyes and trembling through her chin. She leans toward me, willing herself to move even faster.

When she reaches me, she flings her arms around my neck. I hug her back fiercely as the rain washes over us. She's alive. She didn't lose all her Light. And she came like she promised. Why did I ever think I could do this without her?

She pulls back and kisses my cheek. "Promise to trust me and don't worry," she says. I know that tone of voice. With that same gentle strength, she's told me many things. . . .

You don't have to kill the fire salamander if you don't want to.

It's all right to weep over death.

Let me, Sabine. I'll boil the flesh off his bones.

It comes as a comfort at first, an assurance that I don't have to push myself; Ailesse will do the hard work for me. Then she sets her jaw, and my heart jumps up my throat. *No, no, no!*

"Ailesse!" I reach for her.

Her peregrine falcon's speed is greater than my nighthawk's.

She spins to the Gates of the Underworld.

She touches our mother's hand.

21
Ailesse

As soon as my palm touches my mother's, she grips my hand. Her nostrils flare with a deeply inhaled breath. My eyes water. I try to hate her, but I can't find that bitter space inside me. All my life I yearned for the look of approval she's giving me now.

"Ailesse!" Sabine clutches my other hand and pulls. "Please let go. This is a trap!"

"I know." Tyrus's dark siren song funnels marrow-deep in my bones. "But our mother can break the soul-bond."

Sabine grounds her feet on the rain-slick bridge and tugs harder. The storm lashes through the long gap in the ceiling. The three Ferriers shout at us. Souls howl, surging nearer. "If that's true," Sabine says, "she's done so through terrible sacrifices."

I stiffen my jaw and stare into my mother's glimmering black eyes. "I know she meant to sacrifice me."

"But she sacrificed thousands of Unchained instead."

My mouth goes dry. I look back at Sabine. Her black curls are plastered to her forehead. Her face is flushed from all her straining. "What do you mean?"

She exhales, desperate.

A soul crashes into me. I lurch forward. Sabine kicks the man back—Chained. My mother's grip flashes to my wrist and bears down like an iron manacle. Why hasn't she stepped through the Gate yet? She said all I had to do was touch her hand.

"Duck!" Sabine shouts. I do as she says. Without releasing me, she swings her staff at the Chained. He's thrown overhead and barrels through Tyrus's Gate. My mother bats him in with a flick of her strong arm, all the while keeping her shackled hold on me.

The bridge creaks and groans. Ten yards away, a great sliver of stone breaks off the side. My heart pounds. "Mother, hurry! We need your help!"

"You can't trust her," Sabine says. Rain glances off her olive skin, and she secures her grip on my hand. "She didn't sacrifice you, but she would have if there were no other way."

"You judge me harshly, daughter." Odiva's eagle owl feather and talon epaulettes sway in the strange current surrounding her. "I entered the Underworld to spare Ailesse's life."

"Maybe you did," Sabine replies. "But now you want out, and you have your claws in her again."

More souls clamber onto the bridge. Sabine's staff wheels

through the air. She hits a Chained, who hurtles through Tyrus's Gate. "Ailesse, listen to me. Odiva wants to pull you inside. She's trying to give Tyrus the sacrifice he asked for in exchange for resurrecting my father."

"No, she needs my help ferrying." *You are my true daughter when it comes to skill and talent,* she told me.

"She has no intention of ferrying." Sabine hurls an Unchained through Elara's Gate. "I understand now. This is how she'll break the bond with her own *amouré*. It's how she'll teach you—by killing you."

I whirl on my mother. *Prove Sabine wrong,* the look I give her says. But she doesn't have to admit her betrayal. I feel it in the sinking of my stomach, the rising acid in my throat, the furious, heart-wrenching burning in my eyes. I've been such a fool.

"You cannot prevent Ailesse's inevitable fate, when I have spent more than two years trying," my mother tells Sabine. "I will not fight Tyrus any longer."

Sabine's expression hardens. Her gaze cuts to the ledge at the other side of the cavern. "Hold on," she whispers. She releases my hand and bolts for the ledge.

My chest seizes. What is she doing?

"No," Odiva gasps.

Suddenly I understand. She's going to run off the bridge. And when she does, the Gates will close. She was the one who opened them.

My mother tightens her grip and starts pulling me toward her. I wrest, yank, use every measure of my tiger shark strength. But she's so much stronger. She always has been. Her albino bear grace bone is aided by four others, while I only have three.

My crutch drops. My knee throbs from the pressure I'm forced to place on my bad leg. My feet slide on the wet bridge, coming closer, closer to the black dust. "No, Mother, please, please, please . . ."

Halfway across the bridge, Sabine looks over her shoulder. "Ailesse!" She jerks to a stop, curses, and races back to me. A Chained is right behind her.

My mother continues dragging me nearer. I cry out. My muscles burn from struggling against her. Sabine catches my other hand. She desperately fights to tug me back. The Chained springs for the Gate to Paradise. Sabine one-handedly fends him away. My mother pulls with more force. I slip another step closer.

Sabine kicks the Chained off the bridge. Abandons her staff. Grabs my hand with both of hers. The tendons in her neck strain as she pulls with all her might. Even together, eight grace bones between us, we can barely resist our mother.

Tyrus's siren song swells and eclipses Elara's descant. It drowns out the rainfall, the warning cries of the Ferriers, even Sabine's shouts and pleas from right beside me.

My realm will be your great adventure, Ailesse, Tyrus's song sings without words, leaving my imagination to run rampant. His music throws my Light in the darkest shadow. *Surrender, surrender. Discover wonder instead of pain.*

I lurch another inch toward his Gate.

"Ailesse, no!" Sabine's feet dig into the ground, but it's not enough leverage. She's slipping forward, too. She looks wildly around her and releases one of her hands from me. She grabs a bar of Elara's near-invisible Gate.

My mother exhales slowly, exultantly. "Well done, daughters."

An enormous rush of energy blasts through me. My back arches. My head is thrown back. It's lightning powerful, scorching hot, and freezing cold. It surges through my blood and pounds through my skull and through my limbs and fingertips.

I'm still stretched between my mother and my sister. I grit my teeth and turn my head to Sabine. Her body is taut, also under massive stress. Her olive skin starts to glow with *chazoure*, and her eyes widen as she looks back at me. I glance down at my arm. I'm glowing, too.

What's happening?

A high-pitched screech fills my ears. It's deafening, louder than Tyrus's siren song. I cry out as it shudders through me, but I can't even hear my own scream. The grating sound comes from Elara's Gate—the riot of many souls, their shrieks of pain.

The screeching escalates higher and higher, until it crashes like broken glass. Elara's realm—her scrollwork Gate and spiral staircase—pulses in flashes of solid silver, losing its translucency.

The silver owl dives in through the gap in the ceiling. She circles me and Sabine, flapping her wings ferociously. It does nothing to stop the madness within me, all around me.

A flood of *chazoure* souls lashes down the spiral staircase and bursts out from the Gates of Paradise, like a dam has broken. The Unchained purge out of it, but they're not set loose in the mortal world. They're sucked into the Gates of the Underworld.

Their onslaught rakes like icy wind through my hair and dress. Shock closes off my lungs. I can barely breathe. My eyes connect with Sabine's. Her *chazoure* irises reflect my horror. This is wrong. Evil. These souls are Unchained, but they're being pulled from a peaceful eternity into the terrors of Tyrus's realm. Why?

What has my mother done?

More souls flow down the staircase. My mother has me by a death grip. Sabine's hold is almost as unrelenting. I'm caged between them, connecting both realms of the gods.

"We have to stop this!" I shout at Sabine. "Let go of Elara's Gate!" I can't hear myself amid the uproar, but her ears are more graced than mine. She nods, and we both tense our legs to keep purchase on the bridge. She inhales a deep breath and turns to the Gate.

Faintly, I hear Odiva yell something. I can't make out her words. Sabine's about to loosen her grip when two unferried Chained swarm close and wrap their fingers over hers. They bind her hand to the scrollwork bar. Sabine struggles against them, but she can't break their hold. The strain of our channel is exhausting too much of her energy.

The remaining Chained and Unchained who haven't been ferried yet flee the cavern. The raging chaos has broken their lure to the Beyond.

The souls from Paradise keep coursing, siphoning from Elara's realm. They scream and plead and cry, but their screeching isn't ear-shattering anymore. I'm finally able to hear myself when I cry out, "Let go of my hand, Sabine!"

Her eyes fly wide, and she shakes her head. Her glowing curls whip around her face in the rain and wind.

"Please!" My throat burns from having to shout at the top of my lungs. "I can't allow all these souls to suffer just to save myself."

Tears chase down her face. "I'm not sacrificing you! That's exactly what Odiva wants."

"What if it is also Ailesse's desire?" our mother asks Sabine. She doesn't glow with *chazoure* like us, but the color of the dead flickers over her pale face and neck as the souls are sucked past her. "She has always sought for glory to earn my respect. What better way to do that than by becoming a martyr?"

I whirl on her. "I don't want your respect. Your crimes are incomprehensible, unforgivable. I'm ashamed to be your daughter."

The silver owl flies closer, her wing-tip feathers almost touching the black dust. She rasp-screeches at Odiva.

My mother recoils slightly. "Then you should crave respect from the gods," my mother tells me. "Tyrus desires to join kingdoms with his bride. It is what they both wanted, from the dawn of time."

"Well, it appears the goddess has had a change of heart."

Odiva's lip curls, just a scant movement, but it still radiates extreme power and intimidation. That look used to haunt me, drive me to train harder, become more devout. Now it only infuriates me.

"You're not my mother anymore," I bite out as more wailing souls stream by. "I'd rather *die* than become anything like you." I throw all the venom I can into my voice, all the years I've wasted trying to please her and gain her affection.

Odiva grins, though her eyes shine. It's hatred, not love, that forms her tears—rage from hurt pride, not a hurt heart. There's no Light left in her. If she's alive, it's because Tyrus's darkness sustains her from all the souls she's feeding him. "If death is your wish, insolent child," she says, "then I will deliver it."

She applies more pressure on my wrist and pulls harder. The Unchained wail, clawing my arms as they're swept away. Their onslaught drives me closer to her. My left arm and half of my face and body slip into the black.

I painfully turn to Sabine. Tears scald my cheeks. "Let me go."

"No!" she cries, vainly tugging harder.

I whimper, all my energy focused on preventing both my shoulders from dislocating. My tears fall faster. I can't speak anymore. I'm in too much pain. *Thank you*, I mouth, hoping she understands what I'm trying to say. I can't even mouth the rest: *Thank you for fighting to save me—for always fighting. For never giving up on me.*

A sob breaks from her. "I'm sorry," she says, though she doesn't stop pulling. Rain and *chazoure* tears streak down her face.

I shake my head, not wanting her to apologize. She's been the perfect friend, the perfect sister. I'm grateful she's the last person I'll see before I die.

My left leg slides another inch into the black. Sulfurous dust fills my lungs and swims through my vision. Tyrus's siren song thrums through my bones.

"Ailesse!"

My heart jumps. *Bastien.*

I turn, struggling to see him. He runs down the length of the bridge, despite the warning cries of the Ferriers. Vaguely, I see the limestone fissure at his feet. For one terrible moment, I fear he'll fall into the abyss, but then he's right before me, his beautiful sea-blue eyes filled with horror and desperation. His grabs me and pulls, one hand on my forearm, the other over Sabine's hand on mine.

A surge of energy ripples through our three joined hands. Bastien doesn't light up with *chazoure*, like me and Sabine, but he blanches and looks between the two Gates.

"I see them," he gasps. His dark hair lashes against his face from the rainstorm and the torrent of souls. "I see the dead."

22
Bastien

Soul after soul rushes toward me, past me. Rain keeps pouring onto the bridge. I fight to stay balanced on the slick lime-stone. The souls could knock me into the pit at any moment.

Pain throbs behind my eyes, and I strain harder to focus. I blink again and again. The souls glow with a strange color. *Chazoure?* Ailesse described it to me once. How am I seeing it? Why are she and Sabine lit up with it, too?

I yank harder, desperate to save Ailesse. My muscles burn with a surprising spike of strength. Ailesse jerks three inches away from the black dust and screams out in pain. I startle and immediately ease up my hold. I didn't mean to hurt her. I could have torn her arm from its socket just now. I've never felt so much adrenaline pounding through my body, and I'm strangely out of step with it. I don't know how to use my own strength properly.

On the other side of the black dust, I find Odiva staring back at me. I swallow. This is the first time I've seen her since she jumped through the Gate.

She's still disturbingly beautiful, with her black eyes and her crown made from a noctule bat skull and the vertebrae of an asp viper. But she's different, too. More openly vicious. Colder. Even deadlier. Those dark eyes bore into me as she pulls us closer with incredible power. "Pitiful boy," she sneers at me. "Always following Ailesse into danger like a besotted fool."

A few crass retorts come to mind, but I keep my mouth shut. She doesn't deserve to be spoken to. I fix my energy on Ailesse instead. "Hang on," I tell her. "We've got you."

She slides out another inch. Rain streams off the ends of her glowing hair. Her pained eyes lock on me. "Bastien," she rasps on the thinnest breath. Somehow I hear it, just like other things that should be too quiet for my ears. The sound of my heartbeat. Higher pitches than I thought were possible. Souls screaming from far away. A new song . . .

It travels out of the Underworld and grows louder. The screams seem to hush. Ailesse's face fades. I'm only aware of the song . . . then another song that harmonizes with it. They both fight for my attention.

I stagger on my feet. I veer toward Elara's Gate, then Tyrus's. My pulse races. I want to—no, I *need* to—go and explore each realm.

Odiva's mouth curves. "You hear the music, don't you, boy, the siren songs of the Beyond?"

Sabine's hand flinches beneath mine. "Shut it out, Bastien."

"If you listen closely enough," Odiva continues, "you will feel the gods' communion with you."

No. I blow out a tense breath and do as Sabine says. I struggle to block the sound. I put my energy into tugging Ailesse toward me instead.

"Do you know what *I* hear?" Odiva asks.

I won't look at her, so I look at Ailesse. Every muscle in her face, neck, and arms quivers from the pressure she's under. She says nothing to me—I don't think she's able to—but I feel her warning me just the same. I shouldn't listen to her mother.

But it's impossible not to.

"Tyrus knows you," Odiva goes on. "He wants you, like he wants all those with vengeance in their hearts."

"Mother, stop!" Sabine says.

"Why should I, when I am fulfilling my word to you?" Odiva lifts her chin. "Can you not see what is happening? Bastien is experiencing your graces. I told you I knew how to share them."

Sabine stiffens, speechless. I'm just as shocked. *I'm sharing Sabine's graces?* Suddenly my heightened abilities make sense. They're why I can see the dead and hear Tyrus's and Elara's siren songs. They're why my strength is so much more powerful than before.

Armed with that knowledge, I fight harder to drag Ailesse away from the black dust. Together, she, Sabine, and I should be stronger than Odiva. So why isn't Ailesse budging? I squint past her through the Gate. Several Unchained souls are yanking on Odiva, trying to escape past her. She doesn't shake them away. She allows them to strengthen her pull against us.

"Tyrus also knows someone else that you do," she tells me, her voice maddeningly calm, "someone who did not merit chains in his life, though that no longer bears significance. When the kingdoms of the Beyond are joined, all will be Chained. All will give their Light to the gods."

What is she talking about?

"Keep hold of Ailesse!" Sabine commands me. "My mother is trying to distract you. Don't—"

"How many years has it been since you have seen him, Bastien?" Odiva speaks over her. "Eight, yes?"

My heartbeat rushes to my head. *No—*

I turn to Elara's Gate. Look up. At the top of the spiral staircase, a middle-aged man is being forced downward, step by step, caught in the surge of Unchained souls. My sight reaches far— farther than it has in my life. I see in detail every thin wrinkle on his face, the laugh lines around his mouth, the creases of fatigue on his forehead from long hours of chiseling stone. He's still wearing the simple tunic and worn trousers I remember him best in, the same clothes he died in. His boots still have scuff marks from when he fell on the bridge after being stabbed in the heart by a Bone Crier.

But now . . . now my father is moving. He's not lifeless and bleeding out.

He reaches the bottom step too quickly. I'm going to lose him all over again. He hasn't even seen me. My throat is so tight I can barely speak. I manage to croak out, "Papa!" I sound like a child, ten years old again, shouting for him to wake up and not leave me all alone.

His eyes finally fall on me. His brows lift. Terror leaves his face for a moment. I see myself in him now, the same angular jawline and thick mussed-up hair. "Bastien?"

It's too much to hear him say my name. I'm laughing, crying.

Sabine shouts something at me. I don't process it.

My father is swept closer, along with the souls. In a blink, he's at the edge of Elara's Gate, then right before me. "Bastien, what's happeni—?"

He tears past me. I try to grab him. "Papa!"

"Ailesse!" Sabine cries.

My heart drops.

I let her go.

I spin to Tyrus's Gate. Ailesse and my father are sucked through at the same moment.

No! I jump after them. The black dust singes my eyes. The siren song roars in my ears. Ailesse screams my name. I reach. I catch a brief glimpse of her terrified face. Something forces me back. I slam against the soul bridge. The limestone groans and crackles. It'll break soon. I don't care. I shove myself back up to my feet and charge for the Gate again.

Odiva is standing in the way. She's on the bridge now, breathing, truly alive. She stalks toward me, driving me back with powerful strength, while my borrowed strength is gone. That doesn't stop me. I throw my fist at her face, her stomach, her jaw.

She deflects my punches. I rail harder, shouting, cursing her. *This can't be happening. Please, please, please, this can't be happening.*

Impatient, Odiva flings me aside. Sabine snatches me before I fly off the bridge. I'm barely grounded on the limestone when she shrieks in pain. The sleeve by her shoulder is cut. A streak of blood spills through the tear. She turns on her mother, her mouth hanging open. Odiva holds Ailesse's bone knife—she must have stolen it off her.

Terrible quiet fills the cavern. I'm blind to the *chazoure* again, but the Unchained have to have stopped coming, or else I'd hear them with my own graceless ears. Three of the Leurress are standing at the foot of the bridge, utterly horrified, but they keep back on the far ledge. The fissures near them are the most threatening.

"You merciless monster!" Sabine cries at Odiva. "What have you done?"

"You will thank me in the end, child." Odiva's hand lashes out for the crescent-moon pendant dangling from Sabine's antler crown. Sabine beats her hand away, but not before it closes around the grace bone lying next to the pendant—Sabine's fire salamander skull. Odiva rips it off its cord.

Sabine loses her balance for a moment, and then her eyes widen. "Give that back!"

Odiva scrapes the bone knife over the skull. Sabine's blood smears onto it. I watch, breathless and stunned. Nothing makes sense. Odiva has taken Ailesse. She sent my father to the Underworld. What more does she want?

She holds the bloodied skull toward the Gate of dust. Rain pelts her. Wind flaps through her dress. "I have given you the child of my once *amouré*." Her rich voice booms through the cavern. "I have given you thousands upon thousands more souls. It is beyond enough. Keep your promise, Tyrus. Break my soul-bond and give me back the man I love."

She glides closer to the Gate. "Here is my second-born daughter's blood, and one of her grace bones. Let them give my daughter's father back his flesh, bone, and blood. In return, I give you my oath to help you reclaim your bride."

The black dust stirs faster. A figure takes form behind it. A man. *Let it be* my *father, not Sabine's.* A vain prayer to a god I hate, but I beg Tyrus all the same.

The man's eyes cut through the dust. They're golden brown, not sea blue. My chest sinks.

Sabine catches my gaze. She motions me with a subtle tilt of her head. We slowly back away from Odiva. The bridge's fissures snake longer. A crack of lightning masks the sound.

Past the Gate, the man's scarlet-and-black doublet appears, then his well-trimmed beard and shoulder-length graying hair. A strong olive-skinned hand, laden with jeweled rings, reaches through the dust for Odiva.

It isn't until he steps through the glittering dust that I see his crown. Feathers carved of black onyx, each one embedded with a large ruby, form a heavy circle around his head.

Sabine gasps, face pale. "It can't be."

The man—a king, by all appearances—comes to Odiva's side

in the pouring rain. She strokes his face, marveling over him. Her grin is triumphant. "Godart," she murmurs, pressing the salamander skull into his hand. Once it's in his possession, she kisses him passionately.

Godart? I was a small child when he died. Godart Lothaire was the last in a long line of kings who ruled South Galle from Château Creux. The people say he was cursed.

Sabine takes another step back. The bridge grumbles like the earth before a great quake. A silver owl flies above—the same one Ailesse saw by the forest river. It sails out of the cavern through the gap in the ceiling. A split second later, lightning strikes the bridge with a deafening *crack*. A large chunk of the bridge breaks away at Odiva's and Godart's feet. They leap back just in time.

Sabine and I turn and bolt the other way. The Ferriers at the foot of the bridge shout for us to hurry. The limestone beneath me buckles. More sections drop away behind us.

The rain pounds heavier. Something arcs by overhead. The silver owl? No, Odiva and Godart. She's jumped with her graces and pulled him through the air. They land on the bridge ahead of us. The stone crumbles apart. Sabine yanks my hand to speed me up.

The foot of the bridge is twenty feet away. Odiva and Godart make it there first. The three Ferriers have their staffs raised to fight them. Odiva seizes one of the staffs and uses it to attack the Ferriers. I don't watch the fight. I'm too busy dodging gaping cracks.

Reality sets in, even as I race for my life. I do have vengeance in my heart. I'll use it to keep me alive, alert, and ready. I'll plot for justice. Kill Odiva and Godart. Punish a god.

Sabine and I rush onto the foot of the bridge just as the rest of it crashes into the abyss. Rubble and chalky dust fill the air. I lunge through it. Search for Odiva and Godart. Two of the Ferriers are huddled on the ground. They're bent over the third woman, with black braided hair and a bracelet of teeth. The side of her forehead is bleeding. Her brown eyes are glassy and lifeless.

"Maurille!" Sabine falls to her knees and shakes the woman's shoulders.

The rubble and dust clear. Odiva and Godart are gone. The Gates at the other side of the cavern have vanished, too.

Rain continues to pour in through the long gap in the ceiling, but there's no bridge for it to land on.

The water falls away into nothing but the dark and endless pit.

23
Sabine

LIGHTNING ILLUMINATES THE DARK CLOUDS above the ruins of Château Creux. Half the night has passed by the time the Ferriers and I arrive home. I was forced to leave Bastien behind. He refused to leave the cavern. His eyes were hollow and he wouldn't speak as he stared at the wall where the Gates of the Underworld once churned.

Pernelle and Chantae carry Maurille's body as honorably as possible on a litter we made of two staffs with our cloaks stretched between them. A third cloak covers her body and face.

I walk beside the litter and hold Maurille's cold, stiffening hand. *It's a comfort to her,* I tell myself. Although she's dead, her soul still remains with her body. It will rise the next time I open the Gates.

On that new moon, I vow to ferry Maurille to Paradise. No more of the Unchained will be stolen to the Underworld. I'll get them back again. I'll get Ailesse back, too. Leaping through the Gate of dust didn't kill my mother, so I have to believe my sister also found a way to remain alive.

Please, Elara, I pray, although the goddess holds no power in Tyrus's realm, *let Ailesse truly be alive.*

The Ferriers and I walk down the crumbling stone staircase and enter the lower depths of the ancient castle. The engraved crow-and-rose crest of Château Creux stares back at me from the archways that seam the corridors together. I've always known they were symbols of King Godart. Signs of him are everywhere in this place where he once ruled. No wonder my mother chose it as our *famille*'s home. No wonder he gave her a necklace of a crow skull with a ruby caught in its beak. It was another representation of his crest. The ruby must have meant his red rose, and the crow skull should have been obvious. I'm such a fool for not realizing Godart was my father sooner.

The Ferriers and I travel through the tide-carved tunnels below the castle, and then walk into the courtyard. I glance up at the full moon and a few stars that pierce the thinning storm clouds. The great tower of Château Creux once rose above this open cavern, but after Godart died, a massive storm rolled in off the sea and struck it down. Much of the castle's beauty was demolished then, and when Casimir's father came into power, he built Beau Palais and left Château Creux to the curse of the king who worshipped the god of the Underworld more than the god of the sun, Belin.

Maybe it was Belin's wrath that destroyed this place.

Now that I know the depths of Tyrus's cruelty, I like to think Elara helped the sun god.

Roxane and the other elders are waiting for us in the courtyard. Perhaps they noticed our absence, or perhaps they sensed us coming with their graces.

Pernelle and Chantae lower the litter to the ground. Nadine and Dolssa gasp and rush closer when I pull back the cloak from Maurille's face. Damiana and Milicent hang back with bowed heads. They are the oldest of the elders and the most acquainted with death.

Roxane remains where she stands, claiming her position of power at the center of the courtyard, though her eyes are wet with tears. Maurille was a powerful Ferrier and a gentle friend. Everyone loved her.

"The last time you stood among us," Roxane says to me, "you injured Hyacinthe. And now, when you dare to return, you bring Maurille—like this." She opens her hand, gesturing at her body. Light rainfall collects like stars in Maurille's black hair. "What have you done, Sabine?"

I clutch my injured arm. The cut my mother gave me is still bleeding, and I have no more salamander grace to help me close the wound. Maybe the small skull held power to mend a hurting heart as well, because there's nothing I can do to alleviate the wrenching pain in my chest. Roxane is right to blame me for what happened to Maurille. I was warned that Ailesse would come to the bridge, and I understood my mother's cunning. I shouldn't have involved any other Ferriers tonight.

Pernelle steps close and places a hand on my shoulder. "Do not accuse Sabine, Roxane. What happened was . . ." She shakes her head. "It was beyond any of us."

Chantae comes to my other side and faces Roxane. "It was *Matrone* Odiva who killed Maurille."

Roxane's brows slowly draw together. "You are mistaken. Odiva is dead."

"She was," Pernelle says. "But she emerged from the Gates of the Underworld tonight."

"It was unprecedented," Chantae adds, "especially because she resurrected someone else, too."

Roxane looks between the two elders, struggling to understand what they're saying. I shrink in on myself. All my lies have culminated to this point—all the truth I've kept back from my *famille* because I feared their anarchy, because I wanted Ailesse to bear the burden of revealing our mother's crimes instead of me.

"Even if resurrection were possible," Roxane says, "who would Odiva bring back from the dead?" Her lips part. "Do you mean Ailesse?"

No, I can't let her believe that. Odiva would never be so selfless. "Ailesse was already alive," I confess. I flex my hands and step away from Pernelle and Chantae. They won't defend me after I expose everything. "She was taken captive by Prince Casimir—King Casimir—the night she tried to ferry with Odiva. His Majesty is Ailesse's true *amouré*. And Odiva didn't die; she was alive when she leapt through Tyrus's Gate."

Milicent, the elder most loyal to Odiva, frowns from where she kneels beside Maurille's body. "That can't be true. Why would the *matrone* do such a thing?"

I blow out a steadying breath and do my best to explain. About Odiva's forbidden love with another man after she sacrificed her own *amouré*. About the gods cursing him anyway, killing him, and wrapping him in chains. About the terrible pact Odiva made with Tyrus, two years ago, to release her love from the Underworld at the cost of killing Ailesse, and how she resisted, ferrying thousands of Unchained to Tyrus instead. About the continuing sacrifices that happened tonight—thousands more Unchained stolen from Paradise, and Ailesse taken away with them after being tricked into finally satisfying Odiva's pact.

The rain falls softer, unable to hush my shame as the elders stare at me, their shock acute and silent. I've revealed that the greatest Leurress who ever existed among us is a traitor to her own people, but my own betrayal for keeping my mouth shut feels just as disgraceful.

Roxane is the first to break the unbearable quiet. "Why hasn't Odiva returned to us, then? Doesn't she wish to rule as *matrone?*"

"I don't know." But I *do* know my mother is devious and power thirsty. Resurrecting my father can't have been the only reason she returned from the Underworld. She must have some stronger goal.

Roxane's teal eyes narrow as they roam over my face. "You have one more thing to confess, don't you, Sabine? Why did Odiva really choose you as her heir?" My cheeks burn. Whatever resemblance I bear to my mother, she must see it now.

My gaze shifts to Pernelle and Chantae, craving their support in vain; they already overheard this truth tonight. But Chantae glances away from me, her jaw tight, and Pernelle doesn't blink as she stares back at me. She looks sickened and confused, like she doesn't recognize me anymore.

My eyes sting. I swallow a lump in my throat. "Because Odiva had two daughters," I answer Roxane. "I am the child of King Godart, the man Odiva raised from the dead."

Aghast expressions cross the other elders' faces. My shoulders crumple inward. I've always felt like an anomaly among my *famille*, inferior in talent and resistant about the life we lead, but now I feel inferior just for existing. I'm the offspring of Odiva's great betrayal of us. While each of the Leurress had to kill the men they loved in order to become Ferriers, Odiva found a deeper love and hid it from everyone.

Roxane looks down her nose at me. "We will not honor Odiva's bloodline any longer. You will *never* be our *matrone*, Sabine."

My eyes grow hot from the deep blow of her words. "But I have to . . . You can't . . ." I try to breathe, try to draw on my Light for strength. I can't feel it. I only feel the jackal inside me, enraged and tensed to fight. I've worked so hard to prove myself, change myself, be more like Ailesse and less like an imposter. "You don't even know the siren song. Many of the Chained are still loose. Not all of them were ferried tonight."

Roxane opens her mouth to say something as Nadine turns to the tunnel leading outside, her posture stiff. "A man is approaching the castle."

Milicent and Dolssa immediately bolt for the tunnel. The others grab staffs from racks along the courtyard wall. No one questions Nadine's eel-graced sense of smell. Now that I attune myself, my golden jackal grace picks up the same masculine musk in the air. I recognize it as Bastien's scent before Milicent and Dolssa drag him into the courtyard.

"What are you doing here?" I gasp at him. He must know it's a death wish to venture near Château Creux. The locals never come within miles of this place, for fear that it's cursed, and that keeps them protected, whether or not they realize it. Some of the elders claim they wouldn't hesitate to kill a man in order to protect the secret existence of our *famille*.

Bastien flips his wet hair off his brow. There's a flinty and dangerous look in his eyes that I haven't seen since the night he first met Ailesse and fought her at Castelpont, determined to kill a Bone Crier to avenge his father. "What are *you* doing here?" he counters, seething at all of us. "You're huntresses. You have the graces you need to track down Odiva. So track her. Threaten her. Tell her to bring back Ailesse and all the souls she stole with her."

Roxane stalks closer to him. "You are not Ailesse's *amouré*. She is none of your concern."

"Like hell she isn't," he bites out. "I can love and fight for whoever I want. I don't need your twisted gods telling me how to live my life, especially when they marked my father as one of your *amourés*."

Roxane tenses. Pernelle covers her mouth with her hand.

"That's right," Bastien says. "And he's in the Underworld now, thanks to Odiva. So if you're really committed to protecting righteous souls, you're going to get him back where he belongs."

Milicent gapes at him. "We can't rebel against Odiva."

He glares at her. She and Dolssa still have him in their graced grip. "Are you telling me you're going to turn a blind eye to what she's done?"

"I never said that." Milicent lowers her brows. "But you don't understand how powerful she is."

"She killed Maurille," Dolssa adds.

"I was there," Bastien replies flatly. "And I saw her do worse than that. That doesn't give me any excuse to cower instead of challenge her."

"We're not cowering," Roxane says. "We're being wise."

"Wise?" Bastien snaps. "You're the damn Ferriers of the dead! You're under obligation to fix what she's done—to demand she undo it."

"He's right." I speak up. "We can't allow Tyrus to keep Ailesse and all the Unchained souls imprisoned in the Underworld. They don't deserve that."

Roxane sharpens her gaze on me. "It is not your place to command us, Sabine."

My hands ball into fists, the jackal in me snarling, urging me to lunge at her. "I'm not seeking power. I'm reminding us of our sworn duty. As Ferriers, it's our responsibility to send these souls back where they belong."

"And punish the woman who sent them," Bastien adds. "I'll gladly volunteer to be the one to slit her throat."

"Enough!" Roxane cuts the air with her hands. "I will consult with the elders and determine our course of action, but as things stand right now, our priority is to protect the living."

"*Ailesse* is living!" I say. "How can you—?"

"The Chained are still loose upon the land." She talks over me. "That is something within the realm of our control. We will herd and trap them, as we've done before."

I tremble with rage. This is nonsense. The Chained are slippery. You can't keep them in cages for long. Roxane knows that. They all know that. "You're afraid of Odiva. You're just avoiding a confrontation with her."

"Odiva has nothing to do with us anymore. We shun her, as we shun you." Roxane draws herself taller so the tines of her antler crown tower over mine. "Leave this place, Sabine. You are never to return here."

I blink back furious tears. "I can't help who my mother is."

"You lied to us. We might have prevented what happened tonight had you told us the truth from the beginning."

A torrent of images flash to mind: Ailesse yanked into the Gate of dust, Maurille lying on the ledge with her head bleeding, thousands of terrified Unchained souls swept from Elara's peaceful realm, my mother set free, my father beside her, vicious cunning on their faces.

"Go, Sabine," Roxane says. "You are no longer a part of our *famille*."

I flinch slightly and look to Chantae and Pernelle again. They're staring at the ground, along with the other elders. My chest caves inward with terrible hurt, even as my blood rages hotter. "Cowards," I hiss, and turn my back on Roxane. I cross the courtyard to Milicent and Dolssa. "Let him go. Our people have stolen enough from him."

Without a word, Milicent and Dolssa unhand Bastien. I move toward the exiting courtyard tunnel, but he doesn't immediately follow me. First, he strides to Roxane and spits at her feet.

She returns his dark glare. "If you are ever seen near this castle again, I will command my *famille* to kill you without question."

He grins, daring her to try, and then swaggers away to join me. "Formidable Bone Criers? What a joke."

I brush away a few stray tears as we make our way outside. *I'm only angry,* I tell myself. I'm not lost or devastated or completely alone in the world now.

Bastien mumbles a string of foul words, cursing Roxane and the elders. Half of me agrees with him, but the stronger part—the deeper part I've buried all my life—can't abide it. "Stop!" I cut him off once we're outside the castle ruins.

His brows launch up. "They just banished you, Sabine. They refused to help us find Odiva. You're right. They are cowards."

"No, they're just uprooted." I finally feel a flicker of Light in me, and it helps me see reason. "Did you see their faces?" I remember what Odiva told me when she confessed she was my mother, and I repeat it to him: "'What Ferriers are tasked with demands great faith.' This treachery has just *destroyed* their faith. No *matrone* before Odiva ever betrayed our *famille*. It throws everything a Leurress must do into question—sacrificing animals for graces, sacrificing *amourés* to complete rites of passage, risking our lives to ferry the dead."

Bastien crosses his arms. "They should have questioned it, anyway."

I nod, growing thoughtful. "*I* did. It was why I never felt like one of them, why I swore to never become sensitized to bloodshed." I give a mournful laugh. "But now I have the blood of five animals on my hands, and I would have killed Casimir if it meant saving Ailesse." I stiffen and murmur, "Cas . . ."

Bastien frowns. "What about him?"

I rush along the overgrown path that leads from the castle garden to the plateau along the cliffside. "I have to find him."

Bastien tags after me. "No, we have to find Odiva."

"You find Odiva. We'll meet later and form a plan once we know where she is and what she's up to. First, I have to get to the king. Tell me where your hideout is in Dovré."

"Forget about Cas," he grumbles. "At least Ailesse is safe from their soul-bond for the time being."

"No, she isn't."

He stops in his tracks. "What do you mean? She's in the Underworld."

"Yes, but she's *alive*, Bastien." The hard line of his mouth says he doesn't question it, either. "Which means she can die. And if something terrible were to happen to Cas, she *will* die. Then we'll have no hope of saving her."

"*Merde.*" His eyes widen, and he drags his hands through his wet hair. "Sabine, last night Cas escaped my hideout after Ailesse left. He's out in the open now, walking bait for the dead dissenters you weren't able to ferry."

A wave of dizziness slams into me. "I have to get to Beau Palais." I tear away across the plateau, still in the direction of Dovré. Cas surely went home to his castle.

"Wait!" Bastien races after me but quickly falls behind. He can't keep up with my nighthawk speed. "King Godart is probably headed straight there!" he shouts.

"All the more reason for me to hurry!" I call back to him.

I set my jaw like Ailesse would and run faster. I have to protect Casimir.

There's no saving my sister if she loses her soul.

24
Ailesse

I RACE ALONGSIDE SABINE, WAVING my hands in front of her face. "Look at me!" She doesn't turn, doesn't blink. Her hazy image streaks at the edges, like a candle's flame when stared at for too long. Everything around me has that same smeared appearance—the wild grass along the plateau, the clouds pulling away from the full moon, the ruins of Château Creux behind us. But when I glance down at myself, my hands and dress are crisp in my vision. They're also a strange color I've never seen before, nothing like *chazoure*.

"Play the flute again!" I cry, keeping pace with Sabine as she runs faster. I don't need my crutch anymore. My shattered knee feels whole. I'm able to use my peregrine falcon's full speed. Maybe

Sabine unwittingly shared her graces with me, like she shared them with Bastien, when we formed the channel between the Gates. Or maybe bones don't stay broken when you're dead. "Open the Gates again! Try anywhere! Try here!" We're on solid earth, not a bridge of any kind, but I'm desperate. "Please, Sabine, I have to come back!"

She remains focused on the east, toward Beau Palais and Casimir. He must be there if he escaped his bonds in Bastien's quarry room.

Tears pool in my sister's eyes. It's easy to guess what she's feeling. I know her better than I know myself. I always have. She believes she's to blame for losing me. She's guilt ridden over Maurille's death, my mother's escape from the Underworld, King Godart's resurrection, and all the Unchained who were stolen from Paradise.

I touch her arm, but she doesn't feel me, just like Bastien didn't feel me when I sat beside him on the cavern ledge and tried to comfort him. That's when my panic set in. Until that moment, alone beside him, I'd watched everything happen to him and Sabine and the Ferriers in shocked silence. And although I was horrified, I felt strangely removed from it all. I didn't realize I was in the Underworld—I thought I'd evaded the Gate of dust—until Bastien went on ignoring me on the ledge, even when I wept and cursed and screamed for him to stop playing games.

The plateau merges into forestland. I don't see any signs of the places that should exist in Tyrus's realm—no bloodred scalding river or scorching Perpetual Sands or smoke and ash from the Furnace of Justice. Only familiar trees and deer trails surround me. I don't understand. Did I really make it to the Underworld, or am I caught somewhere in between?

My panic flares, bearing down on my ribs and squeezing my heart tight. But it doesn't beat faster. I can't feel my pulse at all. I cry out at the top of my lungs, but don't have to catch my breath afterward. My voice echoes on and on, though it shouldn't reverberate in these woods. Maybe everything I've been taught about the Underworld is all lies, and Tyrus creates a personal hell for each soul he snares here.

I dart faster to keep up with Sabine and tug at her arm, though it doesn't jostle. "Please, bring me back! You have the flute. Why won't you even try?" She doesn't bat an eye at me.

Think, Ailesse. No Leurress has ever been able to open the Gates once they're closed. Sabine will have to wait until the next ferrying night. Calm yourself and be patient.

I stifle a whimper. That's impossible. I'll be driven to madness before the next ferrying night. The new moon won't come for another fourteen days.

A guttural and masculine voice calls out, "You are forbidden in this sphere."

I startle and jerk around. Several yards away, I glimpse a spark of *chazoure*. A man. He rushes behind a wide trunk and hides as heavy footsteps thump nearer, radiating from where the voice came from. If Sabine heard it, she makes no indication and keeps racing eastward. I stop following her. I creep closer to the tree backlit with *chazoure*.

"The Chained belong to Tyrus," the guttural voice continues.

"It is best not to attempt escaping your fate. The god of the Underworld does not look kindly on cowards."

Fifteen yards away, the man who is speaking stalks into view. I slip behind a low-lying branch. He's lit with the same strange color I'm glowing with, and he's a blacksmith, by all appearances. A studded leather apron is draped over his bare chest, and he wears matching wrist cuffs and tall boots. Instead of sooty grime, he's dirty with smudges of *chazoure*. It's smeared across his face, neck, and trousers.

"Any last words before you meet your master?" the blacksmith asks, his short-cropped hair rustling in an eerie breeze that affects only him and me. The ends of my hair and my skirt also billow like I'm underwater. "A show of bravery might make a small difference. Pleading for your chains to be removed won't. I forged them myself, and nothing that exists among the damned has the power to break them."

The hiding soul is quiet for a moment, and then he steps out from behind the tree, his hands clasped in prayer. Chains band diagonally across his tunic like a shameful sash. "I will do anything, kind sir, if you'll only help me. You have a sledgehammer and a sharp chisel on your belt there. Surely there is something you can do."

The blacksmith sighs, a weary and angry rattle from his chest that feels ancient, though he looks to be only ten years older than me. "I can deliver justice, nothing more," he says, and draws the hammer from his belt. He swings it overhead with both hands and slams it against the ground.

Boom!

The thunderous sound ripples in waves throughout the forest. I expect the earth to shake or the trees to topple, but not even a leaf stirs. Only the Chained man trembles. "What have you done?" he asks.

The blacksmith stands tall, his muscled arms flexed from exertion. He doesn't answer. He backs away slowly from the ground he just struck.

Muffled yips and howls rise from below. Sharp claws break through the surface, but they don't disturb the dirt. A pointed canine face emerges next and bares its fangs. I stare, astonished. It's a golden jackal. I've never seen one myself, but its image is engraved in the courtyard of Château Creux.

A few feet away from the jackal, another fanged mouth tears up from the ground, then another one nearby. In a few short seconds, a total of six jackals dig their way up and surround the Chained man. He tries to run, but they herd him in, circling closer, their jaws foaming, their eyes glowing red.

The largest jackal snarls and lunges for the man's neck. The others ambush him, too. They snatch at his limbs and *chazoure* clothes with their teeth. My stomach lurches. The man's horrified scream grates on my ears, but I do nothing to intervene. I've trained all my life to deliver the Chained through the Gates of the Underworld . . . though maybe I would have thought twice about it if I'd witnessed what happened here on the other side.

The jackals drag the man through the unseen portal in the ground. The last part of him I see is his tensed and outstretched hand before it's also sucked away.

The blacksmith exhales and slides his hammer back into the loop on his belt. I expect him to stomp away, but he turns. He looks directly at me.

I can thank Bastien for teaching me the first word that drops off my tongue. "*Merde.*"

The blacksmith narrows his glowing eyes and strides in my direction. I don't hide. I don't run. I find the girl in me who dove into a lagoon to kill a tiger shark, and I square my shoulders. Cowardice is a crime, wherever I am. I will not let it mark me.

When he's three feet away, his stern gaze lowers to the pouch of grace bones around my neck. "Watch yourself in this place, Leurress," he grumbles. "I am all-seeing . . ." Another soul-weary sigh escapes him, but his brows form a hardened line. "Whether I wish it or not."

He walks past me without stopping and travels deeper into the forest.

I stare after him, my mouth unhinged. "Wait!" I blurt. "What do you mean? Watch myself *how?*"

His heavy boots stop. He turns and regards me, his jaw muscle tight. "There is one rule in this realm of the Underworld, girl: no intervening in matters of life and death." He wipes a smear of *chazoure* onto his sleeve before he swaggers away. "It isn't too late for you to form chains."

25

Bastien

I LOWER MYSELF DOWN THE scaffolding to my quarry room and find Marcel and Birdine on their knees, brushing up shattered pieces of my father's figurines. Marcel looks at me and pushes his floppy hair out of his eyes. "Oh, hello there." He flashes a half smile. "We were hoping to have this cleaned up before you got back."

"I told Marcel we should wait," Birdine adds, eyeing me nervously. Her frizzy ginger hair is pulled up in a knot on the top of her head. She wears it like that when she takes a bath in the pool of groundwater off one of the tunnels below. "We know how particular you are about these statues."

"But I told Birdie not to worry." Marcel fidgets with the

decapitated head of the earth goddess. "I said you'd be more angry that Cas escaped." He turns to her. "That's what I said, didn't I?"

"Mm-hmm." Her rosy complexion flushes scarlet. "And I'm awfully sorry about that, Bastien. I didn't realize His Majesty was up here all alone."

Marcel reaches into his pocket. "Seems he got ahold of one of Birdie's hairpins, too." He pulls it out. "We found this by his open shackles. He must have used it to pick the lock."

He chuckles until Birdine shoots him a murderous glare. "I have no idea how he pinched it off me," she says. "Who knew the king was a proper thief?"

I doubt he is. It wouldn't have been so hard to filch a pin. Birdine is always fussing with her hair, and she was usually the one to get Cas something to eat.

I slowly walk into the room and pick up my dolphin statue. I run my finger over the crack in its tail and picture my father's frantic eyes, glowing the color of the dead, and my chest pulls tight. "Cas escaped on my watch," I murmur. "Sabine is on her way to bring him back." Cas knows the way here. If they don't arrive soon, I'll go to Beau Palais and make sure she gets the job done.

"Sabine?" Marcel asks. "We haven't seen her in a while."

"I guess she's been busy," I say.

"It will be good to catch up," he replies. "I actually miss her, you know? She's a sweet girl when she's not trying to kill you."

I nod numbly and set the dolphin statue on the shelf.

Marcel brushes a few more limestone fragments off the ground. "I'm sure Ailesse will be grateful to see her, too."

Ailesse. My palm aches, and I flex my hand. She's slipping out of my grip all over again.

My eyes drift to her white chemise, folded on the floor in the corner of the room. I shuffle over and pick it up. After I brought her new clothes, she used the chemise as a pillow. I wanted so badly to sleep beside her and tuck myself around her body. Instead I gave her space and kept to the opposite wall.

I bring the chemise to my nose, and Ailesse's earth-and-flower scent fills my lungs.

"Are you all right, Bastien?" Birdine tilts her head.

I tear a piece of the chemise away, stuff it in my pocket, and harden my face. "Where's Jules? Bathing now that the pool is free for once?" Birdine flinches at the bite in my voice, and I immediately regret taking out my frustration on her. Now that I know my friends haven't been arrested, I need to leave, start searching for Odiva. I'm betting I'll find her at Beau Palais, if that's where Godart was really headed.

"Jules isn't here." Marcel stands up.

Birdine rises beside him. "We thought she was with Ailesse."

"She's not with Ailesse." I rub the back of my neck. "Dammit, Jules," I curse under my breath and hurry over to the scaffolding. It's almost dawn, which means she's been out all night. If one of the Chained attacked her again . . .

I quickly climb the ladder and call over my shoulder, "Marcel, I dropped my father's knife when I fought Cas."

"You fought the *king*?" Birdine asks, as if that's somehow more criminal than abducting him.

"It's on the floor of the quarry somewhere," I go on. "Could you try to find it for me?"

"Of course," he replies. "But what about Jules . . . Do you think she's all right?"

I open my mouth to say something reassuring—I've always tried to put on a brave face for Marcel and not shatter his optimism—but my throat runs dry. After everything I saw last night, it's hard to hope that Jules will be spared. I climb faster, my pulse racing.

I reach the tunnels and rush through them, as well as the cellar beneath the chapel, and then I push up through the hatch door. The stab wound on my back doesn't even twinge anymore. It hasn't since Sabine's graces flooded into me on the cavern bridge, though that power is gone now. I don't stop to wonder what it all means. I have to find Jules.

Turns out, I don't have to go far. As soon as I shut the hatch door and kick the tattered rug over it, a soft moan comes from the chapel. Jules is hunched over one of the weathered pews and gripping it for support. I bolt over to her. Gray morning light spills in through the boarded-up windows and shows her sickly pale face and her sweaty skin.

"*Merde*, Jules." I wrap my arm around her and help her stand.

She slowly lifts her head and squints at me. "So *now* you turn up," she says, her humor as droll as usual, despite her ragged voice.

"What happened to you? Did a Chained—?"

"I'm just tired, Bastien. I was up all night looking for you."

I frown, glancing over her again. The Jules I used to know could stay awake three nights in a row and not look as bone-weary as this. "Are you sure a Chained didn't steal any more of your Light? Some can be shiftier than others."

She snorts. "Shifty Chained . . . what a world we live in." She coughs a few times and sits on a pew. "Remember when all we had to worry about was the pact we made for revenge? Life was as simple as hunting for Bone Criers on full moons, telling Marcel to shut up if he wanted to tag along . . ."

" . . . telling you to slow down so we could keep up." I sit beside her.

She grins. "Those were the good days."

Was it good that all I lived for was the chance to stick my father's knife between the ribs of a Bone Crier? I get what Jules is saying, though. There was an easy rhythm to our lives back then. The world was smaller. We felt like we had a handle on our place in it.

"You'll never guess who I saw parading down Rue du Palais just now," she says. I wait for her to tell me, too tired to speculate. "The queen of the Leurress. Ailesse's damned mother is back." She coughs, shaking her head. "I warned Ailesse that Odiva wanted to be set free again."

My stomach sinks, and I stare down at the pew, scratching the splintering wood beneath me.

"Bastien?" Jules stiffens and touches my arm. "Ailesse didn't . . . ?"

"Yeah . . ." I laugh, though I don't know why. It's a small and miserable sound that doesn't loosen any of the tightness in my throat. "So . . . she's, uh, gone now." I dig at the pew harder. My stupid chin starts to tremble. I lock my jaw, but it doesn't help. "I was trying to hold her back, I swear to you I was. I thought I had her." I squeeze my hand into a fist. "I was so strong. I wouldn't have let her go for anything, but then . . ." My eyes burn. I drag my hand over my face.

Jules rubs my back, waiting for me to continue. Her touch is light and a little awkward, like she isn't sure how to comfort me. The two of us, we don't talk about pain.

"Then I saw him," I go on, having to choke out the words. A dry sob immediately follows. *Dammit, Bastien, don't start crying.* Jules and I never cry in front of each other, either. Staying strong and angry is what has kept us alive. I lean forward and press my forehead on the back of the pew in front of us. I can barely breathe. "He hasn't seen me in eight years, but he recognized me. He said my name."

Her fingers freeze on my back. "You . . . you saw your father?"

"Mm-hmm." My voice cracks. My face is suddenly too hot. The damn tears start falling. I can't stop them or swallow this pain. There's too much of it. "I tried to save him, too." My sobs punch through my chest. "It all happened too fast, and I . . ." I blow out a rough breath and shake my head. "I lost both of them."

Jules closes her eyes tightly, like she's reliving the moment with me. "I don't know what to say, Bastien. I'm so sorry."

I haven't felt this kind of bitter sadness since I was ten years old and I held my father after he was killed. I slid his head into my lap. I placed my hands on his cheeks. I tried to keep them warm while his skin turned cold. All night long, I cried. I thought my ribs would break.

"How did you even see him?" Jules asks. "Why was he there? I don't understand."

In broken words, I tell her everything that happened on the cavern bridge tonight—how Sabine's graces burst through me and I saw Unchained souls stolen from Paradise and taken into the Underworld, and how Odiva and King Godart came out of the Gate of dust after Ailesse and my father were pulled inside.

I slam my fist into the pew and bury my face in my hands. "I didn't even get to talk to him." My voice pitches high like a child's.

Jules pulls me into her arms and says nothing, just lets me weep against her shoulder. This is the first time I've hugged her since I met Ailesse. I didn't know how to act around her anymore, and until right now, I didn't realize how much I've missed my best friend. She's more than that. She's the person I've loved like a sister for eight years.

Her eyes are wet when I finally pull back from her. She wipes under her nose. "If you tell Marcel we were sniveling together, I'll murder you in your sleep."

I laugh. "It'll be our secret."

She holds up her pinkie finger. I grab it with mine, and we bump our elbows together, then our fists, like we did when we were thirteen.

She releases a long exhale, which sends her into a coughing fit. Once she finally stops, she clears her throat and asks, "So what do we do now?"

I sit back and rake my hands through my hair, thinking. "We reverse everything—figure out a way to get Ailesse back and return my father and all those souls to Paradise. We'll plot a way to do that after we find Odiva."

"That part's done. She was clearly headed to Beau Palais."

"And King Godart, he was with her?"

"Unless Casimir aged overnight and got a new crown."

Burning rage hits my veins. I welcome it. Anger is much more useful than sorrow. Godart is alive and kicking because he traded places with Ailesse. I vow to make him pay.

"Then we also focus on protecting Cas." I take a steadying breath. "He's got more to worry about now than dissenters and losing his Light. Godart is after his throne."

26
Ailesse

I RACE FOR BEAU PALAIS, trying to catch up to Sabine. One moment I'm in the forest near Château Creux, where I saw the blacksmith, and the next I'm at the gate of the castle. I gasp, looking behind me. The city of Dovré has the same smeared and streaked appearance as the forest, like it's a painting, not reality. But how did I get here so fast? I didn't even feel it happen.

I turn back to the castle. The gate is open. At least a dozen guards are strewn about on the ground—dead. A *chazoure* Unchained soul kneels by one of them and strokes his brow. I recognize the soul as another guard, one who was killed during the meadow viper attack. "What happened here?" I ask him.

He startles, realizing I can see him. Then my eyes widen. He can see me, too. "Two people infiltrated the castle. They claimed they were the rightful king and new queen."

I should be shocked that my mother killed these men. She was the one who taught me about the sanctity of life. A Leurress's sacred duty to protect mortals from unferried souls is why the gods charged us to sacrifice animals and kill our *amourés*. "A little death is holy if it saves mankind," she once said when she showed me the bone knife with which she had killed my father. "The gods will bless you for it."

As twisted as her words were then, they're nothing compared to what she's done these past two years—what she's still doing. "I'm so sorry," I tell the Unchained guard, feeling my mother's sins upon my own shoulders. "I'm going to stop her."

His *chazoure* brows pull together. "How?"

I don't have time to answer. As soon as I've had the thought to confront my mother, I find myself standing in the great hall of Beau Palais, the same place where I attended the feast for La Liaison with Casimir. The tables have been cleared, as well as the garlands of late-summer flowers, but the blue banners of the sun god and the green banners of the earth goddess still remain. In light of all the tragedies that have befallen this place, I imagine the people are even more devout in worshipping Belin and Gaëlle, their favored gods.

On a dais at the rear of the room, backed by a rich tapestry of Belin's sun shining over this castle, Casimir is seated on the throne and wearing his father's sapphire-embedded crown. Several of his councillors, captains, and high-ranking nobles are present, as if they were already gathered to discuss matters of great importance before my mother and Godart barged in.

I can tell by the astonished looks in the room that their entrance is fresh. Now they're walking toward the dais. I wish to gain a better look at them, and in a flash, I'm standing at the foot of the dais, close to Cas.

Godart is arrayed like a king in the clothes he must have been buried in, though none of the velvet brocade is moth-eaten. His unique crown of carved onyx feathers and rubies is a testament to his identity just as much as his unmistakable appearance. I never knew the man, but I haven't seen another like him.

Sabine's beauty is apparent in his facial structure and his rich brown eyes, which shine gold when the light hits them. But it isn't Godart's looks that set him apart; it's his countenance. His power. It's the subtle yet dynamic way he holds his broad shoulders perfectly square, along with the puff of his chest and the upward tilt of his chin. The only other person I've seen with that breathtaking bearing is my mother. It's no small surprise that they found each other.

While I'm awestruck by Godart, many in the great hall seem more captivated by my mother. They ogle her asp viper vertebrae and the giant noctule bat skull that form her bone crown, as well as the other claws, talons, and bones that dangle from her tiers of necklaces and feather epaulettes.

When they're ten feet away from the dais, Godart and my mother stop. They do not bow. "Casimir Trencavel," Godart says, his deep and commanding voice resonating into the vaulted ceiling, "you are seated on my throne."

To Cas's credit, he doesn't betray any fear. He doesn't even sit taller in a show of dominance, though I know him well enough to recognize that his cool grin means false bravado. "This is my father's throne and my father's castle. What claim do you have upon it?"

"I am Godart Lothaire, King of South Galle."

"Godart Lothaire died fifteen years ago, the same year the great plague fell upon the land. Some say he brought that curse upon us."

"You brought the curse upon yourself," my mother declares.

Cas's stone-blue eyes cut to her. He taps his fingers on his armrest. "And who are you?" He knows very well who she is. Last month he saw her stab Bastien on the soul bridge and leap through the Gates of the Underworld.

My mother's bloodred lips curve upward. She looks feline and hungry, like she's playing with a field mouse. "I am Odiva, and I will be your queen." I don't understand why she cares about ruling a small nation, except that it means she can live her life with Godart. She once ruled a powerful *famille* of Leurress. She must have some ulterior motive.

Cas's nostrils flare, and a tremor runs through his brow. Odiva has struck a nerve. The last queen of South Galle was his beloved mother. "My father was one of the nobles who laid the late king to rest," Cas says to Godart. "Before you make a play for my throne, you will have to prove that men can be raised from the dead."

Godart steadies his hand on the pommel of his sheathed broadsword. "I never died."

A derisive laugh escapes me, but no one except the *chazoure* souls collecting in the room hear the sound.

"Open my tomb, if you do not believe me," Godart goes on. "You will find it empty."

Cas's brows harden. "My father buried—"

"Durand *said* he buried me, but he lied. And he and the nobles who helped him steal my throne by stratagem are all dead now."

Cas shakes his head, tightening his fists on the armrest. "My father was never part of any coup. This is another claim you cannot prove."

"Look to the history of Dovré. When your father usurped me, the gods cursed the land with the great plague." Godart turns to face those assembled in the room. "And now that his son is on the throne, another plague has descended. There is your proof. Tyrus does not support the Trencavel dynasty. The god of the Underworld has power over life and death, and he has punished South Galle and killed the men responsible for overthrowing me. And he will continue to punish all of you if you do not honor your true king."

The people in the great hall erupt in heated conversation. Chained souls whisper to some of the living, and my mother's eyes follow them. I stiffen when her gaze drifts toward me, but then it passes by without the slightest pause. She doesn't see me. I'm not *chazoure* like the other dead. My shoulders relax a little, but then I notice Godart's eyes also trail some of the Chained. Is he sharing my mother's graces the same way Bastien shared Sabine's? How is it possible? I presumed the Gates to the Beyond had to be opened and channeled together for that to happen.

Cas rises from his throne and lifts his hands to quiet everyone, though only some comply. "If what you say is true, then where have you been these last fifteen years?" he asks Godart. "Why did you wait until now to make a claim for your throne?"

Godart pivots back to him but doesn't answer. For a small moment, I feel pity for the man. He waited until now to reclaim his throne because he was dead. And he died because he loved my mother and the gods punished him for it. His fate wasn't fair.

"You're an imposter," Cas scoffs. "You're playing on people's fears to gain power that isn't yours. I've heard enough. Guards, seize this man and woman at once."

Only seven of the thirteen guards present step forward. Cas's friend and captain, Briand, is among them.

The seven men slowly close in around my mother and Godart, who stand their ground. "I'll show you power," Godart says, "power given to me by Tyrus himself—his gift for being his chosen king and loyal servant." Again, I feel a twinge of sympathy. As a dedicated Leurress, how long did I pride myself on being Tyrus's loyal servant, too?

Three of the guards raise their swords. Godart swiftly draws his broadsword. He cuts the arm off one man with a powerful stroke and leaps over the second. I gape. My sympathy vanishes. Before that man can turn to defend himself, Godart stabs him in the back.

My mouth remains unhinged. He *is* sharing my mother's graces. The third man slices his arm. Godart actually leans into the blade, hissing as it bites deeper, and yanks the sword from the large man's grip. Then Godart crosses both blades at the man's neck and decapitates him. The man's head thuds to the floor and rolls to the foot of the dais, streaking a bloody path.

The people gasp. A nobleman faints. The Chained circle like vultures. I stare in horror, my heart pounding, though I'm not short of breath. How can Godart be gentle Sabine's father? His time in the Underworld has turned him monstrous.

Cas strides off the dais, his face red with rage. "My sword," he commands his guards. They pull back. No one attacks Godart again or hands Cas a weapon. Cas looks to his captain. "Damn you, Briand, give me a sword!"

"Don't do it!" I tell Briand. Cas has no chance against five graces—six, with Sabine's salamander skull. Godart must be siphoning its power to heal, because his wounded arm is barely bleeding now. I still don't understand how he's accessing the graces. Even the women in my *famille* can't share one another's power like that. When each Leurress ritually kills an animal, she has to press her own blood onto its bone. That petitions Tyrus to imbue it with the animal's power—power that can then only be drawn upon by the Leurress with that blood.

As Briand deliberates, I spy the blacksmith from the forest at the fringe of the assembly. He's leaning against a towering column. *When did he arrive?* He isn't watching Godart and Cas; he's watching me. His grip tightens around the handle of his sledgehammer.

Briand finally tosses Cas his sword. Cas catches it by the hilt. He faces Godart. "Too afraid to fight your king with one sword?"

Godart smirks and drops his second blade. "And you, boy? Too timid to strike first?"

The muscles clench along Cas's jawline. He strides forward purposefully.

"Stop, Cas!" I bolt toward him. "If you die, Godart will rule." *If you die, then I'm really dead, too. I'll never be able to come back.* "You can't defeat him like this! He's too powerful."

Cas doesn't hear me. He raises his sword and swings for the left side of Godart's neck, but at the last moment, his blade snaps around and strikes low for Godart's right leg instead. Godart blocks the hit and drives Cas's sword away with my mother's eagle owl speed. She observes without interference. Godart must need to prove himself to his people, or surely she would display her formidable skills for herself.

Godart slashes his sword three times, driving Cas backward. "Will Belin or Gaëlle not lend your their power?" he taunts him. "You have paid them great tribute with this castle. Their colors and symbols can be found everywhere the eye turns."

Cas stumbles, forced to back onto the dais. Godart hops onto it as well. He swings his sword overhead and brings it down toward Cas's head. Cas narrowly dodges it. The blade hacks into the gold-plated wood of the throne.

"It is no wonder Tyrus is angry with you," Godart continues. "You and the people of Dovré have neglected him and his bride in your worship. When I rule from Beau Palais, I will right that wrong. I will drape these halls in black and silver and bring balance back to the land."

"You will curse us." Cas feints for Godart's thigh, then quickly swings for his arm. Godart is surprised by the move, but he's faster than Cas. He spins aside before the blade strikes. So far he's only been sporting with Cas. I dread when he fights in earnest. Cas will be killed as quickly as his guards were. As will I. I have to do something to help, even though I still feel the blacksmith's eyes on me.

Godart rakes his hair out of his face, adjusts his grip on his sword, and grins, flashing his teeth. "Now I end your rule, young king. Now I take back what is mine."

He stalks toward Cas. The heavy throne is between them. With a powerful sweep of his leg, Godart kicks it aside. The throne slams against the back wall.

Desperate, I look for the Unchained in the room and find five souls: three deceased castle guards, a maidservant, and a noblewoman. "Help him!" I cry. Unlike me, they can exert tangible force. They can intervene. "You must have loved ones still alive in South Galle. Do you see what kind of ruler Godart will be? You have to stop him before he kills Casimir!"

The blacksmith frowns at me and unhitches himself from the column.

Godart raises his broadsword and charges at Cas.

"Please!" I shout.

The Unchained rush toward Godart. They leap on Godart's back, grab his sword arm, and slow his blade just enough that Cas is able to block it with his own. Even then, he's knocked down from the force. He rolls aside when Godart's sword comes crashing down again. The five souls are barely thwarting his strength.

The Chained in the room race forward to fend off the Unchained. My mother joins them. Cas's loyal guards spring after her. The blacksmith steadily strides in my direction.

Panic consumes me. I have to get Cas out of here. I frantically look around. There's a gap at the back of the dais, between the platform and the wall. It's just large enough for Cas to squeeze through—and Godart is backing him against that wall now.

I catch the maidservant's attention. "Tell Cas to slip behind the dais and escape. Tell him he must leave Beau Palais. Sabine is on her way here. She will help him find safety."

The maidservant's *chazoure* eyes narrow, determined. She darts over to Cas and whispers what I've told her. "Who are you?" he hisses, unable to see her. He dodges another strike from Godart, who's also wrestling two Unchained guards. "How do you know Sabine?"

I hurry closer. "Tell him Ailesse sent you."

She repeats my words. Cas frowns. He doesn't know what's happened to me, but he *does* know I can see the dead.

Cas's captain, Briand, joins the fight against Godart. The maidservant springs to help them, lashing out with her fists.

Cas slips though the gap behind the hollow dais. A few seconds later, he crawls out again at the front, through its velvet draping. He just misses my mother, who steps onto the dais right before he exits. She charges through the madness, tossing people and souls aside as deftly as she did while ferrying. She reaches Godart and demands, "Where has he gone? Have you let him escape?"

Godart knocks away Briand's sword and yanks back the

captain's arm. His bones snap, and he howls in pain. Godart shoves him aside and scans the dais. "He was here mere moments ago!"

Relief courses through me as I watch Cas sneak out of the great hall. I race after him, wanting to be there when he finds Sabine. But I have only made it to the courtyard when the blacksmith steps in my path. I freeze. He has his sledgehammer raised.

"I warned you," he growls, his mouth set in a stern, unforgiving line.

"Yes, but—"

He grabs my left wrist before I can finish speaking. Then, just as swiftly, he lets go and stalks away.

I stare after him and reach for my wrist to rub it. But instead of warm skin, I feel cool metal.

I look down and go rigid. There's a cuff there—one round, perfect link.

The blacksmith has given me a chain.

27
Sabine

THE GREAT LIMESTONE WALLS OF Beau Palais come into view as I race closer to Dovré. I take the road that leads through Castelpont, not one of the main thoroughfares to the city. This way is faster and less traveled. Once I crest the high arch of the ancient bridge, I spy someone running in my direction from the path that curves around the city wall. *Casimir?*

I stop short. I thought I was going to have to break into Beau Palais, no matter who saw me, and force him to leave. I expected to have to fight off several guards, too. But Cas is alone.

He catches sight of me from forty yards away. I glimpse his eyebrows lift, with my keen vision, but then hard lines crease his forehead. He glances over his shoulder and motions me away, even as he sprints toward me. Is someone chasing him?

I don't run away. I prepare to fight so Cas can flee to safety. That's why I came here—to protect him in order to protect Ailesse.

"Get off the bridge, Sabine!" he shouts, coming nearer. He's holding a bundle of cloth in his arms. "Soldiers are searching for me. We need to hide in the forest."

"Soldiers?" I stare at him. "But—"

"I was usurped."

My stomach drops. "King Godart?"

"How did you . . . ? Never mind. Hurry!"

He reaches me, and we run together off the bridge and into the trees. I pick up the sound of tramping boots and distant shouts. We have a head start, but Cas doesn't have my graced speed. Plus, the ground is muddy from the recent rainfall. It won't be hard for the soldiers to follow our trail. We need to get to the Mirvois River, where we can travel through the water without leaving tracks.

"This way!" I take the lead, racing westward through the forest. Cas follows me without a word. I try not to question his willingness. When did we become allies?

About a mile later, the roar of the river reaches my ears. I adjust our direction to take a shortcut. I can still hear the soldiers a quarter mile behind us.

A gully appears. I can leap the twelve feet, but Cas will have to cross it by a fallen tree that bridges the gap. I point it out to him, and he nods, prepared.

On second thought, I decide to cross it with him. If he slips, I can hoist him up before he falls the twenty feet. We keep running.

We're three feet from the fallen tree when I yelp as the edge of the mud-slick gully breaks away. I plummet. Cas grasps my hand, but I only drag him down with me.

We cling to each other as we slide down the tumbling mud and earth. Seconds later, we crash into the shallow stream below, scraping into it on our backs.

Neither of us moves for a moment. We're lying side by side in a bed of mud. We slowly turn to each other, gasping for breath. His stony eyes look more vividly blue with all the mud caked on his face. The thought pops into my mind that if I were with Ailesse, we would burst into laughter, and then my own laughter bubbles up my throat. I try to suppress it—this shouldn't be funny, especially after all the terrible things that have happened in the last twenty-four hours—but resisting it only makes me snort. I fall into a fit of giggles.

Cas isn't amused. Not at first, anyway. But when I point at him and say, "You should see yourself," his composure cracks.

He shakes his head and starts chuckling. "You're deranged, do you know that?" I nod and laugh harder. A smile splits across his face and makes his teeth gleam. "I think we're both deranged."

I exhale a heavy breath that lands between a groan and a sigh. "Well, being usurped can do that."

He echoes my groan. "True. And what is your excuse?"

"Lack of sleep," I answer tritely, then look away, staring up into the moody blue sky. The storms are gone for now, but the bruised color of the clouds promises they'll be back again. "There's more to blame than sleep," I confess, my voice more sober now. "I was usurped, too." I bite my lip. "It was harder than I expected. I suppose I wasn't ready for another blow right after losing my sister."

When I meet Cas's eyes again, his smile is gone. His brow furrows as he studies me. "You lost Ailesse? How do you mean?"

I don't know where to begin. How much does he even know about the Leurress? "Do you remember how my mother jumped through that swirling black dust at the end of the cavern bridge?" He nods. "That was the Gates of the Underworld, and Ailesse . . ." I swallow hard. "She's there now. My mother tricked her into trading places."

Cas sits up, agitated. "But she can come back, right? Your mother did."

"I hope so." I sit up, too. "But I'm not really sure how my mother accomplished that." At any rate, I have no intention of sacrificing souls, if that was Odiva's method.

He grows thoughtful, gazing around us at the sparkling stream and the dragonflies skipping across the water's surface. "We'll find a way, Sabine. Ailesse is closer than we realize." He looks at me and closes one eye against the brightness of the sun. "She helped me escape Beau Palais."

I frown. "What?"

"She told me how to leave, and that I should look for you afterward."

My pulse kicks faster. "I don't understand. Did you hear her voice?"

"No, it was another girl's voice, but she said Ailesse sent her."

I'm about to reply when the soldiers' boots thump above, squelching through the mud. I hold a finger to my lips and point to the top of the gully. Cas quickly rises and offers his hand. I don't need his strength to help me up, but I grasp his fingers anyway. They're warm, and his grip is confident. My stomach flutters. It's hopefulness, I tell myself. If Ailesse found a way to communicate with him, then there's reason to believe she really is nearby and still retrievable. *I will get her back again.*

Cas and I tuck against the muddy wall of the gully. There isn't time to run without being seen. A moment later, I hear a soldier say, "They've gone into the stream to hide their tracks."

"They're moving toward the river," another one replies.

They set off in that direction, their footfalls fading as they follow the path of the stream from above. We wait until they're far gone before we step out into the open again. I hold my antler crown in place so the muddy wall doesn't suck it off my head. I feel ridiculous. I really need to rearrange my grace bones into a necklace soon.

Cas trudges across the stream and picks up the cloth bundle he brought. He must have dropped it when we fell. "What is that?" I ask.

"My father's crown." He unwraps it. He moves to where the stream runs with clean water and kneels, washing some of the mud off the gold. "What would he think of me if he could see me now?" He sighs. "I couldn't even rule his kingdom for more than a day."

I drift over and sit beside him in the stream. I begin rinsing out the skirt of my dress. "If it makes you feel any better, no king would have been able to prevent what happened today, no matter how long he had ruled." I scratch at a faded stain, the red stag's blood. "I'm guessing my mother was with Godart?"

Cas nods.

"She has five grace bones." I pause. "Grace bones are what give a Leurress—"

"I know what grace bones are." He dips his crown in the water. "Ailesse explained a little, and I learned a lot more after she and her friends took me prisoner."

I give him a pained smile. They haven't given him an easy time, and between threatening to kill him at the cavern bridge and releasing meadow vipers on Beau Palais, I haven't either.

"What I don't understand is how Godart is just as powerful as your mother," he says.

I consider that. "She must be sharing her graces with him. I'm not sure how it's done, but somehow I shared mine with Bastien on the cavern bridge, too."

Cas's brows slowly rise. "Huh." It's a subtle reaction, considering how bizarre all the mysteries of my life must be to him. "Well, perhaps you could figure out how to do that again."

"Perhaps," I reply, even though I highly doubt it. It was probably my mother's dark magic that bled into us from the chain of our joined hands.

Cas goes back to cleaning his father's crown. I watch him quietly for a moment, captivated by the way the sunlight glints against his eyelashes.

"Do you think . . . ?" I twist my dress in the water, unsure why my heart is beating faster. "Do you think you and I can begin again?"

He stops rubbing and lifts his eyes to me. Even with mud smeared through his loose strawberry curls and down his face and neck, he's as handsome as he was when I first met him at Castelpont, when I wondered if he could be my *amouré* instead of Ailesse's.

Heat flushes my cheeks, and my nerves flare like they do when I'm in danger. *Is this danger I'm feeling?* I hated Cas for abducting Ailesse. I didn't care that he thought he was saving her. But now . . . well, I don't hate him anymore.

"We have more in common than you think," I go on, nervous that he hasn't said anything. "You're meant to rule South Galle, even though it first belonged to King Godart. And I'm meant to rule my *famille*, even though Ailesse was the first heir." As soon as the words are out of my mouth, I catch myself. Do I really believe I'm meant to be *matrone*? "We're also both determined to overthrow my mother and father."

Cas blinks, and then his eyes widen. "Wait, King Godart is your *father*?"

I shrug. "I only found out yesterday. My mother sort of resurrected him."

He shakes his head slowly and gives a droll laugh. "Is it strange that I find that comforting? It makes a lot more sense than the story he told me. Godart claimed my father falsified his death in order to seize his throne."

"Oh, Cas . . ." Shame spools inside me, even though I can't help who my father is. "I'm so sorry."

"You realize what this means, don't you?" He arches a brow. "You and I are rivals."

I frown. "Why?"

"You should be ruling more than your *famille*, Sabine. By all rights, you're also the heir of South Galle."

I scoff and roll my eyes.

"I think we're going to have to duel now," he adds.

I smirk. "You know I'd kill you, right?"

"I know." He chuckles.

We smile at each other for a long moment. Warmth slips into my chest and settles there, despite how conscious I am of my mud-drenched appearance.

Cas washes his hand in the water and then offers it to me. I don't think mine will ever be clean again, but I give it to him anyway. He shakes it, and his right cheek dimples. "This is us starting over, Sabine."

"So we're friends now?" I grin.

His thumb brushes over the back of my hand, and I find myself holding my breath. "We're friends."

28
Ailesse

I STAND AT THE BANK of the stream, watching Sabine and Cas wash the mud from their clothes. Sabine has already rinsed her face clean. Her cheeks have a pretty flush from the cool water—and maybe from the way Cas keeps catching her eye and softly grinning at her. I don't mind that he is, I realize.

The separation I'm experiencing from the life I led is already shining more clarity on it. When I look at Cas, I'm not conflicted by what I should or shouldn't be feeling for him. I see him more objectively now, not as my *amouré*, but as a sweet and wise boy who seems to be taking a tentative interest in my sister.

A wistful smile tugs at the corners of my mouth. What I would give to forget all my troubles and steal a moment alone with Sabine.

I would tease her that she's starting to like Cas. She'd deny it until I teased her harder and made her confess. It would be like old times, back when we hid off the road and watched travelers come and go from the city, stifling our giggles as we imagined what their lives were like . . . wondering what *ours* would be like if they were so magically ordinary.

The daydream fades as I look down at the cuff around my left wrist. I yank at it, trying to slip it off my hand, but the band is wide, tight fitted, and hard like iron. Its color isn't *chazoure*, like the chains of the souls I've ferried; instead, it's the new and strange color that the rest of me glows with. I thought the jackals would come for me after the blacksmith marked me, but I haven't even heard a distant howl. Still, a chain link can't be a good thing.

My sixth sense shivers up my right arm, and I turn in that direction. The blacksmith has reappeared, and he's with a beautiful woman who looks as timeless as him, neither young nor old. They're several yards away and standing along the same bank downstream. If the blacksmith were alone, I might be more nervous, but the woman's presence is calming and somehow familiar. Her long and waving hair is loosely braided and pulled in front of her shoulder. It's the same color I am, and the same color as her eyes and skin and all the rest of her.

The blacksmith and the woman stand close together, but not touching. He whispers something to her, and she leans nearer to him. He pulls away slightly as a lock of her hair slips out of her braid and wisps toward his face. They must be talking about me, because they both meet my eyes at the same time, even though I haven't moved or made a sound.

The woman nods at the blacksmith, and I hear her words when she murmurs, "I will see to it." They share a parting glance that lingers, weighted with a yearning that feels ancient and almost tangible. The blacksmith throws me a stern gaze and walks away while the woman walks toward me. I drift closer to her as well. She has answers about this place; I can sense wisdom behind her lovely eyes.

The bank is narrow where we meet, so we stand in the stream. The water rushes over my shoes and her bare feet, but it doesn't part around us like it would around a rock. We have no effect on it whatsoever. The woman glances over me. She doesn't smile, but her expression doesn't pass judgment, either. Soft locks of hair float around her face in the illusionary breeze that also stirs my own hair and dress, and her posture is both elegant and relaxed. "Forgeron told me we had another Leurress in our midst," she says.

"Another one?" I frown. "Oh . . . you must have met my mother when she was here."

She nods, searching my eyes.

"I'm not like my mother," I add, fidgeting with my fingers behind my back.

"Perhaps not in all ways." Her head tilts. "Your mother was at least clever enough not to earn one of those." She gestures at the cuff around my wrist, and I cover it with my hand. A small grin lights upon her mouth and curves the edges of her full upper lip. "I have two of them," she confesses, and holds up her arms. The long sleeves of her dress fall back and reveal a cuff on each wrist. Hers are the same size and color as mine, but they're also beautifully engraved with flowers and scrollwork. "They feel a part of me now. I have had them for centuries."

Centuries? My chest sinks.

Her grin deepens. "My name is Estelle, and I am also a Leurress, the first of our kind."

I feel my eyes grow round. "You mean the first Leurress *ever born*, the Leurress born in a beam of silver moonlight between the Night Heavens and the Underworld—that was *you?*"

"In reality, I *fell* from the Night Heavens *into* the beam of silver moonlight." Her shoulders tremble with silent laughter. "But yes, that was me."

I openly stare at her. "How did you—? Why—? This is no place for . . ." I try to compose myself. "You should be in Paradise, not here." I shift on my feet. "Where *is* here?"

She meanders down the stream. "Walk with me, Ailesse."

She knows my name? I glance behind me at Sabine and Cas. They're deep in conversation, and more important, safe for the time being. I inhale a breath I don't need and follow after Estelle.

As soon as I reach her side, the landscape changes. We're no longer in the gully, but walking along the shore of the Nivous Sea. Tall limestone cliffs rise behind us, and the water laps at the glittering sand. "Do you know this place?" Estelle asks.

I take a closer look around me. The cliffs surround us on all sides but one. Out beyond the distant waves, I spy sea stacks and jagged rocks. Everything still has that hazy and streaked-edge appearance that I'm becoming more accustomed to, but other than that, where I am is the same as I remember. "This is the inlet where the land bridge surfaces at low tide," I reply. I've never seen it in the daylight. It's still beautiful, but far less mystical than it was when I stood on the cliffs above here on the night of the new moon.

"You are correct," Estelle says. "We are in the Miroir, the threshold of the Underworld, and all that surrounds us is the same as it is in the mortal world, only we are not a part of it."

I try to absorb this. "Is that why I'm this color?" I touch my face.

She nods. "*Orvande* is the shade of those who are trapped here, even though they have no chains. Or in our case, those who have not experienced death."

I raise my brows. "You haven't died either?"

She shakes her head, gently kicking her pointed toe through the sand, although the grains don't shift beneath her. "I came here when Forgeron did."

"The blacksmith? Is that his name?"

"It is his title. I fear he has forgotten his name. He forbids anyone to use it."

"Why?" I can't keep my questions from tumbling out.

"Names are the song of the soul. They hold Elara's Light and help us channel it." Estelle tips her head back, as if to bask in the sunlight, but the sun is behind a cloud at the moment. The waning moon, no longer quite full, is a faded footprint in the sky, and when I concentrate, I also feel its muted energy siphoning into me. "Light is scarce and precious in the Miroir," Estelle says, "so we take great care with it. If we use it to help a living person, we will be punished."

I consider the *orvande* cuff around my wrist again. "But I didn't use Light to save Casimir. I don't even know how to use Light. It's just a part of me."

"You used Light last month on the cavern bridge," Estelle counters, and I think back on the first time I discovered that place. "Your grace bones were taken away, yet you still found the strength to fight your mother. I was there," she adds, noting the surprised look I give her. "I watch all ferrying nights of the founding *famille*. You are my descendants."

Growing more awestruck by everything she tells me, I'm not sure how to respond. I follow her as she wades thigh-deep in the sea and trails her fingers through the water. It doesn't stir at her touch. Her dress doesn't swirl from the current, either, but she smiles all the same, as if imagining what it feels like gives her enough satisfaction.

I finally find my voice. "If I used Light to fight my mother, I did it by accident, the same as I did with Casimir today. I shouldn't have been punished." I do my best not to sound petulant. I just don't want Estelle to be disappointed in me. She's the first Leurress, the mother of all of us.

"The laws are strict in the Miroir," she says. "Remember, this is part of the Underworld. I have been punished for far less than what you have done, Ailesse. Any interference in the mortal world is forbidden, whether or not you use Light. Because you still found a way to help Casimir, Forgeron was compelled to give you your first chain link."

I picture the sullen blacksmith I keep crossing paths with. "You make it sound like he didn't have a choice."

She lifts a shoulder. "He believes he doesn't, and perhaps that is true. His duty is his curse, you see. He is the man who wraps all sinners in chains. It has been so for countless ages, ever since his mother and father banished him here for loving me."

I halt, instinctively bracing myself against a large wave, but of course it only washes over me without a jostle or even wetting my hair. "Forgeron is your *amouré?*"

Estelle sighs, as if that word is upsetting, and she shakes her head. "Your *amourés* did not exist in my time. The four gods resolved to introduce the tradition after what became of Forgeron and me. We were the first star-crossed lovers. He was the son of Belin and Gaëlle, and I was the daughter of Tyrus and Elara."

"Was?"

She considers me. "I suppose they are still our parents." I stay in step with her as she wanders back to the shore. "We haven't seen them in many ages, so it is difficult to think of them as family anymore."

I recall what I know of the four gods. At the dawn of time, Tyrus and Elara married in secret against the will of the supreme god, Belin, and as punishment he separated their kingdoms. He cast Heaven into the night sky, and Gaëlle opened her earth to swallow Hell. "So because Belin was still angry with your parents, he cursed his own son to live here forever, and to be the man who forges chains—all because Forgeron loved you?"

"The wrath of a god is no small thing."

"Well, it isn't fair."

A soft laugh escapes her. "I have stopped worrying over what is fair and what is not."

I marvel at the serenity on her beautiful face. "Is that how you've found contentment here, because at least you can be with Forgeron?"

"Is it contentment?" She purses her lips. "I am not sure. I *imagine* joy in this place with the only man I have ever loved. That is what carries me."

Pity stirs within my chest, the kind that would squeeze my heart, if my heart could be pained here. "I'm sorry that all you can do is imagine." I've barely spent any time in the Miroir, and already the inability to speak with Sabine and Bastien is unbearable. "I don't know how other souls tolerate it."

"They are not supposed to. Tyrus designed his threshold to be the first stage of eternal suffering. The Miroir is a mockery of life, you see, a place where you can look upon the world you left behind, but you cannot act upon it, like the blessed can in Paradise."

A dozen questions spring to mind, but before I can ask any, Estelle shifts directions in the sand. The moment I turn with her, our surroundings change. Now we're standing on the rickety wooden bridge in the forest, overlooking the river where I saw the silver owl. "This is where Bastien asked you what you would choose for your life if you weren't born to be the *matrone* of your *famille*." She leans over the railing to gaze at the glistening water.

I glance at the hole in the bridge I fell through, and the memory of the river's coolness trickles back to me, though I can't quite grasp the feeling again. "I remember," I murmur, and close my eyes, trying to recapture the sensation of kissing Bastien one last time before I told him we should just be friends. I was terrified to pull away from him like that, but I felt more desperate to be free—of *something* in my life. And I didn't know how to be free of who I was born to be.

"Your great-grandmother Abella was with you."

I open my eyes. "Pardon?"

"Here on the bridge," Estelle clarifies. "She was also *matrone* in her day, so she understood your burden. I watched her stroke your hair and tell you all would be well if you dreamed of a life larger than the limitations of your birthright. 'Sabine would be a worthy ruler,' Abella whispered, 'if you chose another path.'"

"I never heard her voice," I say quietly, fighting a flicker of hurt. Why is everyone telling me I don't have to be *matrone*? Didn't I do enough in my life to prove myself?

"No, but you felt her truth nudge at your heart. Souls in Paradise have that privilege. They can commune with their loved ones in the mortal world, while souls in the Underworld are not allowed to. The Miroir is the only place where we can even see the living, but our interference is forbidden, especially in matters of *saving* lives." Estelle's *orvande* eyes grow somber and earnest. "This is what Forgeron wishes me to make clear to you, Ailesse; it is why you earned your first chain link. If you earn three, you will be considered fully Chained, and he will be forced to call the jackals on you. They will drag you to the true terrors of the Underworld."

I shudder as the irreversible implications bear down on me. I'd have no hope of returning through the Gates if that happened. I'd never be with Sabine or Bastien or anyone in my *famille* again. "I understand."

"I hope so. The jackals eventually come for every Chained after they are ferried here. Forgeron only calls the jackals when a soul evades them the first time. The beasts are far more ferocious when he has to strike his hammer. I do not wish you to suffer that horror."

"I'll be careful."

"It will be very difficult," Estelle warns me. "You will have to cultivate the restraint you might have developed had you completed your rite of passage."

I stifle a prick of defensiveness. "I can learn self-control without murdering someone."

She grins softly, both amused and sad. "I wish more of my descendants had been like you." She walks off the bridge, and her fingers wrap around one of her wrist cuffs. She already has two, and she told me she has worn them for centuries. One more slip-up would have sent her to the deeper Underworld. It could still happen.

"How did *you* learn restraint?" I ask, drifting after her like a duckling again. If *amourés* didn't exist in her time, then neither did rites of passage.

"Slowly," Estelle says, without looking back. "Painfully." She brushes a loose lock of hair off her face. "It is not the living who tempt me in the Miroir. It is Forgeron." Her shoulders broaden as if she's inhaling a steeling breath, even though she won't be able to feel how it stretches her lungs to capacity. "Twice we have been unable to resist each other here, and twice our weakness gave me chains." She releases the breath, and her shoulders wilt. "When we touch, he forges links around me. It cannot be helped. It is his curse."

I stare after her, speechless at the injustice of her existence.

She gazes back at me again, and if there was any sorrow on her face, it's gone now, replaced by her serene smile. "Do not pity me, daughter of daughters. I would rather be near my love, unable to hold him, than be apart from him in Paradise. It was my choice to come here, and I do not regret it."

My thoughts turn to Bastien and how he danced with me under the ruins of a glass dome in Dovré when the moon was full. I knew I loved him then. "I would choose the same," I say, and then catch myself. Would I really, or would I let Bastien go and choose to be *matrone* of my *famille* instead?

Estelle's smile deepens, and despite how conflicted I feel, Elara's Light fills my chest with warmth. I soak it in, remembering that Light is scarce in the Miroir. "Goodbye for now," she says.

I stop at the bank of the river we've started walking by. "Where are you going?"

She heads for a thicket of trees. "The Miroir is overflowing with Unchained souls, wrongly stolen from Paradise. I must warn who I can of the dangers here, lest they also become wrapped in chains."

I lower my eyes, furious at my mother for what she did to bring them here. I just can't figure out why she did it. *I* was the sacrifice required for Tyrus to resurrect Godart, not the Unchained. Why did she take more of them when she already had me in her grasp at the soul bridge? If she is still serving Tyrus, working to help him join kingdoms with Elara, it must benefit her somehow, too. "Please tell me they can still be saved.

Not just from chains, but from here."

Estelle looks at me one final time before she enters the thicket. "Perhaps . . . if *you* can learn to save and also be saved from this place."

I'm not sure I understand. "Will you teach me?"

"I cannot say more than I have. You are not dead, only trapped. I would earn my third link."

My chest falls.

"Do not despair, Ailesse. You are more than your mother's daughter; you are also mine. I believe in you."

She offers me one last calming smile and turns and disappears.

29
Bastien

"JULES, MARCEL," I CALL, CLIMBING down the scaffolding. "You'll never guess what's happened. All of Dovré is talking about it. King Godart has usurped Casimir." I hop off the ladder and into my quarry room to find the usurped king staring back at me, along with Sabine, Jules, and Marcel. They're all seated comfortably in various places on the floor, like fast friends at a picnic.

Cas waves once, an awkward attempt at a peace offering. "I thought I'd take my chances back here until I can reclaim my title . . . if that's all right."

Sabine gives me a pointed look. "Cas has returned as our friend and ally." She's sitting close beside him on the straw mattress next to the ball and chain that *isn't* shackled around his ankle. "He's not to be your prisoner anymore," she adds. "We need his help, and he needs ours if he wants his throne back."

"And if he wants to stay alive," Marcel chimes in from a few feet away, a stack of open books laid out before him. "A throne isn't much good if you're going to die in ten months from a soulbond—whether or not your soulmate is stuck in the Underworld."

I shift from foot to foot, trying to process all these new developments. "So we're back at trying to break the soul-bond, then?" I avoid eye contact with Cas. It's going to take a moment for me to swallow the idea of him living here again. My side is still smarting from when he bashed it with my dolphin statue.

"Yes," Jules answers with a weary exhale, coughing once into a handkerchief. "And we're running into dead ends, as usual."

"You're forgetting about Cas's books," Marcel says.

Cas's books? What are they talking about?

"I haven't forgotten about them." Jules rolls her eyes. "We just don't know if they're going to help yet."

"When have books ever failed us?"

"When I got possessed by a Chained, when Bastien got stabbed, when Ailesse got hoodwinked by her mom . . ." She lists the reasons on her fingers.

"Well, besides all that life-and-death stuff."

Jules throws her hands in the air. "Why do you think we need these books, Marcel?"

"You brought books with you?" I speak over them and turn to Cas, finally leveling a hard gaze at him. I take a few steps into the room. "How did you manage that? Word on the street is that a brawl broke out in the castle and you barely escaped with your life."

"What you heard was true," he says. "Godart and Odiva killed many of my guards when they stormed the castle. They would have killed me, too, if . . ." He scratches the back of his neck. "Well, I think Sabine can explain better."

She gives him a small but friendly grin. Since when did they become so easy around each other? "An Unchained soul told Cas how to escape," she replies, "and that soul said she was relaying a message from Ailesse."

My chest pulls tight. "W-what?"

Sabine nods, her eyes shining. "She's near, Bastien. We really *are* going to save her. And we have a solid plan. Cas's books are just one part of it."

My hand slips into my pocket around the scrap of Ailesse's chemise. I start pacing the room. "Tell me everything. What's in these books?"

"Stories of Belin and Gaëlle," Marcel answers. "Scripture, poetry, some folktales." He leans back against the side wall and crosses one ankle over another, a wide grin on his face. "Cas pointed out that we've only been studying about the Leurress and Tyrus and Elara. Maybe we're missing part of the puzzle, and the other gods are involved, too."

"Belin and Gaëlle separated Tyrus's and Elara's kingdoms in the first place," Sabine explains. "Perhaps learning more about how they did that is key to breaking the soul-bond."

"But first we have to break back inside Beau Palais," Cas says. "I don't have the books with me yet. They're in a private library near the royal apartments."

I pace in the other direction. "What about confronting Odiva?" I aim my question at Sabine. "That's part of your solid plan, right?" Saving Ailesse has to include threatening her mother to reverse what she did.

"I've got it!" Birdine calls, her muffled voice traveling down to us from above. I turn as she descends the scaffolding ladder and steps into the room. Her eyes are red, like she's been crying. She removes the scarf wrapped around her shoulders and reaches under the low neckline of her dress. She pulls out two glass vials from between her breasts, even though she has a satchel, and passes them to me.

My ears flush with heat. *Why do I have to touch them?* I quickly hand the vials over to Marcel, and Jules bites down a laugh. "What are those?" I ask, and shove my hands in my pockets again.

"Poison and an antidote," Marcel replies, beaming. "Birdie obtained them from her uncle's perfumery."

I raise my brows, impressed. It's no secret that perfumers handle dangerous ingredients to make fragrances. Making poison is illegal, though, and perfumers have to be members of a guild in Dovré that regulates their use of potent herbs and tinctures. "Tell your uncle thanks next time you see him."

Birdine bursts into tears. I shoot Marcel a worried glance. What did I do?

"Aw, Birdie." He rises to his feet. "Come 'ere."

She rushes over to him and cries against his chest. I look at

Jules, wondering what I missed, but she only shrugs.

Birdine finally pulls back and dabs her tears with her scarf. "My uncle has been attacked by one of the Chained, I'm sure of it. He thinks he's hearing voices because he's sick with a fever, but it's more than that." She sniffs. "He couldn't even rise from his chair. I had to mix all these ingredients for him."

Sabine stands and hurries over to her. "I'm so sorry." She knows Birdine a little from the time we spent plotting to free Ailesse from Beau Palais. "I'll ferry all the Chained as soon as I can, I promise."

"Thanks." Birdine forces a tiny smile. "I only pray my uncle isn't dead by then."

I nibble on my lip and consider Sabine. I don't ask her how she thinks she's going to ferry souls without the backing of her *famille*. I don't want to destroy Birdine's hope—or mine—that South Galle can finally be rid of these monsters . . . before it's too late for those suffering from stolen Light. My eyes slide to Jules. She's suddenly intent on stitching a tear in her leggings and acting like she can't hear us.

Cas clears his throat. "The, uh, poison is for Godart," he says, gently breaking the silence with a calm and focused tone. No doubt he learned such diplomatic skills from his royal upbringing. He pushes to his feet to join those of us standing. "Seeing as Godart is in possession of Sabine's salamander skull, we asked Birdine to concoct the strongest tincture possible."

"Godart will need to take a full sip for it to take effect," Birdine adds, "but one drop is enough to knock down a regular person."

I note the way both of them dodge saying "kill," a word Jules,

Marcel, and I came to terms with years ago in our quest for revenge.

"The plan is to slip the poison into Godart's drink," Cas continues, "and then give Odiva an ultimatum: we won't administer the antidote unless she tells us how to free Ailesse."

"*And* free the Unchained," I stipulate, crossing my arms. "We can't win a war without leverage. If we can get the Unchained back, Tyrus will realize we're a threat to him. We'll be in a position to make more demands. We can ask him to end the need for blood sacrifice." I pause, wondering if Cas even knows that more Unchained were stolen. "Has anyone told you what happened on the soul bridge?"

He nods somberly. "Sabine informed me about the transfer of souls, if that's what you mean."

I strive to keep my voice steady. "My father was among them."

His brows slowly draw inward, and he studies me for a long moment. He swallows and takes a deep breath. "If I were you . . . if my father still had a soul, that is . . ." He looks down to compose himself. "I'd do anything to see him rightly returned to the fate he deserves." He meets my gaze again, and his voice lowers in pitch and lines in steel. "We'll bring him back where he belongs, Bastien. I give you my word that I will not rest until we see it done."

My throat tightens as I stare back into his determined eyes. For the first time, I see him as a king I would follow. "And I promise we'll get Godart off your father's throne."

Marcel lifts a finger and clears his throat. "This seems a fitting moment to give you back your father's knife, Bastien. I found it on the quarry floor, where you said it fell."

My heart pounds as he passes me the simple and unwieldy blade I've kept with me for eight years, the blade I've sworn to fulfill my vengeance with. Once it's back in my grip, it feels like a natural extension of my arm. I briefly close my eyes and release a long exhale. "Thanks, Marcel."

He grins. "If this were a folktale, a beam of light would shine on you right now, and all of us would start singing a hero's ballad."

Jules groans. "If you break into song, Marcel, I swear I will cut out your tongue."

He holds up his hands and retreats to stand by Birdine, who whispers, "I wouldn't mind a song."

I sheathe the knife and crack my knuckles, thinking over the poison plan. It's desperate at best, but the longer we wait to come up with something smarter, the stronger a foothold Odiva and Godart will gain in Dovré. That will put Cas in more danger, which will threaten Ailesse in turn. My stomach tenses, and I flex my jaw muscle. I'll do whatever it takes to protect her.

"All right, then. Who's breaking into Beau Palais with me?" I shouldn't have asked, because Jules looks up hopefully. "We should keep our numbers small," I quickly add, "to maintain a low profile." She glares at me and sags back against the wall, coughing into her handkerchief again.

"I agree," Sabine replies. "My mother has the grace of a whip-tail stingray, which gives her sixth sense. She'll pick us out from the servants and guards if we move in a big pack."

Odiva also has a sixth sense for tracking her daughters, though I suppose we can use that to our advantage.

"I'll be coming, of course." Cas stands taller. "I know the quickest routes through the castle and alternate ones, if necessary."

"And we'll need the strength of my graces," Sabine says.

I eye her antler crown, trying to guess which of the tines is the one imbued with power. "Any chance you could string your grace bones on a necklace? I'm not sure how covert we can be with you looking like the queen of the dead."

She arches an unamused brow, but nods. "We'll also need disguises."

"Right. Guards' uniforms would be best."

Cas scratches his chin. "And where are we going to purchase guards' uniforms?"

I smirk. "Who said anything about purchasing them?"

30
Sabine

WE WAIT UNTIL NIGHTFALL TO approach Beau Palais. Dark clouds mask the light from the waning moon as our rowboat pounds through the rapids of the Mirvois River. The strength from my jackal and red stag helps me wrestle the oars and prevent the boat from tipping over.

I guide us to a rocky bank. Bastien jumps out in a spot of calmer water and moors us. Casimir hops out next and drags a large bundle of rope. We're going to enter Beau Palais from the cliff of the hill it's perched on, then climb the castle wall to reach the guards' barracks. A risky endeavor, but we've used the entrance through the dry well too many times. It's surely been compromised.

I set down the oars and step out of the boat last. Until we can steal new disguises, I'm clothed in a pair of Jules's leather leggings and one of Birdine's loose blouses. They're much easier to move about in than the tattered ferrying dress I've been wearing for weeks.

A few curious Chained souls watch us from a distance, but don't venture too near. My grace bones hang in full view from a cord just beneath the hollow of my throat. Once the Chaineds' *chazoure* eyes clap on my crescent-moon pendant, they stop advancing.

Bastien, Cas, and I walk several yards around the base of the cliff, searching for a good place to climb. I'm going to go first. My nighthawk vision will make it easier to see each crag and nook. Bastien and Cas will have to rely more on the rope I'll throw down afterward.

I stop once I spy a route with decent handholds and footholds. Cas passes me the coiled rope, and I drape it over my head and shoulder. He rubs my arm and whispers, "Be careful." His pupils are large in the darkness, but my keen eyes still catch the thin ring of blue around them. It calms my pounding heart. None of my graces give me great skill for climbing, like Ailesse's alpine ibex, and I no longer have my fire salamander skull to give me graced agility—or to heal if I fall. I'll have to depend on my strength to keep me anchored to the rock.

"Thank you," I say, and dry my river-wet hands on my sleeves.

I begin the climb.

Except for a tricky overhanging rock midway up, navigating the cliff isn't too difficult. Perhaps my meadow viper grace is helping after all. Snakes are known to climb rough surfaces. But when I glance above at the towering castle past the cliff, my pulse trips in double time. Those smooth limestone walls are going to be my greater challenge.

I find a deep crevice at the top of the cliff and secure the grappling hook that's attached to the end of the rope. I toss the coil down to Cas and Bastien, and the rope unravels.

My jackal hearing picks up a few of their words. They're arguing over who gets the privilege of climbing up next. I roll my eyes.

While they debate, I slink along the castle wall until I'm closer to the north corner, where the barracks are. I study the architecture. Aside from mortared grooves between the large limestone bricks, there's little to hold on to except for a few arrow slits and ledges of crenelated molding.

Bastien and Cas catch up to me a few minutes later, after they finish the first leg of the climb. Bastien walks ahead of Cas, so he must have won the squabble.

"Proud of yourself?" I tease him.

He shrugs with a smirk. "For the moment."

Cas hands Bastien the rope, and Bastien passes it to me. I take a deep breath. *Here we go again.*

I'm only twelve feet up when my muscles start shaking. I channel all my graced strength into my limbs, toes, and fingertips. I slowly inch myself toward the arched window on the second floor, blessing every slightly protruding brick and slim ledge, anything I can lean my weight on to ease the grueling strain on my muscles. Thankfully, my leather leggings provide a little traction. I already mourn the fact that I'll have to give them back to Jules.

I grab an edge of molding with both hands and start to slide my legs up. The molding under my right hand breaks away. I yelp and swing down, barely hanging on by my left hand. Adrenaline crashes through me. Cas gasps my name. Bastien curses. I scramble for a foothold, but can't find anything. Dizziness rocks my vision. *Calm down and focus,* I command myself. I grit my teeth and reach up, grabbing a more secure spot. Eventually my toes anchor on the mortar between two bricks. I press my forehead against the stones and pant, laboring to steady my racing heartbeat.

You're almost there, Sabine. You can do this.

No, you can't, the weaker half of me whispers in my head. *Ailesse would have already reached the window by now. Stop while you can. This is a fool's errand. You can't outsmart your mother. You're leading Cas and Bastien to their deaths.*

My muscles quiver harder. Perspiration drips down my spine. I can't hold on anymore. I'm going to fall. I whimper, then chide myself for doubting my abilities. It's the jackal grace playing upon my insecurities. If Ailesse were here, she would be the first to say I *can* do this. Perhaps she is here, like she was with Cas when she showed him how to escape. I imagine her smiling and holding her hand out to help me. I tighten my jaw and climb.

The ledge of the window finally comes within reach. I peer inside, and true to Cas's word, this barrack room is empty. We timed our break-in to coincide with the guards' shift change. I pull up on the ledge, attach the grappling hook, and throw down the rope again.

Cas climbs after me first this time, and my sharp eyes focus on his quirked half smile as Bastien begrudgingly waits his turn. Once both boys have made it to the window, we quietly pull up the rope, stash it under a bunk, and tiptoe into the hallway. Cas is familiar with the place, and he leads us to a closet. We shut ourselves in and listen for the guards to return. I'm acutely aware of how close Cas stands beside me. The heat of his skin radiates through his sleeve to mine.

Several minutes pass until my graced ears hear the sound of light snores and rhythmic breathing from the nearest bunks. I reach Cas's hand and squeeze, signaling that we can go now. He squeezes back, then holds my hand longer than he needs to. The nerves along my palm tingle. I try to quell the flush rising through my body. He's in love with Ailesse. If his fingers are lingering on mine, it's probably because he's distracted and trying to listen for the guards himself.

He finally lets go and opens the closet door. I'm thankful for the dimly lit hallway. My cheeks must be flaming red.

We come to the first room, and Bastien sneaks inside. I may have graced lightness on my feet, but he's the thief. This task is his. I studiously avoid Cas's gaze as we wait for Bastien to return with our uniforms.

"You did well out there," he murmurs, breaking the silence.

My eyes lift to his, and my insides melt when I see the soft pride in his expression. Some other emotion is there, too. I glimpse it when the corner of his lip lightly catches on his teeth as he searches my face. Nervousness? Another deeper sentiment? I can't tell. "Thank you."

"I've been meaning to tell you, you have a lovely voice."

It takes me a moment to understand why he's brought that up, and then I wince. "Oh no. Was I singing while I climbed?"

"Here and there." He grins. "It isn't the first time I've caught you softly murmuring a song."

I cringe again, shaking my head at myself. "I don't even realize I'm doing it."

"It isn't anything to be ashamed of. Like I said, your voice is beautiful."

A tingling sensation sweeps through my limbs, and I look down at my hands, fidgeting with the cuff of my sleeve. We grow quiet, and that silence makes my heart thump faster.

Ever since we made peace with each other in the forest gully, I've felt more awkward around Cas, which makes no sense, although I feel that new shyness coming from him, too. We often drift toward each other, but then don't have much to say. I keep finding myself earnestly pretending to be normal—whatever that is—and I can't recall any helpful lessons from my *famille* on my predicament. Ailesse and I were taught that an *amouré* would be chosen for us and belong to us. I never thought I'd have to work at getting to know a boy . . . or what to do if I actually began to like one I didn't need to kill.

"How are you feeling?" I ask Cas. "About tonight," I add, when his brow wrinkles.

"Oh." He quietly chuckles and tugs the collar of his shirt. He's removed the fine doublet he wore earlier and is now in a black shirt and breeches. "I'm, um, working to stay focused, one task at a time. When I pause to dwell on Godart in my father's castle or think of Odiva touching my mother's heirlooms . . ." His nostrils flare, and he shakes his head. "Let's just say it doesn't put me in a charitable mood."

I offer him a quavering smile. "You're lucky you had parents you admired . . . though I'm sorry you lost them the way you did."

He lowers his eyes and softly scuffs the toe of his boot against the floor. "I'm starting to wonder if my mother may have lost her soul, the way my father did. She died during the great plague. What if it wasn't illness that killed her, but the Chained?"

My chest hurts for him. "I wish I could tell you, if it would bring you comfort."

"That's all right." His dimple flashes as he musters a grin. "I've imagined her watching over me for so long." He sighs. "I suppose I was braver and kinder and altogether a better person because I sought her approval, even from Paradise."

"Then you still honored her memory, and she would be proud to see who you've become."

Cas holds my gaze for a long moment. He swallows. "Thank you, Sabine."

I nod, growing warm at the gentle but fervent way he says my name.

"What's more incredible is who you are, given your own parents," he says.

"Another woman raised me," I confess, and lean my shoulder against the wall. "I believed she was my mother for most of my life, though I probably owe any of my better qualities to Ailesse. We were best friends long before we found out we were sisters."

He tilts his head, studying me for another stretched-out moment. I chide myself for bringing up Ailesse and wonder what's taking Bastien so long. "Do you know what I think?" Cas finally asks, and I arch a brow. "You give yourself far too little credit. The world can be a bitter and cruel place. In the end, each of us must decide who we are and what we will do with the lot we're given. And from what I know of you, you have a fierceness and loyalty that can't be inherited or mimicked. They're earned by true devotion and selfless sacrifice. *You*, Sabine—you are the reason you're remarkable."

I'm left speechless, blinking against the heat brimming in my eyes, struggling to see the person he sees in me . . . and yet feeling *seen* in a way I've never experienced before, despite my failings and weaknesses—because Cas has also seen me at my worst. "If you speak like that to all your subjects, your people will follow you anywhere." I laugh, a little breathless.

He chuckles and scratches the back of his neck shyly. "I'm not usually this inspired."

Bastien emerges from the bunk room, quiet as a wildcat, but he may as well be stomping for how rude the intrusion feels after the spell Cas has me under. His arms are piled high with uniforms and boots. "Got them," he says, in case we hadn't noticed. With a tip of his head, he motions us back to the closet.

We take turns changing clothes. I go first, fumbling in the darkness with the buckles on the ill-fitting leather cuirass. I pull a tunic on over that, then a hood piece. The breeches are tight in the hips and baggy everywhere else. I abandon them and the boots, which don't fit either, and stick to my own leggings and the leather shoes Jules loaned me. Last of all, I fasten my own belt around the tunic and push it low on my waist.

I walk out of the closet and shrug. "This will have to do."

Bastien snickers, but Cas grins. "It becomes you," he says, and slips past me to change next.

Once all three of us are dressed, we sneak out of the barracks and stride through the courtyard, adopting the confident bearing of royal guardsmen. We each wear our sheathed weapons of choice: me with my bone knife, Bastien with his father's knife, and Cas with the jeweled Trencavel dagger.

Cas leads us to what looks like a servant's entrance tucked behind a large tower, and we enter a storage room lined with corked barrels and sacks of grain. From there, we take a few branching hallways until we reach a twirling staircase inside a narrow tower. Halfway up the flight, we come across a Chained man. I quickly step in front of Cas and pull out my grace bone necklace from beneath my tunic. The man hisses and races in the other direction.

The only other souls we pass on the way to the third floor, where the royal apartments and the private library are located, are Unchained. Maybe Chained souls are just as afraid of Odiva as they are of me.

Bastien and I wait outside the library while Cas grabs the books about Belin and Gaëlle. A few of the Unchained start to gather at a distance, watching us and whispering among themselves. Many of them are dead castle guards. I'm about to tell them they should leave when Bastien says, "Have you and Cas . . . ?" He shifts on his feet, scratching his jaw as he studies me. "Do you, you know, fancy him?"

I almost snort. "Do I *fancy* him?"

He grins and shoves my shoulder, like I've seen him do with Marcel. "Never mind."

Cas returns with a lumpy sack. There must be at least three books inside. He's also holding two jeweled goblets and a bottle of wine.

Bastien gives a low whistle. "That's some library you have here."

Cas passes him the wine and goblets. "If you see me back on my throne, I welcome you to visit anytime."

Bastien smirks. "Deal."

We leave the Unchained souls behind and continue down the corridor, approaching what must be King Durand's old chambers. Cas explained the castle layout before we set out here. We slow as we near the door. I listen carefully with my graced ears, but hear nothing. The door is ajar, so I creep closer and peer within. My viper heat vision doesn't capture any living thing, either. The room is empty.

I nod at Cas and Bastien, and we enter. If Godart and Odiva had been in here, we had a backup plan to plant the poison in the council room—Cas suspected they might go there next—but so far everything is falling into our hands. *Please, Elara, keep blessing our luck.*

Cas guides us into a private sitting room that adjoins the

bedroom. Two armchairs are drawn near a fireplace, with a small varnished table between them. Cas motions Bastien over quickly. We need to hurry. We only have so much time before my mother senses my presence and comes—which we're counting on, but we have to be ready first.

Bastien sets down the goblets on the varnished table and fills them with crimson wine. According to Cas, any servant worth his wages would offer two drinks, knowing the new king's promised queen would accompany him here.

Cas gives Bastien the sack of books and pulls out a handkerchief from his pocket. He unwraps it partway, just until he exposes the first glass vial, the one with the poison. It's a dark and brackish color that makes my stomach turn.

He struggles to pop off the cork.

"Let me try," Bastien says.

Cas shakes his head. "I almost have it."

My jackal ears catch footsteps from the corridor. "Someone's approaching," I whisper. "It might be them."

Cas continues to wrestle with the vial. Bastien starts pacing. I chew on my lip. Our plan feels more reckless by the minute. What ever made us believe we could pull it off?

The footsteps are at the bedroom door. The door to *this* room is just a few feet away from that one, and both doors are open.

I don't dare give another warning. My mother has graced ears, too, as well as uncanny instincts when it comes to her daughters. I reach for the vial to open it myself.

Cas misreads me and hurriedly shoves me the handkerchief to

free up his hands. I'm unprepared to take it. I barely grasp a corner of the cloth. The antidote wrapped within slips out. Falls to the stones. Shatters.

My heart stops. I share a panicked glance with Cas. He's just uncorked the poison vial. I snatch it from him and mouth, *Hide!*

He springs for the curtains at the window opposite the fireplace. Bastien dives behind a large chest in the corner behind the door. I tip the poison into both goblets with shaking hands. This isn't going to work. My mother will feel Cas's and Bastien's presence with her sixth sense. They weren't supposed to be in the room when she and Godart returned. I wasn't, either, but at least I have a fighting chance to defend myself.

I shove the empty vial in my pocket, then step on the crushed glass to hide the useless antidote. That's all I can do before a large figure appears on the threshold between the rooms, pauses, and slowly walks inside.

"Hello, daughter," Godart says.

31
Ailesse

I STAND BETWEEN SABINE AND her father, my hands out-stretched in a futile attempt to ward them away from each other. I've seen what Godart can do with my mother's graces. I don't doubt he's still able to use them, even though he's come alone.

Sabine remains frozen with her foot over the shattered anti-dote vial, not daring to move. I'm surprised Godart recognized her so quickly in the uniform she's wearing and with her hair tucked back in a hood. He's only seen her once before, on the soul bridge.

"Aren't you going to greet your father?" He takes two steps into the sitting room, his gait loose and overconfident.

"Stay back from her!" I say, but he can't hear me.

Sabine slowly uncurls her fists. "Forgive me. Good evening, F-father."

His eyes sweep over her with mild interest. "What brings you to my castle—and in disguise, no less?"

From the window where Casimir is hiding, the curtain rustles when Godart says "my castle." I inwardly plead for Cas to hold still. If Godart attunes himself to the sixth sense he can access, he'll feel Cas's presence in the room. Thankfully, Bastien remains motionless behind the chest. Sabine needs to trick Godart into drinking the poison, antidote or not. I've followed every step of my friends' journey here and know the depth of their plan.

"I *had* to come in disguise," Sabine answers. "I've invaded Beau Palais once before; the guards know who I am. If they captured me, they would kill me before I had the chance to see you—and I needed to see you. I'm desperate. Ailesse is gone. I have no one else to turn to."

My shoulders relax a little. Sabine actually sounds convincing. I've underestimated her ability to deceive. Perhaps her golden jackal grace is helping.

Godart drifts nearer. I step out of the way, even though he wouldn't feel me if he plowed me over. "You cannot turn to your *famille?*" His eyes narrow on her.

Sabine lowers her head. "They've banished me."

"My daughter, banished?" He frowns, his pride nicked. "Odiva said she named you her heir."

Sabine's mouth struggles into a piteous smile. "She did, but she didn't tell them she was also my mother. I kept that from them, too." She sighs. "I've kept far too many secrets. And because of that, I've lost their trust. There's nothing I can do to earn it back now."

"Women," Godart scoffs. "At the end of the day, they are pack creatures. Betray one, and you betray them all."

Oh, how I hate him.

Sabine's eyes spark, enraged, but she glances away before he can see her reaction.

"There is only one exceptional female," Godart says, "and she puts all others to shame. You are fortunate to share her blood."

Sabine lifts her chin. "I hope one day I can say I'm fortunate to share your blood, too."

He cocks a brow. "One day?"

"I'll have to forgive you first." She takes no pains to mask her anger this time, but she's swift to channel it into sorrow that cracks her voice when she adds, "You're here because Ailesse is gone forever."

"Oh, Sabine," I whisper, and place a hand on her shoulder.

Her lips part, and her eyes dart around the room. I stiffen. Did she hear me?

Another person walks through the doorway. I expect it to be my mother, but it's another man, one who carries a blacksmith's hammer. No one sees him but me.

I step back from Sabine and hold up my hands. "I didn't save her, Forgeron. I only said her name."

His face is as hard as the chain link he gave me when I helped Cas escape. "Did you remember nothing Estelle told you?"

I don't understand what he means at first, but then my breath catches. *Names are the song of the soul,* Estelle said. *They hold Elara's Light.*

Is that how Sabine heard me when I said her name? Through Light?

It doesn't make sense. I've said her name before in the Miroir. Cas's and Bastien's, too. None of them heard me until now.

Godart grows quiet as he contemplates Sabine, the daughter he never had the chance to raise. No father of a Leurress ever did. "You are my heir as much as your mother's," he finally says. "Such a union could only create a child with wondrous potential. If you are willing, Sabine—if you show the strength of your bloodline and let the past be forgotten—I will teach you to be indomitable. You will not mourn your life or who you knew at Château Creux. Surely that is why you came here." His eyes, so like hers, drop to her grace bone necklace, and he inches another step closer. "You will be welcomed into a *new* family."

Sabine bites her lip, considering his offer.

I sneak a glance at Forgeron. He hasn't left yet. He slowly paces at the edge of the room.

"How do I know I can trust you?" Sabine asks.

"Is not the promise of a great king honorable?"

"Perhaps." She lifts a shoulder. "But when a Leurress makes a pact, she seals it in blood."

Godart gives her a cool grin. "You already have my blood, daughter."

"True." She purses her lips, and her gaze falls on the goblets. Perspiration glistens on her brow as she picks one up and offers it to her father. "Will you drink to give me your word?"

I smile at her cleverness.

Godart laughs, both wry and cunning. He doesn't take the goblet from Sabine. He reaches for the other one on the table. As he does, his loose collar droops and reveals a small skull strung on a leather cord around his neck.

My eyes widen. Sabine's fire salamander skull.

I only see it a brief moment before he straightens again, but my keen vision doesn't miss its dark crimson stains. Sabine's blood.

I glance at Forgeron again, and anxiety grips me. He wouldn't be here unless he thought I'd still intervene. Unless he thought Sabine needed saving.

I rapidly glance about the room. No Unchained souls are here. No one can warn Sabine of any danger but me. But *what* danger? What does Godart mean to do?

He raises his cup to Sabine. She raises hers to him. I stand right beside her, watching her every move with the sharpness of my falcon vision. *She won't drink the poison,* I tell myself. She'll only bring the rim of the goblet to her lips. She'll wait for him to drink first.

My sixth sense shudders up my spine. Forgeron paces closer. "Stay back," I tell him. "I've done nothing."

Godart brings his cup near his mouth and pauses. Sabine does the same, stalling for him.

I don't move a muscle. *Drink the poison, Godart!*

Forgeron stares at the king's lower back and frowns. I step around Godart, just in time to see him slip out a knife tucked in his waistband. I gasp. "Sabine, run!"

She presses the goblet to her lips. She can't hear me.

"We warned you, girl," Forgeron growls at me.

I ignore him. He can't chain me. Not yet. "Sabine, listen to me," I say frantically. "It's Ailesse. Your father is trying to kill you."

Godart's goblet hovers at the edge of his mouth. He inches the knife around his body.

"Sabine!" My shout echoes through the Miroir.

She tips her cup higher. The wine swirls against her pressed lips.

"Careful!" I clutch her arm, but she doesn't feel me. Cas warned her how potent that poison is.

Godart drops his goblet. His knife whips out with eagle owl speed.

"SABINE!"

Her eyes bulge. She sees the knife. It slashes for her throat. She sucks in a sharp breath. The wine spills into her mouth.

"No!" I cry, as she knocks his knife away with her cup. She's almost as fast as he is.

He lunges for her neck again, this time with his bare hands. She chokes on the wine and struggles to fend him away. He drives her back against one of the armchairs. She coughs. Gags. She's forced to swallow.

Merde, merde, merde. There's no antidote left.

Godart's fingers tangle around her grace bone necklace. He pulls on the golden jackal bone.

My sixth sense drums. Bastien bursts out from behind the chest, his knife raised. Cas emerges from the curtains, dagger in hand. They converge on Godart.

Godart lets go of the grace bone, dodges Bastien's strike, and kicks him hard in the stomach. Bastien is thrown back as Godart swings for Cas—but not before Cas's dagger slices into Godart's side. He hisses, clutching the wound, but then slowly grins, staring down Cas. He'll heal, I realize. He has Sabine's salamander skull.

I go rigid as a new understanding hits me. Sabine doesn't need an antidote. She just needs the skull back.

She crumples to the floor. Her body starts to seize.

Cas's eyes flood with concern. He can't get to her. Godart is prowling around him, goading him to attack again.

I rush over to Bastien. He's wheezing and doubled over. "I need your help, Bastien!" I kneel beside him. Forgeron frowns when I use his name, but I don't care if he chains me a second time. I can't let Sabine die.

Bastien makes no sign of hearing me. Sabine moans and writhes. Cas swipes his dagger at Godart, but Godart easily side-steps him. He laughs past a grimace. "Did you come here to die, boy?"

"Bastien!" I grab his arm, but can't move him. *Think, Ailesse.* How did Sabine hear me when I said her name? I wasn't panicked or desperate. I was calm and focused. I thought of her with love, as a true sister.

I close my eyes, shutting out the noise of Godart taunting Cas, and Sabine struggling to breathe. I think of Bastien when he asked me to dance under the moonlit dome, when he first looked at me with forgiveness, when he spoke of his father, when he gave me space when I needed it. I have to close that space now to reach him.

Let go, I tell myself. I imagine, for just a moment, the burden I carry as my mother's firstborn daughter falling away from me, like my heavy dress fell away and sank into the depths of the river. I imagine making a different choice than being *matrone*—endless choices, really—and Bastien is one of them.

I open my eyes. Bring my mouth closer. My lips brush his ear. "Bastien," I whisper, using his name to reach his soul, his Light.

His brows jerk together. "Ailesse?"

Forgeron steps closer.

I swallow and refocus, speaking quickly. "Godart is wearing Sabine's salamander skull on a necklace. She needs it to heal."

Bastien blinks. Turns to the king.

"Take it," I say. "Hurry!"

He rises, still short of breath, and tightens his grip on his knife. His eyes shift in my direction, though he can't see me, and he squares his jaw. Catlike, he sneaks toward Godart while the king's back is turned.

I stand to follow him, but Forgeron blocks me. His *orvande* face is stern and unrelenting. "That was foolish."

I jut up my chin. "Perhaps it was brave." I startle when he grabs my right wrist. "What are you doing? Sabine isn't saved yet."

"It does not matter. You used Light. You pierced the barrier of the Miroir, and you did so with the intention to save. The punishment is the same."

He lets go of me, leaving me with another *orvande* cuff, then turns away, eyes pained.

I swallow hard and hasten over to Sabine. I can't think about my chains now. Sabine is thrashing on the floor and choking for breath. Her hood has fallen back. I vainly try to smooth her sweat-damp curls off her brow. "Hold on," I say, and glance at Bastien. "Hurry!"

He's advancing on Godart from behind and searching for his necklace cord, but the collar at Godart's nape is too high. Cas doesn't make eye contact with Bastien, but the two boys approach the king in rhythm. They're coordinating their attack.

"Did you really return from the dead to rule such a small kingdom?" Cas asks Godart, laboring to keep him distracted. Sabine's writhing must be the only reason Godart can't feel Bastien, like I do with my sixth sense. "With Odiva at your side, you could conquer lands greater than South Galle."

"Universal dominion must begin somewhere." Godart gives an easy shrug. "Other kingdoms can be conquered in time. And time is the luxury of the gods."

I finally understand my mother's lasting interest in being Godart's queen. Yes, she loves him, but it's more than that. She believes they can rule the known world together. That must hold more allure for her than governing the small number of Leurress in our *famille*.

Cas shifts nearer with his dagger, lightly bouncing on his feet. "Did you just compare yourself to the gods?" he asks Godart. "You may have been resurrected, but you can still bleed." He nods at the oozing cut on the king's side.

Godart smirks. "For now. When Paradise is empty, it will be another story."

Paradise, empty? What is he talking about?

My sixth sense pounds harder. I stiffen. Someone else is coming.

Cas slashes for Godart. When Godart moves to dodge the dagger, Bastien wraps him in a choke hold and tears open the front of his shirt with his knife.

"Godart!" My mother storms into the room. "What is ha—?" She freezes. Bastien's blade is under the necklace cord that holds the fire salamander skull. Godart holds perfectly still, no arrogance left in his expression. Blood trickles down his throat.

Why doesn't he use his graced strength to knock Bastien away? He'd only lose his ability to heal.

"Bastien . . ." My mother speaks slowly and with forced calm. "Step away from your king."

"He's no king of mine," Bastien spits.

Her black eyes narrow. A bone knife slides into her hand from her sleeve. "If you wish to live, you will do as I say."

"You're in no position to threaten me."

Sabine's back arches. Veins bulge at her temples. She kicks and whimpers.

Odiva belatedly notices her. Her bloodred lips pale. "What is wrong with my daughter?"

Cas is the only one who dares to move. He hurries over to Sabine and kneels beside her. I'm across from him on her other side. "She drank poison meant for Godart," Cas answers. Godart's brow twitches. "The antidote was destroyed," he adds, voice trembling. He turns to Bastien. "We have to get her back to Birdine," he says under his breath.

Odiva takes a tentative step forward. She's unnaturally stiff, and the tendons in her neck are stretched taut. "Give me Sabine's jackal grace bone, and I will allow you to leave."

Godart wasn't trying to kill Sabine earlier, I realize. He was after her crescent pendant. Why are they so desperate to have both bones?

"I'll be the one striking bargains here," Bastien replies. "Tell us how to release Ailesse and the Unchained from the Underworld, and I won't slice Godart's neck open."

My mother's eyes tighten. She presses her lips together.

"Tell me!" he demands.

Sabine's face purples. Her eyes start rolling back while she convulses.

Cas holds her hand in a death grip. "Damn all of you!" he says, and shoots Bastien a frantic glance. "We have to leave. *Now*." He turns to Odiva. "You will let us go if you want your daughter to live."

My mother stares at Sabine. I can't read what she's thinking or feeling. I pray that somewhere in her hardened heart, she still holds affection for the daughter she once favored. For the first time in my life, I don't care that she did. I just want Sabine to survive.

My mother stands taller, feigning a look of indifference. She opens her mouth to speak when my sixth sense starts hammering. She whirls to face the door, feeling it, too.

Several souls burst into the room—Unchained castle soldiers, the men she and Godart killed. At least fifteen of them. They're holding solid weapons that don't glow with *chazoure*.

They lunge for my mother. She swiftly counterattacks. Bastien takes advantage of the diversion and tries to cut away Godart's salamander skull. But his knife never nicks the necklace cord. He's knocked away by six souls converging on the king.

"Bastien, come now!" Cas shouts, and drags Sabine to her feet. Her head droops as she loses consciousness. He lifts her in his arms, like he lifted me on the soul bridge.

"It's all right, Bastien," I say, knowing obtaining the skull is too risky now. I want him to live, too. The Unchained souls won't stall my mother and Godart for long. "Leave!"

Forgeron glares at me but doesn't approach. Bastien didn't hear me this time. I didn't use any Light.

Bastien grabs Cas's sack of books and rushes after him.

My mother seethes, watching them pass her and the souls she's fighting.

They reach the door and run.

32
Sabine

I CAN'T BREATHE. SOMEONE'S HOLDING me under the surface of the water, but it's insufferably hot, not cold like the sea. I thrash, pulling at my clothes. I kick and hit so the person lets go of me.

Sabine . . . Sabine . . . Sabine . . .

Cas? No, it's Ailesse. Why are they hurting me?

My muscles seize and cramp. I cry out, my voice battered.

An acrid taste fills my mouth. I try to spit, but someone shuts my jaw and plugs my nose. I gag and swallow. I'm being poisoned all over again.

Cas's handsome face appears, hovering in my blurred vision. "It's going to be all right." His hand warms my cheek. I whimper, and my head sags against him. I'm so tired, but I can't rest. I have to ferry the souls of the dead. The new moon is tonight. Or is it the full moon? Either way, I must go and open the Gates, even though I'm going to fail again. The silver owl won't help me. She's long abandoned me.

"I'm not enough, not enough . . ." I struggle to form words past the emotions strangling my throat. "Ailesse has to come back." Hot tears leak from my eyes. "We have to bring her back."

"Shh, shh," Cas whispers, but I pull away from his gentle hand. I don't want his pity or his comfort. I want to be strong like Ailesse and the elders—even my mother and father.

My eyelids start to flutter closed. "I can't . . . make a difference . . . if I'm weak."

Darkness envelops me.

The catacombs? No, the pit beneath the cavern bridge. I float, weightless, buoyed up by the glittering black dust in the depths. The siren song warbles harrowingly from above, sounding the way it can only when played on a bone flute.

The black dust lifts me higher, called by the music, carrying me to the Underworld.

Glimpses of my life flash before me. I'm a small girl of five when I see my first dead body; I was too young to remember those who passed away earlier, during the great plague. It's Liliane, who had the most beautiful voice, but she can't sing anymore. Her eyes are glassy and fixed. Her mouth hangs rigidly open. When I'm eight, Emelisse's body is dragged into the cavern beneath Château Creux. I'm ten when Ashena, who loved Jules and Marcel's father, is also brought lifeless before *Matrone* Odiva. These three died for failing to kill their *amourés*. By the time I'm thirteen, three more in my *famille* meet their deaths by ferrying. I'm fourteen when I lose Ciana, who I believed to be my mother. She kisses my forehead, and Odiva's dark gaze lingers, making my blood chill. The next time I see Ciana, her body is limp and wet from the Nivous Sea. She also perished on the land bridge.

Year by year, each death affects me deeper. I stop eating meat. My ferrying training slackens. I stick closer to Ailesse, who excels in everything. Her confidence and acceptance are a shield from the others who scorn or shake their heads at me.

A fire salamander darts midair across my vision, leaving a sparkling trail as the black dust continues to pull me upward. I see a moving image of myself, too. I chase the salamander and trap it. I sob as I stab it with my bone knife. Ailesse hugs me, and I bury my head against her shoulder.

The nighthawk soars overhead. The golden jackal bounds toward me. The meadow viper slithers out of a sack. Each kill at my ritual blade comes more thoughtlessly than the last. Finally, the majestic red stag with sixteen antler tines springs through the forest. I craved his death. I look monstrous when I kill him viciously and mercilessly. It doesn't matter that I thought I was dreaming.

The animals vanish. I stare down at myself. Why am I not bound in *chazoure* chains? I must be dead if I'm being forced to watch my sins. I haven't even seen all of them yet. Where are the people who died in Beau Palais because I loosed poisonous vipers on them? Where are those who lost their souls because I couldn't ferry the Chained?

I rise to the rim of the pit. The soul bridge is re-formed. The Gate of dust lies at its end, but the translucent Gates to Paradise are missing. Chained or not, it seems the Underworld is the only place that awaits me.

The glittering black points me toward Tyrus's realm and sets me on my feet. I advance toward the doorway. No siren song calls to lure me from within. It doesn't need to. I walk of my own accord, knowing it's useless to outrun my fate. My mother warned me what would happen if I bore the jackal grace alone: *He will bury you, daughter.*

I am the jackal. I will bury myself.

"Sabine," someone murmurs when I reach the swirling black Gate.

I look through the doorway and gasp. "Ailesse."

Her auburn hair drifts about her shoulders like she's underwater. Her umber eyes glow with Light that shouldn't exist where she is. "Don't say you're not enough," she tells me. "I wouldn't be who I am without you. I never had a mother's love, but I had yours. Your strength carried me."

My breath catches on a sob. I miss her desperately. I saw her a few days ago, but it's been months since we've been together for more than a few stolen moments. "Nothing makes sense without you," I say. "I can't be who I'm supposed to be without you."

Her smile trembles as she watches me weep. "Yes, you can. We'll always be together. You're my sister. You're a part of me."

I reach for her, but she takes a step away. I exhale, weary. "Just let me come to you."

"No," she replies. "I will come to you. Rest now. Heal. You don't need your salamander skull, Sabine. You have Light. It's always been your strongest gift. Hold on to it."

Powerful fatigue washes over me. I wilt down to the bridge and lay my face against its cool stone. Ailesse sings me a lullaby about the first daughter of the gods and calls her Estelle. *Star.*

I let that song seep inside me. Faintly, almost incoherently, I sing back the refrain with Ailesse. My voice is a thin croak, but I continue singing. Even when I no longer hear myself, the song about Estelle reverberates inside me and burgeons with Light.

I cling to the image of her name, a star, a pinprick of hope against the darkness, and I close my eyes.

33
Ailesse

I'M SINGING A SONG I'VE never sung before. I make it up, word by word, note by note, wishing I had the power to step out of the Gate of dust and stroke Sabine's hair while she sleeps on the soul bridge. But then my hand *is* on her hair, and her black curls are no longer perfectly arranged and glossy, like they were a moment ago; they're damp with sweat and hazy in my vision, each ringlet blurred and streaked at the edges.

"Beware of visions," Forgeron says. I startle to find he's standing right behind me, where I sit beside Sabine. But I'm not on the soul bridge in the underground cavern anymore; I'm in the quarry room beneath Chapelle du Pauvre. Sabine is lying on the straw mattress by the relief of Château Creux and the four gods, her face pale as she sleeps fitfully.

"I—I didn't know I had entered a vision." The last thing I remember, before I spoke with Sabine, was vainly trying to help Cas hold her still as Birdine administered a new tincture of antidote. The next thing I knew, I was on the other side of the Gate of dust. I didn't think the sudden shift was so unusual. In the Miroir, I travel to different places in the blink of an eye.

I glance around the room, still struggling to orient myself. Bastien and Jules are sleeping. It must be the middle of the night. Birdine is gone. I have a vague memory of her leaving to tend to her sick uncle. The only people awake are Marcel, who is reading from one of the books Cas brought back, and Cas, who is sitting close by me near Sabine. He adjusts the blanket over her, his eyes heavy with fatigue.

"You fell asleep," Forgeron explains to me.

I blink at him. "I need *sleep* here?"

"No, but that doesn't prevent you from sleeping when you wish to forget your troubles." He leans against the wall as if he'd like to nod off himself. "I would caution you to stay awake, though. The veil between the Miroir and the mortal world is thin. Dreams have a tendency to slip into visions here, and communicating with the living while in that state can be considered interference."

I stare down at the cuffs around my wrists. If I earn one more link, I'll be fully Chained. Forgeron will have to strike his hammer and call the jackals on me. "Why didn't you chain my mother?" I ask, remembering what Estelle told me: Odiva was clever enough to avoid Forgeron's punishments. "The vision she sent me was calculated," I say. "She tricked me into freeing her from the Underworld without even receiving a single link."

"Your mother did not use Light." Forgeron rubs a stubborn smear of *orvande* soot on his forearm. "Tyrus does not ask me to punish those who wield his darkness here."

"I didn't know darkness could be wielded."

"Everything has its opposite."

I study him. His manner isn't as abrasive as usual. Maybe he hasn't had to forge as many chains lately, or maybe he's not always in a dismal mood . . . not that I'd call his current mood pleasant. At least he doesn't look like the whole world of the living and the dead is pressing down on his shoulders. "What happens if you defy Tyrus?" I ask, remembering what Estelle said. Forgeron doesn't believe he has a choice. His duty is his curse.

He grows quiet and picks at the handle of his hammer. "I will remain in the Miroir, but Tyrus will mask my view of the mortal world forever. It will be nothing more than a fog of endless streaks and blurs. He will do the same to Estelle; he tied our fates when she followed me here." His mouth quavers until he flexes his jaw muscle. "I could bear the punishment if she didn't have to suffer, too."

I picture Estelle trailing her fingers through the sea she can't feel, tipping her head back to the sun that doesn't warm her, telling me she watches her descendants each ferrying night. Despite her contented nature, it's clear she wants what she doesn't have, even though what she wants most is happiness with Forgeron. I imagine *joy in this place with the only man I have ever loved,* she said.

That is what carries me. "I think she'd prefer a real life here with you rather than only pretending at living."

"A real life?" Forgeron's deep voice almost breaks. He covers it with a growl. "I can't even touch her without giving her chains."

"Even if you defy Tyrus about that as well?"

"I do not dare tempt him to find out."

I glance at Bastien, asleep on the pillow of my folded chemise. He's curled up like a child. The dolphin statue his father carved for him is close beside him on the floor. "Some people would choose to be Chained if it meant being with the person they loved forever."

Forgeron scoffs. "Even if it meant calling the jackals on them?"

"You are not without agency. Whether you strike your hammer is up to you. You should trust the choice Estelle already made. She was ready to give up life among the living when she joined you here long ago. She's been waiting ages for you to accept her reasoning."

His temper flares. He unhitches himself from the wall and glares down at me, his *orvande* eyes rock hard. "I have been trapped in the Miroir for millennia. I do not need a child who has scarcely set foot here telling me what to do."

He swings up his hammer. I wince, afraid he'll bring it down on the ground just for making him angry. Instead, the hammer falls back to rest on his shoulder with a heavy *thud*. He stalks away and disappears from sight before he reaches the drop-off of the quarry room.

I sigh. I'm not doing myself any favors by making enemies with the blacksmith of the Underworld.

Bastien rustles, murmuring something unintelligible in his sleep. I drift over and sit beside him. His brows are pinched and his eyelids flutter, like he's having a bad dream. I have the urge to sing to him, like I sang to Sabine, but I keep my lips sealed. I might use Light—I yearn to use it—but if I did this time, it wouldn't be in an unwitting vision. Forgeron would come back for me.

Bastien settles back into peaceful sleep. His forehead smoothes, and his right fist relaxes. A slip of white cloth peeks out from his fingers. Curious, I touch it, but I can't feel its texture, and I've no ability to nudge Bastien's hand open wider.

I study the edge of the cloth with my falcon vision. The threads are fine like soft linen, and the weave of the fabric has a subtle scalloped pattern. It's a small piece of my chemise.

I rest my hand over Bastien's and lie down so our faces are close together. I wish there was something I could also hold that belonged to him, something to help me cling to the memory of his touch.

I lean close and kiss his lips gently, but I can't feel the warmth of his mouth or his breath stirring mine. My chest sinks. I hate that I can't feel the physical pain of missing him. The ache is trapped inside my useless body.

"I'm sorry I was so afraid to share my heart with you," I whisper. "I thought I didn't have enough room within me to keep hold of both my dreams and my duty. If you can give me another chance, I want to prove my soul is big enough."

What if I can't? What if I never escape this place?

I squeeze my eyes shut. I can't think thoughts like that. I'm *going* to escape. And when I do, I'll help Bastien and my friends free the Unchained. Estelle gave me hope I could do that if I learned how to save others from the Underworld, as well as myself. So I *will* learn. I'll come out of the Miroir with the knowledge my friends need to defeat my mother and Godart, and together we'll stop Tyrus's growing tyranny.

Marcel yawns. His head bobs as he starts to drift off. The heavy book propped on his bent knees slides to the floor. *Thunk!*

Bastien jerks awake and whips out his knife. Marcel startles with a snort. They look at each other for a moment, and then Bastien exhales and sheaths his blade. It's looped on his belt, lying on the floor beside him. He picks up the scrap of my chemise he's dropped and brushes his thumb over it tenderly. He rises to his feet and stuffs the scrap in his pocket. "How's Sabine doing?" he asks Cas.

Cas shrugs and rubs his tired eyes. "She's not writhing quite as much, but she's still a little feverish."

Bastien stares at Sabine with furrowed brows before he nods and turns to Marcel. "How about you? Read anything helpful in those new books?"

"Shut up, will you?" Jules rolls over and coughs into her sleeve. "It's the middle of the blasted night."

"Morning, actually," Marcel replies. "Dawn should have risen an hour ago."

Jules groans. "I hate this place."

Marcel is unruffled by his sister. "Nothing helpful yet," he replies to Bastien. "I say we reconsider my missing-element theory." I recall what he told me a few days ago: the Gates to the Beyond are made up of four of the five elements—water, wind, earth, and spirit. "There has to be a way to use fire as a weapon against Tyrus."

"How would we do that?" Cas frowns. "The only place left to ferry is on the land bridge, right?"

"And the Gate of water would only extinguish fire," Bastien adds.

"How else can we threaten Tyrus?" Marcel sounds a little put out that no one will entertain his theory. "We need *some* leverage if we want to save Ailesse and all those souls."

Jules rises into a sitting position. "What if saving Ailesse is as simple as pulling her out of the Underworld"—she coughs twice—"just like she pulled out Odiva?"

"I didn't pull my mother out," I say, though no one hears me. "I took her hand, and she pulled me in, despite all my struggle." And Bastien's and Sabine's.

"That only worked because Ailesse took her place," Bastien replies.

"Yes," Marcel adds. "There has to be an exchange."

"So why can't Odiva be the exchange?" Jules rummages beneath her blanket and pulls out her handkerchief. Her thin shoulders rack as she coughs into it. "We push her in and pull Ailesse out." The three boys stare at her, considering. "I'm not saying it would be easy," she goes on. "Odiva is powerful, but—"

"Sabine could help us once she's feeling better." Bastien's face brightens. "It might work."

A measure of hope takes hold in me.

"What about Godart?" Cas asks.

"Odiva was the one who resurrected him," Marcel replies. "If she's taken back to the Underworld, maybe he'll die again. The resurrection will be reversed."

Cas mulls that over. "Even if it isn't, he wouldn't be able to share Odiva's graces anymore. It would be a fair fight when I confront him."

Bastien starts pacing. "This plan still doesn't help us free the Unchained."

"Not necessarily," Marcel says. "Freeing Ailesse might open the channel between the Gates again."

"And if Ailesse is free," Jules adds, "she can help Sabine link the two Gates together, like they did before. The Unchained will have a chance to escape while the channel is open."

I lift my brows at Jules. Marcel isn't the only one who's brilliant in their family.

"Wait." Marcel's expression falls. "The channel could do the opposite, too. It could pull the rest of the Unchained out of Paradise and into the Underworld. That could be what Tyrus needs to force Elara's kingdom to join his."

Oh. I didn't think of that.

Bastien blows out a heavy breath. "I'm sure that's exactly what Tyrus wants—and Odiva and Godart will try to help him. Whatever pact she's made, she'll want to finish it."

"Good," Cas says, a dark tone of challenge in his voice. "That means they'll come to the land bridge of their own accord. We won't have to trick them into it."

A hoarse voice joins the conversation. "They'll come for my golden jackal pendant, too."

I gasp. Sabine's eyes are finally open. Cas jerks around and grips her hand. I rush over and kneel at her side. She lies limp, no strength left in her body, but there's a spark of fight in her eyes. Her gaze locks with Cas's. Something almost tangible passes between them. The strength of its Light is so pure it penetrates the Miroir to me. I haven't sensed that kind of Light since Bastien kissed me for the first time, in the tunnel above the cavern bridge. This is no passing flirtation, whether Sabine and Cas realize it or not.

"What special graces does a golden jackal have?" Marcel asks Sabine, imperceptive as usual to his bad timing.

"Let's not press her with questions just yet," Cas says.

"It's all right," she rasps, clearing her throat. "The jackal doesn't give me any extraordinary graces," she answers. "I'm not sure why my mother and father need it, except . . ." She takes a labored breath, and Cas rubs the back of her hand. ". . . except it's Tyrus's sacred animal." Bastien brings her a cup of water. She takes a sip. "All I know is that Godart was after the pendant when he attacked me."

I can't determine why the pendant is so crucial. If anyone else has a guess, they don't share it.

Bastien takes up pacing again, his fingers laced at the nape of his neck. "All right," he says. "Let's go back to our plan. Say we *can* force Odiva to switch places with Ailesse, and say the exchange reverses Godart's resurrection. None of that gives us leverage to bargain with Tyrus. We still need to figure out how to stop him from demanding blood sacrifice, or else the cycle goes on. Ailesse and Cas die within ten months." He swallows hard. "More fathers die. More brothers. More friends."

"More of the Leurress who won't kill their *amourés*," Sabine murmurs.

Jules sighs. "Look, we don't have to solve everything today. We still have time to plot a way to defeat Tyrus."

"Time?" Bastien gives a miserable laugh.

"Yes," she replies. "We can't do any of this until ferrying night, remember? The new moon doesn't come for . . ."

"Twelve more days," Marcel supplies.

"Sabine needs that long to recover, anyway," Cas says, still holding her hand.

Bastien takes another turn around the quarry room. Everyone's eyes are on him, waiting for him to give the final word—even Cas, who has come to respect Bastien's authority in the small kingdom of his quarry.

"This plan is your best shot," Jules says.

"She's right." I stand and walk toward him. Maybe it's just reckless hope building inside me or obstinate faith in my friends, but I feel an almost tangible certainty that our efforts are going to succeed. Whatever I have to do to escape the Miroir and help them defeat Tyrus—and my mother—I'm going to make that happen.

Bastien finally looks at everyone and crosses his arms. I also turn to face them, at his side. "So are we all on board?" Each of them nods. He exhales a pent-up breath. "All right, then. Prepare yourselves. We leave nothing to chance."

"Nothing," I echo. "There's no room for failure."

"We have twelve days to come up with a strategy to cast Odiva into the Underworld."

"We've accomplished harder tasks in less time," I chime in.

"I'll start by digging deeper in these books." Marcel opens one of the volumes from Beau Palais. "There's bound to be something useful in them."

"Good," Bastien and I say together. "I want to make sure Sabine and Ailesse can really connect the Gates again," he adds. "See what you can find out about linking them."

Marcel salutes him and eases into a comfortable position.

"I'll take up knife practice and strength training again," Bastien continues. "My mind works better when I keep my body in motion."

"I'll do the same," Cas replies. "I have my throne to win back, and I can't do that without challenging Godart."

"Maybe I can learn how to share my graces with all of you," Sabine suggests. "If my mother can, then it's possible. We'll have a much better chance to succeed."

"I believe in you." I smile at her.

"Excellent." Bastien claps his hands together. "Everyone get to work."

"Hold on." Jules rises and sets her fisted hands on her hips. "Don't you want to know what *I'm* going to do?"

"Oh." Bastien eyes the way her legs wobble with weakness. "Well, I figured you'd help Marcel. Those are some big books he's got."

She pins him with an icy look. "Have you forgotten that I'm your best sparring partner, and I have a father I'd like to avenge, too?"

He rocks back on his heels. "Definitely haven't forgotten."

"Good, then . . ." A sudden coughing attack seizes her. Her handkerchief flies to her mouth, and she bends over, hacking for a long moment.

"Are you all right?" He moves closer.

She turns away and coughs a few times before she wipes her mouth clean. "Course I'm all right." She stares down at her handkerchief. "Get your knife. We'll practice in the church."

"You sure you don't want to—?"

She whirls on him. "Get. Your. Knife."

He holds up his hands and spins around to do as she says. After an awkward pause, everyone else returns to what they were doing. Everyone but me.

I drift over to her and peer around Jules's back at the handkerchief she's hiding in her tensed grip.

It's soaked in the middle with a bright ring of blood.

34

Bastien

I SIT ON A PEW in the nave of Chapelle du Pauvre, sharpening my father's knife on a whetstone. Thunder rumbles outside, and rain drips through the cracks in the vaulted ceiling. The twilight seeping through the boarded-up windows is quickly turning to black. I don't light a lantern. Lanterns can be snuffed out. I need my eyes to adjust to the darkness.

The new moon is here. It's ferrying night. Twelve days have passed since my friends and I concocted our plan, and it's just as reckless and half-formed as it was then. We've had no break-throughs on how to defeat Tyrus. Our only hope is that if we take back the souls stolen from Paradise, he'll feel threatened and be willing to bargain with us.

I slip my hand in my pocket and feel the scrap of Ailesse's chemise. "Be there tonight," I whisper, hoping she'll be ready at the
Gate when Sabine and I shove Odiva through it. Maybe, with all
the graces of the Ferriers, they won't need my help, but I'll be
damned if I'm not there to bring Ailesse out.

The hatch door behind the altar creaks open. Sabine climbs
out from the cellar with a lantern. I sigh. So much for adjusting
my eyes to the dark.

Cas, who has been practicing parrying moves in the chapel,
sheaths his sword and wanders over to her like she's just played
him a siren song.

Sabine has changed into a new white dress, one I stole for her.
I didn't tell her it's the bridal dress of a soon-to-be duchess. That
might be upsetting, and I need her to be focused. The crux of
our plan depends on her tonight. She's the one who has to open
the Gates and channel them together. Maybe that means forcing
Odiva to help her. Or maybe it means switching out Odiva and
Ailesse first, so Ailesse can help Sabine connect the two realms
of the Beyond.

Merde, I hate that we don't know what we're doing.

Jules steps out from the hatch next, with her own lantern. I
stand as she saunters over to me and take in her tightly braided
hair and washed blouse, and the two slim knives on the belt
around her hips. This is how she dressed every full moon when
we scouted bridges for Bone Criers. "You're not coming tonight."
I cross my arms.

She shrugs. "Doesn't mean I can't have one last knife fight with my best friend." She sets a foot on the pew and tightens the laces on her tall boots. Her leather leggings, tucked inside, have grown a little loose over the past few days. Her cheeks are more sunken, too. While Sabine has been reviving, Jules keeps withering. It scares the hell out of me. "Your technique was sloppy last time," she adds. "I'm not going to send you off to face the queen of the Bone Criers if you can't even beat me in a practice round."

"Hey, now, I won most of those matches."

"Not the last three."

"Those don't count." I laugh. "You woke me up in the middle of the night."

"I had to catch you off guard somehow. Do you think Odiva will go easy on you?"

I force another chuckle. The truth is *I've* gone easy on Jules. I could have knocked her knife away with no effort each time she took me by surprise, but I keep humoring her. Her pride is her greatest strength, and I won't take that away.

She draws one of her knives and lunges at me. I delay half a beat before I sidestep her. She swipes for my head, and I duck that as well.

"Come on, Bastien." She coughs into her handkerchief. "You can do more than dodge me. Pick up your knife."

I grab it from the pew and move into the aisle. How should I strike? What will look like I'm trying?

I'm about to swing for her left thigh when Marcel bursts into the chapel through the hatch. He's holding one of the fat books from Beau Palais. "Listen, everyone!" He trips on a moth-eaten rug. "You'll never guess what I've discovered!"

"How to connect the Gates?" I sheathe my blade. Thank the gods I have an excuse not to fight Jules anymore.

"Or the secret to sharing graces?" Sabine moves closer. She's had no luck finding a way to do so. Each of us has nicked our hands and arms several times, testing our blood on her bones.

"You're both wrong," Marcel answers cheerfully. He hops up to sit on the dusty altar and opens the book. "Though it *does* have to do with your graces, Sabine—specifically those from your golden jackal. I've figured out why Odiva and Godart want that grace bone so badly."

She exchanges a tense glance with Cas. "Go on."

Marcel waves everyone over, and we gather around him. Jules hangs back a step, annoyed that her brother is interrupting our practice.

"Listen to this." He flips the pages until he reaches the one he's looking for. "'Gaëlle grew a majestic pear tree, the first in her orchard and the first to break soil from her virgin earth. All the beasts wanted to taste its fruit, but it was the golden jackal that crept into the orchard while Gaëlle was sleeping and bit into its flesh. Tyrus praised him for his cunning and claimed the jackal for his own.'"

Marcel leans back and crosses his ankles over each other. "Guess what a pear represents."

No one answers.

"The renewal of life. Immortality."

Sabine's eyes grow large. Cas pinches the bridge of his nose. I glance behind me at Jules, whose mouth hangs open. I'm the only one not following. "How is that important?"

Cas hangs his head. "Godart wants the jackal pendant so he can rule forever."

"And Odiva, too, if they can share the grace," Jules adds soberly.

"But . . . Sabine doesn't have immortality." I glance around at everyone. They seem to be forgetting that.

"Maybe she does." Marcel closes his book. "Birdine said the poison she drank should have killed her long before we gave her the antidote."

"So let me get this straight." I hold up a hand. My brain is spinning. "You're saying Sabine can't die?"

Marcel's smile splits wide. "Yep."

Overwhelmed, Sabine sits on the edge of the platform surrounding the altar. Jules gives a low whistle. Cas stands frozen. I stumble back a step and rub my brow. "*Merde.*"

Sabine's fingers shake as she touches the jackal grace bone hanging from her neck.

"This is good news, right?" Marcel hops down from the altar and claps a hand on her shoulder. "It should give you an advantage when you confront your mother."

"Not if she steals the jackal pendant." Sabine tucks her necklace deep inside the front of her dress.

I take up pacing. One part of Marcel's theory still doesn't add up. "How can immortality be a grace? Golden jackals don't live forever. If they did, Sabine wouldn't have been able to kill one."

"But *Tyrus* lives forever," Marcel says. "And the golden jackal represents him. Sabine's blood on the jackal bone is what first invoked its graces in her—Tyrus's graces—including immortality."

Cas sighs bitterly. "Now I understand what Godart meant when he compared himself to a god. He said he'd no longer bleed when Paradise is empty. He won't require Sabine's salamander skull if Tyrus can make him indestructible." He sits beside her, placing a gentle hand on her back.

I think about what happened on the last full moon. "I'm not so sure about that. On the cavern bridge, Odiva smeared Sabine's blood onto the salamander skull and asked Tyrus to give her 'daughter's father back his flesh, bone, and blood.'"

Sabine nods numbly. "The skull sealed his resurrection."

"And if he and Odiva get the jackal pendant," I add, "then Godart stays alive forever, along with her." Cas's jaw muscle tics. "They need both grace bones."

Jules steps forward. "Well, we're not going to let them live forever, are we?"

I frown at her. "We?"

She sets her hand on her hip. "You better give me some credit for helping to save the world, even if I can't be with you tonight."

Before I can reply, the heavy door to the church opens and Birdine slips inside. Her cloak is damp with rain. I can't remember a summer that's been so wet. The storms keep rolling through, one after another.

"Bad news." Birdine's airy voice drifts across the chapel to us. Sabine and Cas stand. I curse under my breath. What now?

Marcel hurries over to her, meeting her halfway down the aisle.

If this were any other time, I might crack a joke about how they look like they're about to get hitched. They might just do that, young as they are, if Jules gives them her blessing. Marcel's ready to make a living at his scribe work, and Birdine wants to help him. They have their lives figured out, which is more than the rest of us can say.

Marcel rubs her arms. "Is it your uncle?"

"He's all right." The lantern light glints on her red and puffy eyes. She's been anticipating his death for days, and she tears up easily. "It's the tides that are the trouble." She turns to the rest of us. "I overheard a few fishermen in the city. They were complaining about the high level of the sea. South Galle has had too many storms. The beaches are flooded." She swallows. "What if the land bridge doesn't surface by midnight?"

I scratch the back of my neck and turn my heavy stare on Sabine. "Can the Gates open if they're underwater?"

She tugs her lip between her teeth. "I think so. The bridge rarely floods, but I've heard of it happening once or twice, and it didn't stop the ferrying. It will be much more difficult, though. Some of the Leurress have graces to help them swim or hold their breath, but you . . . ?" She shakes her head.

"I'll be fine."

Cas folds his arms. "I can help Bastien haul a rowboat to the inlet."

"Good. Then the plan stays the same." We can't wait another month until the next new moon. Odiva and Godart will be at the land bridge tonight, flooded or not, to make their final attempt to drain Paradise of its souls. "We have to get moving," I tell Cas and Sabine. "Dragging a rowboat over seven miles is going to slow us down—not to mention exhaust us."

Sabine lifts a brow. "Not if I drag it."

Cas chuckles, and I shrug. "Fair enough."

Birdine starts crying. She gives the three of us farewell hugs, like we're being sent to our deaths. She and Marcel are going to stay back with Jules. They're not fighters like the rest of us, and Jules couldn't even make the journey to the inlet without collapsing into a coughing fit. I don't want them anywhere near Odiva and Godart and the hordes of the Chained.

While Sabine comforts Birdine, Jules gives Marcel a long and affectionate embrace. His smiles, brow wrinkled. "What's this for?"

"For all the times I should have hugged you more," I hear her whisper. "Now seemed as good a time as any."

He pats her back. "Oh. Well . . . thanks."

She pulls away and coughs several times into her handkerchief. I catch a flash of red on the cloth when she straightens up. My heart kicks.

"Was that blood?" I hiss as she comes over to say goodbye.

She stiffens and slides the handkerchief behind her back. "It's nothing to worry about."

"Nothing to worry about?" My voice rises. She smacks my arm to keep me quiet. "*Merde*, Jules, why didn't you tell me?"

"What difference would it have made?"

"You shouldn't have been helping me train, for one thing."

She rolls her eyes.

"We'd better be going," Cas calls to me. He and Sabine are already headed for the door. She's got her quarterstaff in hand.

I force a deep breath and try to not panic. The rest of the Chained are going to be ferried soon, and then Jules will be safe from the threat of any more attacks. She's going to heal. I'll make her. "Promise you'll rest while I'm gone."

She waits a beat too long to answer. "Promise."

I stifle a grumble and throw on my cloak. Before I leave the church, I veer over to Marcel and whisper in his ear, "Don't let your sister out of your sight."

35
Sabine

DARK CLOUDS LOOM OVER THE plateau leading to the cliffs above the inlet. The growing storm blots out Elara's starlight. If not for my graced eyes, the night would be near black. I feel that darkness crowding in on me, quashing my Light. The closer we come to the land bridge, the more suffocating it becomes.

Find your confidence, Sabine. You have the jackal bone. As long as you keep hold of it, you're safe.

My shoulders fall. If only I'd learned to share that grace with Cas and Bastien.

I tug on the cord of my necklace. My grace bones don't budge; I've tucked them under the tight neckline of my dress.

"Do you sense your *famille* yet?" Cas asks, walking beside me.

He's carrying my staff while I drag the rowboat by a rope. He and Bastien helped me carry it for the first three miles, but then I forced them to let me do it alone. They were exhausting themselves, and it isn't so much of a strain on me.

"No." My stomach knots. "I'm sure I will soon." It's hard to imagine Roxane and the elders will allow me to lead them again . . . or even let me into their presence. If they don't, I won't have a chance of freeing Ailesse tonight—or of defeating my mother and Godart and Tyrus and freeing thousands of Unchained souls.

My chest seizes up. I realize I've stopped breathing, and I force a slow inhale. *Relax, Sabine. Focus on one task at a time.*

I attune my senses to my jackal grace, checking once more to see if I can pick up any conversation from the Leurress. It's close to midnight, and I'm not sure whether the Ferriers have arrived on the shore yet. I'm just out of range to be able to hear them. I'm counting on them to be there, desperately trying to open the Gates, even if they don't know how to without me. My friends and I need their help. I can't defeat my mother alone.

Cas nibbles on his lip and casts a glance at Bastien, several yards ahead of us. He slows his footsteps. "Can I talk to you for a moment?"

The shy tone of his voice awakens some of the buried Light inside me. I drift closer as we walk side by side, and our shoulders brush. "You've been talking to me." I grin, letting myself slip under the warm spell he's always able to cast over me. Maybe it will give me courage. Tonight I need to perform my duties as *matrone*, even if my *famille* doesn't give me back that title.

"You know what I mean," he says.

Do I? His eyes grow soft, and my heart skips. If it weren't for the rope in my hands, hauling the boat behind me, would Cas try to hold one of them? My nerve endings tingle at the thought. I want him to, the way he did when I first woke up after I was poisoned. I'll never forget that feeling of being the vital center of his attention.

He sets down my staff and moves nearer to me. I'm not breathing again. He touches my face, sweeping a wispy curl of hair behind my ear. His fingers are cool and slightly damp from the moisture in the air. "Drop the rope, Sabine," he whispers.

"W-why?" I ask, but I think I know why. Cas wants to do more than hold my hand.

He chuckles quietly, his breath fanning across my face. "Trust me."

I clutch the rope tighter. I don't know the first thing about kissing. What if I'm terrible at it?

"Trust me," he murmurs again. His thumb brushes across my cheekbone.

My knees knock as I let the rope go. I suddenly don't know what to do with my hands. Cas does. He takes both of them, and twines our fingers together. He draws me even closer. A rush of heat shoots up from my belly to my chest and neck and ears. *Help me, Elara.*

His hands shift to my waist. I'm hyperaware of his thumbs as they slide up from a spot just above my navel to rest on my lower rib cage. A thousand butterflies take flight inside me.

He leans his head nearer, pausing when our faces are almost touching, like he's gazing at me. How well can he see me in the darkness?

His mouth slowly lowers . . . mine rises . . .

It would be so easy for Cas to pretend I was my sister right now.

The fullest part of his lip grazes the end of my nose by accident. He's missed my mouth.

I can't do this.

I shrug away from him.

He stands stunned, his cheeks flushed. "What's wrong?"

"This—it isn't the right time." I fold my arms against my chest and hold my muscles rigid like armor. "If we succeed tonight . . ." I draw a tense breath. *We're* going *to succeed.* "Ailesse will be back, and well, she's your *amouré.*"

She's more than that. She's the daughter who should be *matrone.*

"Your lives are still bound together," I say.

"Ailesse doesn't love me."

"You love her."

He shakes his head. A strawberry curl tumbles across his brow. I fight the urge to touch his hair like he touched mine. "Sabine . . ." He sighs.

"The gods designed her for you," I rush on before my defenses break. "I can't compete with that. I don't want to be the one you fall back on because you can't have what you want."

"That's not what—" He reaches for me, but I take another backward step.

"I mean it," I say. "I'm tired of being second best." *Even if I am.*

The muscles tighten along my jawline. I suddenly realize what I have to do after Ailesse is free: accept my place within the *famille* and let the fiercer, stronger daughter be *matrone*.

Bastien ambles back in our direction. "Did I lose you two?" he calls.

"No, we're right behind you." I pick up the rope and start tugging the rowboat again. "We have to hurry," I tell Cas, without meeting his eyes. "Come on."

Bastien reaches us and squints at me in the darkness. "You're going to have to take the lead from here, Sabine. I don't know where the entrance to the hidden stairs is."

I nod and walk past him, biting my quivering lip as I drag the boat. *Don't say you're not enough.* I repeat Ailesse's words from my vision, but it's still my first instinct, still my reality. Maybe the golden jackal grace is preying on my doubts, seeking to grind me underfoot even while it grants me perpetual life. But I can't imagine I'd feel any different if I cast off the bone—which I'd never do, anyway. I need every ounce of its power and protection tonight.

Soon I come to the two boulders that conceal the hidden stairs and pause, staring at them. I'm lightly panting, finally feeling the toll of walking seven miles with this boat. My mother won't be weary like I am when we come face-to-face.

I'll never defeat her. I'm going to fail at freeing my sister and saving the Unchained.

"Why have we stopped?" Bastien asks.

I swallow and point at the narrow gap between the two boulders. "The pathway isn't wide enough for the rowboat. I didn't think this through."

I didn't think anything through. We know what we want to have happen at the land bridge, but we have no real strategy on how to accomplish it. We should run while we still can and come back next month, better prepared. If we don't, Bastien and Cas will die tonight, and it will be my fault.

I hear it then . . . a beautiful melody echoing up from the shore: the siren song to open the Gates. Except some of the notes are off and not held out long enough.

Footsteps pound up the stairs. Adrenaline flares through my veins. The Ferriers have sensed our arrival.

I drop the rowboat. Kick it up on its side. Yank the bone knife from a sheath at my thigh. "Take cover," I tell Bastien and Cas. They duck behind the boat just as Dolssa and Vivienne burst out from between the two boulders. I stand my ground.

Dolssa flings a dagger at me. I react fast and knock it away with my blade. Vivienne raises her staff, ready to strike, but then freezes. "Sabine?"

"Yes." My voice is suddenly hoarse, but I clear my throat. "I've come to help. I'm the only one who can open the Gates. You know it." *Stay calm. Be strong and follow through tonight. You won't have to act as* matrone *for long.*

Vivienne looks to Dolssa, one of the elders. Dolssa sighs. "Roxane banished you, Sabine, and for good reason."

"I know, but I'm here to prove myself. Give me this one last chance. If you aren't satisfied, I'll relinquish my title and teach Roxane the siren song before the next ferrying night."

Dolssa rubs her snake rib necklace. "Who is behind the rowboat?"

I swallow, bracing for their reaction. "Bastien Colbert and the usurped king of South Galle."

The two boys slowly rise to their feet and hold up their hands to show they're not a threat.

Dolssa's eyes widen. Vivienne gasps. "They are forbidden to come here."

"I need their help," I say. "I need yours, too. Ailesse is alive. We know how to bring her back from the Underworld and free the imprisoned Unchained, but only if the Ferriers take a united stand against my mother." I take a fortifying breath. "Because Odiva and King Godart are also coming tonight."

Vivienne and Dolssa exchange a pensive look. Finally Dolssa says, "Follow me."

"What about the rowboat?" Bastien asks.

Cas picks up my staff and nods politely at the two Leurress. "The rowboat is essential to our plan."

Vivienne studies him, intrigued by the son of King Durand. "I will find a way to bring it to shore," she replies.

We leave her to manage the boat while Dolssa escorts us between the boulders and down the hidden stairs to the inlet.

When we walk out of the cave at the bottom and onto the beach, I see Roxane standing ankle-deep in the shallows, playing the bone flute I left behind at Château Creux. Pernelle holds a woolen blanket over Roxane's head, like she did with me, to keep the instrument out of the rain.

Roxane still struggles with the siren song. Beyond her, I see Birdine was right about the tide. It would need to lower at least another seven feet for the land bridge to surface, but this is the lowest it will recede tonight.

Ten of the Ferriers, the strongest swimmers, are already out at sea. They're staggered in a line that leads to the place where the Gates should rise. The other twenty Ferriers, not including Dolssa and Vivienne, are waiting on the shore. Their plan must be to herd the souls there, then send them in controlled numbers to the Ferriers treading water. It won't be easy. Many of the Chained have grown in power from stealing Light over the last month. But no souls are here yet. The song isn't working to lure them.

Our arrival is noticed at once. Several Ferriers gape. No boys or men—no living ones, anyway—have ever been to this place. Bastien and Marcel came the closest two months ago, but they only made it as far as the cliffs above. Now Cas and Bastien are standing in the middle of the beach, in the very heart of the place most sacred to my *famille*.

I hold my shoulders square against all the mounting pressure, and I channel the jackal inside me. I have the strongest grace bone of any Leurress. Even Ailesse. Even my mother. I take hold of its fierceness and feel my blood quicken. I'll use that strength to win my *famille*'s trust. I won't let them underestimate me.

Dolssa holds up a hand, preventing the nearest Ferrier from attacking Cas. Roxane turns and pulls the flute from her mouth. In addition to her three grace bones—an antler wreath, her spotted eagle wing bone earrings, and a bracelet made of fangs from a gray wolf—she's wearing two new pendants on a necklace. The five bones officially declare her the new *matrone*.

I stifle a flare of resentment.

Dolssa brings us closer to the shoreline, then motions for us to stay back as she wades into the water to reach Roxane. She relays everything I've told her. Roxane narrows her eyes on me. "Why would Odiva and King Godart come here?"

I stand taller, wishing I'd taken the time to tie my grace bones back onto my own antler crown. "My mother still serves Tyrus, but not Elara. She wants to steal the rest of the souls from Paradise and force the goddess to join kingdoms with the Underworld. Tyrus is taking extreme measures to reunite with his bride."

The Ferriers break into tense murmurs.

"Joined kingdoms?" Élodie asks.

"But all souls would be Chained," Maïa says.

Roxane lifts a hand to silence them. "Perhaps you shouldn't raise the Gates then, Sabine."

You, she just said. She's acknowledging she can't do it on her own. "The Gates *will* be raised tonight," I reply, "whether by me or by my mother. Odiva has the original bone flute." She took it with her when she entered the Underworld, and she would have brought it back.

"These matters concern only our *famille*." Roxane's gaze cuts to Cas. "The usurped king should challenge Godart elsewhere and take that commoner with him." She spares Bastien a glance.

Cas steps forward, addressing Roxane with a diplomatic bow. "If you will permit me to speak, I'll have you know that a Chained killed my father, King Durand, body and soul. Hordes of the dead also ravaged my people. As for my friend"—Cas gestures at Bastien, who stands with his arms crossed and legs planted wide—"he also has a keen interest in ensuring that the Chained face justice. His father, one of your deceased *amourés*, is now in the Underworld, along with the other trapped Unchained."

"And along with Ailesse." Bastien glares at Roxane like all this trouble is her fault. "I have a keen interest in her, too, and I don't need any soul-bond to prove it."

I hastily shift in front of him so he'll bite his tongue. "We plan to throw Odiva through Tyrus's Gate and bring Ailesse out again," I explain. "It's how Odiva switched places with her before," I add, looking around at all the Leurress. "We need your help. I can't overpower my mother without the strength of several Ferriers working alongside me."

Roxane frowns. "And does this command come from him?" She turns her hardened gaze on Cas. "We are not accustomed to taking orders from men—especially mere boys."

"They aren't my orders," Cas replies.

"They're mine," I say, lining my voice in steel. "*I* am the *matrone* of this *famille*. I will not be banished or ignored. We will save Ailesse. We'll ferry souls, as well. And when Ailesse is free, she will help me connect the Gates and return the Unchained to Paradise." I try not to think about how a reversal might inadvertently happen instead, or the thousand other things that might go wrong. "We are daughters of Elara. We should honor her by protecting her kingdom and returning her souls."

Roxane twists the bone flute in her hands, deliberating. Beside her, Pernelle speaks up. "Sabine is right. We can't call ourselves true Ferriers if we don't give the righteous dead a safe passage home."

Roxane's brows furrow as she turns the flute over one more time. She finally walks out of the shallows and onto the sand. She passes me the flute.

Warmth shivers into my chest as I take hold of it. I look into her eyes. I don't see my rival anymore; I see the elder I've always admired, someone who has tried her best to help the Leurress, like me. "Thank you."

Bastien grins. "We need to hurry." He turns around to scan the shore and mutters, "Where's that Leurress with my rowboat?"

"Up here!" Vivienne calls, her graced ears acutely sharp. She's standing on the cliff backing the inlet. She pushes the rowboat to the edge of the limestone. "Catch!" she shouts to the Ferriers right below her.

Bastien stiffens, watching the boat drop a hundred feet to the beach.

I'm not worried. I know the strength of my sisters. Four of them converge, and the boat lands safely in their arms. Vivienne tosses down the oars next. The Ferriers place them in the boat and bring it to the water's edge. Bastien steps inside and sits on the plank seat. Two of the Leurress give the boat a strong push and help him launch against the tide.

Cas touches my arm, and I shiver with warmth. "Ready?" he asks.

I meet his gaze. A few of the storm clouds have parted, and gentle starlight shines down on us. He must be able to see me a little better, because he's looking directly at me now. The sprinkling rain mists across his face and clings to his loose curls. My chest tightens with the familiar ache of wanting something I can't have.

I wish I'd let him kiss me on the plateau. I wish I'd believed I was someone he could love without comparison.

"Ready." I swallow.

He squeezes my shoulder and takes a few steps back, allowing me room. Pernelle brings the woolen blanket and holds it over me. I shake out my hands, clear my throat, and bring the flute to my lips.

Now is your moment, Sabine. Now I show my *famille* I can be their *matrone* without running away.

Now I finally save my sister.

I blow a focused breath into the mouth hole, and I play the siren song.

36
Ailesse

SABINE IS LIMNED IN FAINT silver starlight as she plays the bone flute, but pulsing storm clouds above the inlet creep together and cast a black shadow over her, driving away that beautiful Light.

I stand beside my sister, rubbing her arm, whispering encouraging words, fidgeting as I keep watch on the sea and wait for the Gates to rise. I'm not nervous that she'll be able to open the Gates—she's done it twice before. I'm anxious about the immense tasks my friends and I hope to achieve after she does. And I won't be able to help if I can't escape the Miroir.

The siren song reverberates in the air and floats across the lapping waves of the sea. When Sabine lends her breath to the last haunting note, the water above the end of the submerged land bridge churns and bubbles. The Gate lifts in a wave three feet above the water and darkens to silky black. It hovers at that height, unable to rise any higher. The lower part of the Gate must be hidden beneath the surface. It doesn't matter. It's open.

To the right of the suspended wave, the near-invisible Gates to Paradise barely peek above the water, but the spiral staircase to Elara's realm can be seen stretching high into the Night Heavens.

I exhale a breath I don't feel leave my lungs, but I still imagine it gives me relief. "Well done," I tell Sabine. A fleeting grin crosses her face. She hurriedly wraps the flute in the lambswool Pernelle provides and slips it into a pouch on her own belt. Cas gives her back her staff, and she looks to the cliffs and the cave off the shore, waiting for the dead to arrive.

I take a quick glance myself, then gaze out to the sea to check on Bastien. He's fifteen yards from the shore, rowing against the tide toward Tyrus's Gate, which is another twenty-five yards away. None of the Leurress have joined him in his boat, but several keep watch on him. I trust they'll help if he's attacked by any Chained.

I don't rush to meet him at the end of the land bridge. He can't attempt to free me until my mother takes my place. I turn back to the cliffs and the cave entrance. "Don't come yet," I murmur. Sabine needs to position herself near Tyrus's Gate first.

Deep thrums of music pulse against my ears, throbbing from the depths of the Miroir and the Underworld beneath it. I stiffen and anchor my feet, bracing myself against the powerful urge to wander away in search of the deeper realms of the Underworld.

Tyrus's siren song always grips me by my longing for adventure and draws me closer to him.

But instead of yearning, I'm repulsed with bitterness. It doesn't seize me with nausea, but I sense its sickness all the same. Tyrus's spell can't work on me, not when he's already trapped me here. I latch onto Elara's beautiful descant instead, and it instills me with courage. She's rooting for my friends and me to succeed and save her kingdom.

Forgeron and Estelle appear on opposite sides of the beach. They stare up at the cliffs as the landscape illuminates with an otherworldly glow, overwhelmingly *orvande* in color, not *chazoure*. A massive number of imprisoned souls are swarming to the edge of the cliffs that wrap the inlet.

These aren't the Chained. Forgeron and the jackals must have sent all those souls to the Underworld's deeper realms. These are the Unchained in the Miroir. I scarcely notice a place where they're not packed shoulder to shoulder. They've been scattered until now, perhaps watching their loved ones, like me. Now they're desperately amassing at the call of Sabine's siren song, frantic to escape the Underworld and return to Paradise.

I gasp as they start plunging off the cliffs. They don't take the time to crawl down headfirst like I've seen the Chained do. Instead, dozens of them fall into the sea. Dozens more tumble after them. Some crash onto the shore from a hundred feet above. I wince. I know they can't die again, but they'll feel the pain. *Won't they?* Maybe not, if I can't, and I'm *orvande* like them.

As they flood toward the Gate of water, Sabine and the

Ferriers don't notice them. They can only see the *chazoure* souls who also start to converge. For a ferrying night, their numbers are significant—some have been loose in the mortal world for longer than a month—but they only look like flickers of lightning against the thunderous storm of the Miroir's Unchained.

The Leurress in my *famille* begin ferrying the dead. Most manage them on the shore. They pass them in small groups down the line of ten Ferriers with the best graces to swim at sea. None have rowboats like Bastien. Even if the Leurress kept a supply for rare nights like tonight, I doubt the Ferriers would use them. They're better able to fight without having to maneuver a boat against the waves at the same time.

Throngs of *orvande* souls pummel over the Chained, also headed for the bridge's end, but they're not tangible to the Leurress or even the *chazoure* souls they ferry. The *orvande* souls can't disturb them or penetrate the Gate of water. Whatever power held my mother back when she was in the Miroir also keeps them at bay, despite their growing numbers. Already, at least two thousand imprisoned Unchained are in the inlet, trying to escape the Underworld. Perhaps Bastien's father is among them. I've yet to see him in this realm.

While Forgeron keeps an eye on me, Estelle dashes along the beach and calls out to the panicked souls. She's trying to calm them, but they ignore her and continue to flood into the sea. They don't bob or rock on its waves. They're not even floating. They sink to the seafloor, while the only ones who break the surface are piled on top of the others.

This is madness. How will I reach Tyrus's Gate when the time comes? The *orvande* souls aren't a disturbance to the Ferriers, but they can restrain me.

I lurch forward as one rams into me from behind. He nearly plows me over in his desperate race toward the Gates. Another one batters against my side when I stumble into her path. I press toward the cliff that backs the shore, hoping I can stay out of the chaos until my mother arrives. But then my keen eyes catch a glimpse of Bastien.

He's only advanced another fifteen feet in the sea. Two *chazoure* Chained are in the water surrounding his rowboat, unavoidably drawn to the Underworld, but its pull angers them, and they're taking out their frustration on him. No Ferriers go to help him. They're inundated with other souls.

One of the Chained—a man, bearded and thick-armed—grabs the right edge of the boat. Bastien pitches sideways. I shout his name as he scrambles to ground himself in the hull. Rebalanced, he snatches an oar and blindly attacks the Chained, then shoves him off into the water. But the second Chained slips inside the boat without Bastien realizing.

I run toward the sea, doing my best not to trample the *orvande* souls in my way, but there are too many, and my graced strength overpowers them. I accidentally knock three down and almost barrel into Forgeron. His grim eyes stare back at me. "Take care, Leurress." His deep voice rumbles against the screeching wails of the dead. "You only have one more chance before you're Chained. Do not force my hand."

I pinch my lips together and look past him to Bastien. Still unable to see his opponents, he's locked in combat with the second *chazoure* man. They're wrestling for control of his oar, while the first Chained swims back for the boat again. If the two of them get Bastien into the water, they'll drown him. The nearest Ferriers don't notice his trouble. They're battling more of the powerful Chained.

I meet Forgeron's eyes again and set my jaw. "I'm not forcing your hand. You have a choice, remember?" Before he can reply, I push past him and hurry toward Bastien.

My progress is difficult among the panicked *orvande* souls, but I channel my ibex agility and falcon speed. I charge forward and cut through the masses. I'm still not fast enough. Both Chained men are in Bastien's rowboat now. It's twenty yards away, drifting with the tide toward the shore, and I'm only knee-deep in the water. A girl with a golden braid streaks past me and dives into the sea. My eyes fly wide. *Jules?*

She swims toward the rowboat. Her strokes come shaky but determined. I race after her—after Bastien—battling my way through swarms of *orvande* dead that don't impede Jules.

Bastien has his knife out when he sees her. He's blindly stabbing men who don't bleed when his face blanches in the darkness. "Jules?" He gapes. "What the hell are you doing here?"

She's too winded to reply. She keeps swimming to him. She ducks through the waves when they crest, but some of the stronger currents hold her underwater. She coughs when she surfaces, arms wildly flailing.

I curse as I fight my way forward, now waist-deep in the sea. Why did Jules come? She's too weak to help Bastien. I've watched her cough up blood for days. She'll only distract him.

Another wave crashes over her and shoves her underwater again. Bastien watches for too long. The bearded Chained cuffs him across the jaw. He buckles to the hull of the boat and blinks hard.

I shout his name again. I'm neck-deep now. A wave rolls over my head. I try to swim, but I can't act upon the water. I paddle and kick but can't propel myself to the surface. I only break above it when a wave barrels past me.

The rowboat keeps drifting toward the shore. Jules is now six feet away from it. I'm twenty. The second Chained man abandons Bastien and jumps after her. He grabs her shoulders and pulls her down.

I take another step, and the seafloor declines steeply. I'm fully underwater now. On instinct, I hold my breath, then catch myself. I don't need to breathe. Determined, I keep plunging deeper into the sea.

I wrestle past the Unchained. Their *orvande* limbs and faces flash before me as I push forward. Twelve feet ahead, I find Jules. She's slowly sinking from the weight of the Chained man. Bubbles stream from her mouth as she thrashes. She stabs him with one of her thin knives. He lets go. She kicks to the surface and gulps in air.

I make it another five feet before I'm barricaded by a wall of *orvande* souls, piled high on each other. More climb on top of them, frantic to reach Tyrus's Gate. I do the same, quick and nimble with my ibex grace. When I reach the peak of their writhing bodies, I emerge from the water.

The rowboat is closer, now seven feet away. I can't see Jules anywhere. Bastien and the bearded Chained are on their knees in the hull, in a tense struggle for the knife. The man is driving it toward Bastien's throat.

I leap off the piled souls with my falcon grace, hating that I have to use them as leverage to reach Bastien. Just as I spring away, they shift beneath me. I topple and slide underwater.

Jules and the Chained man are below the surface again, twenty feet down. He's pinning her against the seafloor. My sixth sense drums up my spine as I fight my way toward her.

I grab at the Chained, but I can't move him like I can the *orvande* souls. I'm just as intangible to him as I am to Jules when I vainly reach for her, too. Only Bastien can save her. But how can I get to him?

My mind races, thinking through the natural laws of the Miroir. I picture Estelle kicking the sand without disturbing it; somehow that sand still held us on our feet, even though we were in a separate realm. No, the sand didn't hold us. We stood on it because our minds told us we should.

I *can* swim. In fact, I don't even have to.

I imagine myself in the rowboat, and suddenly I'm there beside Bastien.

I strive for calm, despite the blade bearing down on him and almost nicking his neck. Despite Jules, who is seconds from drowning. "Bastien," I say, and reach for the Light in his soul.

His brows quiver. He hears me.

"Call for Isla," I tell him. "Ask for help." I've never liked Isla—she's been my rival since childhood—but she's the closest Ferrier in the water, and she has wolf-graced ears.

"Isla!" Bastien shouts at once. "Help!" His voice is half-strangled, but twenty-five feet away, Isla turns from the Unchained *chazoure* soul she's guiding. Her eyes widen.

I forgive her for every scornful word or look she's given me as she immediately launches for the rowboat. The swordfish jawbone on her necklace gives her powerful speed in the water. She reaches the boat in mere seconds. She springs inside, yanks the Chained man off Bastien, grabs the knife from his grip, and hurls him toward the path of the Ferriers above the land bridge.

"The knife." Bastien opens his hand, no time to thank her. Isla passes it. He dives into the water for Jules. Isla dives after him. I direct my mind back to the seafloor, and in a blink, I'm there.

Isla reaches Jules before Bastien does. She wrestles the Chained man off her. Jules is barely conscious. Bastien grabs her, kicks off the seafloor, and swims for the surface. Isla zips up to help them. She seizes Jules's other limp arm and races them upward for air.

I'm about to follow when I see Forgeron underwater. His blacksmith's hammer hangs from his belt. He walks on a bed of coral that doesn't cut him, and he charges toward me, adeptly dodging *orvande* souls in his way.

Merde.

I think myself back to the surface. He can't chain me if he can't catch me.

My surroundings change in a flash. I'm sitting in the rowboat, but Bastien and Jules aren't in it. They're at least above water. Isla is still helping them toward the boat.

I scan the depths below and search for Forgeron. An *orvande* glow flares behind me. I whirl around. The blacksmith is on top of the water—*standing* on it. From four yards away, he strides a steady course toward me. "You don't have to do this." I squirm to my feet. "You can choose who you chain."

His brows lower in a rigid line. "No, I can't, and you know why."

He reaches for me. I flash away before his large hand grabs my arm.

Now I'm near the end of the flooded land bridge—and *I'm* standing on the water. Panic sets in. I fumble to grab hold of something, but there's nothing solid nearby. I start to sink, but then I fist my hands and tighten my jaw. *Stop*, I tell myself. *This isn't really water, not in the Miroir. I'm in a separate place from the Nivous Sea and the inlet and the rainstorm. They can't overpower me.*

I rise up. My feet balance on the surface. I glance around, expecting to find Sabine swimming near the two Gates. She's *matrone*. She should be performing the final ferrying. Instead, Pernelle and Roxane are in her position.

I look to the shore and my body goes stiff. Among the masses of *orvande* and *chazoure* souls, I spy a viper and bat skull crown, a sheet of raven hair, and epaulettes of eagle owl feathers and talons.

My mother. She's already here.

She faces Sabine. A few yards away, King Godart turns and locks eyes with Cas across the beach. Both men draw their weapons. *No, no, no.* This wasn't the plan. My *famille* is supposed to be helping Sabine. She can't drag my mother to Tyrus's Gate on her own. But the Ferriers are overwhelmed and battling the Chained in their heightened power.

I'm racing across the water toward my sister when Forgeron finds me again. He cuts across my path. "You have chosen your fate. You can't escape it now."

I flash back from him ten feet. A split second later, he's before me again. I try two more times. It's no use. Now I'm on the far side of the Gate of water, inches from the three-foot wave that hovers above the surface. Forgeron has me backed against it.

"Wait, please!" I hold up my hands, then realize what I'm doing and quickly hide them behind me. But he doesn't need to grab my hands. He reaches for my neck.

"Forgeron, don't touch her!"

Estelle.

She appears beside him, and he freezes. "Ailesse is my daughter of daughters," she says. "She is yours as well."

Despite my panic, awe fills me. Of course Forgeron is my father, several generations back. Estelle told me she'd never loved another.

"We owe our allegiance to our *familles*, not Tyrus," she says.

Forgeron's brow twists. He won't look at her. His eyes hold fast on me. "If I disobey him," he replies, "you will never see your posterity again."

"I made that choice when I came here. I chose you above all

else." She slips a step closer to him. "Is it not time to let go of the past and embrace the present?"

He clenches his jaw.

"Our daughters are strong, Forgeron. They don't need me. But you do."

His chin trembles, but he isn't deterred. He slowly reaches for me.

"Aurélien." Estelle's voice is only a hush, but it carries the weight of countless ages.

Anguish tears across Forgeron's face. "Do not call me that."

"It is your name."

"Not anymore. I'm a blacksmith, a weapon, a forger of chains."

"You're my soul's song. My only love. My life eternal."

"You're my father," I also whisper.

Estelle moves even closer to him, her lithe feet gliding on the water. "Give me your chains, Aurélien. Give Ailesse her life."

He painstakingly turns to her. "But the jackals . . ."

"You won't strike your hammer," she says calmly. "Tyrus can cut us off from the living, but he cannot make you act."

The tension limning his broad shoulders ebbs. "Estelle," he murmurs, and tentatively draws nearer to her. Their faces are almost touching. "Are you sure?"

She leans into him and kisses his mouth. His hands reach to cup her face. A slender *orvande* ring forms around her brow, engraved with beautiful scrollwork. It isn't a third chain link. It's a crown for a queen.

Bastien's rowboat reaches Tyrus's Gate. He and Jules search for

Sabine, but she isn't there with Odiva. My sister and my mother are fighting on the beach. Cas and Godart are also there, pressing through the masses, intent on dueling each other. The Ferriers battle the *chazoure* Chained in the sea and on the shore, while the imprisoned Unchained roll toward Tyrus's Gate. Their bodies clamber over each other like *orvande*-capped waves.

Urgency seizes me. "I need your help," I say to Estelle and Aurélien, wishing I didn't have to interrupt them, especially after how long they've waited for this moment.

They pull apart and stare at me and their surroundings, a little disoriented. I imagine what they must be seeing—only me and the trapped Unchained in the barren Miroir, their view of the Ferriers and the inlet and the *chazoure* souls in the mortal world cut off.

"Can you hold back the Unchained when I try to escape?" *Please, Elara, let me out of this place so I can help my friends.* "Then I can free all these souls and send them back to Paradise."

I'll need Sabine's flute and a miracle to make that happen, but I'm staking my faith on the power of ritual music. Several siren songs exist: one for a rite of passage, one to open the Gates, one to lure souls to the Underworld, and one to lure souls to Paradise. Who's to say more siren songs can't be written? What if I played a new one tonight and used Elara's Light to guide me? A new song might be able to break the barrier of Tyrus's realm and call out the wrongly trapped souls.

Estelle turns to Aurélien and arches a brow. He grins, sliding his large hand around hers. "Together, we are strong enough."

I study the Unchained again. Even though they've grown

countless in number, there must be this many or more of the Chained rightly locked in the deeper realms of the Underworld.

"Good," I reply. "Then prepare yourselves."

I can do more than free innocent souls tonight. I've just realized how my friends and I can defeat Tyrus.

37

Bastien

HOLD ON, AILESSE. I'M COMING *for you.* My pulse hasn't stopped racing since I heard her voice. She's really here. And she's depending on me.

I dig my oars into the water and hold the rowboat steady against the tide. "Come on, Ferriers." I strain my eyes to focus on the dark beach. Ailesse needs their help, too.

I catch a flash of Sabine's white dress as she ducks a strike from Odiva's staff. Her *famille* should be helping her, but they're busy fighting an invisible army of the Chained. It can't be easy, but I have no patience. Forcing Odiva to Tyrus's Gate is more important. Meanwhile, down the beach, Cas's and Godart's weapons collide. They've started their duel.

"Sabine and the Ferriers aren't going to come in time," Jules says. She's seated across from me, the loose hair from her braid plastered to her forehead and neck. We're both soaked to the bone. "The Gate won't stay open forever."

The black wave hovers six feet to my left. Roxane and another Ferrier I don't know are in the water in front of it. I can't see the soul they're trying to ferry, but he must be powerful if it takes both of them to wrangle him.

"You're right." I turn the boat around with my oars.

"What are you doing?"

"We have to help Sabine. *I* have to help her," I correct myself. "You're getting off at the other end of the shore." My teeth grind together. "I don't know what you were thinking coming here. You nearly got yourself killed."

"Don't go back to the shore."

"You have a better idea?"

"Yes." She takes a focused breath. It sounds like paper shredding in her chest. "We get Ailesse on our own."

My fingers clench the oars so tightly my hands throb. My muscles burn with building rage. I finally realize why Jules has had almost manic energy these past several days, despite being so sick. She's figured out a way to really help: she wants to exchange herself for Ailesse. "If you think I'm going to let you pass through the Gate of the Underworld, you've lost your damn mind."

Her small and resigned smile makes me want to throttle her. "I'm dying, Bastien."

"No. You're healing. And once the Chained are gone—"

"I'm not healing! The damage is done." She coughs hard into her sleeve, and blood spreads through the wet cloth. "My soul is hanging by a thread. I feel that thread unraveling. Let me die on my own terms."

"Death in the Underworld?" I try to scoff, but my throat is too choked. "It would be torture."

"It would be *temporary*. You'll free me when you free the other Unchained. I'll find your father among them, and I'll go with him to Paradise." Her eyes glitter with tears. "Think about it. I'll be with *my* father there, too."

My head sags. I drop one of the oars and pinch the inner corners of my eyes.

"You and I made a pact eight years ago to get our revenge," she goes on. "This is my last stand—the last thing I can do to fight for what we've worked so hard for."

"Stop, Jules!" My voice breaks. "I won't hear this."

"You have to." She grabs my hand. "Ailesse has to be free to help Sabine defeat Odiva and connect the two Gates."

"We'll find another way."

"Let me go, Bastien." She moves closer, kneeling in the hull of the rowboat. "I trust you to save my soul."

I gaze at her through my hot and blurry eyes. I can't . . . I won't let my best friend die.

I clench my jaw, shake off her hand, and grab the oars. I give them a strong pull.

"Fine," Jules says, and quickly rises. "Then we'll do this my way."

She leaps out of the boat.

I gape in horror. The dark water by the Gate swallows her from sight. "Jules!" Adrenaline jolts through me. I drop the oars and dive in after her.

My vision floods with black. I grope blindly, searching for an arm, a leg—anything I can grab on to so I can pull her away.

My eyes adjust a little. I see the white dresses of the two nearby Ferriers. They're still fighting the Chained. Then I glimpse Jules's braid. It trails behind her as she swims for the Gate. The rushing black veil is even darker than the water. I can't resist staring into it. For a brief moment, all my muscles go slack. I drift weightless in the current. *Ailesse.*

From the other side of the Gate, her eyes meet mine, and my chest squeezes tight. She's backlit by a strange glow, and her auburn hair swirls in the water like fire.

She looks to Jules, who's darting straight toward her, and her eyes widen. "No!" The water muffles her voice.

I swim hard again. Jules is three feet from the Gate. I grab hold of her boot when she kicks to move faster. She jerks her leg, and her heel smacks my arm away.

"Jules, don't!" Ailesse throws up her hands, trying to stop her. She can't, trapped inside the Gate. Jules reaches through it and seizes her wrist. I snag Jules's other arm.

"Please!" I shout, but my voice is lost in a spray of bubbles.

I pull her, but she won't let go of Ailesse. She thrashes a moment before her body goes still. I worry she's on the verge of drowning, but her expression is alert . . . and peaceful. The anger that's fueled her—that's kept her alive since we were twelve—is gone. A faint smile touches her mouth. She looks between Ailesse and me, like she's asking for permission.

Permission to die.

My heart is in my throat. It's all I can do to hold in a broken sob so I don't lose any more air. It wasn't supposed to end like this for Jules. But the least I can do is help her keep her soul—before the rest of her Light is drained away.

My pulse pounds slower as I loosen my hold on her arm. It slides through my grip until I catch her hand again. Just for a moment. *I'll save you*, I mouth. I'll do what she asked. I'll see her brought back to Paradise with my father, even if it kills me.

I love you, she mouths back.

I see the girl who raced through the streets of the poor districts with me, who practiced knife fighting until the Dovré boys respected her, who followed me every full moon while we hunted for a Bone Crier.

My fingers open . . . and I let her slip away.

Jules yanks herself through the Gate, keeping her grip on Ailesse. A moment later, Ailesse is shoved out, shock written all over her face. We grab hands and kick to the surface.

Our heads emerge. I gasp for breath, and then those breaths hitch. "Ailesse . . ."

Her arms slide under mine. I bury my head against her neck, sobbing openly now. Her graced strength bears me up so I don't sink. Losing Jules . . . holding Ailesse again . . . it's all too much.

There's chaos all around us—the unearthly howls of the Chained, the battle cries of the Ferriers, the rumbling sky as the storm grows heavier—but Ailesse is a calm force against everything. She doesn't chide me for falling apart. She doesn't rally me, either. She just carries me in the water, her lips pressing again and again to the side of my face, until I get ahold of myself.

It's not too long before I gather my strength and breathe steadier. Fierce determination builds inside me. I can't let Jules's sacrifice be in vain.

I rest my forehead against Ailesse's, taking in her warmth one more moment before I say, "I'm ready."

She kisses my mouth tenderly. I don't know what it means for us, but I close my eyes and let myself hope. When she pulls back to look at me, I see the fearless warrior I met at Castelpont three months ago. "I know how to defeat Tyrus," she says.

I lift my brows. "We'll have to defeat your mother first."

Her hand lowers to the pouch of grace bones around her neck. "I think I can give us a fighting chance."

38
Sabine

I LUNGE WITH MY STAFF and strike for my mother's stomach, another desperate attempt to prod her into the sea and toward Tyrus's Gate. Her staff swings with impressive speed. She blocks the hit. Her eagle owl is faster than my nighthawk, but my red stag is quicker than her noctule bat. Except for her greater experience with her graces, our abilities are evenly matched.

She leaps over me and lands a jab to my arm. I hiss, though she could have struck my head. She doesn't want to kill me. Not yet, anyway. She hits me again while I'm still smarting. I stumble toward the shoreline. She's intent on driving me toward the Gates, too. Does she need me to form another channel between Paradise and the Underworld? All I know is that Tyrus wants the rest of

Elara's souls, and my mother has become his willing servant.

I dodge her next strike. Our staffs collide. I grab hers with one hand, and she grabs mine. We wrestle against each other in a pushing match. "Why did you even ask me to be your heir?" I pant for breath. Rain streams down my face. "Our *famille* isn't even sacred to you anymore."

"The world will always need Ferriers." My mother grits her teeth, her black eyes mere inches from mine. "What happens to Paradise doesn't change that."

"Do you really want all souls to be Chained?"

"It is the fate intended for all mortals. The realms of the Beyond were never meant to be divided."

"Think of what you're saying, Mother!" My feet dig into the sand as I push harder. "The Leurress are mortal, too. If the realms join, then when we die, we'll also become Chained. That would mean eternal torture. You can't want that for us."

Her face hardens with stubbornness. "Tyrus will honor the souls of the Leurress."

"There is no honorable place in the Underworld."

"Tyrus promised—"

"Tyrus is a liar!" I break away and shuffle backward to give myself more room to fight. "He will say anything to get what he wants. I should know; his golden jackal grace floods me with doubts and confusion as much as it does with false pride. If this is immortality, it isn't worth it."

My mother's gaze flickers to the lump where my crescent-moon pendant is tucked under the neckline of my dress. She moistens her lips. "Then relinquish the bone to me, daughter." She shifts her weight onto her back leg, holding her staff low behind her. Her rain-soaked dress doesn't impede her flawless agility. "I am prepared to bear it."

Panic shoots through my veins. "I'll never give it to you."

I strike for her neck. She swings her staff around her hip and snaps my weapon away. She pivots to hit my shoulder next. I'm scrambling to block the blow when I hear a loud noise like wood shattering. A girl cries, "Bastien!"

Ailesse?

My mother's staff whips into me. I'm thrown to the sand. I grimace, but quickly roll over, purposefully launching myself into the chaos of Ferriers battling souls. I hurry past them and crawl around the other side of a five-foot boulder to hide.

I scan the sea, and my heart jumps. I'm not imagining things. Ailesse really is out there. She's in the water, fifteen yards away. She and Bastien are swimming alongside the broken remains of his rowboat. A Chained is trying to drown him, but Ailesse attacks the soul and shoves him off toward another Ferrier.

I don't understand. How did Bastien free her? And where is Jules? I saw her with him after I opened the Gates.

A rasp-screech catches my attention above the calamitous sounds of battle. I gasp. A surge of hope runs through my body. The silver owl. She's come. She flaps her wings, hovering over where Cas is fighting King Godart.

She dives between them just as Godart lunges to stab Cas with his sword. The distraction gives Cas the opportunity to deflect the attack. Before Godart can strike again, the silver owl flies in his face and drags her talons across his cheek. He cries out, but it's a noise of fury, not pain.

"Sabine!" Ailesse again. If she can see me at this distance—in the dark—she still has her grace bones.

I turn to her, but I don't dare shout back. I'd reveal my hiding place. Despite my jackal endurance, I'm not ready to fight my mother again. I didn't think I'd have to do this alone.

"Throw me the flute!" Ailesse is ten yards from the shoreline. Bastien is right behind her, the water at chest level. "I know how to free the Unchained!"

I feel my eyes widen. *The flute can free them?* I pull the instrument from the pouch on my belt. *Throw it,* I command myself, but my muscles lock and my grip on the flute squeezes tighter. If I give it to my sister, I may as well be handing over the title of *matrone*.

That's what I've already decided to do. So why can't I let it go? I try to throw it again, but I can't make myself move. I'm paralyzed, pulse hammering. Blood rushes to my head. *What's the matter with me?* I killed the jackal and carved the flute from its femur, but this instrument was never meant to be mine. I should give it up.

I narrow my gaze on Ailesse. It shouldn't surprise me that she would be the one to claim victory tonight. She was always the better leader, the better fighter, the better Leurress. My stomach burns. I didn't even get the chance to help save her.

"Hurry!" Her eyes dart to the other side of the boulder.

I suck in a breath through clenched teeth. *Move, Sabine. Let the flute go. This won't be the last time you can save someone.*

The tension in my body eases. I push to my feet and arc my arm back. Just as I move to hurl the flute, something hard and slim presses against my windpipe. I'm jerked backward by my mother's staff. She's standing right behind me, choking me with it.

"Drop the flute." Her breath is hot in my ear.

I blink against the pain and building pressure in my lungs, but I don't drop it. It isn't mine, and I can't let it be hers.

In one quick movement, she whips the staff away from my neck and strikes my wrist. My grip weakens. The flute tumbles to the sand.

I lunge to grab it back, but I'm too late. She plucks it up and snaps it into two pieces.

I freeze, reeling in shock.

The sky thunders. My heart drumrolls with it.

It's all right, it's all right. My mother has the original bone flute and—

She pulls the other flute from her dress pocket and also breaks it in two. "The Unchained stay with Tyrus," she says, her declaration loud and bold.

Five yards from the shore, Ailesse also stands stunned, eyes horrified.

Beyond her in the distant sea, where the flooded land bridge ends, the jutting black Gates of the Underworld collapse, and the shimmering Gates and spiral staircase to Paradise also disappear.

39

Ailesse

I GO RIGID. "WHAT JUST happened?" Bastien asks. His eyes aren't graced. He can't see my mother on the shore in the darkness. He doesn't know what she's done.

"She—she broke them." The tide crashes into my back. Bastien stumbles forward a step, but I stand stone-still against its force. "We needed them to . . ." I shake my head. Fight to catch my breath. I'm not used to the demand on my lungs or the way my heart slams against my rib cage. I can't gather my thoughts. "How will we free them now?"

"I don't understand." Rain streaks down the planes of his face. "What broke? Who broke it?"

"The flutes. My mother . . . she destroyed both of them."

Bastien's mouth falls slack. *"Merde."*

My sentiments exactly.

For one staggered, stunned moment, the fighting in the sea and on the shore ceases. The *chazoure* souls don't feel the pull of the Gates anymore. There are no Gates. The Unchained stop advancing. The Chained stop resisting. I can't see the *orvande* souls in the Miroir anymore, but I imagine they've halted, too.

The Ferriers rapidly assess what's changed. Then one soul—an emaciated Unchained man—shuffles backward in the sand. That small movement spurs a ripple of commotion among the dead. More backtrack. Some turn around in the sea. The first man breaks into a run. Shouts of panic arise. The ripple launches a riptide. All the souls start fleeing the inlet.

Not again. Many souls have already been ferried tonight, but at least a hundred are still unmoored.

The Ferriers spring to action, trying to herd them together. A Chained woman rushes past me. I'm instinctively reaching for her when a shrill screech grabs my attention.

The silver owl is here. She's flying over Cas. She launches herself at Godart. His face is already cut up from her talons. She rakes them across his right eye. He howls, covering it with his hand. My mother gasps and runs toward him, leaving Sabine. "Godart!"

"Come on, Ailesse!" Bastien grabs my arm. "If Cas dies, you die."

Cold perspiration flashes across my chest. We race to the shore.

My knee doesn't even twinge once I'm out of the water. I expected my injury to return once I came back through Tyrus's

Gate, but my leg is strong. Whole.

I inhale a steadying breath. I can defeat my mother. I will. *We* will.

I pick up speed. She's just reached Godart. The white of his eye is red with blood, and the silver owl is swooping in for another attack. My mother grabs the owl's leg and hurls her away. The owl catapults through the air and crash-lands in the shallow tide.

I gasp. That's Elara's sacred bird. My mother is in full revolt with the goddess.

I run faster. She and Godart will turn on Cas soon.

Sabine bolts toward me. Her eyes are wild. She's rain drenched and shaking all over. "I'm sorry, Ailesse. I'm so sorry. It's my fault Odiva broke the flutes. I didn't act fast enough. I—"

My arms fly around her. "Shh, shh." We're children again. She's waking from another night terror. She dreamed another Leurress died for failing to kill her *amouré*. She swears she'll never do what it takes to become a Ferrier. "I'm here. Everything is all right now." But it isn't. And it never was. Only Sabine had the sensitivity to recognize that. She was the one who truly understood Elara's Light, long before I learned how to call on its power.

My skin prickles. *Light.* It's still the answer.

I pull back from Sabine and hold her shoulders tight. "You don't need the flute. You have a voice. Open the Gates again. You already know the siren song."

She blinks twice, her brows scrunched together. "It doesn't work like that. I can't just sing the song."

"Yes, you can. Elara's Light has the power to penetrate Tyrus's realm. That's how I spoke to you in the vision. It's how I spoke to Bastien. Light has more power than anyone in our *famille* realizes. Odiva didn't want us to know that. She wanted us dependent on Tyrus." I rub her arms to encourage her. "Draw on the Light inside you. *Sing*, Sabine."

She clutches the lump under the neckline of her dress, where her grace bones are tucked away. Her face clouds with doubt.

"You can do this." I kiss her cheek quickly. I have to hurry and help Cas. The silver owl is still floundering in the water, and my mother has drawn a bone knife. She's stalking toward my *amouré*. "No one else in our *famille* discerns Light like you do. You were meant to be *matrone*."

She swallows. "Do you really mean that?"

"Yes." I truly do. I hope my fleeting smile is enough to convince her. I channel all the love and truth I can into it before I take up her fallen staff and race away. Bastien catches up to me, and I grasp his hand.

"Wait!" Sabine shouts. "Even if I *can* open the Gates, how will I free the Unchained without you? We have to connect the Gates together."

I don't stop running. I call over my shoulder, "Sing a new song if you need to, and use the Ferriers. They're also daughters of Elara. Their Light is powerful." United, I have to believe we're stronger than Tyrus. "I'll join you when I can."

When I do, I'll assault the god of the Underworld, like he assaulted his bride by stealing the Unchained from her kingdom. I'll demand an end to this war and all the blood sacrifice.

Bastien glances at me as we race onward. "About that fighting chance you said we had against your mother—I'm ready when you are."

I nod and take a deep breath to focus myself. I reach for the Light inside Bastien, the song of his soul, knowing both of us are willing to give love and receive it.

I furrow my brow, struggling to form a connection. My stomach is tense, and my legs are restless. I'm about to face my mother. But once I murmur Bastien's name, I'm centered on the glowing embers inside him. I fan them brighter with my own Light and share what I have, with no need for blood or bones or sacrifice.

I exhale, meeting his gaze. "Can you feel them?"

He grins and squeezes my hand, his grip tiger shark strong.

We're a formidable team now. We're both sharing my graces.

40
Sabine

I HASTEN TO THE EDGE of the shore overlooking the flooded land bridge and fold my arms across my roiling stomach. The tide laps at my feet, but I'm numb to the cold. *Sing the Gates open?* I might laugh if the situation weren't so pressing.

Pernelle notices me struggling. "I saw Odiva break the flutes." She hurries over. "It wasn't your fault, Sabine. Don't let it trouble you. We need your help with the Chained. They're escaping again."

I feign confidence I don't have and lift my chin. "I know how to call them back."

Her brow wrinkles. "But that's impossible."

"Ailesse learned how to do it when she was in the Underworld."

Not exactly true. "She taught me."

Pernelle's gaze travels across the shore to my sister and Bastien, moving closer to Odiva. She purses her lips for a moment, then nods to herself. She raises her voice to the other Ferriers. "All is well! Sabine can call the souls back."

"No, don't!" I grab Pernelle's arm. "I'm not ready for . . ." *I wanted to try it without everyone watching me.*

It's too late. The nearby Ferriers stare expectantly. Some, like Roxane, are in the water. She wades closer. "How can you call them back?" She frowns.

I want a shell to hide in, a dark cave, the deepest tunnel of the catacombs. "I'm going to open the Gates again by . . . singing the siren song."

Roxane's slender brow arches. "Singing?"

I nod mutely, my cheeks on fire.

Word spreads fast among the Leurress. All thirty-two Ferriers gather around me. Some, like Pernelle, have desperate hope in their eyes. Most look as doubtful as I feel, but they keep converging. None go to aid Ailesse, Bastien, or Cas. They're too fearful of our old *matrone* and King Godart, who's sharing her graces.

My heartbeat races as I glance at everyone. I suppose I have to begin now.

I clear my throat . . . and start to hum. I don't know what else to do. This song has no words. It was meant to be played on a bone flute, not desecrated by the youngest Ferrier of the founding *famille*.

Pernelle rubs my back, which makes me feel like a child. "I

think you'll have to be louder, dear."

I nod, shivering in the pelting rain. There's no safe place to gaze—everywhere I look I find skeptical eyes staring back at me—so I look down at my feet.

It's impossible to hum any louder. I have to open my mouth. I voice the melody with no other lyrics than a tentative "ahhhh" for every phrase.

The song has never felt so long and shaky, so breathy and dissonant. I'm too nervous to stay on pitch. I haven't captured the siren song's hauntingly beautiful essence at all. If the Chained or Unchained can hear me, they must be cringing.

When the song ends, I chance a peek at the dark sea. The tide has settled. Barely a wave skims the surface. Nothing stirs in the water where the Gates should rise except ripples from the rainfall.

I chide myself, *Did you really believe you could call on divine power with your voice?*

Whatever Ailesse learned in the Underworld is beyond me. I turn to look at her. She and Bastien are circling Odiva, drawing her away from Cas and Godart, but my mother's haughty expression says she isn't worried. My stomach wrenches. I should go help my friends. Cas's right arm is bleeding, and he's limping. It's pointless trying to open the Gates.

But if I don't, the Chained will be loose for another fortnight, and more deaths will be on my head. How many of the dead already blame me for losing their lives? How many more can't even point a finger at me because they no longer have a soul?

"Try again," Pernelle says. She musters a smile, but her brow twitches. Does she really believe in me, or do I only represent her last shreds of faith? She saw my mother's sacrilege firsthand when Odiva raised Godart from the dead, when she killed Maurille and broke both flutes. Pernelle has also seen the Chained evade the Ferriers again and again. There's little hope left to salvage what my *famille* has sacrificed so long for . . . except for me.

"Yes, Sabine." Vivienne steps forward. Her chestnut hair clings to her face in the rain. "Try again."

The words are echoed, Ferrier by Ferrier, their desperate prayers that I can do something to help them finish their duty to protect the living from the dead.

Roxane is the last to say something. She bows her head, the tines of her antler crown sagging before she stands taller and looks me squarely in the eye. "Try again, Sabine."

My heart thrums faster. Pressure builds on my shoulders. Everyone is counting on me.

I squeeze my eyes shut. Force my pinched lungs to open. *Draw on the Light inside you*, Ailesse told me.

Where is that Light? All I feel are my crushing doubts, the golden jackal grace burying me deeper beside the stream in the hollow.

My words to my mother echo back to me. *Why did you even ask me to be your heir?* I know the answer now: because I'm the weaker daughter. She knew I wouldn't be able to lead our *famille* in rebellion against her.

I sing the first phrase of the siren song again. I can't even hold the last note. My mouth goes dry, my throat closes, my eyes burn.

Hot tears slip down my cheeks. I furiously scrub them away.

Distantly, a corner of my mind screams, *This is the golden jackal, not you! Destroy it!*

Panic jolts through me. *No!* I can't destroy the crescent-moon pendant. Its strength is the only thing keeping me standing against all my insecurities. It can protect me from the dead and channel the power of the Underworld. Immortal life. Only a fool would sabotage that gift.

You don't need immortality. The red stag gives you enough strength.

Stop! I command myself. I'm *matrone*. I should have five grace bones. I've already lost my salamander skull; I can't lose another one.

Twelve feet to my right, something washes up on the tide. A dark gray bundle. No, it's silver.

I gasp and rush over to the owl, drawing her into my lap. Her wings are waterlogged, her eyelids slit with exhaustion. My graced ears catch the slight and rattled rasp of her breathing. More tears scald my face to see such a beautiful and proud creature so wilted and fragile.

This is Light, I realize, naming my pain. It's the same anguish that made me weep from all the blood and death I've seen in my life. It's my anger and shame for being born what I am—a girl meant to sacrifice majestic animals like this, a girl destined to slaughter the boy she'll come to love. I've ached for a better way. I've mourned that there wasn't one.

But what if . . . what if the better way begins with me?

"I'm sorry," I whisper to the silver owl. She hasn't guided me or given me visions in weeks. "I want to do better. Will you help me?" I can't believe I'm asking this of her, but I push onward before I lose my courage—or, more important, my tremulous grasp on my Light. "Will you share your graces with me?"

Her lovely eyes crack open wider.

"I don't want your death. I don't want your bones. I don't want to steal anything from you. I want us to work together." I stroke her wet feathers. "You have the graces of Elara. This is your chance to take back from Tyrus what is rightfully yours."

She screeches so faintly it sounds like a purr, but I sense her Light pulse brighter. I wait for her dignity and power to flow into me, but nothing happens. Her head bobs lower. Her eyes stare directly at the lump under the front of my dress where my crescent-moon pendant is hidden. I understand the problem now. My jackal grace is blocking my Light—and blocking her power.

I pull out my necklace and clutch the pendant. My muscles harden, freezing me into paralysis again. I can't give it up. The jackal gave me the boldness to crash through a stained-glass window. It gave me the fortitude to set vipers on Beau Palais, and the viciousness to kill the red stag so I had a *matrone*'s five grace bones. I'd be no one but Ailesse's weak sister without it.

Don't say you're not enough.

But what if I'm not?

You have Light. Ailesse's words again. *Hold on to it.*

I hesitate. Can Light really be stronger than the strength of Tyrus?

The silver owl rasps again, a soft but stalwart cry. I feel the sound reverberate through me, like it's my own voice, my own song.

I exhale slowly. Untie the pendant from my necklace with shaking fingers.

"Pernelle," I say. The elder Leurress comes to me. "May I borrow your staff?" I gently set the silver owl down on the sand.

She passes it to me. I swallow and place my pendant on a nearby stone. I hold it there a long moment, not letting go. Perspiration flashes over me, hot and cold. *Elara, help me.*

I focus all my energy. My head throbs, heart quickens. Finally my muscles go limber. I painstakingly drag my hand away from the pendant.

The moment I let it go, I no longer feel its power. But that's not good enough. I can't let my mother or father be granted immortality.

I stand up tall, broaden my shoulders, and inhale a shuddering breath.

I slam the end of the staff down on my golden jackal grace bone.

41
Bastien

MY TIGER SHARK VISION CUTS through the darkness and sheets of rain. With Ailesse's graces, the moonless sky looks more like a gray dawn, even with all the storm clouds. My eyes snag on every detail of Odiva's knife when she swipes for me—the aged color of the bone, the jagged teeth at end of the blade, a pack of jackals carved on the hilt.

I leap back, and my breath catches. My reflexes are startlingly fast. The knife nicks my shirt, but not my skin. Odiva keeps driving me back toward the wall of the cliff behind me. I'm close to touching it.

"Jump, Bastien!" Ailesse shouts. She scrambles up to her feet. Odiva has thrown her several yards away.

Jump. That's right, I can almost fly.

I tense my muscles and kick hard off the limestone. I slingshot through the air. It's all I can do not to whoop from all the adrenaline. I spin over Odiva's head and hurtle toward the ground. My landing is a mess. I roll over and skid into wet sand, but I'm up again quickly, a dazed grin on my face. My pulse races, ready for more. With this much energy pounding through me, anything is possible. *Revenge* is possible.

I crack my knuckles. Tighten my fists. Meet Odiva's black eyes across the twelve feet between us. *This is the night you finally die.*

Her bloodred lips curve. "The boy you love is overconfident," she says to Ailesse, who moves into a tactical position on her right. "Is that why you desire him more than your own *amouré?*" Odiva tilts her head at me like a hawk. "I do not blame you. Bastien may be arrogant, but at least he has a strong inclination to survive, regardless of the graces he gleans from you. I cannot say the same for poor Casimir."

I look fifteen yards past Ailesse to where Cas is fighting Godart. He's putting in a decent effort, but Godart has the clear upper hand, with five graces in his arsenal. Cas drips with rain and a good amount of blood. His arm and leg are wounded. Badly. Godart's got Cas backed against a boulder, and he's inching closer, using his sword to toy with him. He nicks him with small cuts. Hits his arms and legs with the flat of his blade to bruise him.

"Go help him!" I tell Ailesse. She's not any weaker, which means Cas hasn't lost Light. But their lives are still soul-bound. He dies, she dies. That would just as well as kill me, too. "I can handle your mother."

Her pointed look says Odiva hasn't even started to challenge us. She shifts on her feet, glances between me and Cas, then sucks in a quick breath, like she's remembered something. "The salamander skull!" she shouts to Cas. "Cut it away! Godart can't live without it."

Odiva's grin falls. Cas's expression hardens. He swiftly butts heads with Godart, then catches the cord of his necklace and slices it with his own blade. The skull drops to the sand. Godart reaches for it, but Cas cuts his hand and grabs the skull. He smashes it against the boulder with the pommel of his sword. It cracks into small pieces.

I watch, holding my breath. I'm not sure what to expect— maybe for Godart's flesh to melt off his bones and those bones to turn to ashes—but nothing happens. He growls and attacks Cas again. Their swords clash.

Vibrations thump up my spine and left shoulder. My sixth sense. This is how Ailesse described it. I look in that direction. Odiva is slowly stalking toward her daughter. "Foolish girl."

Ailesse steals another glance at Godart, frowning. She's just as confused as I am. "At least they're closer to having a fair fight now," she says. "Godart won't be able to heal."

"Heal?" Odiva's nostrils flare. "Your *amouré* stole *all* his graces."

Ailesse narrows her eyes. "The salamander skull . . . it was binding your graces to him," she says in realization. "But how? It was Sabine's grace bone, not yours."

Odiva draws herself taller. "You forget it had Sabine's blood on it, and through hers, mine."

I don't follow the finer points of Odiva's dark magic, but one thing is clear—it *is* a fair fight now. For Cas, anyway.

Odiva charges at Ailesse with her bone knife. A new rage has taken hold of her. The games are over.

Ailesse swings her staff to block her mother's strike. Odiva leaps over it and slashes Ailesse's upper arm. She gasps and drops her weapon. I bolt for her. Blood gushes from the wound. *Merde*, the cut is deep.

Odiva smoothes a lock of dripping black hair off her face. "This is not what I wanted for you."

"No." Ailesse clutches her bloody arm. "You wanted me to spend eternity in the Underworld."

Odiva lifts a shoulder. "You would have had a semblance of real life in the Miroir."

"Stop making excuses! You sacrificed me coldheartedly, knowing full well I would become Chained there."

"And yet you are here." Odiva's nose wrinkles as she stares Ailesse down. If Odiva ever had any love for her, it's been obliterated. Nothing but pure hatred courses off her now. "Which means, first-born daughter, I must kill you with my own hands, after all."

Ailesse fumbles for her staff. She's slow with her injured arm. I try to grab it for her, but Odiva beats me to it, noctule bat fast. She whips the staff against Ailesse's side—and her ribs break with a sickening *snap*. Ailesse is thrown down on the sand, writhing.

"Ailesse!" My blood lights on fire. I turn furious eyes on Odiva. She's dead. I'll make sure of it.

I fly at her, wildly slashing and stabbing with my father's knife. Her staff blocks me at every turn. "I will kill you, too, boy." Her black eyes are flat, no life or Light, just darkness. "The same way my *famille* killed your pitiful father."

My heartbeat roars in my ears. "Don't you dare speak about his death."

The side of her mouth curves. "Very well." She pummels me backward until I fall to the ground. She plants her staff in the sand, draws her bone knife, and pins me with one knee. "Then I will speak of *your* death, Bastien. Or better yet, I will deliver it."

She aims her blade at my heart. Rain slides off the sharp tip. "And this time, I will make certain you die."

42
Sabine

THE LIGHT INSIDE ME RADIATES with the graces of the silver owl. The night sky brightens—I'm seeing even better in the dark—and my hearing also sharpens. But it's the changes in my bearing and frame of mind I notice most.

I walk along the sand on silent huntress feet, no longer weighed down by lies or doubts. My new graces don't compel me to feel differently; they gently persuade me to own who I am and what I believe in. And I'll sing of that confidence now.

The siren song pours out of me, each note articulate and unwavering. I lend it strength from my lungs and the power of my convictions. I give it Elara's rage at a millennia-old marriage to a tyrant god.

I turn away from the sea. Some instinct inside me says the Gates don't need a sunken land bridge to stand on. I am the bridge. The Ferriers of my *famille* are the pillars of its foundation. We carry the torch of Elara's Light. It shines brightest in us. We are the daughters of the goddess.

In the middle of our gathering, two brilliant columns of flame shoot up from the sand. They curve at the top and join together to form a towering fifteen-foot arch.

Prickling awe showers over me. It's a Gate of fire—the missing element, like Marcel said. Or more accurately, the last element that could create a doorway to the Underworld.

The rainfall lashes at the blazing arch, but its fire doesn't hiss or extinguish. It's inexplicably stable, like the wind that blasted up from the cavern pit and held the glittering dust together, or the silky black wave that stayed hovering when it should have crashed. I look to my right and see that Elara's translucent Gate has also risen. The silvery shimmer of her spiral staircase stretches high to the Night Heavens.

"Sing with me," I say to Pernelle and Roxane.

"We don't know the siren song," Pernelle replies.

"The Gates are already open," Roxane adds.

The silver owl hops near the Gate of fire. Her feathers dry in its rippling heat. She faces Tyrus's Underworld, unfurls the full span of her wings, and points the feathered tips toward the sand. It's a battle stance. She's declaring war. She's ready for her Unchained souls to come home.

"She still needs us to sing," I tell Pernelle and Roxane. I turn to the rest of the Ferriers. "She needs all our Light and strength."

The Leurress gather closer, positioning themselves behind me. They're bruised and bleeding and drenched from the storm, but they're also stalwart and noble, my unified *famille*.

I start singing again. I follow a new melody, a song of my own creation. It's wordless, a cry in the night set to a fervent melody. I infuse it with what I believe in most: human dignity, respect for life, sisterhood, devotion.

The Ferriers join in, one by one, falling into its rhythm and repeating the musical phrases. But then their voices grow bolder. They add their own harmonies and soaring descants. Our chorus swells, more beautiful than any siren song played on bones, more powerful than the deep and angry chant that pulses from the Underworld, resisting us.

I take Pernelle's hand. She clasps Roxane's. Soon all thirty-two Ferriers and I are linked in a winding path. Chantae and I stand at each end. I'm nearest to the Gate of fire, and she's closest to the Paradise. She seems to understand what to do next, because she grabs a bar of Elara's scrollwork Gate. I turn to the rippling arch of fire and hesitate, feeling its heat scorch my face.

The silver owl lifts into the air and flaps her wings at me. She's urging me, telling me I'll be safe.

I grit my teeth. *Our Light is stronger than your flames, Tyrus.*

I seize the column of fire.

It burns and sears, but I can endure it. I continue singing with my sisters, and each of us transforms, incandescent with *chazoure*. The silver owl zooms overhead and screeches triumphantly. The channel between the Underworld and Paradise is open.

Unchained souls crash through the Gate of fire like a battering ram. They flood out in wave after wave, crying with a surge of freedom.

More souls flock near from the cliffs and the cave off the shore, the Chained and Unchained still trapped in the mortal world. The open Gates are calling them back.

"Some of you need to break away and ferry them," I shout to the Leurress. "The rest of us will keep the Gates linked."

Roxane, Nadine, Dolssa, and eleven other Ferriers pull away from the channel, but not before the Leurress on either side of them scoot together and join hands. The fourteen Ferriers grab their staffs and start guiding the oncoming souls.

I see a beautiful *chazoure* woman with a bracelet of dolphin teeth drift down the beach with the other Unchained. I gasp, seeing the Leurress who died at the cavern bridge. *Maurille.*

Damiana embraces her and gently leads her to Paradise. My eyes sting. I wish I could ferry her myself, but I'm more grateful she can be at peace now. She smiles at me before she passes through the silvery Gate. "Stay strong, child," she says, and shimmers away inside.

I draw a steeling breath and continue singing with my sisters. The song builds, thrumming faster and sharp edged and raging. It's our demand that Tyrus free every last one of Elara's Unchained in his realm. Her trapped souls keep coursing out of his Gate of fire, weeping tears of relief.

Hope builds inside my chest. Maurille being ferried feels like a sign. We're going to win. Victory is almost in our grasp.

A crack of lightning flashes. It pulls my gaze to the distant shore where my friends are fighting. But the only one I see standing is Ailesse. Bastien is crumpled at her feet. And Cas . . .

My heart gives a hard pound.

Cas is lying in the blood-soaked sand.

43
Ailesse

Fifteen yards behind me, Cas crawls out of the pool of his own blood. He rises to face Godart again. I don't know where he's found the stamina to keep battling him for so long. Godart can't access my mother's graces anymore, but Cas is still the weaker of the two. He was already badly injured when he crushed the salamander skull, so it hasn't been a fight of equals, after all.

I wish I could do something to help, but I can't leave Bastien to fight my mother alone. At my feet, he's been unconscious for over a minute.

Wake up, wake up. His left temple is bruising from my mother's staff strike. She came close to stabbing him—I barely shoved her away in time—but she's still intent on killing him. The only thing preventing her is a group of eight Unchained. They rushed to my aid when I called for help, but they won't be able to hold my mother back for long. She's swiftly fighting them off, and the relentless lure of the Beyond also pulls them away, one by one.

Down shore, the rest of the Unchained are flooding to Paradise through the open channel between the Gates. When the arch of fire blazed up from the sand, my mother audibly gasped. I almost burst into tears. I've never been prouder of my sister.

Bastien's eyes finally crack open. I release a huge breath. *Thank you, Elara.*

I reach to pull him up, my broken ribs smarting, and my mother sneers as she fends off the last three Unchained. She wants Bastien dead before she kills me, I'm sure of it. That way I'll suffer more. She's become monstrous, nothing like the woman I once admired as a child. But I'm done with suffering at her hand. I can channel Light like my sister, like I did in the Miroir and when I fought my mother on the cavern bridge.

I call on my own soul, my own name. My mother gave it to me, but its power runs deeper than the word uttered at my birth. My name is separate from her now. It's bright with Light passed down to me from Estelle, and before her, the goddess Elara. And it's me, not my mother, who chooses to keep that glory in me burning.

Strength flows into my limbs, more graced than my tiger shark or alpine ibex or peregrine falcon. But I hold on to that power, too. I'll fight with everything I can draw upon. My mother's dark reign ends tonight.

She strides toward Bastien, staff raised. He's kneeling, barely coherent. He's not ready for her.

I am.

I bury the pain of my broken ribs and bleeding arm. I charge at her before she can reach him. We're two raging forces about to collide.

She yanks her staff up like a skewering pike. I grab hold of its end and swing around it. I kick away her upper hand, then jerk the staff down. Its other end slams into her chin with a loud *crack*.

Shocked, she staggers backward. Before she can recover, I tear away her three-tiered necklace and its tooth band, claws, and pendants; her epaulettes of feathers and talons; her skull and vertebrae crown. I cast them out of reach beyond a cluster of boulders. The grace bones of her whiptail stingray, albino bear, eagle owl, noctule bat, and asp viper—they're gone.

Her black eyes are pits of seething rage. "You wretched, abominable girl." It's a violation to remove a Leurress's grace bones without consent, but I've done nothing more than my mother did when she stole Sabine's salamander skull.

She pulls out her bone knife, but she's lost her speed and strength. I grab her wrist and wrench the blade away. I place its sharp tip at the base of her neck. Her pulse flutters madly. She inhales a careful breath through her nose. "I brought you into this world, Ailesse. Is this how you will honor me?"

I scoff. "I've learned no honor from you. You're the hypocrite who cast me out of this world. You're a threat to your own *famille* and a danger to every Unchained who ever walked this earth. This can't go on, Mother. You . . . *you* can't go on."

My knife trembles. I've never killed another person, but I need to now. Surely that's what Elara has sanctioned me to do. But this feels wrong, premeditated. My mother is defenseless. She's small and thin without her formidable grace bones. She looks younger, too. It's easy to imagine her being a novice once, a girl who never played a bone flute, or lured a man onto a forest bridge, or conceived a daughter before she killed the father, or met and fell in love with another man, or lost him before she could make a life with him.

"Do not taint yourself with my death," my mother says, her voice a shameful croak. "Be better than me, Ailesse. You cannot want what I have endured."

I scrutinize her shimmering tears. She's manipulating me, I know it. So why does my chest pang, my throat tighten, my own eyes blur with emotion? "I wanted so very much to love you," I whisper.

A tear streaks down her cheek, but it's quickly swept away by the rainfall. "I know."

My shoulders curl inward. I exhale and pull away the knife. It hangs from my limp hand. "Go. Take Godart with you. Leave South Galle and the Leurress forever. At least you can be with your love."

I start to turn away. She can't hurt me or my friends anymore.

"Ailesse!" Bastien shouts a cry of warning.

My sixth sense pounds. I glance behind me. Odiva whips out another knife from a hidden sheath on her back. Her tears still fall, but they're tears of fury.

Her knife slashes for me. I'm faster. Just before she can kill me, I stab her through the base of her throat.

Her eyes startle wide. Her grip slackens. Her own knife drops. She collapses to her knees and tries to speak. No words come out, just a horrible ragged gasp. I've cut through her windpipe and sliced an artery.

Crimson blood blooms down her neck. She chokes on it, drowns in it. Her enraged and astonished gaze bores into me. She careens to the sand.

My mouth is agape, my hands splayed. I'm unsure what to do. I openly stare at my mother as she writhes and gags, my knife still stuck in her neck. I've given her a fatal wound, but it could be minutes more before she finally dies.

Bastien rushes over to me. I stifle burning sobs as my mother gurgles on more blood. I can't bear watching her like this. "Make it stop," I say, my voice a frail whisper.

He slowly pulls away from me and kneels beside my mother. He points the sharpened end of his father's knife directly over her heart. The simple hilt trembles in his grip. She stares frantically at him, convulsing harder. He looks to me for permission. Hot tears stream down my face. I nod.

The knife drives into my mother's chest, sure and swift. She buckles with one last convulsion. Then her expression goes vacant. Her body stills. Her head droops to the side.

I clap my hand over my mouth and shake my head again and again.

"Ailesse . . ." Bastien's eyes fill with pain. He comes to me and folds me into his arms, kissing the top of my head.

Anguish racks my broken ribs and turns all my muscles to water. It's Bastien who holds me up now, like I held him in the sea. He strokes my rain-drenched hair and whispers words of comfort. This can't be how he imagined culminating his revenge, but that makes his gentle embrace all the more meaningful.

My graced ears catch the sound of another person breathing, panting. My sixth sense patters up my spine from their weak movements. Then a stronger pummeling hits my lower back. I look behind me to where Cas and Godart are fighting. They're both badly wounded and bleeding.

Cas leans against a boulder. He clutches a stab wound on his side. Godart limps toward him, dragging his sword in the sand. Cas unhitches himself from the boulder, but he's scarcely able to stand without support.

"Go," I tell Bastien, and quickly wipe away my tears.

He nods, leaving his knife in my mother's chest. He picks up her fallen blade, and I grab her staff. We run for Cas, but he's fifteen yards away, and Godart is less than three yards from him.

Godart flexes his jaw muscle. Raises his sword. Cas's eyes are hooded, barely open. My keen vision focuses on the feeble twitch of his fingers over the hilt. He doesn't even have the strength to lift his blade.

"Cas!" Bastien shouts, urging him to not give up. My life is still at stake tonight, tied to his.

Now three feet from my *amouré*, Godart hefts his sword overhead with both hands. Blood drips from his hairline into his mangled right eye. "Now you die, bastard prince."

"Cas!" I cry, as Godart's sword plunges down.

Cas's expression flashes with steel. He jerks away from the boulder, spins to dodge Godart's strike, and thrusts his own sword into Godart's back. The silver blade runs clean through him and juts out of his chest. Godart's face twists in horrific shock. Cas yanks out his sword. "Not a bastard," he says. "Not a prince. A *king*. Son of Durand Trencavel. Ruler of South Galle."

Blood burbles from Godart's mouth. He collapses facedown in the sand.

Bastien and I finally reach Cas. Bastien pulls him into a fierce hug. "Well done."

Cas grins, but then his knees start to buckle. He clutches his bleeding side again. "Easy on the brotherly affection, all right?"

Bastien chuckles. "Yes, Your Majesty."

I wrap my arm beneath Cas's to help him stand. "Come on. We're not finished."

Bastien and I help him walk across the shore to where Sabine and the Leurress are still holding the channel open between the Gates. Only a slow trickle of souls now passes out of the blazing arch and into the delicate shimmer of Paradise. No more *chazoure* Chained or Unchained roam the inlet. The Ferriers' work is almost done. Mine isn't.

Sabine's eyes squeeze shut in concentration. Her hand shakes, gripping the burning Gate. I call out her name, and she looks at me. She quickly takes in the three of us approaching—and who we've left behind. Our mother. Her father. Their souls haven't risen from their bodies yet, but they're bound to soon. "Oh, Ailesse." Her brows lift inward.

She says something to Pernelle, and the silver owl flies closer, hovering near the elder Leurress. Pernelle nods, breathing in deeply, and takes Sabine's place holding the Gate of fire.

Sabine races across the sand to me, and I break into sobs again, hearing her cry. I'm sorry to cause her fresh pain, but I'm also filled with overwhelming relief. The two of us have survived.

She barrels into me with a powerful embrace. I hug her back with all my graced strength. "We're going to be all right." I stroke her hair. "You're all the family I need."

"You, too." She nods against my neck. "Thank you for believing in me tonight."

"I'll always believe in you. You're my sister, my *matrone*."

Cas comes over to us, and Sabine turns to him, still weeping. I let him comfort her, as well. As they embrace, I share a glance with Bastien. He nods. We haven't conquered everything yet. We've restored the balance between the realms of the Beyond, and we've removed the dead from the land of the living, but I'm still soul-bound to Casimir. My *famille* is still enslaved to Tyrus, as well.

I wait until the last of the Unchained escapes the Underworld, and then I plant my feet in front of Tyrus's Gate. His flames lick at my dress and hair, but they don't catch fire. I'm blazing with too much Light. The silver owl swoops in and lands on my shoulder, and I stroke her wings. "I think your bride has a message for you, Tyrus," I call past the churning storm of embers. "She will not suffer her souls to be abused by you any longer." The silver owl screeches.

Tyrus ignores us. His siren song wafts its dark music without a hitch in the melody. I feel the lure of its pull once more, but the temptation to go to him is only a weak desire now. I'm too aware of his corruptness to be tricked into walking through his Gate.

I stand taller. "You have threatened Elara and tormented your own Leurress daughters for centuries. You've thrust your own misery upon us, and twisted our sacred duty into a mockery. We are soul guardians and defenders of the living, and we won't be compelled to kill any longer. And so now we threaten you."

Behind me, I feel the Light of all my sisters, urging me on. Each of them is here because they killed their own *amourés*, because they were told they had to.

"We will keep this channel open!" I shout into the embers. "There are souls still within your kingdom for the reaping. We will drain the Underworld of every Chained in your grasp and leave you abandoned—alone for the rest of eternity with nothing but your own despair to keep you company—unless you end your demand for blood sacrifice. There will be no more rites of passage, no more soul-bonds tied to death, no more slaughtering of any life for power."

Tyrus's siren song warbles, like he's laughing at me.

I dig in my feet. "Don't you believe me? Elara will gladly receive your souls. Paradise is boundless. She can surely find a place to hold them." The silver owl releases an explosive screech, backing my claim. "Perhaps many don't deserve your chains to begin with." How much mercy did Tyrus extend to mortals for the mistakes they made while they were living? Not much, if his strictness in the Miroir is any indication. "And the goddess will do something more. After we purge you of your souls, she will leave her kingdom unjoined from yours. You will rule an empty, desolate realm, and Elara will rejoice."

The flames of the arch retract slightly, a deadly simmer. Now I've angered Tyrus. It's a start.

I look to Sabine. "Do it. Sing to release the Chained."

Her eyes widen. I've had no time to explain my plan, but Tyrus needs to see that this isn't an idle threat. We have the power to strip him dry.

Sabine quickly composes herself and hardens her brow. She inhales a steadying breath and sings a song I've never heard. No one has. It's all minor notes and violent staccato. It speaks wordlessly of the worst of the Chained, the most wretched and murderous and greedy. The Ferriers join her, their harmonies discordant and out of rhythm. It's just what the song needs. The silver owl pushes off my shoulder and flaps around them, lending her own high-pitched screams.

Past the flashing embers beyond the Gate, the vilest *chazoure* Chained start to converge. They're howling and raging. They want to escape the Underworld, too.

The flaming arch swells in size, blazing higher and hotter and more vicious. The heat scorches my face and sears my eyes, but I don't back away. I won't let Tyrus intimidate me.

The Ferriers' song becomes a chant of shrieks and wails, the language of the Chained. It's horrific and cacophonous and terribly perfect.

Two souls stagger down the beach, my mother and Godart.

Newly forged chains encumber their limbs and throats. No Ferrier fights them. They don't need to. Odiva and Godart can't resist Tyrus's siren song. It rages raucous and bitter. It forces his servants to face their fate.

I meet my mother's desperate gaze, and my heart squeezes. Would she have made the same awful choices in life if she'd been allowed to love who she wanted from the beginning?

She's swept past me, sucked near Tyrus's Gate. At the last moment, I grab her hand. She gasps and seizes Godart's in turn. Her eyes aren't black anymore; they're *chazoure*, and they glitter with tears. "Forgive me, Ailesse."

I hesitate, my pulse racing. "I want to." Holding on to the bitterness of the past won't bring me any peace. If I can forgive my mother, can Elara do the same? Can her kingdom really welcome a Chained soul and offer a path to redemption?

There's one way to find out.

I slowly backtrack in the sand, using all my Light and graced strength. I drag my mother and Godart away from the fiery arch, then pivot and launch them in the other direction—toward the shimmering Gate to Paradise.

They stumble inside the goddess's kingdom. No blast of energy shoots them out again. Their bodies relax. Their strained expressions ease. My mother exhales and offers me an elegant nod and fragile smile. Hand in hand with Godart, she turns and ascends the staircase to Paradise.

My chest swells with hope. Perhaps she and I *will* grow to love each other one day.

The flames of Tyrus's Gate roar stronger, build wider. The shrieks in the Underworld intensify. I rush back to the fiery arch, and it almost engulfs me. My hair whips around my shoulders. My feet blister in the sand. I clench my jaw and hold on to the brighter blaze of Elara's Light inside me.

Warped, disfigured faces press closer from the other side of the Gate—the most vicious of the Chained that Tyrus has tortured in the deepest realms of his kingdom. Somewhere beyond their *chazoure* bodies are two *orvande* souls I can no longer see, just like they can no longer see me. But Estelle and Aurélien are ancient and wise. They must know what is happening. I can picture Aurélien now, his hammer raised and ready.

The soul closest to the Gate—a man with gouged-out eyes and sewn-shut lips—blindly staggers forward. He claws out for me past the embers. His hand is missing two fingers.

The flames of the Gate lash madly. Tyrus's siren song clashes and pounds in frenetic, furious turbulence. If the Gate becomes fully breeched—if Sabine and the Ferriers allow that barrier to fall—there will be no holding back the violent Chained. Yes, Tyrus will have lost, but we'll also surely be killed.

"Do you want this to end?" I shout at the top of my lungs. A fingernail on the mangled hand snags my blouse. I don't shrink away. "It's simple, Tyrus. Stop coercing your bride to join you. If you love her, show her. Let your rage and hatred go. Break my soul-bond. End your reign of blood sacrifice."

The Gate of fire pulses. The flames surge and contract, like he's undecided.

The withered hand trails up to my throat. It may only have three fingers, but they're long and stretched. They can easily strangle me. They clutch my neck. Squeeze like a vise.

I hold my ground. My heart drumrolls. My vision flickers with black stars. *Please, please, Elara. Don't let me die like this.*

The rippling arch blasts to a towering height. It shoots at least fifty yards into the night sky. Tyrus's siren song crescendos, a deafening rail on my eardrums.

The Ferriers sing louder, their voices full-scale blaring. At the core of their defiance, I feel their powerful and unified Light. Elara's Gate and the translucent staircase flash with opaque bursts of silver. The stars in the Night Heavens penetrate the storm clouds. The goddess is sending us all her strength, too.

I can't speak to Tyrus aloud, so I speak in my mind, hoping my words will still reach him. *Elara might give you a second chance if you learned to show long-suffering affection,* I say. *Perhaps then your kingdoms could rejoin, and you could grant the penitent Chained forgiveness. The Beyond could become a place where redemption is possible for all.*

The withered hand clenches tighter. Darkness crowds my vision. I'm about to lose consciousness. About to die. Tyrus hasn't heard me. Either that, or he doesn't care. He'll never change.

All at once, the flames crash. The siren song ends. The arch collapses to its former size. The clawing hand retracts.

My muscles go slack. I release a trembling exhale and breathe in heavily.

He did it. Tyrus surrendered.

I slowly stand taller. Warmth radiates inside me. I stare into the embers and call to Aurélien by his blacksmith's name, "Strike your hammer, Forgeron. It is done."

I can't see his weapon, but I hear its earth-shuddering *slam* against the ground. The howls and yips of the jackals rise. They've come to return the Chained to the depths of the Underworld.

I cling to the hope that Tyrus will prove himself and grant his souls more mercy. Perhaps then they'll advance to the Miroir once more. I picture Forgeron in a new role: the breaker of chains. I envision Estelle ushering forgiven souls out of the Underworld and back to her daughters, the living Ferriers. My *famille* and I could guide them into Paradise.

Sabine and the Ferriers stop singing. Pernelle lets go of the burning column. The other Leurress break their hands apart. The channel closes. The Gate of fire vanishes. Nothing but charred smoke curls up from the sand.

My legs wobble. I press my palm to my chest. I can't believe we did it.

Bastien rushes to me and catches me up in his arms. He laughs, kissing my mouth, my cheeks, my forehead. My broken ribs ache. I don't care. "You were incredible!" he says.

I smile, light-headed. I'm still quaking in shock. "We just . . . we *won*, right?"

He laughs again and cradles my face in his hands. "We more than won. We brought Hell to its knees." He kisses me a second time, deep and tender and beautifully dizzying. I lean into him, and finally—*finally*—the last of my tension, months in the making, melts away.

I pull back and gaze serenely into his eyes. "I never want to be your friend again." His brow wrinkles. "No, that wasn't right." I frown at myself. My head is still in a daze. "I meant I don't like being just friends . . . but I like *you*. Actually, I love you." How did Estelle say it to Forgeron? "You're my song's soul." I blink. "My soul's song."

Bastien chuckles and wraps me in another embrace. "Please keep talking. I've never been more entertained." I slug his arm, and he laughs harder, kissing my cheek. "I love you, too," he says.

I grin and look past him for Sabine, but she's not where I last saw her. I scan the Ferriers, and the ringing in my ears fades. It's replaced by the soft and lovely descant from Paradise. A few feet away, Elara's shimmering Gate is still standing. The silver owl is perched before it like a sentinel, her heart-shaped face tilted at me. Is she keeping it open? Why?

I search the shore again and finally find my sister. She and Cas are several yards away at the edge of the lapping sea. They're not alone, either, though Cas doesn't have the vision to see the two *chazoure* souls who are with them. One I know. The other I recognize, even though we've never met, because he has Bastien's chiseled jawline and his same head of tousled hair.

I look into Bastien's sea-blue eyes, kiss him gently, and smile. "Would you like to share my graces again?"

He quirks a brow. "Why?"

I draw a long breath and squeeze his hands. "Your father and Jules are still here, and I thought you'd like to see them one last time."

44

Bastien

I'VE FORGOTTEN HOW TO BREATHE. Or think. Or walk. Somehow my legs carry me down to the shoreline.

He's here. She's back.

My father. Jules.

Ailesse's falcon vision is my vision now. I see the world with a violet tint again, and within it, the color of souls.

Sabine and Cas step away to give me space. I look between the two people I've loved the longest in my life. My heart won't stop pounding. My throat runs dry despite the drizzling rain. I don't know what to say. I don't know who to hug first. *Can I hug them?*

Jules finally rolls her eyes. "It's still me, Bastien."

I laugh and brush the tears off my cheek. "Right."

She wraps me in a tight embrace. It's good to feel her strength again. She's been so weak. "See?" she says. "I knew I could trust you. You didn't even leave me in the Underworld long enough for me to tell any good stories."

I snort. "You're welcome, I guess."

She waves a hand up and down at herself. "So how do I look in *chazoure*?"

I glance over her braided hair, fitted leggings, low-cut blouse, and tall boots, all glowing in different shades of the color. "I think you're ready to take on Paradise and challenge any boys who dare to call you Julienne."

She smirks. "Damn straight." But then her expression sobers, and she fidgets with her sleeve. "Can you pass along a message to Marcel for me?"

I take a deep breath. I don't know how I'm going to break the news to him. "Of course."

"Tell him . . ." Jules's voice goes hoarse. She can't speak for a long moment. She lowers her head and shifts from foot to foot. When her chin stops quivering, she meets my eyes again. "Tell him he's going to make a fine scribe. Tell him I want him and Birdine to have twelve children and grow old and fat together."

I nod, smiling. That future is easy to picture—Marcel and Birdine living in Dovré, their house overflowing with books and smelling of rose water, too many kids running amok. "What about you?" My voice chokes up again. "Will you be happy?"

Her eyes gleam. "Don't doubt it for a minute. I'll eat cake and sleep in a soft bed and never have to thieve again. I'll be with my father, Bastien." She bites her lip and glances over her shoulder at *my* father. "I'll let you have this moment with yours."

She swaggers back, and I turn to him, running my hand through my rain-soaked hair. I'm a mess of nerves. I have no idea how to begin a conversation. For eight long years I prepared how to exact my revenge, but I never spent a moment preparing for this. In no part of my mind did I imagine I'd have this stolen time with him.

We both take a shy step toward each other, lean our weight on our left legs, and shove our hands in our pockets. I give a flustered chuckle. Like father, like son.

I'm still struggling for words, so I find myself staring at him, desperately trying to memorize the tiny details I've somehow forgotten over the years. The bridge of his nose is a little crooked. He has a long scar on the back of his hand, maybe from a slip with his chisel and hammer. His hair isn't as thick as I remember, and the skin under his eyes is thin and a little saggy. He was starting to get old when he died, and I didn't even realize it. I'd held on to a younger picture of him in my mind, the father who could race through a field with me on his back, the man who sculpted all day and still had the energy to tell me stories beside our hearth every night.

"Did you suffer long?" I suddenly blurt.

He tilts his head. "Pardon?"

"When you were killed, I mean." My mouth trembles. I rub it, but it won't hold still. "Did you suffer lo—" My throat closes.

Merde, here come the tears again. I can't help them. More than anything, it's the agony he felt when he was stabbed that's haunted me all this time.

His eyes brim with pain. "Bastien . . ." He sighs and shakes his head. "That was just one small moment out of *millions* of moments. When I think of my life, I don't dwell on my death. I don't want you to dwell on it, either." His brows tug inward. "I hope I gave you more than that."

I swipe beneath my nose. "You did. I couldn't have asked for a happier childhood."

His smile is heavy, even a bit weary. Doesn't he believe me? He steps closer and places his large sculptor's hands on each side of my face. "I'm grateful for the time we had together, and I'm so proud of you. You spent the hardest years that a boy must live raising yourself—taking care of your friends, too. But I want more for you than just surviving." He lowers his head a little so we're eye to eye. "Thank you for doing your best to honor my life, son. Now I want you to honor *yours*."

I inhale and solemnly nod. "I understand. I promise I will." I look behind me at Ailesse. She's a few feet away and watching us. Warmth rushes through my chest at her soft smile. "Father, I want you to meet someone."

She presses her lips together, smoothes her skirt, and drifts closer. "Hello."

I take her hand and weave her fingers through mine. "Father, this is Ailesse."

He grins slyly. "She's not a stranger."

"She's not?"

"I'm still part of your life, Bastien." He crosses his arms. "And I've had my eye on you two."

"Oh." A few heated moments pop to mind, and my ears burn. "But not *all* the time, right?"

He chuckles and folds me against him. I forgot that he hugged like this, his strong arms almost crushing me. I don't want him to let go. "I've been waiting for you to take her to see the dolphins," he says. He pulls away and gives my face a hearty pat.

I scratch the back of my neck. "Well, she hasn't exactly been available lately."

Ailesse cocks a brow.

My father laughs and extends a hand to her. She embraces him instead. Before he can squeeze too tight, I say, "Careful with her broken ribs."

He's gentle with her. He even kisses her hand afterward, like a fine gentleman. "Take care of each other," he says, returning Ailesse to me. I wrap my arm around her waist, and she leans her head against my shoulder.

Just when everything feels comfortable and right, the silver owl flies past us and rasp-screeches. Ailesse turns to me and whispers, "It's time to say goodbye."

I take a steeling breath. I hug my father and Jules one last time. Ailesse also embraces Jules and says, "Thank you for my life."

We walk them both to Elara's Gate and watch them enter side by side.

Long after the other Ferriers leave, Ailesse and I stay standing in the sprinkling rain. We gaze into the night sky until the last silvery glimpses can be seen of my father and Jules as they climb the spiral staircase to Paradise.

Their peace is my peace, and it satisfies far deeper than revenge.

45
Sabine

"Can you come down from there?" I ask Ailesse, trying not to panic as she walks the thin parapet of Castelpont. The stones of the bridge are dry from the late morning sun—the summer storms have finally blown away—but I can't stop picturing her slipping and falling forty feet into the barren riverbed. It's good to see Ailesse so free and herself again, but—"I can't heal a cracked-open head, you know."

"Maybe you can." She pivots on one toe and walks in the other direction. The limestone walls of Beau Palais gleam behind her from the castle's perch beyond the city wall. "I wouldn't put it past you. I'm counting on you to heal my cracked ribs, anyway." Beneath her laced bodice, her torso is wrapped in a tight linen bandage. I tied it on myself.

"Well, I need to catch this fire salamander first." I'm crouched on the bank in the shade of a willow tree. I hold myself rigid as a yellow-spotted black tail peeks out from the mulch by the tree trunk. My salamander skull was crushed in Cas's fight with Godart, and I'm eager to get my healing power back.

The silver owl set a high standard for allowing me to share her graces without any bloodshed, but I'm determined to reach it once more. So many people in Dovré still suffer from Light they've lost. If I can obtain a fire salamander's graces again—if I can share them with others—I can restore their Light. From the visionary dreams I keep having over the last five days, I truly believe it's possible.

Ailesse laughs the way she always has with me, not cutting or condescending, but affectionately amused. "Oh, Sabine. You don't need to catch him."

"How else am I supposed to go about this? He won't stay still."

I lean close again, but as soon as I'm within a yard of him, the salamander darts out from the mulch and skitters down the bank. He hides under a fallen branch.

I sigh. How will I show my *famille* they don't have to sacrifice animals anymore if I can't prove that my experience with the silver owl wasn't a one-time occurrence? None of the Leurress lost their graces when Tyrus surrendered, but aspiring Ferriers will need to obtain new graces in the future, and I want to show them there's a better way.

I creep toward the fallen branch when Ailesse asks, "Have you kissed him yet?"

"The salamander?"

"No." She giggles and walks another length of the parapet, her feet ibex elegant and agile. "Cas, of course. I can't spy on you two anymore, so you have to divulge everything."

I shake my head at her, but I can't hold back a grin that makes me feel twelve years old again. "When would I have kissed him? He's been shut up in Beau Palais, having meetings with his councillors . . . or whatever it is a king does to restore order in his castle. I haven't even seen him since the new moon." The five days that have passed feel like forever.

Ailesse's brow arches. "No secret rendezvous in the forest, then, after everyone is sleeping?"

"No!" I snort. "What would our *famille* think if they saw me sneaking out at night?"

"They'd think it's refreshing to have a *matrone* so young and passionate."

I laugh and rub my cheeks, which must be flaming red. Ailesse makes kissy faces at me, and I laugh harder. "Stop!"

A few days ago, I couldn't have imagined such a lighthearted moment between us. The Sabine who wore the jackal pendant wouldn't have let Ailesse talk her into continuing forward as *matrone*, let alone allowed her to tease me about how smitten I am with her former *amouré*. Her soul-bond with Cas broke when Tyrus surrendered to us, and Ailesse has been practically dancing ever since.

The fire salamander streaks out from beneath the fallen branch. I curse and start running. "Get him!" I call to Ailesse as he tears onto the bridge.

"But he'll drop his tail."

"Then don't catch him by his tail!"

She lowers herself off the parapet, careful with her ribs. As she sets foot below, she quickly swipes for the salamander, but he dodges her and scurries up the half wall to where she was just standing. I rush over the moment he slips between a deep crack in the stones.

I blow out a heated breath and set my fists on my hips.

"Are you sure he's really a fire salamander and not the spawn of a Chained?" Ailesse asks.

I scoff and poke her in the shoulder. We both burst into laughter.

Someone walks toward us. I hear the distant footsteps the moment Ailesse shivers from her sixth sense. We both turn to the path that curves around the city wall. She gasps, and my heart somersaults in my chest. *Cas.*

Ailesse squeals and squeezes my hands. "Promise to tell me everything!"

Before I can reply, she kisses my cheek and hurries off the bridge in the other direction. I roll my eyes, but stifle a giggle.

As Cas comes nearer, I exhale a steadying breath and tuck a few stray curls into the knot that half of my hair is wound up in. I hope I'm not too sweaty. The day is already hot, and I've been chasing the fire salamander for over an hour.

He reaches the foot of the bridge and shyly smiles at me, his dimple caving deep. Another flush of heat rushes through my body.

He's still a little pale and has a hitch in his step when his left side jostles—I'll help him recover from his injuries soon—but other than that, he looks well. He's wearing a fine scarlet doublet and soft breeches tucked into his polished boots. I wish I was clothed in something nicer than my simple brown hunting dress, but Cas doesn't seem to mind. His blue eyes are rapt on me as he walks toward the crown of the bridge where I'm standing. "I saw you from Beau Palais," he says, trailing his finger along the parapet. "Is this going to be our new meeting place?"

"Perhaps." I grin. Maybe it's why I came here of all places to catch a fire salamander.

He joins me, and we stare at each other for a stretched-out moment. His loose strawberry curls shine blonder in the sun, and a gentle breeze sends a lock tumbling across his brow. My stomach flutters. "How is everything with your *famille*?" he asks.

"They're well." I turn and lean my folded arms against the parapet. "Though some are a little nervous that the king of South Galle knows where they ferry now."

He nods and also leans on the half wall the way I do. Our elbows are almost touching. "I hope, in time, they will come to trust me. I envision the Leurress and myself as allies. I promise you I'll never expose their way of life."

I never doubted it. Well, maybe a month ago I doubted it, but not now. "Thank you." We share another look that leaves me slightly breathless. "And you? Is everything well in Dovré?" I quickly amend, "As well as it can be, anyway." I'm still determined to heal the people.

He nods again, winking against the bright sunlight. "The dissenter movement has weakened. As it turns out, most weren't overly fond of King Godart." He grows quiet a moment, and then clears his throat. "My, um, coronation will be in three days." He idly kicks his toe against the wall. "Would you . . . ?"

My stomach twists. My heart patters faster.

"Would you like to join me as my special guest?"

My brows rise, and I purse my lips. "Define special." I suppress a smile. "*How* special?"

Cas makes a noise between a groan and a laugh, and his head drops into his hands. His ears are the most endearing shade of red. "Sabine . . ." He sighs. "I want you to know I've thought a lot about what you said the other night." He meets my eyes again. "About you thinking you're second best, that's not how I—"

I cut him off with a kiss. He stiffens, surprised, but then his hands slide up to my jaw and cradle my face. He melds into me, kissing me so tenderly and spellbindingly that I wonder if he has his own magic, much stronger than a siren song.

When he finally draws back to gaze at me, something black and yellow catches the corner of my vision. I tense. "Don't move, Cas."

He cautiously looks where I'm looking. The fire salamander has returned. He's peeking up at us from the crack in the parapet.

"Hello," I whisper gently, and reach for the Light inside the tiny creature. "May I talk to you about your graces?"

46
Ailesse

I MEET BASTIEN AT SUNSET in a field of blue mist flowers. Marcel and Birdine are also there. The four of us work together to lift a heavy three-foot pillar of limestone out of a wooden cart, and we set it upright on the ground in the shade of a hazel tree.

Bastien kneels and brushes a little dust from the fresh engraving he chiseled with his father's tools. It's a picture of the Gates to Paradise, with a staircase spiraling up into the clouds.

Bastien says the work is flawed and simple, but if they were here with us, I know his father would be proud and Jules would be beaming.

They probably are.

Seven days later, at the harbor near the royal shipyard, the sun is still shining. I can't get enough of it after so many weeks spent underground, indoors, or in the rain. My nose and cheeks have a light sprinkling of freckles and even the hint of a burn. It's glorious.

Bastien and I stand on the dock near *La Petite Rose*, waiting for the ship's final boarding call. New adventures await us. We're going to see the volcano on the Ember Isles and the colossal waterfalls off the coast of the Dagulu rain forest. From there, who knows?

Sabine and Cas have come to see us off, but right now she's sitting on a bench with a frail-looking sailor. I can't hear what they're saying amid the commotion of gathered passengers and a few merchants watching their last barrels being loaded onto the ship. But from Sabine's earnest expression and her gentle hand placed on the sailor's arm, it's easy to guess what is happening, though I doubt the sailor knows it. She's healing him, restoring his Light.

She's been going about it quietly these past few days, in simple and unobtrusive moments just like this. Her patients have no idea that the kind and beautiful girl who listens to their troubles is a Bone Crier from myth and Old Gallish fairy tales. She wouldn't want them to. She's content to know that they will wake up the next morning, and each one after, feeling stronger. I'm proof of that. She's already healed me of the little Light I lost—Cas, too— not to mention my broken ribs, his sword wound, Bastien's bruised head, and all the other aches and pains we've endured since the new moon. She even managed to revive Birdine's uncle from his deathbed. Birdine cried for a solid day.

Cas gives Sabine and the sailor a few more moments alone

and ambles over to me and Bastien. The coronated king of South Galle is wearing inconspicuous clothing today, as well as a woolen cap to hide his hair. So far no one has recognized him.

He passes Bastien a rough-spun sack with two loaves of bread that poke out from the top, and my graced nose picks up the smell of salted meat and hard cheese. "Some food for your journey."

Bastien's arm sags once he takes hold of it, unprepared for its weight. He wrinkles his brow and peeks inside. I look with him, curious. A considerable pile of gold coins lies at the bottom of the sack.

"Cas, this is too much." Bastien shakes his head. "You already secured our passage."

"Consider it payback for locking you in my dungeons."

"I think we're even, since you were our prisoner, too."

"Well, then consider it a gift from a friend. It might help you start an honest life."

Bastien smirks. "So I can't say I robbed a king?"

Cas shrugs. "If it helps your reputation. You never know. Your ship could get set upon by pirates."

Bastien chuckles and gives the sack a little shake, jangling the coins. "Thanks, Cas."

Sabine joins us and pulls Bastien aside to say goodbye to him first. Cas and I are left awkwardly staring at each other. I clear my throat. "So . . . we're still friends, right?" I'm under no illusions that he has any remaining attachment to me, but I don't want him thinking his tenderness to me wasn't meaningful or that I was callous toward his affections.

"Of course." He grins. "We're most assuredly not enemies, so we must be friends. There's no middle ground after mutual abduction, forging and breaking soul-bonds, and all our other death-defying experiences."

A small laugh escapes me. "That's true." I sneak a glance at Sabine, and then bite my lip. "Listen, I never knew your mother, Cas," I say, remembering his reason for being attracted to me after the power of my siren song faded. "I don't know how much I really am like her, but I *do* know there's no one in the world better than Sabine. Your mother, if she really was like me, would have no doubt about that. She would be so happy for you."

His smile softens, and he looks down at his feet for a moment before he nods and whispers, "Thank you."

Sabine walks over to me and sniffs. "Promise this isn't goodbye forever."

I take both her hands in mine. "I promise. I might even come back with stories of the other Leurress I meet. I can tell them everything that the founding *famille* has accomplished, so they can share our blessings." I want the rest of our people to know that they can live like us, without the burden of blood sacrifice.

Sabine and I embrace each other. I hold on tightly as a rush of affection makes my eyes grow hot. "Thank you for being my best friend . . . and the best sister I could ever have asked for."

She hiccups with a soft sob. "I love you, Ailesse."

"I love you, too."

Someone from the ship calls for the final passengers to board. I take a steeling breath, pull away from Sabine, and wipe my nose. "Ready?" I ask Bastien.

He already has our bags slung over his shoulder, but then he scans the busy docks and frowns. "Marcel said he would be . . . ah, there he is."

I can't pick Marcel out of the crowd with my sixth sense; I'm prickling all over from too many people. But soon enough I spy a head of floppy hair and an easygoing swagger. Marcel is in no rush, oblivious to the mild panic of everyone else at the harbor. He spots us and quirks a smile, waving what looks like a scroll of parchment at us.

"I made something for you." He catches up to us as we walk toward the boarding plank. "I copied it out of *Ballads of Old Galle.*"

Bastien grins. "Just like a proper scribe."

Marcel nods, bouncing lightly on his toes. "Remember when we were all sequestered together in the catacombs," he says, like the days I was held captive there are among his fondest memories. He unrolls the parchment. "This is that song about the Leurress that I showed both of you. That was the moment we figured out just how dire the soul-bond was—even though you ended up not being Ailesse's *amouré*," he adds to Bastien. With a chuckle, Marcel flips his hair out of his face before reading:

> *The fair maiden on the bridge, the doomed man she must slay,*
> *Their souls sewn together, ne'er a stitch that can fray,*
> *His death hers and none other 'cross vale, sea, and shore,*
> *Lest her breath catch his shadow evermore, evermore.*

He smiles broadly, rolls the parchment back up, and passes it Bastien. "Anyway, I thought this might serve as a type of good-luck charm . . . you know, to remind you, if you're having a rough day, that nothing can be as bad as what you've already been through."

Speechless, I turn to Bastien, whose bewildered and amused expression matches my inward reaction perfectly. But his voice is heartfelt when he replies, "Well, thanks, Marcel."

"Anytime." He reaches the boarding plank before us and absently walks up it.

"Are you coming with us?" I tease.

"Whoops." He hops down.

I laugh and give him a hug. When Bastien hugs him next, his eyes grow a little misty. "Take care of yourself, all right?"

Marcel closes his eyes, his chin tucked over Bastien's shoulder. "All right."

Bastien and I board the ship and find a spot on the side to wave goodbye to our friends. Sabine is nestled against Cas, his arms folded around her waist. She blows me a kiss.

As La Petite Rose sails out of the harbor, I give Bastien a sly look while leaning back against the rail. "You still have it, don't you?"

"Have what?"

I grab his trouser pocket, yank him forward, and dig my hand inside.

He jumps. "Ailesse, what are you—?"

I pull out the scrap of my chemise and wave it in front of him. "Do you really need this anymore?"

His mouth parts, and he blushes. "How did you know about . . . ?" He laughs and shakes his head at me. "How much did you see while you were in the Underworld, anyway?"

I shrug coyly. "Let's just say I numbered your baths."

"Oh really?"

I nod. "And, sadly, you never bathed."

He snorts and pulls me closer by the waist. He tucks my hair behind my ears and kisses me, grinning against my lips. "Come on." He grabs my hand, and I race with him to the forecastle deck, where it's less crowded. "Maybe we'll see some dolphins."

It takes two hours of waiting, but the time passes quickly between more stolen kisses, stories of Bastien's father, and my stories about Sabine. And then, sure enough, dolphins start leaping in pairs along the wake of the ship.

When night falls, Bastien and I remain on deck, all wrapped up in each other and too excited about our journey to fall asleep. The waxing moon basks us in her silvery light, and our ship sails forward under the constellations of Elara's Night Heavens.

The starry claws of the Jackal continue to reach for the Huntress. Perhaps the gap will close between them in time. Regardless, she isn't dissuaded. She sets her own path, she is her own north, and the lodestar rests on her brow.

Acknowledgments

Writing the conclusion of Ailesse, Sabine, and Bastien's story was a great challenge, but one that brought me immense joy. Many thanks to those who gave a helping hand:

My agent, Josh Adams, who has been in my corner for over seven years now. You're more than my agent; you're my friend. Thank you for continuing to make my dreams a reality.

My editor, Maria Barbo, whom I've had the pleasure to learn from since our first book together, *Burning Glass*. Four books later, you're still my amazing emperor editor.

My publisher, Katherine Tegen, and her incredible team at Katherine Tegen Books HarperCollins, especially assistant editor Sara Schonfeld. Thank you for all your talents and generous support.

The fantastic design team: art director Joel Tippie, Amy Ryan, and Charlie Bowater, who illustrated another gorgeous book cover. I am beyond thankful to each of you.

The incredible authors who helped launch this series with their wonderful blurbs: Stephanie Garber, Mary E. Pearson, A. G. Howard, Evelyn Skye, Jodi Meadows, and Sara B. Larson.

The book subscription box companies who introduced this series to several thousand new readers. Extra-special thanks goes to OwlCrate, FairyLoot, LitJoy Crate, and The Bookish Box.

My husband, Jason, who continues to show me tremendous support and who is my most passionate reader. His overprotectiveness of my main characters is adorable.

My children: Isabelle, for inspiring me with her music; Aidan, for helping me choreograph tricky moves in fight scenes; and Ivy, for reminding me what is most important in life.

My writing friends, especially Jodi Meadows, Erin Summerill, Lindsey Leavitt Brown, Kerry Kletter, Ilima Todd, Robin Hall, and Emily Prusso. Here's a shout-out to my besties, Sara B. Larson and Emily R. King, who deserve the sweetest spot in Elara's Paradise for all the time and love they have given me this past year.

My French friends, Sylvie, Karine, and Agnés. This series wouldn't exist without the impact each of you had on me when I was a teenager. Thank you for your genuine sisterhood.

My father, Larry. I felt you with me when I wrote the scene where Bastien speaks with his deceased father at the end of the book. His words to Bastien became your words to me.

My mother, Elizabeth (Buffie). You are a goddess, through and through. Thank you for raising me to believe I was capable of wonders. I still depend on your unshakable belief in me.

And to God. I can't imagine living a single day without knowing You are real, infinitely merciful, and rooting for me with perfect love and patience. Thank You for true grace.